SPACE VAULT
The Seed Eclipse
Jeremy Clift

ElleWon
PRESS

ElleWon Press

The Sci-Fi Galaxy Series Awards and Accolades

Jeremy Clift

Winner Best New Sci-Fi Series – Born in Space, BookFest Awards, Fall, 2024

Distinguished Favorite, Independent Press Awards, May 2025

Cygnus Award Finalist, 2025

Pacific Book Awards, Best Sci-fi (Galactic Empires), 2025

IBPA Bill Fisher Award – Born in Space, 2025 Silver Winner.

Born in Space – "A prophetic novel that is uniquely elaborate and immersive, breaking new ground in the science fiction genre."

The Independent Review of Books

"More than a sci-fi story; it's a profound, thrilling examination of motherhood, power, and the far-reaching consequences of ambition in an ever-expanding universe."

The Prairies Book Review

"Clift's shrewd writing loads the book with SF tech .... and engaging touches. A profound and full-bodied futuristic story of love, technology, and infinite outer space."

Kirkus Review

Space Vault: The Seed Eclipse – "Clift brilliantly combines cutting-edge science with raw human emotion. You'll find themes of genetic engineering, climate catastrophe, political unrest, and alien diplomacy all woven into a narrative that never forgets its beating heart: a mother's love. Teagan is fierce, wounded, and real and her struggle to protect Diana amidst collapsing ecosystems and hostile factions reminded me of how powerful a parent's love can be in the face of impossible odds.

"What really elevates this book is the philosophical undercurrent: **Who owns life?** In an era when corporations and governments increasingly control the food we eat, the air we breathe, and even our genetic future, this question becomes more than a fiction; it becomes urgent. Whether you're a sci-fi fanatic, a parent, or simply someone who loves gripping stories about resilience and the human spirit, this book is for you."

—Melissa Caudle, Dr. Mel
Editor, Blogger, Sci-Fi Enthusiast

"Blending sharp science fiction with deep emotional stakes, this novel explores identity, legacy, and the unyielding power of maternal love."

—*NewInBooks.com*

"A remarkable novel, centred on a stunningly original idea."

—John Fullerton, author.

"Clift expertly merges thrilling narrative with compelling philosophical inquiry. Who holds the rights to genetic codes that determine survival? How should consciousness and DNA be valued in a future driven by technological advancement? ***Space Vault: The Seed Eclipse*** challenges readers to contemplate these provocative ethical dilemmas, unraveling complex issues surrounding human identity and bioengineering.

—PaxJones blog

PUBLISHED BY ELLEWON PRESS

BORN IN SPACE; UNLOCKING DESTINY
COLLISION IN SPACE (free ebook)
SPACE VAULT: THE SEED ECLIPSE

https://www.jeremycliftbooks.com/

SPACE VAULT

THE SEED ECLIPSE

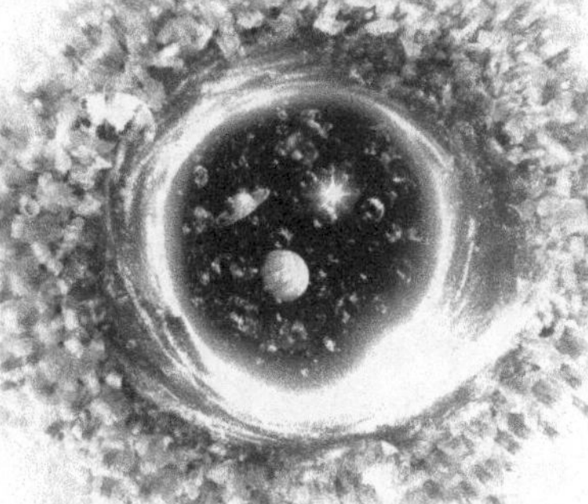

JEREMY CLIFT

ISBN (hardback) 979-8-9900107-7-2

ISBN (paperback 6 x 9) 979-8-9900107-8-9

ISBN (Paperback 5.24 x 8) 979-8-9900107-5-8

ISBN (eBook) 979-8-9900107-6-5

Cover design by: BookcoverZone

Visit: www.jeremycliftbooks.com

To Ronita —

for your unwavering patience, undeniable strength, and steadfast
support. Thank you for seamlessly keeping the wheels turning
while I grasped for the stars.

And to everyone who dares to envision a future beyond our planet — this
story is dedicated to you.

Contents

The Story So Far ...

AFTER A LONG and painful struggle to remain part of the lives of seven children born from a controversial genetic experiment aboard the Quivira space lab, Teagan Ward has settled in California with her partner, Julian.

Though Dr. César de Luca—who once directed the program—is presumed dead following the crash of an asteroid into the Moon, Quivira continues to operate under the leadership of Professor Olga Polyakov and the asteroid mining magnate, Howie Rich.

Love is space and time measured by the heart.

Marcel Proust (1871–1922)

Out beyond our world there are, elsewhere, other assemblages of matter making other worlds. Ours is not the only one in air's embrace.

Titus Lucretius Carus (c. 99– 55 BC)

1

THE RAGTAG ARMY

Lagos, Nigeria, April 4, 2102

BANJO ADE WORE THE forlorn expression of a man who knew his fate was sealed; his large frame shivered slightly under a loose-fitting, intricately embroidered traditional Nigerian agbada that draped over him, giving him the appearance of a colorful, walking tent. The vibrant fabric billowed around his ungainly body, as he shifted nervously from foot to foot, his wide eyes darting towards the advancing lightly armed protesters.

Beads of sweat glistened on his forehead, catching the light and betraying his inner turmoil, his lively attire doing little to armor him against the apprehension he felt gnawing inside. The approaching protesters were a ragtag army of destitute farmers and displaced rural laborers, their crinkled sweat-stained garments and tired faces bearing the marks of a wearying journey as they dismounted haphazardly from a convoy of yellow and blue buses and battered trucks that had snaked its way across the bridges to Victoria Island, the upmarket commercial district of Lagos — the largest city on the African continent.

After clambering down, their legs stiff from the long ride, the demonstrators began to raise their voices, their chants and shouts drifted through the air, along with the occasional honking of passing cars and the distant sounds of construction. The odor of discarded food left out overnight and nearby sewage mixed with the scent of the early morning ocean air.

The convening crowd—a chaotic but determined sea of disgruntled individuals united in their discontent—was a mismatched patchwork of restrained fury and frustration. Many protesters carried farming tools, the wooden handles rough and splintered in their calloused hands. The pavement beneath their feet was cracked and uneven as the column meandered slowly along. As they passed, their weathered faces and worn clothes contrasted with the stylish nightclubs, affluent bars, and high-end boutiques and businesses that surrounded them, and to which they could never have access.

Their target was a white, German-built concrete-and-glass building that housed the local headquarters of West Africa's main seed distribution company. The edifice loomed over them, a symbol of wealth and power that seemed worlds away from their current struggles.

Nearby residents, attracted by the noise, watched as the seething crowd marched down Akin Adesola St before turning right toward the diplomatic quarter. A gentle breeze wafted from the lagoon as hover droids and securitybots armed with tasers and teargas lined up outside what locals called the NIPAH complex.

NIPAH was short for *The Network for Indigenous Plants, Agriculture, and Horticulture*. Although the company sounded like it was a network of cooperative farmers, NIPAH's ownership structure was shrouded in secrecy; rumor had it that top people in government and powerful oligarchs owned the monopoly distributor.

Banjo tried to read some of the agitators' signs illuminated by the early morning light: "Nature, Not NIPAH, Knows Best!"; "We Reject Foreign Seeds! Support Local Agriculture!"; "Farmers' Rights Over Profit/Greed!"; and "Our Land, Our Crops, Our Choice!".

For about three decades, NIPAH had been Africa's sole distributor of agricultural seeds marketed by the Global Seed Company Inc. (a vast conglomerate better known as GLOSCOM, based in Des Moines, Iowa). NIPAH had outlets across the region, including a headquarters in Nairobi, Kenya, and a large warehouse and administrative complex in Dar es Salaam, Tanzania, a port city on the Indian Ocean.

Farmers across Africa relied on NIPAH for their seeds, but they were becoming increasingly disgruntled by repeated crop failures. Many farmers blamed genetically modified seeds that were effectively single-use and would not propagate. And now they were outside NIPAH's gates, upset and not afraid to show it.

But instead of sending any of the company's higher-ups to address the crowd of angry farmers, NIPAH had dispatched Banjo, a spokesman who was only authorized to parrot the corporate spin.

Banjo tried not to let his emotions show as he mentally cursed his bosses. Striving for calm, he addressed the motley group. He bit his upper lip and called for quiet. Some paid attention; others booed him

He held up his hands: "Good morning, friends. We are facing some tough times. But, despite various malicious rumors, I want to assure you that our seeds aren't sterile. You *can* propagate for the season from your harvest. If you can't see results, it must be due to environmental degradation and climatic factors. Our seeds are of the highest quality. However, I want to assure you that we take your complaints seriously. We—"

What Banjo was about to say was drowned out in a chorus of further boos.

He wiped the beads of perspiration from his forehead. The crowd had so far been peaceful, but Banjo feared things could turn violent at the drop of a metaphorical hat. He was just a PR person—he didn't know why the farmers had seen dismal harvests or if the seeds really were bad, as they claimed. That knowledge was above his station. Indeed, he didn't care to know. His job was just to disperse the crowd and avoid an incident. Whatever he said or did to achieve that, the company would back him up.

He waited for the heckling to die down before continuing.

"Friends, I understand your frustrations. I also have a millet farm up north. I planted NIPAH seeds and had a bountiful harvest. I also used seeds prepared from my harvest this planting season. The other planters in my cluster had a great harvest as well, and they did the same thing I did. So I think this has to do with your cluster. Maybe there's something wrong locally. We have a seasoned agronomist who will check with you, and—"

The boos rang out again, mixed with shouts of "Liar!" But it was a shout of "We want to meet with who's in charge!" that made Banjo fall quiet once more.

Among the crowd, a woman raised her hand. She had dark skin, cropped hair, hard brown eyes, and a mouth set in a thin line. The crowd abruptly fell quiet. If Banjo had doubts about who was in charge of these protesters, they had been dispelled. The woman held Banjo's gaze; it was clear she wanted to say something.

Banjo thought about ignoring her and continuing his speech, but he knew this stern-faced woman could cause him trouble. Banjo idly wondered why the farmers would acknowledge someone like her as their leader. She didn't seem to have either flair or charisma. But he didn't see any problems with letting her speak, so he nodded and ceded the floor to her.

"Mr. NIPAH, I have three simple requests for you. First, I would like the location of this phantom millet farm up north where you recorded bountiful harvests. We also want you to confirm or deny that your genetically modified seeds have a DNA sequence infused in them that makes them useless to farmers for propagation after their first harvest. Finally, we want to know why NIPAH sent a mid-level officer to address their customers when the people we really want to see are safely ensconced in their plush offices?"

Banjo shifted uncomfortably, silently cursing again. He wondered how a day that had started so calmly was turning to shit. Of course he didn't have a millet farm up north; he had made it up. He didn't know of any farm clusters up north in fact, but he wasn't about to tell this bitch that.

"Ms..."

The woman shook her head. "I don't go by titles, Mr. Ade. Just call me Tandy."

Banjo took a deep breath. He recognized the tactic. Going without titles made this woman's minions feel like she was accessible to them, gave them the impression she was fighting for their cause when she was actually fighting for herself and her credit line.

Banjo knew his job depended on how well he handled this matter, so he grit his teeth, gave Tandy a fake smile, and proceeded with his spin.

"Tandy, thank you for your questions. Regarding your first question, you know I can't tell you the location of my farm or the cluster for security and privacy reasons." He fiddled with the microphone in his hands and clicked on a video he had ready. "However, I can show live footage of the pilot farm projects run by NIPAH with the same seeds you buy."

As the images played on the screen, he said, "In this case, look at how big the corn cobs are. These plants are from second-generation seeds, seeds that came from harvest. Each plant has at least six cobs on them. Which again leads me to ask, why are these farms doing well while yours aren't? Go to farms in Ibadan, Tema, Aflao, Accra, Cotonou, Bouake, and Abidjan. In all these places, NIPAH seeds are used, and in all these places, record harvests have been recorded from second-generation seeds. These locations cut across hundreds of thousands of hectares, at least four countries, and various climatic belts. This is why I wonder if it's just your cluster having these problems."

Banjo was getting into his stride, about to show more slides of lush green maize plantations and hectares of dwarf oil palms, but again Tandy raised her hand to interrupt him.

Banjo let out a frustrated breath and gave her a look of irritation. He knew several people in the crowd were recording the exchange — if he came across as brash and aggressive, the higher-ups might not like it. So he smiled and held up his hand to signal she should hang on while he finished.

He expected her to insist on speaking, but Tandy instead waited patiently for him to wrap up, an unnatural calmness that threw him off. He rambled on about seeds and soils before losing his train of thought and finishing his rebuttal rather lamely.

Banjo was beginning to hate this Tandy woman for her unnatural calmness. It was clear she was angry, but she was also in control of her temper.

The moment he stopped speaking, Tandy jumped nimbly over the barricade. All the bots trained their weapons on her and, for a fraction of a second, it seemed as if the bots would mow her down with their pulse blasters. But Tandy calmed her people with a shake of her head, and everyone on the other side of the barrier fell silent. Banjo had no choice but to tell the armed bots to stand down.

Tandy gave him a cold smile as she walked toward him. "Pardon me for being a little forward, but when I become invested in a cause, I tend to forget where I am. Since we are showing video evidence, why don't I show you mine?"

Tandy queued up her video without actually asking for permission, and Banjo watched in horror as he saw vast barren fields. What shocked him wasn't the fact that there was video evidence to prove he was lying; it was the fact that he hadn't known the scope of the disaster. It wasn't just in one part of western Africa.

The more footage Tandy showed, the more restless the crowd became, shouting and waving their signs angrily. Banjo began to fear for his safety. The guards were ill-equipped against a mob, and he knew it.

After the presentation ended, Tandy stood on the steps of NIPAH headquarters and watched the crowd impassively. Banjo would have thought she'd whip them into a frenzy, but she just stood there and watched as the crowd grew restless and the tension grew unbearable. He almost pleaded with her to say something to douse the uncomfortable atmosphere, but he kept himself in check.

Finally, Tandy decided it was time to speak. Banjo watched in amazement as everyone instantly fell quiet. He felt a grudging respect. The woman knew how to play a crowd.

"Sir, we thank you for meeting with us, although it is apparent that NIPAH doesn't rate us particularly highly since the ones in charge couldn't even bother to move their asses and meet with the people keeping them in a job." She paused to look in the direction of a probable camera, her face gaunt and defiant.

"I know we are being recorded, so I will speak directly to them. You have seen our videos. All those empty fields you see are from second-generation seeds, seeds bought from your company. In all cases, not a single seed germinated. We aren't talking about a bad batch; we are talking of a system in place here at NIPAH to ensure that farmers come back every planting season to buy new seeds and seedlings. This has to stop.

"We are giving NIPAH until the start of the next planting season to clean up their act, or they will face the wrath of the farmers." Tandy looked directly at Banjo, then at the probable camera, the threat evident in her eyes. "That is our message to you."

As soon as she finished, Tandy walked down through the guards, hopped back over the barricade, and yelled, "Let's go home, people."

Like a well-drilled army, the ragtag protesters immediately dispersed.

Banjo knew they were in for trouble.

* * *

A couple of hours later, three diverse groups examined Tandy's performance.

The first group reviewed the footage recorded by one of the hover droids. This group contained two women and a man. They didn't have a specific role in NIPAH; they were simply called the Committee. No one knew exactly what they did or why they met regularly in a tiny room at the NIPAH penthouse and made decisions that instantly became classified.

As they watched the footage for the third time, the Committee members became more impressed with Tandy's composure and control while increasingly disappointed with Banjo. One of the women, Dr. Vivien Chinelo, shook her head in disgust as she watched Banjo wipe his brow for the umpteenth time.

"What kind of negotiator shows this much weakness? Look at how he stands helplessly while this woman takes over his stage. She walks through a cordon of guards and steals his podium, she uses his projector to turn the tables on him. Look at how shocked he looks when she starts to show barren fields. Whose side is this idiot supposed to be on? I don't understand how GLOSCOM—and NIPAH, in particular—task these incompetent idiots to do their jobs. They could have just released a statement and got it over with.

"We're going to have to embrace this Tandy bitch, and make sure we whittle down her influence on the farmers' groups; she's the glue that holds them together. If we don't discredit her, our own monopoly will be tenuous at best."

The other two nodded several times. There were rarely divergent views among the Committee members because their only interest was the perpetuation of GLOSCOM's dominance across the globe. Most of Africa's farmers had already accepted that they had to buy seeds every season. The east and western African regions just had to see the light. If GLOSCOM could get Tandy on their side, that could be a reality.

The second group that reviewed Tandy's performance on the steps of NIPAH's headquarters was no less sinister than the Committee, though their goals were different. Instead of convening in a plush penthouse office, the group of nine met at an abandoned farm on the outskirts of the city of Ibadan, about one hundred and twenty kilometers north of Lagos.

Much like the Committee, this group also met in secret and came from diverse backgrounds. However, it had only one purpose: ending the NIPAH monopoly once and for all. How that was to be accomplished was something to be decided now. The choices: a prolonged political campaign through the press in support of the Green Dawn Collective or else a shock campaign of violence and confusion during a coming solar eclipse designed to force the company to fold.

"It's clear this Banjo is just a distraction. They will not change unless they are forced to," said one of the collective's leaders. "It's time to put an end to the greed and humiliation."

Others murmured assent.

The third group observed from a Tritan scoutship in orbit high over Earth. The cosmotic drive thrusters of the *ArcturusPathfinder 4* strained to hover in place long enough so that they could assess the topography and ecology of the region..

The gangly observers aboard the starship analyzed the scene, their rust-colored exoskeletons gleaming under dim console lights. Their hooked mandibles clicked in quiet deliberation. Through the bridge's reinforced viewports, the fields appeared to be barren. Data showed exhausted soils and repeated crop failures.

Perched in her command chair, Captain Calytricx Draeven's twin-elbowed antennae flicked in agitation atop her elongated, heart-shaped head. Currently on a mission to scout for a new Tritan homeland, she studied the holographic star map projected before her, its shifting constellations reflecting in her large, protruding eyes.

Around her, the crew—a mix of seasoned Tritan explorers and cybernetically enhanced specialists—worked with silent precision, observing the data from the location below.

The place appeared to have few prospects.

"No potential in the vicinity here," said the chief data analyst. "Time to move on. Maybe other parts of the planet are more promising."

In an instant, the mysterious vessel vanished into the void with a flash of metallic brilliance.

2
THE APPRENTICE

Sнiко Tanaka fidgeted in his seat, the frayed cuffs of his emerald-blue shirt catching on his fingertips. He ran the soft fabric between his fingers as he sat upright in his contoured reclinable chair, equipped with an unused entertainment system. Biting his nails, he gazed out of the tinted viewport with a mixture of excitement and apprehension.

Born as part of Dr. César's Heavenly Babies Project and raised in the controlled environment of Quivira's rotating space habitat, he had only ever seen and read about Earth from afar. Now, at almost twenty-five, he was on a shuttle flying straight toward the familiar blue-green orb. This would be his first visit; naturally, he was nervous. He was about to embark on a new chapter of his life: work experience in the heartland of America.

The bustling cityscape stretched out beneath him, a maze of towering buildings and snaking highways that seemed to pulse with energy. Shiko's shuttle descended smoothly, its engines humming softly as it nestled down on the landing pad. After the pilot had powered down the thrusters, Shiko gathered up a simple bag containing his few belongings and headed for the exit.

Stepping into the skybridge, Shiko felt the rush of Earth's atmosphere against his skin, the scent of soil and vegetation combined with a whiff of rocket fuel filling his senses. Just walking through the bright spaceport, crowded with travelers and brightly lit cafes, was exciting.

He was greeted at the exit by his new supervisor, Dr. Elena Canek, a seasoned agronomist and genome specialist. She flashed him a warm smile that radiated confidence and a handshake so firm it felt like an unspoken challenge, signaling the intensity and high expectations to come.

"Welcome to Des Moines, Shiko," said Dr. Canek reassuringly. "I'll be guiding you. We're excited to have you join us at Global Seeds."

Although her back was rigid and her jaw appeared clenched from habitual restraint, Canek's voice matched the buzzing energy of the city around them, and Shiko couldn't wait to begin his work with the renowned agricultural company.

"Thank you, Dr. Canek," Shiko replied, returning the handshake. "I'm eager to get started."

They sat together in the car, but, although Dr. Canek tried to make conversation, Shiko was mostly silent and avoided eye contact. He matched her rigid posture, despite the comfort of the seat.

"You must be tired after your trip," Dr. Canek said.

Shiko accepted that as a good explanation for his reticence.

She tried to ask him about Maureen, but he had little new information. The Quivira administrator, Maureen Grau, had secured the secondment from GLOSCOM through her personal contacts at the firm in the months before her retirement. Maureen had also briefed Shiko about his assignment, giving Shiko the impression that Dr. Canek was a formidable figure within GLOSCOM, wielding considerable power and influence as a high-ranking executive in the company's Research and Development division.

If Shiko played his cards right, she would be a good mentor.

Shiko was the last of the children born as part of Dr. César's path-breaking project to incubate babies in space to get a work assignment off Quivira, where they had been raised: Nevie was a radiation specialist on the ElleWon space station; Gabby was at an animal sanctuary in Ghana; Liam was training as a doctor in advanced neurobiology or quantum bioinformatics, or something; Arturo was learning the mining business; Ved was investigating genetic engineering; and Tara was working as an environmental engineer for an organization focused on sustainable agriculture and water management in rural India.

GLOSCOM's headquarters, near the confluence of Iowa's Racoon and Des Moines rivers, occupied a prime piece of real estate, commanding attention with its futuristic design and imposing presence. Surrounded by bustling streets lined with shops, cafes, and luxury boutiques, the building stood as a symbol of corporate power and influence. Its proximity to major transportation hubs, including high-speed rail networks and orbital spaceports, ensured seamless connectivity with the rest of the world.

In a nice touch, it was also not far from a magnificent Beaux-Arts memorial to Nobel Prize-winning agronomist Norman Borlaug, known as the Father of the Green Revolution and the man who saved more than a billion lives with his innovations in agriculture in the twentieth century.

Shiko thought he was lucky to get the job in Des Moines, in the heart of the rural Midwest. His assignment at the company was to learn about Earth's agricultural practices and apply his expertise in hydroponics and vertical farming to improve crop yields. From his diligent preparatory research, he had learned that GLOSCOM was a massive conglomerate that controlled most of the world's seed research and production, and much of the resulting food manufacturing and distribution.

Shiko admired the huge glass building that housed GLOSCOM's head-quarters. They'd already downloaded his biometrics to enable him to enter the building unhindered and given him a desk on the sixth floor in Room 174.

"6174," mused Shiko, remembering his studies in mathematics. "Kaprekar's constant."

A smile tugged at his lips as he took it to be a good omen for his new job.

Over the next few weeks, Shiko immersed himself in his work, spending long hours in the company's state-of-the-art research labs and greenhouses. He was determined to do well, and lost track of time as he delved deeper into his projects, feeling grateful for the opportunity to be part of such an innovative company. He marveled at the variety of plant species cultivated by GLOSCOM, from genetically modified grains to drought-resistant vegetables.

One day, while analyzing data in the company's research facility, Shiko began chatting with Doctor Santiago Nevarez, an agronomist known for his no-nonsense approach.

"You see, Shiko," Dr. Nevarez said, gesturing to the screen displaying crop yield projections, "our genetically modified strains are the future of agriculture. They're resistant to pests, droughts, and diseases, ensuring food security for billions."

Shiko listened intently, his mind swamped with questions.

"But what about biodiversity?" he countered, aware of scientist Clara Ward's work in preserving heirloom seeds in her moon vault. "Aren't we risking the loss of genetic diversity by relying solely on a handful of engineered crops?"

Dr. Nevarez frowned, unused to being questioned.

"It's a valid concern," he conceded, "but sometimes sacrifices must be made to tackle immediate issues, such as climate change and pests. We're working to address these issues through our research, but it's a delicate balance. Feed the billions now or preserve the diversity for future generations."

GLOSCOM provided Shiko with an apartment in a modern complex not far from headquarters, offering convenient access to his workplace and the busy city center. He was able to walk to work, although sometimes he found the sidewalk smells hard the bear.

The apartment was modest but comfortable, with modern furnishings and large windows that flooded the space with natural light. It quickly became Shiko's sanctuary amidst the hustle and bustle of city life. He decorated the space with potted plants and personal mementos, infusing it with warmth and personality. And though he missed the endless expanse of stars outside his window on Quivira, Shiko found solace in the vibrant energy of Des Moines, embracing each day as an adventure waiting to unfold. This was the beginning of a new chapter in his life, and he was eager to see where it would take him.

As Shiko began unpacking his belongings, he caught snippets of conversation drifting through the thin walls of the apartment. He paused, listening intently, and realized that the voices were coming from the unit nextdoor. Curiosity piqued, he ventured into the hallway and knocked on the neighboring door. It swung open to reveal a young woman.

"Hi there," she greeted him. "You must be the new neighbor." She was attractive, with striking features and an encouraging smile that lit up her face.

Shiko nodded, returning her smile. "Yes, I just moved in," he replied. "I'm Shiko."

"I'm Katrina," the woman said, extending her hand. "Nice to meet you, Shiko. You can call me Kat. Are you settling in okay?"

Shiko nodded, grateful for her friendly vibe. "Yes, thank you. It's been a long day, but I'm glad to finally be here."

"Where are you from? You look Japanese."

Katrina seemed full of curiosity.

"I'm from Quivira. It's a space habitat in LEO."

"Oh, I've heard of those. They're for rich people, right?"

"Not really. At least, I'm not rich. I was born there."

"So you've never been to Earth before?"

Shiko shook his head.

"Wow! An Earth virgin. I can be your first Earth woman."

Shiko blushed.

"Not like that, stupid. I mean, I can be your first Earth friend."

"Just friends?"

"We'll see."

Kat smiled at him, delighted by his reticence and modesty. He had a lot to learn, but she wouldn't mind helping him.

"What are you doing here?" she asked.

"I specialize in hydroponics and vertical farming."

"Hydro-what?" she said with a dimpled grin.

Kat had a way of making those around her feel instantly at ease, as if they'd known her for a lifetime, but in her presence, Shiko talked a bit like a robot.

"Hydroponics — it's a method of growing plants without soil, using nutrient-rich water solutions instead. I'm pretty good at it now, from basic setups for home gardening to large-scale commercial operations."

Having grown up in the controlled environment of a space habitat, Shiko had developed a keen interest in sustainable agriculture and innovative farming techniques. He'd been drawn to the idea of growing food in controlled environments, where factors like light, water, and nutrients could be carefully managed to optimize plant growth and yield. He had also specialized in vertical farming, a practice that involved growing crops in stacked layers or vertically inclined surfaces, maximizing space efficiency and output.

"Sounds like a good catch for GLOSCOM!" Kat said. "Maybe you can give my plants some attention. I always kill them!"

Ignoring her invitation, Shiko parroted the explanations he'd been given; he hadn't had to explain himself before. "My work at GLOSCOM allows me to apply my specialized knowledge to real-world problems, from improving crop yields and resource efficiency to exploring innovative solutions for feeding growing populations in an increasingly urbanized world... What about you?"

Kat eyed him, not wanting to match his earnest recitations, but not sure he would grasp her light-heated banter.

"Oh, I'm a seven," Kat responded.

"A what?"

"Based on numerology, I'm a seven."

"What does that mean?"

"If you break down the letters of the alphabet in my name, Katrina Merrick, and add them into a single number, I'm a seven."

Shiko looked nonplussed. "Sounds very complicated."

She giggled.

"What's it mean though?" he asked.

"It means that I am a Truth Finder."

"I've never heard of that before! I'm impressed," he said, not sure whether to believe her.

"People with a destiny number of seven are natural analysts who are always seeking to understand the deeper meaning of life."

"Seems profound!"

"Is that code for BS?"

Shiko didn't respond.

"You just need some clues for life, some signposts," Kat tried to explain. "It's only meant to be a bit of fun!"

3
THE GLASS HOUSE

Quivira, June 17, 2102

ON QUIVIRA, PROFESSOR POLYAKOV'S lab was eerily quiet, save for the whirring of machines and occasional beeping from a bank of monitors. Howie Rich's disembodied brain floated within a green perfusion fluid inside a glass case. Tethered by an array of tubes and wires, it was hooked up to a powerful computer interface that kept his mind alive and connected him directly to the digital world.

Before his "accident," Howie had run his Space Consortium with a firm hand. But now, he was no longer even human—or at least less so. The fight on Halona had left him unable to walk, breathe, or function on his own.

Professor Polyakov, however, had saved his brain and enabled Howie to "live" on. It seemed almost poetic how this once-proud man had been reduced to nothing more than a floating cerebrum connected by wires.

But, despite this physical limitation, some things never changed. Howie still held power over everyone in the office, just like before, except now he wielded it with even greater force, fueled by rage at those who had defied him when he was alive and able to move around, coupled with newfound strength from being freed from mortality's shackles.

Though some thought this would be the end for Howie's empire, they were wrong—very wrong.

The directors wanted to avoid a fight for succession, and the Consortium continued to thrive under Howie's guidance as he carried out all decisions remotely from his new residence that had become known as the Glass House. Few knew about his "accident" though, and those who did were sworn to secrecy.

Howie called the board meeting with his directors to order. His disembodied voice came through the speakers, booming and clear.

"Colleagues, I'm sorry I'm late. I had to take my dog for a walk."

Laughter erupted around the table.

"Still the same sense of humor," quipped Carl Howard, overall head of the moon mining operation, his casual dress camouflaging his shrewd and detail-oriented mind. Chris Stackpole reported to him.

Polyakov sat at the head of the table, taking notes on everything that was said. She monitored the conversation closely, making sure that Howie had all the information he needed to make decisions.

Some of the board members had initially found it strange that they were talking to a disembodied brain, but they quickly got used to it. Howie was a quick-witted CEO, and he always managed to keep them on track.

The discussion at the board meetings grew heated at times, but Howie's calm robotic voice never faltered. It seemed as if he had never been away.

Only his long-time deputy, Ofentse Mataka, was missing.

Some said he was taking a much-needed holiday in South Africa. Others believed he was inspecting some Consortium lunar mines. No one seemed curious about his absence.

The meeting finally adjourned and the other board members filed out of the room, leaving the image of Howie's face floating on the screen.

Even though his physical body was gone, his mind was still curious, still searching.

"I need more, though," Howie declared.

Apart from keeping the company going, Howie's first thought was always revenge and retribution for those who had crossed him.

"Bring me those snakes who have betrayed me," he instructed Polyakov after everyone else had left. "They will wish they had never been born."

"I'll look into it," she muttered.

Howie smiled. Or at least, his facial image did. His real brain, floating in the tank, pulsed with slow, steady certainty.

"Good girl."

Howie tried to laugh, but it sounded disembodied and electronic (which of course it was). Nevertheless, his command set in progress a series of events that would span a small part of the universe and attract the notice of some unwanted visitors.

"What exactly did we create?" Polyakov whispered.

The nutrient tank emitted a slow pulse as Howie's organic brain responded, activity flickering across the monitors.

"The future."

Polyakov's fingers curled against the desk. She wanted to walk away, to burn this entire project to the ground. But she knew better.

She was trapped in a nightmare of her own making.

She switched off the screen showing his face.

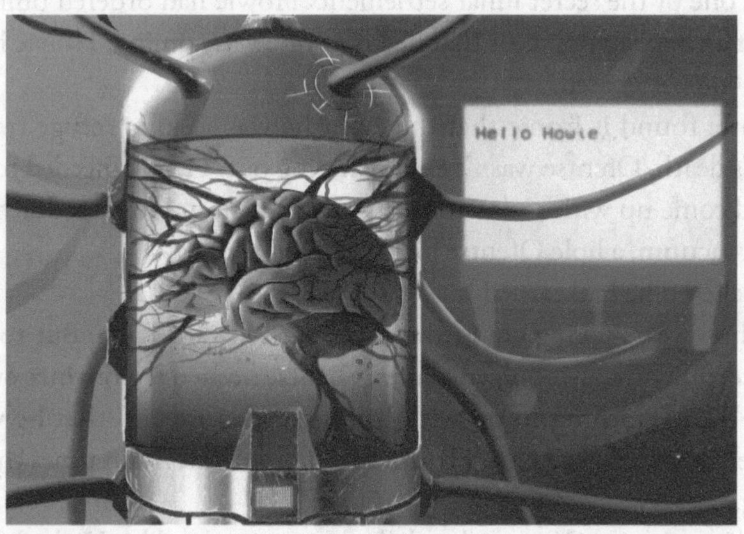

4

THE REFUGE

Tricala Lunar Base, June 18, 2102

UNAWARE OF HOWIE'S LIFE-SAVING operation, his former deputy Ofentse Mataka sat in a bunker concealed amid the gentle hills in Tricala, one of the secret lunar settlements Howie had ordered built in the event of an apocalypse. Not that he knew one was coming; Howie had just wanted to be prepared.

Ofentse found it ironic that the event he was seeking refuge from was Howie's death. Ofentse wasn't exactly hiding out. He just needed to strategize and come up with a plan for his own succession. Howie's death would create a vacuum, a hole Ofentse intended to fill.

He believed he had earned it.

All those years taking crap from the great Howard Rich. But to fill the man's corpulent, self-indulgent shoes, Ofentse needed to convince everyone that he'd had nothing to do with his boss's demise and that he was the right person to lead the Consortium through the uncertain times that were coming.

For the first part, Ofentse already had a watertight alibi. He had forged a memo with Howie's signature, ordering Ofentse to visit three lunar mines. He had left for ElleWon en route to the lunar surface on the night of the murder, but the record would show he had departed several hours earlier, putting him in the clear. He had also scrubbed the surveillance footage and had the security forces issue a trace order for both Clara Ward and her vengeful daughter, Teagan, as wanted fugitives.

A bot offered to bring Ofentse a drink as he huddled near the control center, trying to be unobtrusive. He was expecting the news of Howie's death any moment now.

He tried to guess who would make the call. Was it that slab of granite Howie insisted he make Head of Security? Or César? Ofentse knew Howie and Doctor César de Luca were close. Or maybe that other one, the intrusive Professor Polyakov. Maybe it would be the obsequious Carl Howard, Head of Lunar Mining. In the end, they would beg Ofentse to take over because it was a crisis and he knew everything. He knew "where the bodies were buried."

Ha ha, that would be funny.

Smiling to himself, he began to think up a befitting memorial speech for his mentor and leader, Howie Rich. He would give him a great send off, one that underlined all the achievements Ofentse had helped with.

Ofentse wondered if he should feel some sort of remorse for killing Howie in cold blood. The truth was, he didn't feel anything. Howie had outlived his usefulness; his secrecy and recent erratic behavior meant Howie was no longer the best person to lead the Consortium. Ofentse had catalogued various errors in judgment in recent times, though most worrisome was Howie's promise to eventually hand over the reins to Arturo, his idiot protégé.

When the time came, Ofentse had assumed that either he or the Quivira admin chief, Maureen Grau, would take Howie's place. They were the closest to Howie, and the most senior on the ladder. At worst, Ofentse had thought Howie would hand the reins over to Dr. César.

Ofentse could have lived with working for de Luca or Grau, although the good news was that the latter was retiring. After all, they were brilliant and competent administrators. Dr. César had masterminded the Heavenly Babies project and had brought in all the income from medical innovation. In Ofentse's book, that gave him a pass to head the Consortium.

But not Arturo. Arturo was a fumbling idiot. Why Howie had thought of *that* Heavenly Baby—who lagged Nevaeh, Gabby, Tara, Liam, Ved, and even Shiko—was beyond him.

That was when Ofentse had decided to take matters into his own hands and start making plans to dispose of Howie Rich. He needed to preserve the Consortium and some of the most thriving communities on the Moon. Of course, he hoped to get rich while doing so, but that would be a bonus.

Naturally, he'd need some friends on the board. The six board members were himself, Dr. César, Umar, Chris, the ever-bubbly Aussie Randy Quarles, and Howie's sycophant Carl Howard. Ofentse knew he couldn't count on votes from Carl and Dr. César. He wasn't sure about Chris, but he thought he could count on votes from Randy and, with the right pitch, Umar. The plan was to have three on his side by the time the board convened.

And he had a plan to make that happen. Ofentse had summoned Gignotek, his personal bot, to set up meetings with all of them.

He had already scheduled a private meeting with Umar Sadiq, the taciturn genius. Umar was one of the most influential men in the Consortium, having brought down energy costs with his water ice propellants. Not only had Umar cut the price of mining propellants, but he had also created a near monopoly, with virtually all lunar mining operations dependent on him. When Howie brought Umar into the Consortium, it had been a significant coup; Ofentse didn't have Howie's charm, but he knew that the thought of a more considerable bite of the pie would appeal to anyone.

Then there was Chris Stackpole, the Canadian responsible for running the three biggest mines on the Moon. He reported to Carl and was also the only one Ofentse didn't know how to approach. Even when Howie was in charge, no one knew whose side Chris was on. He just did what was asked of him. His voting pattern showed he wasn't a Howie man, but he wasn't against him either. Bringing Chris to his side would be important.

Ofentse had assumed that he would be asked to take over the running of the conglomerate. He knew how it worked and every aspect of its operations. So he was puzzled when he did not get the notification. Something must be up. But he was unsure what.

* * *

The next morning, Ofentse felt the vibration alert of an incoming call. It was from Umar. Ofentse patted down his hair and tried to smile. "Hello, Umar, how are you doing?"

Umar didn't return his smile. "Mr. Mataka, I received your encrypted message asking for a face-to-face meeting. What's this about?"

Though Ofentse kept his smile in place, inside he was seething. Umar wouldn't have dared to question Howie this way. It showed the other board members didn't see him at the head of the table yet. He needed to appoint a seventh, deciding vote. He thought Toni Demirci, his old protégé, would be a safe choice.

"Umar, I believe the message you received was clear enough, so I'm not going to repeat myself. We need to move quickly. The longer you stay away, the longer the vacuum at the head of the Consortium will obstruct us. The Consortium is bleeding money. The Chinese are silently plotting to take over our business and our mines. They think that, with Howie dead, we are weak. We need to plug that hole as soon as possible."

Umar's face was still expressionless. "I'm currently on my way to Earth. I need to deal with a problem in a propellant factory there. Why don't we schedule a meeting on Halona at this time next Sunday?"

Ofentse's smile warmed. "I'll be honored to receive you, Umar. I wish you luck on your jour—"

Umar ended the call before Ofentse could finish his statement.

"Stupid prick. I hope he chokes on his water ice and freezes his balls off."

Ofentse knew he didn't need to like Umar to work with him, but Umar needed to respect him. Ofentse had been working mines before Umar had had his first kiss; he knew more about mines, propellants, and the dynamics and politics that ran those mines than anyone, except Howie Rich. To be disrespected by someone who wouldn't even matter if he hadn't been lucky enough to find a better alternative to propellant rubbed Ofentse the wrong way.

Next on the list was Randy Quarles. Randy was always the life of the party — the perennial optimist could see a rainbow over the shittiest cloud. He was also a second-generation miner, whose knowledge of the mines could mean he'd be a worthy successor to Howie. Ofentse had arranged to meet Randy on his turf, a sign of respect that Randy would understand and appreciate; he'd also brought along a bottle of whiskey—exceedingly rare in these parts—that would put him very high on Randy's favored list.

As soon as Randy saw Ofentse, he embraced him with a bear hug.

"Ofentse, boyo, what are you doing here slumming with the dirty folk instead enjoying the view from Halona?"

Ofentse laughed and returned the hug. As soon as they pulled apart, Randy led Ofentse to his office where, with a flourish, Ofentse produced the bottle of whiskey. He smiled to himself as Randy's eyes sparkled and the man rubbed his hands together with glee.

"Today must be Christmas, Independence Day, and my luckiest day all rolled into one," Randy said. "Ofentse, what do you want from me? No one gifts whiskey as fine as this for free."

Ofentse chuckled. Randy was nobody's fool, but Ofentse knew the right cards to play. So he got straight to the point.

"Randy, we have known each other long enough for me to appreciate that I wouldn't get anywhere bullshitting you. I want your support at the board meeting in three weeks. I want you to support my bid to become Head of the Consortium."

It was Randy's turn to laugh. He got up from his chair, went to the table to fetch cups, and came back to face Ofentse. Before speaking, Randy opened the whiskey bottle, sniffed it appreciatively, and poured generous portions into the two cups.

As he handed one of the cups to Ofentse, Randy said, "I'm sorry I don't have the best crystal to serve the drinks with, but these will have to do."

Ofentse, who rarely drank alcohol, took a sip while watching Randy take a healthy gulp and smack his lips.

"You know, Ofentse," Randy said, "you have my support. I've been hearing unsettling rumors about the Chinese and their plans to weaken us. We need someone who can be as ruthless as Howie was. I'm sure you can do it."

At the rate things were going, Ofentse thought he would have his majority within the week. He didn't need to force his smile this time around as he said, "Thank you, Randy, I was sure I would have you in my corner. I assure you that I will make more use of your many talents, instead of just shutting you out in the mines."

Randy gave a booming laugh. "Boyo, you and Howie aren't so different after all. He also tried to take me away from the mines, but that is what I do best. It's what I grew up doing; it's what I'll die doing. Being on the board is enough for me. I have no intention of being another Ofentse Mataka. No offense intended."

Ofentse's smile dimmed, but he forced it to stay in place even though his face was hurting from the effort.

"Randy, my dear friend, I said the same thing when I was in the African mines. One thing I realized, though, is that we never give ourselves credit for how much we can evolve if we offer ourselves the chance to do so." With his plastic smile still in place, he took another sip of his drink and rose. "I would have loved to spend the rest of the day with you, but I have some boring office stuff to do on Halona, so I'll get out of your hair. Thank you once again, Randy."

Before Ofentse could leave, Randy held out a hand and dropped his voice down to a whisper. "I might be at the asshole of the Moon, but I hear things. And one of the things I've heard is that Howie isn't dead, although he might be an avatar."

Ofentse looked at Randy for a long time, his mind racing, then started to laugh. "I'm sorry, Randy, but I think the whiskey has gone straight to your head. I've heard they plan to make a statue to commemorate him on Halona."

Randy looked a little embarrassed and smiled sheepishly. "Well, you can't blame a man for being hopeful. I heard Carl tried to save him by getting him to Quivira for emergency medical assistance. Maybe Polyakov achieved a miracle."

Ofentse, trying to humor Randy, nodded. "Yeah, Professor Polyakov tried her best, but there was nothing she could do. No one wishes Howie was still with us more than me, Randy. He was much more than a mentor to me."

Ofentse considered his conversation with Randy. There was no way Howie was still alive. Howie wasn't one to stay in the background— if he was alive, he would have found a way to exact his revenge. But doubts began to plague him. *What if it had all gone wrong?*

Ofentse tried to put the thought of Howie being alive out of his mind so he could work on convincing Umar and Chris, but his conversation with Randy began to gnaw at Ofentse as the days passed. Was it possible that Howie was still alive?

Driven by a mix of curiosity and dread, Ofentse conducted some discreet investigations. The outcome was astonishing: damnation, it was true—Howie, the old bastard, was indeed still among the living. That treacherous viper Polyakov had intervened, saving him from the jaws of death. Even if Howie was some kind of floating avatar, his presence remained a formidable force that could not be underestimated. The realization sent a tremble down Ofentse's spine, and he felt his hand begin to tremble with an involuntary shiver.

Ofentse knew Howie would track him down and come after him.

He didn't have to wait long.

Ofentse was having a quick snack when his communicator vibrated. Ofentse checked the caller: Professor Olga Polyakov, Dr. César's deputy. Ofentse practiced his surprised face before accepting the call. He knew it was the summons.

"Olga, how's everything in Quivira? I have to say, I wasn't expecting your call. Is everything all right? What plans—"

Olga cut him off. "Ofentse, this isn't a social call. I need to know where you are and if you're alone."

It took everything within Ofentse to stay in character. He put on his concerned face and asked, "What's wrong, Olga? I'm at Tricala, on Howie's orders. I'll be going to our mines for a week before heading back to Halona. I'm sorry, but I can't tell you the details of my mission, it's between Howie and me."

"Howie and César are dead."

Ofentse didn't have to feign surprise — the shock that registered on his face was genuine.

"What? When? César? Who could have killed him? I know Howie had a lot of enemies, but everyone loved César. He's the father of the Heavenly Babies, the great innovator, and one of the greatest minds out there. How did it happen?"

Olga looked confused. She shook her head, then closed her eyes for a moment. "I don't know what happened. But what I do know is we need you on Halona as soon as possible. Get the fastest form of transport there that you can. Howie has been moved to Quivira. An autopsy will be performed, and he will then be atomized. César has already had a natural cremation at the location." She paused. "What's your ETA, Ofentse?"

Ofentse pretended to think about it. He had made private arrangements to get back to Halona as soon as he was informed of Howie's death. Dr. César's death, though shocking, would have been good news for Ofentse; it meant the road to the top would have been a little clearer. But now he realized it was all a trap. Polyakov was trying to lure him back. Then he would be a doomed man, at Howie's mercy.

Ofentse took a deep, dramatic sigh. "I'll leave here immediately. Where are you?"

"I'm on Quivira, trying to get things in place. We need you to set up logistics for a memorial for Howie, and inform the rest of the Consortium. We'll talk when you get to Halona."

With that brief conversation, Ofentse knew Howie was alive and Olga was his agent. He needed to go into hiding somewhere Howie couldn't find him, but where could he go? It wouldn't be easy. He knew he didn't have much time before Howie came looking for him. Ofentse started to panic.

Then, like an epiphany, it hit him. The only person he could trust was the person who had replaced him as the head of the African mines: His sidekick and protégé, Toni Demirci.

He chuckled to himself. The good thing was that she wasn't on the board, so she probably wouldn't know about Howie's accident. They had got on pretty well too; Ofentse had always fancied her. He would not mind taking refuge with her.

Ofentse had given Toni the opportunity of a lifetime by proposing her to Dr. César as one of the egg donors for the Heavenly Babies when he was looking for contributors. Unlike Teagan Ward, Toni wanted nothing to do with "her" baby; she did not want to be a surrogate mother. As soon as she was paid and got the promotion she was promised, Toni had left to head up one of the Consortium's Earth operations, where she had produced a string of successes.

Ofentse wondered why he hadn't thought of Toni before. It probably had to do with everything that had happened lately.

Feeling a sudden sense of urgency, Ofentse used a secure link to place a call to Toni.

"Ofentse, how are you doing? Haven't heard from you in a while."

"I've been visiting Tricala. Comms are a bit more difficult on the far side." Ofentse knew it was a weak excuse, but it would have to do.

"I heard about Howie. That must have been terrible for you."

So she did know, but thought Howie was dead.

"We were all shocked," he replied.

She hesitated a moment before saying, "Not to sound rude, Ofentse, but why are you calling me?"

Ofentse smiled. Toni had always been blunt, maybe even too direct. Some might be offended by Toni's abrupt manner, but Ofentse was used to it. He didn't have time for frivolities either.

"Do you know MaureenGrau?" he asked.

"Ofentse, I don't have time to go down memory lane or reminisce about old flames. Why are you calling me?"

Ofentse mentally kicked himself. He had been getting easily distracted recently and losing his train of thought. Nevertheless, Ofentse reminded himself he had to be at the top of his game if he was to outsmart Howie.

"I'm sorry, Toni, the events of the past few days have affected me. Anyway, I want you to be my Maureen Grau. Before Howie died, he and I were planning a new city, one that would rival both Quivira and Halona in human and artificial intelligence and amenities."

Ofentse saw the spark of interest in Toni's eyes. Now to reel her in.

"I have reliable sources that have assured me that demand and price for real estate on the Moon are about to skyrocket. If we are perfectly positioned by the time this surge happens, we will not only be filthy rich, but will be in a position of immense influence and power."

Ofentse could see that Toni was considering his proposal. It pleased him that she trusted him enough not to think of his plan as the ramblings of a madman.

"I'm guessing this isn't Consortium business," Toni finally said. "If I'm going to run this, it means I have to leave a well-paying job with a huge prospect for advancement. Why would I want to leave that for what is essentially a pipe dream? Apart from a potential loss of income, there's also the lack of challenge. What exactly would be the scope of my job?"

Ofentse smiled at her questions. She was clearly taking him seriously.

"I wouldn't have thought of you if I thought this job wouldn't be a challenge to your vast talents. As for the financial remuneration, let's say a fifty percent increase in your basic salary. Like you correctly assumed, this will be a privately owned venture. I represent a group of anonymous investors, and we are also willing to give you a five percent stake to be the face of the city. I'll send you all you need to know, Toni. Please give me a response by the end of tomorrow."

"Tomorrow, Ofentse? Give me 'til the end of the week. I'll check out your proposal and inform you of my decision."

Ofentse shook his head. "No offense, Toni, but I don't have the luxury of time. I've sent you the documents. Read them and get back to me. Have a great day."

Ofentse smiled to himself. Getting Toni on board would be a master stroke. If everything went according to plan, she would be his cover while they both made a profit.

5

THE LURE

Des Moines, Iowa, July 10, 2102

THE DECISION TO SEND Shiko to GLOSCOM was driven by a combination of factors.

First, the practical: The Consortium had commercial ties with GLOSCOM. Second, the personal: Maureen had links from the old days with the Head of Finance. And third, the strategic: Understanding food in space seemed essential.

Maureen had personally coached Shiko about his new role. The job was meant to provide him a rich and meaningful learning experience that would not only expand his technical skills, but also amplify his understanding of the complex interplay between science, the corporate world, and society, all while enabling the Consortium to deepen its ties with a long-time partner.

"Just remember who you are," Maureen told him, although what she'd meant by that was not clear to Shiko and he'd not had the foresight to ask.

From the start, Shiko eagerly plunged into his work at GLOSCOM, keen to learn from the experts and contribute to cutting-edge research in agricultural science. He was captivated by the company's scientific achievements and the potential they held for addressing global food security challenges. He specifically wanted to study seeds that could be used in space and low-gravity environments. After all, as well as being a source of food, plants played a crucial role in maintaining life support systems on space habitats by absorbing carbon dioxide and releasing oxygen through photosynthesis.

One plant variety that especially attracted Shiko was tomatoes. What intrigued him was that they were classified as both fruit and vegetables, depending on who you were talking to, and seemed to be related to potatoes, even though they didn't look alike. Yet, strangely, their flowers were the same.

Like other plants, tomatoes contributed to the replenishment of oxygen levels in the habitat, helping to create a more livable environment for crew members and residents. Tomatoes were also a popular part of the diet on Quivira, and Shiko had decided to see how to improve the varieties that already grew well.

Although he had his own office, Shika also had a seat in the lab near Ravina Patel, a plant biologist with a background in agricultural science and genetics. Ravina had grown up in a rural village near the city of Satara in India, nestled amidst the greenery of the Western Ghats mountain range in the state of Maharashtra. Shiko would bring her coffee and tell her jokes, and Ravina had quickly become fascinated by his life on Quivira.

"I can't believe this is your first time on Earth. It must be so weird!"

Shiko didn't know what to say, so he just smiled.

He learned from Ravina that her home region was prone to droughts and water scarcity, particularly during the dry months between monsoon seasons. Farmers struggled to irrigate their crops and often relied on traditional rainwater harvesting techniques to conserve precious water resources.

One day, while analyzing the genetic sequences of the modified tomatoes, Shiko noticed a puzzling anomaly in the data: Certain genes that were supposed to enhance pest resistance and improve fruit quality appeared to have been altered in unexpected ways, resulting in unintended side effects and potential health risks.

He showed the data to Ravina, who was sitting near him with an air of attentive curiosity. Her back was straight, shoulders slightly squared, projecting an aura of confidence and poise. As her eyes scanned the figures on the screen, she leaned forward ever so slightly, her brow furrowing in concentration.

A moment later, a spark of understanding lit up her expression, and her lips curled into a satisfied smile. "These modifications are not aimed at improving nutritional value or agricultural productivity," she said, "but simply at generating more sales."

"Yeah, like I thought," responded Shiko. "Although, to play devil's advocate, what's wrong with making things taste better?"

"On the surface, making crops taste better might seem harmless," she said, "but the implications go far beyond simply enhancing flavor." She gestured toward the data on his screen, indicating the patterns of genetic modifications. "These alterations aren't just about improving taste," she explained.

"They're about fundamentally changing the nutritional composition of the crops and prioritizing certain traits over others."

"But why does that matter?" he pressed. "Isn't that the idea?"

"Think about it this way," she said. "By prioritizing traits like caloric content and palatability, these genetic modifications are potentially contributing to the prevalence of unhealthy, processed foods in the global food supply."

Ravina—whose expertise in plant genetics and molecularbiology made her a valuable asset to the company—pointed to a graph displaying rising rates of obesity and diet-related diseases. "We're facing a global health crisis," she continued. "Obesity, diabetes, heart disease: these are all linked to poor dietary habits and overconsumption of foods high in sugar, fat, and empty calories."

"So by manipulating crops to make them more palatable, we're essentially fueling this crisis," Shiko surmised.

"Exactly," Ravina affirmed. "And it's not just about health. These practices also contribute to environmental degradation, loss of biodiversity, and socioeconomic inequalities in access to nutritious food." Shiko leaned back in his chair, processing the information. "I never realized how interconnected it all is," he admitted. "But what can we do about it?"

"Nothing," advised Ravina as she got ready to leave for home. "Take the money and shut up!" She had known hardship, and she wasn't about to give up a great job in a big multinational like GLOSCOM.

She paused, then added before leaving, "But I'm not a sellout. I'm still committed to upholding scientific integrity and prioritizing the wellbeing of people and the planet. Just so you know!" She wiggled her head endearingly.

Shiko sat, looking at the data, and decided to download part of it via the Cryptex neural interface embedded under the skin of his forearm. The implant was linked to his peripheral nervous system and brain, and only activated with Shiko's unique neural and physiological signature. He assumed it could not be accessed by GLOSCOM. Shiko preferred this type of interface to total neural integration — he'd heard of corporate implants being exploited to brainwash or control individuals, and GLOSCOM's reputation made him cautious.

As he delved deeper into his work, Shiko began to grapple with some of the ethical questions surrounding GLOSCOM's practices.

When he got home, he passed Kat in the hallway.

"Hi #7!" he shouted at her.

She grinned. "Want some lumpia?" Kat asked.

"Lump of what?"

"Not lump, lumpia. I've been cooking."

Kat let him into her apartment, where Shiko immediately got a whiff of cabbage.

As he followed behind, Kat's long dark hair flowing ahead of him, he noticed again that she had a striking natural beauty. Her features were delicate yet expressive, with eyes that gleamed with intelligence and empathy. She sat him next to the kitchen table and offered him a plate of crispy fried rolls stuffed with some kind of filling.

Shiko hesitated.

"Try it," Kat directed. "It's a Filipino snack." She dipped it into a sauce in a bowl and handed the thin roll to him with her fingers.

He took a bite. It crunched in his mouth as he tried to taste what was in it.

"It's made of pork, with carrots and cabbage," she explained.

"Delicious," he said politely. "No tomatoes?"

She ignored his question. "Have some more."

"I've never had this before. What's the sauce?"

"Spicy garlic chili."

"I like it. Better than the bland food on Quivira." Shiko paused.

He began to look at her, as if for the first time, then asked, "So where's this food from?"

"The Philippines."

"You're Filipino?"

"No," she said, "but I was brought up in Palawan, which is an island in the Philippines."

"So how come you're here?" Shiko asked. Kat laughed. "Palawan is a slice of heaven. I have a deep connection to our islands. But I knew that we would have to actively defend our land and the seas surrounding them."

"Defend them from what?"

"From ecological destruction. I knew we were in a fight and, to respond, I needed training. That's why I opted for a degree in Environmental Science and Policy at the University of California. Driven by my love for the outdoors and a desire to make a difference."

"What did you learn there?"

"I immersed myself in the study of ecology, sustainability,and environmental justice, gaining a comprehensive understanding of the complex interplay between human society and the natural environment."

Shiko was impressed.

"Just kidding! Mostly I chased boys and had a good time." Kat laughed.

Shiko looked disappointed, but pushed past it and said, "You know, I probably looked down on you every day. Quivira mostly flies over the equator."

"You might have looked down on us, but we're equals now," Kat told him. "In fact, in my heels, I might even be taller!"

He laughed. Despite her slender frame, Shiko had noticed that Kat possessed a quiet strength and confidence that shone through every time she moved. He was pleased they were neighbors.

Lining up for coffee the next morning, he found himself standing behind Dr. Canek and decided to discuss his findings with her. Her hair was coiled into a perfect silver-black twist at the nape of her neck, not a strand out of place.

"Elena," he said, after clearing his throat and getting her attention. " I've noticed some strange things in my research and wanted to get your opinion."

"Sure, happy to discuss anything. Glad that you're getting stuck into your work."

"I've been noticing some weird things in the data," Shiko began.

"Like what?" She turned to him, her eyes unsettling—cold, unblinking, and pale gray, like mist trapped in glass. They didn't just look at him—they dissected him, catalogued him.

"Some genes seem to have been altered in unexpected ways."

"Why would that be unexpected?" Dr. Canek asked. "That's what we do, Shiko. We alter plants to make them better, as well as giving them more shelf-life."

"Yes," Shiko pressed, "but this could actually cause sickness in humans."

"You've just started here, Shiko," she said after a moment."I think you should spend a bit of time finding your feet."

Shiko looked at her. Her stare made him feel less like a man and more like one of her lab results. "Take care, Shiko," Dr. Canek added. "Everything we do is safe and effective. There's no need to imagine things that aren't there." She paid for her coffee and left.

Shiko didn't want to challenge her or stir up trouble, so instead he decided to dig a little deeper.

He began to stay behind in the evenings to access the data, and it didn't take long from him to begin to uncover disturbing patterns of genetic modifications designed to increase the caloric content and taste or palatability of certain crops, such as corn and soybeans.

But maybe he wasn't uncovering anything new. As Dr. Canek had said, "that's what we do."

THE DECAYING PLANET

Tethys, Lyra Constellation, July 12, 2102

O**N A SPACESHIP NESTLED** behind Tethys, part of the Lyra constellation in the Milky Way, seven Tritan leaders were gathered around a large circular table, their insect-like heads twitching with anticipation and worry. Their faces were set with determination, but their bulging eyes betrayed fear and desperation.

The Tritans didn'thave a single ruler; they were run by a High Council, and all decisions were made by voting. Every Tritan at this meeting had been selected by each of the seven districts to sit on the Council. Asmegin Krognar, a botanist and the youngest member, was the Council Chair.

"Order, order," he called out, trying to get members to settle down, but the muffled chatter between them continued. He used his four upper limbs expressively: his two dominant manipulators that resemble elongated hands with jointed, claw-like digits, and two smaller limbs he reserved for precision tasks or particular gestures that he now curled in a request for calm.

The seats at the round table were smooth and cool to the touch, each one designed to fit the unique physical features of the Tritans. Their exoskeletons provided a hard outer shell, but their sensitive antennae showed signs of nervousness as they twitched and fidgeted. They knew they were living on borrowed time: Their home planet, Trita Prime, was dying, and they needed decisions fast.

The Tritans had taken just a few millennia to build a technologically advanced, planet-wide society functioning in harmony with nature. Despite being fully capable of interstellar space travel, the Tritans had no desire to leave their planet. They were clever, inventive, and evolved.

But a while ago, everything began to change. The once-thriving motherland started to turn barren. Fallout from an advancing black hole meant they did not have much time to shore up their defenses or find another home.

They had begun a search, and now it was time to hear the results of the reconnaissance probes.

Their scientists had told them they either needed to revive their planet or move to another one. They had sent out several probes to locate a suitable new homeland, and now it was time to see if their faith in the experts would be rewarded.

They heard that two probes had crashed on the moon of a promising blue planet; one of the teams had narrowly escaped being crushed by a falling asteroid after taking refuge in a convenient lunar lava tube. The omens were not good.

The Tritans' homeworld, Trita Prime, was behind a dead star to one side of the Lyra constellation, ensuring the Tritans prospered without interference from outsiders. The planet's soaring crystalline formations radiated hues of purple and green. Travelers used the bright star Vega as a guidepost to reach Trita Prime, and only the Draxid, occupying Cygnus, ever bothered them.

The High Council gathered around a glowing holographic map of the galaxy, with Trita Prime at the center. The walls were covered in blinking screens, and the air was filled with a hushed tension. The fate of their species hung in the balance as they waited for an answer from their specialists.

As soon as the last member of the High Council was seated, they plugged themselves into the artificial intelligence and listened.

"Welcome. The scoutships have brought in their reports. We have found four viable planets in this solar system," said the team coordinator, Captain Calytricx Draeven.

"One scout ship found a planet just at the edge of the solar system. Its inhabitants have died out, affected by some virus. It is smaller than Trita Prime, but it is ready for occupation. A bit of an effort to get to.

"The second one is a promising blue planet called Earth by the inhabitants, orbiting an unassuming yellow dwarf. It has a moon that can also be exploited. The blue planet is inhabited by a primitive mammalian species known as humans that has spent thousands of years slaughtering each other. Fortunately for us, they are on the verge of destroying their habitat and each other. The elevated levels of pollution mean it is already becoming uninhabitable for them. They are an obstacle easily cleared. The land is still productive, although patches are barren after being planted with sterile seeds.

"Another is a red planet known as Mars, with two moons. It is barren and would need terraforming. Its atmosphere is rather thin, and we may be in competition with the humans for it. They have already begun creating minor settlements.

"In all three cases, we will need suitable vegetation to reproduce and thrive. Most of the resources on Trita Prime are withering or have already been wiped out. A fourth option is the Veridian Delta, but it may be geologically unstable. We need tests."

The coordinator looked around. Her chitinous exoskeleton gleamed a deep bronze-black under the ambient light, segmented and organically armored like sculpted plate mail.

"Thank you for the report," Asmegin said. "Any questions?" He waved his elongated index finger in the air as if summoning responses. "We need to evaluate which site is best for us and how to secure the necessary nutrition for continued existence at the new location," he continued. "Although some of our expeditions have survived off minerals in the soil, we will need vegetation for a normal diet."

"Our seeds are all sterile and won't germinate," Vrillon Zorvaxya, the longest serving member on the Council, observed.

"We'll just have to change our diet," said Aak'iks Nebbxchi, the de facto Head of Intelligence, who had been munching on a small tablet of lava that had been distributed in bowls around the table. Aak'iks, tall and astute, but often off-putting by being too direct, was still awaiting formal confirmation on the High Council.

"Not very practical," said Pell Cciottix, the Tritans' chief engineer, who had been on one of the scouting missions and had been invited to the council session.

Asmegin sat pensively, his eyes wide but his antenna drooping. When he had been asked to join the High Council, he had taken it as an honor. Today, he wasn't so sure. As Chair of the Council, his job was to see to the wellbeing of the Tritans, but it was now proving to be an almost impossible task.

"I was being facetious. But I do have a suggestion," Aak'iks said.

"Chairman Asmegin, what do you know about the Seeds of Life project?"

Asmegin straightened in his seat. "Although I'm a botanist, I don't think I have ever come across the phrase." He looked to the other members of the High Council to see if they had heard of it before, but they also looked blank.

"The Seeds of Life project is a way to ensure that the Tritans continue to exist," said Aak'iks. "One of our expeditions became aware of it when they crash landed on the Earth's moon some time ago. While awaiting rescue, they came into contact with a few humans. One in particular has various hardy seeds preserved in her care: Clara Ward. She's keeping those seeds to revive the Earth in the future, given all of its pollution and climate problems. Their continuous wars don't help either. She has a ready-made storehouse of the seeds that could possibly heal our ailing ecosystems and restore balance to our planet."

As Aak'iks spoke, a human woman's picture showed on the screen. They scanned her in both natural light and infrared, but picked up nothing unusual. Clara Ward appeared kindly.

"How accessible are these seeds?" asked Vrillon.

"I'm not sure. I don't think the seeds are guarded," responded Aak'iks. "We need two types of seed, known by ancient names, according to my report: The twin remedies of Sigillaria and Silphium. Sigillaria to revive the soil and Silphium to replenish our bodies, as we are getting weaker by the day.

"Sigillaria grows rapidly and is ideal for our soil. It reproduces from spores distributed by cones. Although it went extinct on Earth, technicians at the seed bank have extracted fragments of its genetic code. Most importantly, Sigillaria is not just a plant, it is a conduit for the mystical energies that define Trita Prime.

"Sigillaria's rootsystem can harness the crystalline formations in the soil, summoning the cosmic forces within our home world. When summoned to the surface through the rituals performed by the Tritan priestesses, Sigillaria takes on several distinct forms that can resonate with cosmic frequencies, making it a versatile defensive tool in the hands of those who understand the ancient arts to protect our planet and way of life."

A long silence followed Aak'iks's explanation. No one was certain how relevant all this was.

"How long will it take?" called out one member of the public who had been allowed in as an observer. "We're getting desperate."

"That we will have to study, but we can survive until then," responded Nokaen Craxaddin, the top cosmologist on the Council.

"Other ideas?"

"The moons of Saturn offer some hope. But moving there will require more resources and adaptation than we can muster," said Craxaddin,

Nobody said anything.

"Sounds like we have no alternative suggestions," Asmegin observed.

In the end, the High Council had to make a decision.

"You will pick a team, and go to this human and get the seeds of life from her. Try to make it amicable," directed Asmegin to the expedition team leaders Asimov and Draeven.

"If she resists?" asked Draeven.

Aak'iks answered before Asmegin could. "If she resists, you may apply force. Our future depends on it."

The directive triggered uproar among members of the High Council.

"Might I say a word?" asked Asimov, the expedition commander who had experienced a hard landing on the Earth's moon.

"We recognize your courage in your recent expedition, Commander. The floor is yours," said Asmegin.

"Aak'iks has made his opinion known," Asimov said, "and he has a point. This human would never easily part with what she regards as her life's work. I agree our technology is far superior, but we are about to have no home. We need friends, not enemies. In my view, diplomacy will be better than violence. We must at least recognize that the humans have had the foresight to create a reserve that we do not have."

Aak'iks looked at the commander with disdain. "And who are you? Aren't you the one who managed to crash your scout craft on the surface of a minor moon, thus delaying our urgent reconnaissance missions? What do you know of tactics? The human life form is beneath us; their technology is basic at best. You don't negotiate with a lower lifeform, you simply take what you want from it. We will not go to this human to bargain. If we don't secure our future, the Draxid will be at our door."

The members of the High Council looked around, as if to consult.

"Is there a better way?" Thaldor Eoxonus—a representative from an outer region—asked while scratching his face with one long nail. "Can we develop the seeds ourselves?"

"We don't have time," responded Nokaen. "The advancing decay means our doom if we do not act. Our beloved planet cannot be saved."

Asmegin tried to look impassive, but his mind was racing. He was in a conundrum. His people needed the seeds to secure their future, but he wasn't comfortable with grabbing them through violence. That was not their way. He watched the images of Clara Ward again. She looked well-meaning and sincere. Peace was a better route than war.

"Do we know what seeds they have?" Asmegin asked.

"When I did a scan of her brain, Dr. Ward seemed proudest of her recovery of spores from a Sigillaria cone," said Asimov. "Sigillaria is long-extinct on Earth, but it's ideal for our atmosphere on Trita Prime. Its long roots have a regenerative effect on the soil, and it is very hardy; the trunk is protected by diamond-shaped scales. It grows quickly, and has long, slender, grass-like leaves that capture dwindling sunlight with unprecedented efficiency. These leaves utilize not only visible light, but also various parts of the electromagnetic spectrum, including infrared and ultraviolet radiation."

Asmegin raised his hand to call for silence. "I suggest we equip some new ships to return to the Earth's moon to find Dr. Clara Ward and ask for her assistance. "

"By any means necessary?" asked Aak'iks.

"Firmly, but politely. Am I clear now, Aak'iks?"

"I second that," said Nokaen, anxious to be reasonable in the face of adversity.

7

CLARA'S SEED BANK

Philolaus Crater, near the Moon's North Pole, July 16, 2102

As she did every morning, Clara Ward took the elevator down from the barren, angular entrance in the Moon's Philolaus Crater to the large underground vault system housing her seed bank, one of the biggest collections of seeds from all over the world. The vault was a treasure trove, the result of a love of humankind and a lifetime of diligent and dedicated collecting in pursuit of biodiversity.

Clara's footsteps echoed on the stark concrete floor of the huge subterranean cavern. As she walked through rows of neatly stacked shelves holding vacuum-packed silver packets, sealed jars, and test tubes, she could hear the hum of the air conditioning keeping the seed bank's temperature at a constant chill.

She stopped at a workbench where bots were sorting and filing recently contributed seeds from Earth; the seeds were stored in neatly stacked boxes on shelves that stretched from the concrete floor to the white ceiling. Making her way through the rows of seeds, Clara could detect a faint hint of earthy mushrooms from the new acquisitions from Sumatra.

"Those go on the top shelf of Room D," she told one of the bots.

"Yes, ma'am."

Here in this vault lay wild and ancient varieties that couldn't be easily found on Earth but whose DNA was priceless for future generations. What Noel had dubbed the Seeds of Life project had started almost as a hobby for Clara. While she was at her home in Arizona, she had started collecting and cataloging seeds when she went on her daily walks. But, once she had started at the Malapert moonbase, the project took on a life of its own.

Now it wasn't just a hobby, it was a project that might determine the survival of Earth. Greenhouse gases were at record levels, and almost all humans living on the planet had some amount of microplastics in their bodies. Climate change had turned swathes of vegetation into deserts or swamps, and many areas were no longer habitable for humans, either through flooding or extreme temperatures. Flora and fauna were going extinct at an alarming rate, and vast stretches of coral reef had simply calcified and died.

Clara believed her seeds might aid the slow process of restoration and revival, and ultimately halt the death of Earth. She had accumulated millions of samples from farmers and well-wishers over the years; generous gene banks around the world, under threat of closure or being bought by GLOSCOM, had sent shipments. Every day, new varieties of seeds would be flown in for safe keeping.

Clara carefully sorted through newly arrived packets from places such as Indonesia, Brazil, Siberia, and southern Africa. The bots would handle the repacking and storage.

Then she came across a packet with familiar handwriting —Teagan's.

Her daughter had been a great help with her Seeds of Life project since moving to California with her partner, the artist, Julian Trace. Teagan had helped gather heirloom seeds for her, classifying and hermetically sealing the contributions before forwarding the seeds for registration and storing in the moon vault. Sometimes she would add a personal note about why this seed or variety was important.

Clara smiled fondly; Teagan's interest in the project had touched her deeply, making her feel it was all worthwhile.

"Open-pollinated and particularly delicious," Teagan had written on the latest shipment. "Nothing cardboard about this one!"

As Clara turned over a small container pot made by Teagan in her hands, she thought about how their family's lives had changed over the years. She and her husband, Noel, had initially been academics, envisioning a life in the Arizona suburbs with their two children, Hunter and Teagan. But now, Clara's pale skin—speckled with age spots—had a slight blue tint to it, caused by low blood oxygen from living in the lunar colony for so long. She was one of the pioneers after all, having lived half her life on the Moon, dedicated to preserving plant diversity for future generations. And she was still at it, though walking a bit less steadily.

Climate change and industrial farming practices on Earth had dramatically reduced plant diversity. Huge monopoly seed corporations had increased crop yields at the expense of biodiversity, and monoculture agriculture had left food supplies more susceptible to crippling diseases and drought, putting the future of humankind at risk. Shops sold fewer varieties of fruit and vegetables that were increasingly tasteless.

Clara heard a bot at the entrance and buzzed the new delivery in. Despite installing a security pass system, it was still too easy to enter and exit the vault. *But who would go through such trouble for seeds in such a remote and inaccessible location?* she thought.

Even as one of the pioneers of space colonization, Clara had never expected to end up here. But then came the Great Unraveling — climate change, violence, and resource depletion had ravaged Earth. The race to colonize lower Earth orbit or LEO, the Moon, Mars, and beyond had intensified. And Clara had been recruited by a research facility at the Malapert Lunar Base, near the Moon's South Pole.

She laughed to herself as she remembered her boss Alain Gagnon's bushy, protruding eyebrows. *Weird how some memories stick with you.*

Clara had always been a strong-willed woman, determined to make a life for herself on the Moon. But as she held Teagan's handmade pot in her hands, memories of their family and how everything had changed flooded her mind. The Great Unraveling had turned their lives upside down, forcing them to leave Earth behind and start anew.

At first, it had seemed like a good idea — a fresh start away from the violence and chaos back home. But now, as she thought about all the 'what ifs,' Clara couldn't help but wonder if they had made the wrong choice. If they had stayed on Earth, Teagan wouldn't have had her eggs harvested by that doctor and fallen into a depression.

Maybe Clara could have prevented everything from spiraling out of control. Ultimately, Clara's decision to move to Malapert had caused a ripple effect that turned her daughter into a fugitive, her husband into an obsessed man, and herself into a survivalist. Hunter, meanwhile, had joined a multinational team that cleaned up space junk, called Starfire, which meant he was out of contact for what seemed like ages, separating the family by time and space.

Melancholy filled Clara as she wondered if there were things she should have done differently. Had her ambition torn the family apart?

But, as usual, Clara pushed these thoughts away. There was nothing gained in regrets, and if things hadn't happened the way they did, she would never have had the chance to build a cherished bond with her wonderful grandchildren, Nevaeh and Liam, who'd been born in space.

She scratched her hand. A little bit of blood dripped to the floor.

More DNA to clear up, Clara thought.

She went to get a dehydrated packet soup from the kitchen. All she had to do was add water. She wondered how many times the precious H_2O had been recycled.

8
MRS JOHNSON

Des Moines, September 12, 2102

S HIKO DECIDED TO GIVE his work on the tomatoes a break. Instead, he began to look at the great American staple: Corn, otherwise known to the rest of the world as maize. He wanted to know why it was so popular worldwide.

He found that most maize grown now had been genetically modified to be more disease-resistant and have greater yields. That was good. But one small fact bothered him, a seemingly innocuous discrepancy in the data regarding the genetic modifications made to a particular strain of corn developed by GLOSCOM.

One afternoon, Shiko chose to go for a walk through the fields outside Des Moines. The sun created shapes through the tall grasses swaying gently in the breeze. The walk was a welcome escape from the odors of the city, where the smell of industrial fumes often hung heavy in the air. Here, though, the wind carried the scent of wildflowers and fresh earth, filling Shiko's lungs with a sense of peace.

He breathed deeply, closing his eyes for a moment, feeling the weight of the world slip away. With a sudden burst of energy, he waved his arms in the air as though he was about to begin a workout routine, laughing at the sheer freedom he felt. Earth was wonderful.

After wandering for a while, he arrived at a small clearing. There, nestled between the fields, was a community garden. Rows of vegetables, herbs, and flowers stretched out in neat beds, lovingly tended by local volunteers. A group of people—some old, some young—moved slowly between the plants, their hands deep in the soil. Shiko was drawn in by the simplicity of the scene, the way everyone seemed to be in tune with the land, with something ancient and grounding.

One elderly woman, her hair pulled back into a loose bun, caught his eye. She was bent over a bed of tomatoes, her hands stained brown from the earth. Shiko felt an impulse to speak to her.

"Hi there," he called out, stepping closer. "What a beautiful day!"

"Indeed," the lady replied, wiping her stained hands on her faded apron.

"This is amazing. How long have you been doing this?"

The woman straightened slowly, a kind smile spreading across her face. "Oh, we've been growing our own food here for years," she said, cleaning the tips of her fingers on the apron. "Just gathering in before the first frosts. Name's Mrs. Johnson. We started this garden as a way to give back to the community, but it's become much more than that."

Shiko was intrigued. "What do you mean?" he asked, after introducing himself without mentioning anything about his off-Earth upbringing.

Mrs. Johnson chuckled softly. "Well, it's not just about the food. These seeds we plant -- they're symbols of independence and perseverance. In a world that's always telling us what to buy, where to go, how to live, we've chosen to take control of something small but powerful. We believe in the power of seeds, not as commodities but as living things, carrying the promise of tomorrow." Her hand brushed over the packet of seeds in her pocket.

Shiko listened intently. He had never thought about it like that, how planting something in the earth was an act of defiance, of hope. And as they continued to talk, he found himself drawn in by the woman's calm wisdom and the weight of her words. He couldn't deny the significance of planting seeds, of taking control in a world that constantly tried to dictate your actions.

Mrs. Johnson described the plants she treasured and how she loved the smell of the soil. As she spoke about her love for their garden, her voice grew softer, almost as though she was about to share a dark secret, one that had been weighing on her for years.

"I can tell you're on a journey. You're on your way somewhere. With six steps forward, one step back," she said, her voice taking on a mystical quality. "Seven stars will light your track." Her eyes seemed far away, lost in memories as she recited the words. "The four winds whisper secrets true," she continued, her voice now barely above a whisper. "The path ahead is made for you."

The air around them seemed to hold its breath as she spoke, as if the words held some deep and ancient magic. Shiko couldn't shake off the feeling of unease that crept over him. Was it just a cryptic poem, or was there a hidden meaning within? As much as he wanted to know more, he also feared what he might discover.

Shiko blinked, hesitating, but his curiosity got the better of him. "What does that mean?"

Mrs. Johnson smiled again, but this time there was a hint of mystery on her face. "It's an old saying of my grandmother's," she explained. "A reminder that life is a journey — one where you might stumble, but the stars are always there to guide you if you pay attention. The winds will speak, if you listen closely enough. The path may be uncertain, but it's yours to walk."

Shiko felt a shiver run down his spine. It was as though Mrs. Johnson had spoken directly to a part of him he hadn't even realized was searching for something. He looked back at the garden, at the vibrant life bursting from the soil, and thought of how much it reflected what Mrs. Johnson had said. Seeds planted today, nurtured with care, could grow into something much greater than themselves, even through setbacks and uncertainty.

"Thank you," Shiko said softly, unsure if words could fully capture what he felt in that moment.

Mrs. Johnson simply nodded, her hands returning to the earth. "Keep walking, Shiko," she murmured. "And don't forget to look up at the stars."

Shiko turned her cryptic words over as he headed back to his small apartment. How did she know his name. Had he mentioned it and it had slipped his mind?

Her words began to take on added meaning as he thought more about them. Her mention of *"Six steps forward, one step back"* hinted that Shiko's journey would involve progress, but not without setbacks. However, the *"seven stars"* lighting his path suggested that despite the challenges, guidance and opportunities would appear, perhaps even from unexpected places.

The *"four winds whisper secrets true"* pointed to Shiko needing to listen closely to the subtle clues or advice that life and the world around him would offer; these *"whispers"* could be key to unlocking the deeper truths he needed to move forward.

Six, one, seven, four. That number again. What is that about?

Finally, her prediction that *the path ahead is made for you* implied that no matter how uncertain or difficult Shiko's future might become, the path was uniquely his. Possibly a message of reassurance, one that encouraged him to embrace his destiny with confidence, knowing that every experience—good or bad—was shaping him for something significant.

Inspired by Mrs. Johnson's words and her intimate garden, Shiko began to question his allegiance to GLOSCOM. Were genetically engineered crops truly the solution to Earth's food security challenges, or were they merely a symptom of a larger problem: The commodification of nature itself?

9
NOEL'S PACT

Tricala Lunar Base, November 21, 2102

THE ASTEROID ATTACK THAT destroyed Doctor César de Luca's moon lab a year before had not only obliterated all verifiable records of the Tritans after their crash landing at Marius Hills, but had also shattered Noel's hopes and dreams.

In an instant, Noel's work of recording his encounter with the Tritans had been rendered meaningless. All his hard work and data collection had been for nothing, erased in a matter of seconds. No one would believe his tale of the Tritans now. It would sound like the ravings of a madman. Colleagues would just say he had been dreaming; they would think that it was all a hallucination, the fictional imaginings of an old man who had been away from Earth too long.

It would not help that Noel's daughter, Teagan, had served as the Tritans' priestess, or that his wife had engaged in conversations with these remarkable and intelligent extraterrestrial beings. Their testimony would not be believable in the absence of tangible evidence. The recognition he had longed for was now lost forever, leaving him conflicted about his future and purpose.

Noel knew he had been lacking as a father. While ostensibly seeking security, he had prioritized his career over his daughter's future. His own son hardly spoke to him, and his wife lived in her own world — a world of seeds and the potential of life.

But what was his potential? What could he do now to recover? He wracked his brain, trying to think of a way to secure his legacy and gain the academic recognition that he craved.

An idea crept into Noel's mind like a whisper, a way to reclaim his standing in the academic realm, though it danced on the edge of ethical compromise.

He knew professors back in Arizona who had connections to corporate funding. He could do the same. If he could get a new lab, he'd be on his way to reclaiming his position. He knew that the Consortium had space on the far side of the Moon — ideal for an observatory of his own. A former professor of planetary sciences at the University of Arizona, Noel had always dreamed of making a significant discovery in space, something he could attach his name to.

Maybe he could use the observatory to reconnect with the Tritans and then his research would be published. Maybe he wouldn't have wasted his life.

But where would the money come from?

Maureen had friends inside GLOSCOM. They would finance him, no questions asked, but Clara would never abide by it. GLOSCOM was the enemy of sustainability and the enemy of honesty.

But GLOSCOM couldn't be all bad, he figured. Didn't they feed the world? And they had a really good philanthropic program. Did he really believe the tales of their shadowy agenda, even when collaboration could bring him status and funding?

Clara didn't have to find out.

Noel meticulously crafted a narrative that would present him as a reluctant hero. He would position himself as a discoverer of secrets, a scientist burdened with knowledge that the world needed but was not ready to accept. The story would be one of tragedy, personal sacrifice, and the burden of holding the key to humanity's future.

Assisted by Maureen and some other corporate friends, Noel orchestrated clandestine meetings, navigating the shadows where secrets and ambitions intertwined. GLOSCOM, sensing an opportunity to acquire untapped knowledge for its own purposes, welcomed him into its stifling fold, like the jaws of a Venus flytrap closing over its prey.

As the pact was sealed, Noel felt a shiver down his spine, a chilling mixture of trepidation and exhilaration. The weight of his family's disappointment, his daughter's disillusionment, and his son's distant resentment pressed heavily on his conscience. Yet the intoxicating allure of academic redemption and the potential for a place in history clouded his moral compass.

Where Quivira was a place for intellectuals and science, and Halona was a seat of art and music, Howie Rich had wanted Tricala to be a city of the stars. Howie had instructed Toni to coordinate construction.

It was an ideal location for Noel's project. The lunar surface, shielded from Earth's radio interference, offered a pristine environment for celestial observations. Noel had always dreamed of exploring the cosmos.

He assembled a team to support him, turning first to the kids he had helped educate on Quivira, who were now in their mid-twenties. Nevie was the queen of numbers, but she wasn't available. So, instead, Noel asked Liam, along with Tara. Tara, a virtual twin of Gabby, was full of sparkle and energy. He also tried to get in touch with Shiko, but he was on Earth on secondment in Des Moines and probably not recruitable, though Noel thought he would have been useful on vibrational waves. He would get him involved later.

Hunter's partner Kiana—who had successfully infiltrated and defanged the Iron Hornets—dropped in occasionally, but was forever on the move. She could help with security. At least Toni—like Teagan, one of the egg donors for Dr. César's project—was usually on hand as the current administrator of Tricala.

Through his contacts on Quivira and in Arizona, Noel gathered a small team of skilled engineers, scientists, and technicians to help him design a state-of-the-art observatory equipped with cutting-edge telescopes, detectors, and communication systems. Its purpose was to unlock the mysteries of the universe by observing celestial phenomena with unprecedented clarity.

The construction and transportation of the observatory components was a big undertaking, assisted by the Consortium. Howie had instructed Chris Stackpole, who ran moon mining operations, to provide all assistance.

Noel adjusted the calibration of the primary lens, his hands steady despite the weight of the moment. Noel had heard the good news that Teagan was pregnant with Julian's baby, and the thought of the news warmed him in the cold, silent expanse of the lunar far side. A natural birth — her own child.

He smiled to himself, imagining the joy it would bring to the family. The observatory might be his legacy to the stars, but Teagan's baby would be a legacy of love, a light as enduring and precious as any he might discover in the cosmos.

The lunar landscape echoed with the hum of machinery as the team worked diligently to piece together the observatory. Solar panels unfolded like delicate petals, absorbing the meager sunlight on the Moon's surface to power the facility. Telescopic arrays extended into the lunar sky, ready to capture the beauty of distant galaxies and elusive cosmic events.

And as the observatory took shape, that lunar night sky became a canvas for Noel's team to explore the wonders of the cosmos.

The team faced numerous challenges, from the harsh lunar environment to the logistical intricacies of transporting equipment across space. Undeterred, Noel and his crew developed innovative solutions, including modular structures that could be assembled on the Moon's surface from super-heated regolith.

With the help of large construction drones, Noel set up his Tricala observatory to study deep-space gravitational waves and strange patterns in cosmic background radiation, suspecting they may hold answers to unsolved mysteries in astrophysics. And once the observatory was fully operational, Noel and his team conducted a series of calibration tests, eagerly turning their gaze toward the cosmos.

The observatory became a window to the universe, capturing breathtaking images of distant galaxies, nebulae, and celestial phenomena.

Noel's dedication to his lunar observatory project was unwavering, but as the launch date approached, Clara expressed in a few conversations a growing sense of concern about the funding behind this ambitious venture. Who was behind it and what did they want in return?

One time, Clara had asked him directly: "Where's the money coming from?"

Noel had been evasive. "Supportive friends," he replied.

"Rich ones," she said.

"There's always a price to pay."

10
ARTURO'S HUMILIATION

Quivira, November 22, 2102

THE PERIOD AFTER HOWIE'S "accident" was one of perpetual humiliation for Arturo.

Arturo felt that he had saved Howie's life. He had been the one who discovered Howie's immobile body trapped in the blades of Halona's diaphragm door and brought help immediately. The body was rushed away, but nobody had thanked him. He had just been ignored.

Arturo had expected to succeed Howie. Surely it was his birthright? After all, wasn't the great man his real father? But no one had said anything. Arturo felt more neglected and lonely than normal. He had put in the time to gain expertise (everyone said he needed experience and smarts), but whatever he did was not good enough.

He had learned from the grapevine that Howie was thinking of appointing someone else. Maybe Chris Stackpole, the Canadian who ran the three biggest mines on the Moon. But Arturo had even heard talk of Howie appointing that bitch Toni. Chris he could stomach, but Toni? Never.

What infuriated Arturo even more was that everyone he talked to seemed to genuinely like Toni. She had always been quick with a joke; now, she had added charm and charisma to the mix. Arturo had to admit that Toni was an able deputy: Smart, workaholic, not afraid to offer her opinion to Howie even if she knew Howie wouldn't like it. But that didn't change Arturo's opinion about Toni. She would still be a usurper stealing his inheritance.

To please Howie, Arturo had taken up a liaison position. His job was to go to various lunar mines and understand the workings firsthand. It would have been an exciting and fulfilling job for Arturo if he'd had a bit more responsibility. But Howie had made if clear it was either the moon, reporting to Chris or head back to Earth and, in Howie's words, "continue to be unspectacular."

So Arturo had taken the job; he decided he would show Chris and Howie he wasn't so easily dismissed.

Arturo had thought of removing Toni, having her meet some sort of accident, but the thought of Howie's reaction stopped him. Besides, there were better ways of getting his inheritance back. All he had to do was figure out a way.

Standing before a screen linked to Howie's brain a few days after arriving on Quivira, Arturo paused for dramatic effect. "I have learned the lessons you wanted me to learn on Earth, and the records speak for themselves. I think it is time I took the next step in my education and learned from you directly."

Howie typed, "I like ambition. Inordinate ambition, not so much." A report appeared on the screen before Arturo. "Here's your report. Your department experienced steady but unspectacular growth under your supervision. There's no report of innovation or trying new things. In effect, you are a great company man, but not a leader. Why would you think I'll leave the company I've put my sweat, blood, and life into in the hands of someone like you?"

"But you promised me—"

"I promised you nothing," Howie typed. "I have made my decision. Now, if that will be all, I will advise you to avail yourself of the delights of Quivira; and, if you are interested, dinner is at eight."

"So you've decided to bypass me?" Arturo snapped. "I don't know if I should feel angry or insulted. I used to think you were the smartest man alive; this decision smacks of ineptitude, something I would never have associated with you." He immediately knew he had crossed a line and quickly tried to rally by adding, "I don't mean any offense by what I said."

"No offense is taken, Arturo," came Howie's reply. "Venting your mind is good for the soul. But all I hear are childish insults. Now, I run a consortium with a budget bigger than most countries in the world, so if you aren't going to tell me why you are here, then I guess it was nice seeing you."

Arturo calmed himself and tried to regroup. "I'm sorry, Howie. I'm here because I'm ready to take my place."

"Your place is still on the ladder. Maybe you can try for one of our Mars outposts. That would test you."

"Mars? That would be tough and dangerous."

"Precisely."

Rejected again, Arturo decided to team up with Ofentse, if he could find him. Maybe he would get some respect from him. Perhaps the hated Toni would know his whereabouts.

* * *

In one of Quivira's private rooms, Ved held in his hands a duffel bag containing a wooden box. Inside the box was a strange crystal that could determine his future.

He took the casket out and turned it over in his hand, the faint shimmer of its core catching the light. It was a gift from Maureen, given with quiet insistence, as if she had known what it would awaken in him.

For years, Ved had pushed aside the whispers, the side glances, the uneasy silences that followed him. He had always been "different," and people had theories — a tragic accident repaired by medical miracles, a child saved by genius and innovation. But beneath the stories lay a darker suspicion: That his survival was due to something not entirely ... human.

He clenched the box tightly and looked out of the habitat's portal, his reflection faintly visible in the glass. His face was familiar yet alien, even to himself.

Before it had become home to the crystal, somebody must have left the box on ElleWon. Something had stained one corner of it, and it looked like someone had tried to scrub it clean, though not very successfully. It looked like it was made of eastern red aromatic cedar. Ved held it up to his nose and sniffed. It still had a beautiful scent.

Ved had heard that the crystal had been found on the surface of the captured Valdenia asteroid, but how it got there was unclear. He remembered what Maureen had told him when she gave the box to him: "*This stone has created lots of trouble. But it is also the key for you to return home. I believe they will welcome you. Keep it safe, and use it when the time comes. It will unlock your future.*"

Return home? He'd been born in a sterile white lab on Quivira. He didn't have any other home. But Ved had to admit that he felt a strange power when he held the crystal in his hands.

Maureen had also told him Dr. César had injected him with alien DNA. Was that true? And if so, what kind? He had to find out. Maybe that was why he felt so different. But how could he find out where his DNA was from? Dr. César was probably dead.

Ved knew there was one person who could help with his journey: Hunter, the most experienced pilot of all of them, with a knack for finding secrets hidden among the stars. If there was any chance of success, he had to persuade Hunter to help him.

Ved stared at the crystal, his hand trembling as he cradled it with his fingers. He knew he held his future in his hands, if he just had the courage.

Would Hunter believe him, or just think he'd gone mad?

Ved decided it didn't matter. Either way, he had made up his mind, and nothing would stop him from seeing this quest through until the end — even if that meant risking both of their lives in the search for answers. He had to know where he belonged.

11

GABBY'S CALLING

Owabi, Ghana, November 28, 2102

"TROUBLE IS COMING, MILTON. If I do what I must do, it will mean leaving everything I hold dear, including you. This sanctuary is my life; I wish I didn't have to leave here for the unknown. But what can I do, Milton?"

Milton, her pet Roloway monkey, gave Gabby a soulful look and yawned. She laughed. Even her best friend wasn't interested in her troubles.

After growing up together on Quivira, the sisters Gabby and Nevie had taken different tracks: While Nevie had become a radiation specialist on ElleWon, Gabriella had chosen to gain experience on Earth. She had made her home at a jungle wildlife sanctuary near Kumasi, Ghana. No one there knew that she was one of the seven original Heavenly Babies. Now, while ostensibly working at the wildlife sanctuary, she was part of an environmental resistance network with tentacles across Africa

Since she was a child, Gabriella had been blessed with the gift of clairvoyance. Back on Quivira, her siblings had called her weird because she saw things that hadn't happened yet. While it was endearing as a child—a bit of a party trick—it didn't help her much as she grew older. In fact, it left her disturbed, someone who didn't fit in.

Then Gabby had moved to Earth. She'd found a job at an animal sanctuary, initially as a vet's assistant and later as something of a wildlife expert. Gabby had finally found her calling. She loved the animals; they were her life. Her likely mother, Toni, had secured the post at the Owabi Wildlife Sanctuary for her, where she helped look after some of the monkeys. Gabby had in particular adopted a handsome and endangered Roloway monkey with a beautiful white beard and striking, long tail whom she called Milton.

Gabby and the animals she cared for forged a relationship that nobody else could. Whenever there was a troublesome animal, no matter the species,

Gabby was the one they turned to first. Gabby found animals trusted her in ways humans didn't.

One night, after Milton had drifted to sleep in her lap, Gabby sat in the quiet of her small, wooden cabin at the edge of the sanctuary. She thought of her mother, Toni, who had arranged this placement for her, and of Dr. César, who had delivered her and the other Heavenly Babies on Quivira. What was César doing now? Nobody seemed to know. He had just disappeared. Rumor had it that he died in an asteroid strike.

Gabby enjoyed life at the sanctuary, but it hadn't taken her long to develop wider interests. With farmers encroaching on the sanctuary land, she had noticed how they struggled to make ends meet while the seed producers and the middle agents profited off their labor. And they weren't the only ones who had these problems; other farmers in Ghana complained about the same thing.

When Gabby had asked why they couldn't just change companies if the problem was with their seeds, one of the farmers had looked at her like she had been living in space all her life. When the elderly man with leathery skin and a strong, sun-hardened frame had given her that look of disbelief, Gabby knew she had missed something fundamental.

"You think we *choose* this, little miss?" he had asked, incredulous. "They own us. Without their seeds, we don't plant. Without planting, we don't eat."

From then on, Gabby began noticing the imbalances in Ghanaian society. It seemed she had lived in a bubble while she was on Quivira, and she was shocked by the injustice in the world.

It didn't take her long to realize the scam that was going on: NIPAH had intentionally made their seeds sterile, and with their monopoly, that meant the farmers had no choice but to buy fresh seeds from them every season. In the past three years, NIPAH had raised the seed prices every year. Yet the farmers couldn't raise the price of their products because of a price control board that was run by middle agents who had government officials in their pockets.

It was during one of her visits to the local market that Gabby had first met Hana, a young woman with a sharp gaze and a no-nonsense demeanor. Hana sold fruit, but she moved with a quiet confidence, a way of seeing the world that intrigued Gabby. After they'd spoken a few times, Gabby began to suspect there was more to Hana than just the market stall.

"You're not from around here, are you?" Hana asked one day, her tone light but her eyes calculating.

Gabby hesitated, unsure how much to reveal. "No, I grew up ... in an isolated place. High up in the sky, you could say."

Hana chuckled, but looked at her closely. "I thought so. People here ... we see things you might not. We know how to look out for each other. We have to, or else they'll bleed us dry."

Gabby realized that she'd found a kindred spirit. Over the next few weeks, she and Hana spoke more often and, bit by bit, Hana revealed the network she was a part of—a quiet but resilient resistance movement determined to counteract the power of NIPAH and others like them. It wasn't much, but it was something.

The resistance worked in the shadows, disrupting NIPAH's operations, coordinating with sympathetic government insiders, and sharing knowledge on ways to resist dependency. Gabby felt an exhilaration she hadn't known she was missing. For the first time, her life felt like it had a clear purpose.

One night, Hana brought Gabby to a meeting deep in the hills. They walked through thick brush, the only sounds the soft rustling of leaves and the occasional call of a night bird. Gabby felt her heart pounding. They reached a clearing where several people were waiting. Hana introduced Gabby with a quick nod.

A man named Kwesi, one of the leaders, stepped forward; his face was lined with age. He studied her, his gaze both wary and piercing.

"So, you're one of the Heavenly Babies," he said, as if testing her.

Gabby was taken aback. "How did you...?"

"We know more than you think, child. We've checked on you. We've been watching NIPAH and their operations for years, and when someone with your background comes sniffing around, we notice."

Gabby held his gaze, unflinching. "Then you know why I'm here." She straightened, her resolve strengthening. "Teach me. I don't want to stand by and watch this happen anymore."

Over the next few months, Gabby became deeply involved. She learned to collect information subtly, tracking NIPAH's movements and identifying which agents were pressuring farmers to stay in line. She connected with people across villages, listening to their stories and sharing knowledge she'd gained on Quivira about sustainable agriculture. Though she knew she had to be careful—revealing too much would give away her background—she felt she was finally becoming the person she was meant to be.

Her messages to Clara became more urgent, relaying details of NIPAH's hold over the farmers and the resistance's efforts to break free. And then there came the message that had urged Clara to join the fight back on Earth and would trigger Nevie's return instead.

As Gabby looked out over the sanctuary one night, Milton curled up beside her, she knew that she was in this fight for the long haul. The seeds of change were slow to grow, but she could feel them sprouting in the soil of Ghana, in the hearts of the people, and within herself.

Slowly, a scheme began to form to deal a deadly blow to NIPAH and GLOSCOM. It was how Gabby, using her computer skills, ended up tracking down Talabi Adedamola, also known as Tandy.

According to the search, Talabi Adedamola had been at the forefront of the struggle for farmers' rights for over ten years. She'd started out as a supervisor on a rice paddy, and from there had moved up to being a farmer manager. In that position, she'd learned firsthand what farmers had to go through with sterile seeds, and had even tried several times to organize farmers to create a viable competitor to NIPAH.

Not only was Tandy fired from her job for trying to organize farmers, she was blacklisted by plantation owners in Benue, Yobe, and Oyo, the biggest farming states in Nigeria. After being declared persona non grata, Tandy had gone underground for three years until she'd resurfaced helping small farmers get organized and eliminate middle agents in their community in Aflao, a border city between Togo and Ghana. There, Tandy had established links with consumers who came to buy the harvest directly from the farms, and also established lines of credit for these smallholding farmers to allow them to expand.

Gabby was impressed with Tandy's perseverance. Others would have given up after being banned by the mega farm owners. She couldn't find anything to show if Tandy was averse to violence, though that didn't bother Gabby; she just wanted to know if Tandy was clean, willing to join their cause, and, most importantly, not on the radar of the far-reaching oligarchs and power brokers. So far, Tandy didn't have any baggage, and everything Gabby had read indicated that she wouldn't mind bringing NIPAH to its capitalist knees.

Gabby ran a cursory look through more restricted deep sites for any more news on Tandy, and after she was satisfied she had all the information she needed, she logged out from all networks and shut down her comms. Gabby was always careful. She knew the reach of the enemy, so she was naturally paranoid. She believed thinking someone was out to get you ensured you were always on your guard.

Gabby's decision to do something about NIPAH hadn't come all at once. It had crept up on her, like the shadow of the baobab trees stretching across the sanctuary at dusk.

What began as irritation had deepened into a simmering anger every time she visited the farmers nearby. Their complaints had once seemed abstract to her, but now, they struck home. The beauty of the sanctuary had once seemed like enough, but now it felt like a comfortable illusion — one that needed to be shattered.

Gabby decided to talk to her sister, Nevie, about it. Nevie was a scientist, and practical. She always had good advice.

12
THE VISITOR

As she liked to do every morning, Clara glanced at the picture on her desk of Teagan and Julian smiling in front of their cottage by the sea. She missed her family terribly, particularly her grandchildren.

Speaking of the devils, Clara's Auryx comms link informed her that someone from Earth was trying to call her. Clara accepted the call, smiling when she saw Nevaeh's face.

"Nevie, I was just thinking about you. How's Earth? Still treating you well?"

"Yeah, Grams, you know I love it here."

Clara felt a pang as Nevie smiled. For the umpteenth time, she thought Nevie was the spitting image of her darling Pumpkin, the pet name the family used for Teagan.

"How are you doing?" Clara asked. "Is your mom okay?"

"Mom's fine; she's the reason I'm calling." Probably sensing Clara's alarm, Nevie rushed on, "She and Julian are going on a little Christmas vacation. They invited me to come, but I don't want to impose. Anyway, last night she told me about your Seeds of Life project. I thought it was a brilliant idea, something we could use to bring about Earth's renewal. If you don't mind, I thought I could join you on the Moon as your assistant, help around a bit."

The news pleased Clara in no small way, but she said, "As much as I want that, Nevie, we must be careful not to attract attention. There are powerful organizations that oppose this project. It could be disastrous if it gets on their radar, and you coming here may attract attention."

Nevie laughed. "Don't worry, Grams, I've got that under control. I'll brief you when I get there. If you'll have me?"

Clara didn't need further convincing. She and Nevie were on the same wavelength; she knew that working with her would be a stimulating experience.

"Sure, Nevie, I'll be looking forward to it. We won't have a Christmas tree, but I'm sure you're used to that after all your time on ElleWon."

"Just seeing you is fine."

Maybe I could pass the torch to Nevaeh, Clara thought.

Noel supported her implicitly, but thought that it was time she retired. Clara, though, was determined to see the project through, despite the growing resistance from her longstanding nemesis, the Global Seed Company Inc. At least with Nevie, the project would be in safe hands.

Nevie was experienced and knew how to run things. She had been trained under the watchful and demanding eye of Commander Bancroft after all.

Clara welcomed Nevie when she arrived just before Christmas, needing both the help and the company. She got up when she heard the airlock's final hiss and gave Nevie a big smile as she stepped forward to hug her.

"I'm glad you could finally make it," Clara said, smiling warmly. "I've been looking forward to showing you around."

Nevie's eyes widened as she took in the high, arched ceilings, illuminated by soft, blue-tinted lights that curved along the walls. It was strangely beautiful, a mix of nature and technology — an impression Clara knew would only deepen as they moved through the different chambers.

"It's even more incredible than I imagined," Nevie replied, her gaze lingering on a row of luminescent panels displaying images of various seeds, each with a brief description of their origin and genetic properties. "The last living seeds from Earth. I... I didn't expect it to feel so..."

"Sacred?" Clara finished with a knowing smile.

"That's how I felt the first time too. There's something about these seeds that goes beyond science. They're not just dormant plants; they're a memory of everything that used to live, of what Earth once was. And now, thanks to this place, maybe a little of it can be restored one day."

Clara led Nevie through the corridors. As they walked, she pointed to the reinforced glass windows that lined the passage and said, "Through here, you'll see our temperature-controlled vaults. Each one is precisely calibrated to keep the seeds viable for as long as possible — some of these can remain dormant for centuries if we do our jobs right.”

They paused in front of one of the larger vaults, and Nevie peered in. Rows upon rows of shelves, each with carefully labeled packets, were stacked floor to ceiling.

Each packet was tagged with a barcode, and a holographic display above showed a rotating 3D image of the seed species within, along with critical data like optimal growth conditions and conservation history.

Clara and Nevie sat on the cool, metallic floor, illuminated by a soft blue glow. Rows upon rows of sealed compartments surrounded them, each holding carefully preserved packets of seeds that could one day bring life back to a struggling Earth — or beyond.

“These seeds represent genetic diversity from every continent,” Clara explained. “Some are extinct on Earth, others critically endangered. Everything here has been meticulously cataloged, from desert scrub to tropical hardwoods. We’re doing more than just preservation, though; we’re also testing viability in simulated environments.”

Nevie inspected a frosted vial in her hands. The label read: *Cichorium intybus — Wild Chicory.* “Grandma, how come some of these seeds look so normal, like stuff we’d grow in our garden, and others have crazy names?”

“The ‘crazy’ names are the Latin.” Clara smiled, her face lit with the kind of quiet pride only a gardener—or a seed vault custodian—could understand. She gently took the vial from Nevie’s hands and replaced it in its slot, then pulled another vial from the shelf. This one was labeled simply: Silphium.

“We have chicory. And we’ve even got some Silphium; know what that is?” Clara asked, her tone conspiratorial, as though she were sharing a grand secret.

Nevie raised an eyebrow but didn’t say anything, knowing her grandmother would fill her in regardless.

Clara grinned and leaned back against a crate. “Silphium has been considered extinct since Roman times. The Romans prized it so much they used it for everything, from cooking to medicine. It was even supposed to be an aphrodisiac.” She waggled her eyebrows dramatically, earning a snicker from Nevie. “But you know what else people say?”

Nevie shrugged, though her curiosity was clearly piqued. “What?”

"Well," Clara said, her voice dropping to a whisper, "some folks think the Romans didn't destroy it all with overuse. The real story might be that visitors from another planet discovered its unique properties and decided to take it all for themselves. Imagine that! Silphium farms on some faraway world, guarded by alien botanists."

Nevie giggled at the thought. "Aliens growing plants just so they can cook fancy Italian dinners?"

"Or," Clara said, wagging a finger, "because Silphium might've been more than just a kitchen herb. Some researchers think it could've cured diseases we're still battling today. What if the alien visitors took it for its medicinal properties, or for something we can't even imagine?"

Nevie's eyes widened slightly, and she peered at the tiny vial of preserved DNA. "So this is like... super important?"

"Very," Clara said, her tone growing serious. "We were lucky enough to find some DNA of the plant preserved in ancient artifacts and fossils. It's incomplete, but even the fragments are priceless. This tiny bit of Silphium could help us restore biodiversity on Earth — or even discover something entirely new."

Nevie stared at the vial for a moment, her delicate fingers tracing the edges of the shelf it rested on.

"It's kind of sad, though. Like, all this effort just to save something people let disappear in the first place."

Clara nodded, her expression softening. "It is sad, sweetheart. But it's also hopeful. Every seed in this vault is a second chance. For Silphium, for Earth... and maybe for us too."

Nevie looked up at Clara with a glimmer of determination in her eyes. "Do you think I could help bring it back someday? Like, grow it?"

Clara reached out and ruffled her granddaughter's hair, as though she were still a small child, her heart swelling with pride.

"I think you could do anything you set your mind to, Nevie."

They moved into another chamber, where biorobots worked at glowing terminals, each analyzing data or adjusting simulations on their screens.

"This is the monitoring room," Clara said, nodding toward the staff. "We're constantly tracking germination rates, adjusting storage conditions, and, when possible, even running growth tests in lunar soil. We need to be sure that if—when—these seeds are needed again, they'll be ready."

Nevie looked around, captivated. "So every seed is cataloged, checked, and... tested?"

"Exactly," Clara confirmed. "And we also have an automatic distribution system. In an emergency, if some place needs certain seeds for food or medical plants, we can quickly pack and ship them out. It's taken years to get it all operational, but we're finally there."

Clara noticed Nevie's gaze had fallen on a small plaque on the far side of the room, engraved with the words:

"To preserve life, we sacrifice nothing; we simply cherish it."

Nevie took a deep breath. "Thank you, Clara. For keeping this hope alive."

Clara put a reassuring hand on Nevie's shoulder. "We're all part of this, Nevie. I'm just glad you're here to help." She nodded toward a nearby console, where a map of Earth's biomes glowed softly. "Ready to get started?"

Nevie smiled. "Absolutely."

* * *

Noel arrived for Christmas and was delighted to see Nevie again. They did their best to turn the sterile environment into something resembling a festive setting. A small, scrappy Christmas tree stood in the corner, its "branches" a collection of carefully bent hydroponic tubing wrapped in copper wiring. The lights flickered unpredictably, but Noel declared it added "character."

Nevie stood staring at the tree with a mix of amusement and dismay. "You know," she said, hands on her hips, "I'm pretty sure Santa hasn't seen *this* before!"

Clara chuckled as she placed a plate of moon rations—reconstituted turkey paste and vacuum-sealed cranberry gel—on the table. "Well, we're a bit far from Santa's workshop, dear."

"Santa doesn't visit the Moon," Nevie said matter-of-factly. "No chimneys. Plus, his reindeer can't breathe up here."

"Rudolph's nose has built-in oxygen," Noel said, grinning as he fiddled with a service bot. The bot—a squat, boxy thing named SP4RK—wore a tinfoil hat shaped like a star and beeped in protest. "I'm telling you," Noel went on, "Santa has the best tech in the galaxy. Got it from the elves, of course."

Nevie rolled her eyes but giggled. She turned to another bot, a taller, sleeker model named CH1M3 ("Chime"). It had been tasked with playing Christmas carols, but something had clearly gone awry in its programming.

"*Jingle bells, jingle bells, jingle all the way,*" it warbled, before abruptly switching to a mournful rendition of "Greensleeves."

Clara sighed, placing a comforting hand on Nevie's shoulder. "Well, at least the bots are trying. And look, we still have each other. That's the most important thing."

Nevie glanced at the corner of the room, where a small crate held carefully sealed packets of Earth's soil. She knew inside were the seeds her grandparents had worked so hard to protect — their family's legacy, the reason they were here.

"I guess it's kind of like Earth Christmas," she said softly, "except no snow. And no cousins. And no—"

"Now, don't you start making a list," Noel interrupted, "or we'll be here all day. It's a miracle we even managed to find a bit of tinsel!" He pointed triumphantly at the ceiling, where a strand of foil shimmered precariously. It had been taped up with lunar sealant and already drooped like a tired flower.

SP4RK beeped suddenly, wheeling toward the tree. Its claw extended, dropping a small package wrapped in what appeared to be insulation foam. "Gift protocol activated. Merry Chris—MA—MA—MALFUNCTION DETECTED!" With a loud pop, SP4RK spun in circles, scattering tiny bolts across the room.

Nevie burst out laughing, tears of mirth and something deeper sparkling in her eyes. Clara smiled, though her heart ached at the sight of her granddaughter's fragile joy.

Noel waved his arms, trying to calm the bot. "Spark, for moon's sake, you're supposed to bring *cheer*, not chaos!"

As Noel wrestled SP4RK back into its docking station, CH1M3 abruptly began playing "Silent Night." The room fell still. The melancholy notes echoed softly in the lunar stillness, blending with the distant hum of the seed vault's life support system.

Nevie rested her head against her grandmother's shoulder. "Do you think we'll ever go back to Earth?" she whispered.

Clara kissed the top of her head, her voice steady but tinged with sadness. "I don't know, sweetheart. But wherever we are, as long as we're together, it's home."

Noel returned, brushing a stray bolt from his sleeve. "Alright, let's open these presents before another bot decides to combust."

The gifts were humble: A moon rock polished smooth for Nevie, a hand-stitched pouch for Clara, and a meticulously etched metal plaque for Noel. SP4RK's gift turned out to be a piece of wire it had salvaged — unintentionally symbolic, Noel joked, of holding things together.

As they sat around the flickering tree, munching on gelatinous rations and laughing at CH1M3's off-key carols, the little family found a fragile peace. It wasn't Earth.

It wasn't perfect. But on the barren moon, amidst seeds of hope, it was enough.

* * *

The celebrations were a joy, but within a few days, Clara started to become flustered and erratic a bit like one of her bots.

"What's wrong, Grandma?" Nevie asked.

"I know you've only just arrived, but you have to get to the Omo River Basin in Ethiopia, ASAP. I don't have anyone else I can trust."

"Omo what?" Nevie frowned. "Isn't that a detergent?"

"I know it's sudden," Clara said, "but one of my contacts just informed me that they've discovered a rare variety of edible mushroom that could be extremely valuable and therefore sought after by you-know-who."

Nevie's frown only deepened, and she shook her head. "I don't know who. I need a bit more to go on."

"Those mothers at GLOSCOM. If we don't get there first, they will snap up everything, hook, line, and mushroom spores, and then sell them like they've owned them for eons."

As far as Nevie was concerned, Clara was speaking gibberish. "What's a spore?" she asked.

"It's like a seed," Clara explained feverishly. "It's the way mushrooms propagate. And don't get me started on the deceptions of GLOSCOM!

They're creating a global monopoly, but it's disguised as public good. 'We're saving the planet.' Fiddlesticks! They're not saving anything.

"And the annoying thing is that they've convinced the world's governments that the best way to combat the harms of climate change is through hardier seeds. All the old heirloom varieties are being sidelined and replaced by varieties that they control. I could go on and on, but you need to get there as fast as possible."

Nevie was startled by the sudden passion in Clara's voice. "Sure. I just have to catalog these seeds and store them, then I'll be on my way."

Clara moved to the workbench where Nevie had been stacking boxes and nudged her. "Leave that to me. You need to go now. Unfortunately, our window of opportunity is very small."

Nevie smiled and hugged Clara. "All right, Grandma, I'll get going."

She knew how much Clara hated to be called grandma; she always said it made her feel old. In her mind, Clara was still in her early thirties.

"If things go well, maybe I can drop by to see Gabby as well," Nevie added.

"I doubt you have time for a side-trip to Ghana. We have a lot to do here, so get back soon," Clara said.

"And remember, keep in touch."

Clara didn't mention it, but the Auryx alert that triggered Nevie's abrupt departure for Ethiopia had come from Gabby.

13

FEEDING KAT

Des Moines, February 28, 2103

Mrs. Johnson's words from the autumn lingered in Shiko's mind like a faint but sweet fragrance.

Attracted by the colorful tents and stalls, he began frequenting a farmer's market every Saturday near his apartment to support local farmers, picking out fresh vegetables directly from the hands of the proud growers. He even struck up conversations with them, learning about their hard work and dedication to sustainable farming practices.

Shiko's fingers delicately ran over the smooth skin of a ripe tomato, feeling its plumpness and imagining the burst of flavor it would bring to his dishes. He had a sense of fulfillment as he walked home carrying his canvas bag of locally grown produce, knowing he was making a difference in his community.

He didn't eat much on his own, and in his enthusiasm he had bought too much, so he decided to invite Kat round for a meal.

With his building's elevator not working, Shiko struggled to carry his three bags—packed with peppers, fresh mushrooms, garlic, tomatoes, broccoli, and a side of Mangalitsa pork—up several flights of stairs.

"What you got there?" Kat asked as he passed her in the stairwell. "Planning a cook up?"

"I found this Mangalitsa pork. I was hoping you would come round for a meal."

A little terrier dog bounced up and began smelling the packages.

"That's truly kind, but I can't tonight. I'm attending a meeting. Get down," she ordered the dog, whose lower teeth protruded from a cute underbite.

"Oh, that's too bad. The meat of the Mangalitsa pig is highly marbled with creamy white fat, and is high in Omega-3 fatty acids and natural antioxidants," Shiko said in the dictionary style he adopted when he was nervous. "I think you'll love it," he added, realizing he was throwing in too much detail.

"Sounds delicious."

"How about tomorrow night? Eight?"

Kat beamed at him. "It's a deal." The dog wagged his tail as though the invitation was for him.

"Who's the dog?" Shiko asked.

"Spencer." Kat paused, looking down at the tawny-coated terrier. "He's been acting strange lately." When she looked back at Shiko, she had tears in her eyes. "I think he's dying."

Shiko frowned. "Who is?"

"Spencer. He's got a large tumor."

"I'm sure the vet can help," Shiko offered.

"I don't know." She gave her dog a hug and waved adieu to Shiko. "Tomorrow night. Eight," she repeated.

Shiko prepared meticulously for the date, looking up what a girl might expect. Kat was special, and he wanted to impress her. He slow cooked the pork to bring out the flavors, and the aroma of herbs and spices filled his kitchen as he then worked on creating the perfect gravy.

Simmering white wine with the juices from the casserole, he then passed the softened vegetables through a food mill before stirring them back into the mixture. He debated skimming off the excess fat, but in the end decided to leave it all in for an extra burst of flavor.

He set the table, looking up the placement of cutlery; paper napkins were placed on the sides of the plates. With those preparations complete, Shiko lit a candle and set it on the table––adding a touch of romance to their evening––then anxiously waited, listening intently for any sign of Kat's arrival.

Minutes turned into an hour, and there was no sound.

What if she's forgotten? Shiko wondered as he watched the wax slowly drip down the stem of the candle, pooling at the bottom. *Or worse, has she changed her mind?* He checked the time, now ninety minutes past their agreed meeting time.

Then a message came through: ***On my way.***

Relieved, Shiko quickly took a taste of the pork, savoring its deliciousness.

Time ticked by slowly until, finally, he heard her footsteps on the stairs. Panting, she burst through the door with a radiant smile. Shiko thought that she looked like a vision of Heaven.

"I'm so sorry," she stuttered. "I couldn't escape. The meeting went on so long."

"What meeting?"

"Didn't I tell you? The meeting of the GLOSCOM protesters."

Though relieved that Kat hadn't forgotten about him, Shiko had a nagging feeling of disappointment and hurt that she had kept waiting for so long in favor of a group of activists. Probably dirty, lazy wasters. And as they sat down to eat, Shiko struggled to hide his conflicting emotions and put on a happy face for Kat's sake.

Once they got to the meal, Shiko was proud that it tasted incredible, but it was hard to fully enjoy it knowing that Kat's mind was still consumed by the protest meeting. Deep down, he knew this was just the beginning of many difficult conversations to come.

Was this the future of their relationship, always coming second to her causes?

"This is so good," Kat said, her eyes flashing happily. "Such intense flavors. Maybe I can take a bone for Spence?"

"Of course," he replied. But Kat's compliments only added to Shiko's inner confusion as he struggled between enjoying her company and grappling with her involvement in something he didn't agree with.

Shiko forced a smile, trying to push aside his conflicted feelings and focus on the present. Deciding to play it cool, he said, "So tell me about the meeting you attended. What was it about?"

"Oh, the evils of GLOSCOM, things like that."

"Evils? Why's it evil to help eliminate starvation, to make sure people get fed?"

"Why don't you work there for a bit and find out?"

"Find out what?"

"What they're doing."

Shiko was silent. He looked at her. Around her neck was a pendant that looked like a tiny bracelet.

"What's that?" he asked, leaning forward to examine the pendant.

Kat lifted it off her cleavage to show him. "It was given to me by a woman who rescued me from a fire. I was the only survivor. The rest of my family died that day."

"I'm so sorry," Shiko said.

"This is my keepsake."

"What's that symbol in the middle?"

"An eye. It keeps me safe. It wards off evil glances."

Later, Shiko began to steer the conversation back to why Kat had been late. When she finally began to open up about the protests, Shiko realized just how deep her involvement went.

Kat wasn't just some casual dissenter; she was a key player, quietly helping to organize efforts to expose GLOSCOM's stranglehold on the global food supply.

The more he listened to her, the more he began to see the cracks in the corporation's carefully curated image. She was sharp—brilliant, actually—and passionate about what she believed in.

He looked at her curiously.

"I can see I've said too much," she said, getting up to go.

"It's getting late. I should get back and feed my dog. That dinner was delicious."

Kat kissed him gently on the cheek and let herself out.

Shiko sat in silence, trying to decide what to do next. Since she mentioned him, Shiko's mind drifted to Spencer. Why was Kat's dog dying? What was there to find out, and how much did Kat know already?

Then it dawned on him. Despite his own doubts, he would have to report this to his superiors at GLOSCOM — just to be safe. He didn't want his boss to somehow think that he was sympathetic to the protests.

After clearing up, Shiko struggled to get to sleep. Just out of curiosity, he looked up how dog food was made. Sure enough, GLOSCOM had a big market share. *Very convenient*, he thought. Anything that humans didn't want, they stuck it in the pet food. Nothing went to waste at GLOSCOM.

14
SCIENTIST AT WORK

Tricala Lunar Base, May 14, 2103

Noel was investigating a cluster of anomalous light readings originating from a sector of space over a hundred million lightyears away. His face illuminated by the dim glow of console screens and spectral data maps, he was fully absorbed in the latest data streaming in from the observatory's array of deep-space telescopes.

The now-finished observatory had a low, angular design. A small fusion reactor provided consistent power during the extended lunar night, and panels of adaptive regolith coated the outer structure, helping it blend with the landscape and regulate its temperature. Located on the Moon's far side, the observatory was built into a lunar crater to shield it from meteor impacts and to provide additional insulation.

Small rovers scouted the surrounding area to monitor dust levels, seismic activity, and other environmental factors. They were programmed to report any irregularities—such as minor meteor impacts or rising radiation levels—that might interfere with the observatory's functioning.

Noel's focus narrowed as he ran a series of calculations on the observatory's central AI system. As the data began to resolve, Noel realized he was seeing hints of something extraordinary: An unusual gravitational wave pattern that suggested the presence of a supermassive black hole, but with a shape unlike any he'd seen before.

"Initiate system sweep of observational arrays," Noel commanded.

The central AI acknowledged in its calm, mechanical voice, "System sweep initiated. Robotic Telescope Maintenance Units Four, Six, and Nine are online and adjusting dome optics to enhance resolution in Sector A36."

Noel leaned back, watching as the RTMUs--small, multi-limbed machines designed to maintain the telescopes--moved along the inner track of

Dome 4. Their slender arms extended to clean and adjust lenses, each motion precise, refined by countless hours of calibration. He knew the data they gathered would be relayed through the adaptive imaging software, sharpening the details of the mysterious source of gravitational waves.

Outside, the construction drones hovered nearby, a standby force ready to perform structural adjustments or emergency repairs if needed. Noel took comfort in knowing that, out here on the Moon's far side, every machine had a purpose, and every system was optimized to keep operations smooth even in his solitude.

"New data stream detected," the AI reported.

Noel looked over to see a surge of data appearing on his display. This was unexpected. He had focused the observatory on a known stellar cluster, yet now, deep within the images, a strange formation began to take shape that he'd never seen before. Tiny, interlocking beams of light spread out across the frame, dim but unmistakably there.

"Cross reference this formation against known galactic structures," Noel ordered.

"Searching... No known matches found. Analyzing potential compositions. Possibilities: Energy-based structure, gravitational anomaly, or artificial formation."

"RTMUs, initiate continuous monitoring on this location," Noel said, his voice breaking the quiet hum of the observatory.

The maintenance robots adjusted accordingly, their sensors now trained to gather readings from this sector. Meanwhile, the adaptive imaging software processed the data into sharper visuals. The lattice pattern became clearer, revealing almost crystalline formations stretching across the stars––almost biological in nature––with patterns and folds that seemed purposeful, as if designed to harness energy from the surrounding universe.

Suddenly, an alert flashed on Noel's console.

"Cosmic radiation surge detected," the AI intoned. "Potentially hazardous to unshielded systems. Activating contingency protocols."

The entire observatory hummed to life as shielding systems engaged. The quantum relay was briefly paused to prevent data corruption, and all non-essential systems were redirected to the fusion battery backup. The robots outside retracted to safe zones within the facility, while the telescopes' sensitive lenses were shielded by retractable panels.

Noel felt the observatory settle into a protective stasis, a reminder of the isolation and the hostile environment he worked in. But he wasn't worried; the AI, robots, and systems had been designed for moments like these.

As the radiation subsided, Noel turned back to the lattice. The cosmic wave had cleared, and the imaging was better than ever. This was his chance to capture the highest resolution images of this structure yet.

He said, "Lock in on Sector A36 and maximize all observational capacities."

The telescopes moved with precision, aligning perfectly with the AI's guidance. The RTMUs adjusted optics to optimal resolution, while the data filtering algorithms processed streams of information in real-time, enhancing clarity as the images formed.

What Noel saw next defied all reason. Within the formation was a faint but distinct pulse, a repeating sequence that he quickly noted wasn't random. Each flash was too regular, too precise. It was a signal —— a message, perhaps, meant to be deciphered. Was it the Tritans reconnecting? Or a signal from elsewhere, something yet unidentified? Anything was possible.

He called Liam and Tara, inviting them to the observatory to take a look, and after months of data collection and analysis, they all became convinced they'd stumbled upon something extraordinary.

The data revealed a complex web of energy signatures spread across lightyears. It was as if these points were deliberately arranged, each one pulsing with faint, rhythmic energy that suggested some kind of connection between them.

Tara looked over Noel's shoulder, her eyes widening as she took in the readouts. "This can't be arbitrary," she said. "There's an intelligence to this pattern, Noel. Look at the symmetry, the intervals between the points. It's like... a neural network, but on a galactic scale."

Noel nodded, feeling a thrill of excitement and apprehension. "Exactly. It's almost like... a giant brain. A neural network built for a purpose."

Noel glanced at his instruments. The analyzer was showing faint but steady readings, signals, soft and rhythmic, like a heartbeat just on the edge of perception.

"Hold on," he muttered, adjusting the sensitivity further. As he tuned the analyzer, the signals became clearer, forming an unmistakable pattern of sound waves. He leaned forward, almost mesmerized. "This isn't random. These are harmonic frequencies. It's as if..." He paused, listening to the delicate, haunting melody emitted by the analyzer.

Tara's voice softened. "As if it's alive."

Their work consumed them, each breakthrough pulling them deeper into the mystery of the formation. As they mapped more connections, they discovered something even more astounding: The formation seemed to have nodes, key points where energy surged with far greater intensity. These nodes formed intersections within the lattice, and according to their calculations, these intersections were the locations of unexplained anomalies recorded in earlier missions — ships disappearing, gravitational distortions, and strange cosmic phenomena that had baffled scientists.

Over the next few nights, Noel mapped out the pulse patterns. To his surprise, he discovered that the frequencies created overlapping harmonic patterns, each one building on the other.

"These pulses are more than signals. They're a symphony," he whispered, watching the waveform dance across his screen. "Each frequency is harmonizing with the next. This can't be random."

Tara sounded excited and a bit fanciful. "What if it's an alien communication network? Or some kind of interstellar language?"

But Noel shook his head, pondering. "It's not transmitting information, at least not directly. It's creating a resonant field."

He adjusted his equipment to emit a low-frequency hum of its own, mimicking the patterns. When he played it back through the analyzer, the pulse responded, increasing its frequency. His pulse had somehow been absorbed into the larger pattern, amplified and redirected back in their direction.

Hours later, exhausted but exhilarated, Noel began formulating a hypothesis.

"If these frequencies are harmonizing, they can't only be decorative. They're forming a structure — a lattice of sound that binds different points in space."

"Like a framework?" Liam asked.

"Yes, but not physical. Think of it as... an Astral Lattice, a sound-based structure that's barely visible yet all-encompassing. This resonance could bind locations together, almost like a web."

Tara leaned back from the monitor, staring at the map they had compiled. "It's like a highway, or maybe a system of gates," she mused, a sense of awe in her voice. "If this is intentional, whoever built it could move across galaxies as easily as we cross star systems."

They dug deeper, tracking the energy pulses through advanced sensors and quantum spectrometers, pushing their equipment to its limits. What they discovered next was even more unsettling: The Lattice had been encrypted. Each node seemed to carry a unique energy signature, one that would only allow access to those who matched a specific frequency –– like a key. But this encryption wasn't digital; it was biological. The Lattice required certain genetic markers to activate, as though it had been designed to recognize a specific species, or even specific individuals.

"It's a safeguard," Noel realized. "This Lattice wasn't just built as a means of travel. It's a defense mechanism, and maybe even a test."

Liam's eyes widened as the realization sank in. "Then it wasn't meant for us," he whispered. "Not originally. This Lattice could have been created by beings who have mastered intergalactic communication and hid it from less advanced civilizations until they proved worthy... or compatible."

The enormity of their discovery weighed on them. The Astral Lattice represented both an incredible opportunity and a terrifying danger. If humanity learned to unlock it, they could access worlds and technologies beyond imagination. But if they misused it or failed to understand its complexities, they might unleash forces far beyond their control.

Tara glanced at Noel. "We can't keep this a secret. But we also shouldn't just make it available to anyone who might abuse it."

Noel nodded slowly, his mind getting ahead of himself as it raced with possibilities. "Then we find a way to explore it safely, to understand it and its capabilities before deciding what to do. The Astral Lattice might hold the keys to humanity's next step ... but not if it falls into the wrong hands."

15

THE BARB

Quivira, May 16, 2103

"MR. RICH, I HAVE something I think will please you greatly," Professor Polyakov said to the monitor connected to the glass tank.

As the monitor came on, letters began to form words. Then words became sentences, and Olga read what Howie Rich's brain was typing on the monitor. "Great, Poly, I need some good news. Does that traitor, Ofentse, still think I'm dead? What are his plans?"

Olga hated being called anything other than her correct name. A lot of sacrifice and dedication had gone into making that name one of the most recognized in her profession, and she did not care to be demeaned by anyone, not even the inventive Howie Rich.

"It's Professor Olga Polyakov, Mr. Rich." She paused, and then said, "Mr. Mataka still believes you are dead. He's trying to become the Head of the Consortium. I know for a fact he's sought the help of Umar Sadiq and Chris Stackpole, though neither have given him a response yet."

"We need to know what he's doing," Howie responded. "Ofentse is a wily bastard. He knows you and Carl aren't on his side, so he won't seek you out. Anyway, that's beside the point. Ofentse is a tiny fly. I'll swat him away when the time is right."

"Mr. Rich," Olga said carefully, "if I can make a suggestion here, I think underestimating Ofentse is what got us here in the first place. Taking back full control of the Consortium and letting your enemies know you are back and strong — that's your first step."

There was silence for a while, and then the screen sprang to life again.

"Step? How can I make any steps at all? I don't have a body! I'm stuck in this tank. You need to get to work on making me a body. It shouldn't take forever. César could probably do it with both hands tied behind his back and one eye closed."

The insult stung. César de Luca, though a renowned doctor, couldn't match Olga's abilities. Hadn't she been the one who'd brought this ungrateful pig back from the edge of death? Wasn't she the one keeping his brain alive and active? Yet now Howie Rich was comparing her to a man whose most outstanding achievement was incubating seven babies. Instead, she was working on an evolutionary leap that would populate the universe.

She could just unplug him now. Olga stared at the green tank. Howie Rich was a great businessman with the mind of a poker player. But even poker players might have trouble mastering their emotions from time to time.

Under her breath, Olga cursed Howie in Ukrainian, the language of her father. She had learned from a tender age that anger, jealousy, and hatred were wasted emotions that drained the mind. The only thing that anyone needed to strive for was power.

"That's a bit of a tall order, Mr. Rich," she finally said. "I've given you a speaking brain. How can we arrange a body?"

There was a mechanical sound from the monitor that resembled the cawing of a crow. The digitized face of Howie appeared on the screen. It seemed to laugh at her. Finally, instead of typing, the face spoke. It sounded like Howie's voice, if he was using a synthesizer or digitizer.

"Poly, it's finally great to see a crack in that icy exterior. If I wanted to talk to someone without emotion, I would hold a conversation with one of the many bots available. I see your point though."

Olga was confused. It wasn't a feeling she was used to.

"Get me Julian Trace," Howie said. "He can sculpt me a body."

"I thought you would want Julian Trace eliminated."

Howie laughed again; the laughter was beginning to grate on Olga's nerves. She willed herself to remain calm by visualizing a flowing stream, its currents taking her anger away. Soon, she regained her composure and looked at Howie's face dispassionately once more.

"He is much more useful alive," Howie told her. Olga adjusted the flow of oxygenated saline into the neural tank, her gloved hands steady despite the weight of exhaustion pressing on her. Keeping Howie Rich's mind alive was a miracle of modern science, but a grotesque one. Even in corporal death, the old man refused to fade. And now he wanted a body.

She turned toward a small, refrigerated compartment, pulling out a petri dish. Inside, a mass of pale, wriggling maggots squirmed over slivers of synthetic brain tissue. The research team had been experimenting with neuro-regeneration, testing how bioengineered larvae could break down damaged cells while leaving healthy tissue intact. If they could refine the process, it could lead to breakthroughs in repairing neural decay —perhaps even a way to maintain Rich's brain indefinitely.

A chime sounded as Medibot-6 entered the lab, rolling toward her on quiet wheels. "Professor, your requested solution is ready for administration," the bot chirped, extending a robotic arm.

Olga barely acknowledged it, too focused on placing a new tissue sample into the dish. But then—

A metallic limb jerked.

A miscalculation in movement. A clumsy *swipe*.

The petri dish flipped into the air.

Time slowed as Olga watched the maggots spill forth, tumbling like grotesque raindrops before splattering onto the lab floor. Some landed on her shoes, others on her gloves. But most squirmed freely, a repulsive, writhing invasion of the sterile space.

Her breath hitched. A deep, visceral disgust crawled up her spine.

Then she stepped back. And felt the *pop* beneath her heel.

A scream ripped from her throat. Her vision tunneled, rage eclipsing reason as she stomped down harder, grinding the creatures into the tile. Her body shook, her breaths turning ragged.

"YOU USELESS MACHINE!" she shrieked, grabbing the nearest object––a diagnostic tablet––and flinging it at Medibot-6. It struck the bot's chassis with a dull *clang*, sending it wobbling back.

The machine twitched, recalibrating. "Professor Polyakov, your vitals indicate extreme stress. Would you like me to—"

"SHUT UP!"

Olga stumbled backward, chest heaving, eyes locked onto the smear of pulped larvae. Her skin itched as if they were still crawling over her. She *hated* maggots. Not just because they were revolting — but because they reminded her of *him*.

Howie Rich.

He had been the kind of man who devoured everything, burrowing into the lives of others, consuming, multiplying his influence until there was nothing left but *him*. She had spent years in his employ, watching his wealth infect every field of research, twisting science into a monument to his own ego.

And now, even in a tank, he clung on — refusing to rot, refusing to *end*.

A flicker of neural activity spiked in the glass cage. The monitors buzzed.

Olga turned, eyes narrowing at the floating brain.

Had he *felt* that?

She stepped closer, placing her palms flat on the glass. "You think this is funny, don't you?" she whispered, voice thick with loathing.

A beep of acknowledgement from Howie. His brain pulsed in its bath.

Olga clenched her fists, nails biting into her palms. She forced herself to step away, forced herself to breathe.

"Medibot," she said finally, voice ice-cold, "clean up this mess. And order a new batch of test larvae."

The machine beeped its compliance as Olga walked to the sink, scrubbing her hands with a fury that left her skin raw.

This experiment would continue. But so help her, if she ever saw another maggot in this lab—.

She might just pull the plug on Howie Rich herself.

16
THE MEMORIAL

"**G**ET ME JULIAN TRACE," Howie had ordered. "He's one of the best sculptors in the world. Tell him it's for my memorial."

Professor Polyakov didn't question Howie's instruction further, and got in touch with Julian in California.

"We have a strange request," she said. "We want a memorial sculpture of Howard Rich. But not static. It needs to look like he is doing something."

Julian was confused. On the one hand, Julian had heard Howie died in an accident on Halona. But then he and Teagan had received that disturbing threat: *"Return to me what you have taken. I will track you down. Mark my words."*

It must be a trap, Julian thought.

Polyakov could sense his unease. "Don't worry, Julian. This is strictly professional. Just a memorial for Howard Rich. He selected you because he admires you. He's left you a considerable amount in his will, but it is contingent on you creating the statue."

Julian wavered when he heard that — he and Teagan could use the money. They didn't have much to live on.

"She said it's contingent on me doing the statue," Julian told Teagan later. "I know we were planning to get away for a bit, but we need the money."

Despite his hatred for Howie and the torture he had put Teagan through, he still admired the old toad and was intrigued by the commission. Howie had given him a leg up when he first needed it. No harm in creating a memorial. Maybe he could give it some character.

Eventually, Teagan had agreed he should go, but insisted he be back for the birth.

"I will," he told her. "I won't miss it for anything."

Kissing Teagan on the cheek, Julian flew to his old stomping ground on Halona to work on the commission. He found his former room, glad to see it uninhabited.

Strangely, he felt happy to be back in familiar surroundings, although most of his artist friends had moved on. He loved California, but the beach every day grew monotonous.

Although he had known Howie personally, Julian spent hours studying the mogul's virtual avatar and talking with Professor Polyakov and others who had worked with him. He wanted to make sure he understood the magnate's innermost personality and desires before starting the sculpture. For some reason, he found that Ofentse, the person who had known Howie best, was not available.

What was unnerving was the massive presence of security that surrounded him, from securitybots to human guards to drones.

Halona was more like a prison than a haven for creatives now; the artists' colony was a shadow of its former self. Julian discovered that some of his former friends had in fact left Halona because of the new security measures.

Once he got organized, Julian finally began to work on the sculpture.

He'd asked for his old studio, but Professor Polyakov had said his work must be kept secret. Using clay stored on Halona and wire frames from the metalworking shop, Julian began crafting a beautiful sculpture inspired by memories of the tycoon and his captivating smile.

Every hour spent laboring over the work was emotionally draining yet therapeutic as Julian began to understand more about what had driven the man who had ruthlessly defeated the late Jack Rush, built some of the earliest mines on the Moon, and whose hero was William Andrews Clark, the nineteenth century copper king who had become one of America's richest mining barons and elbowed his way into New York high society. Howie had similarly taken the lead in harnessing the riches of the asteroids.

Many people had underestimated Howie Rich, to their own cost.

Julian crafted the sculpture with care, using the latest technology to create a body that was both realistic and functional. He wanted to make sure the sculpture not only looked like the billionaire, but felt like him as well, as though the statue might come to life at any moment.

When Julian was halfway through, Professor Polyakov contacted him with an unusual request.

"We atomized his body, but we have some remaining dust particles in a tube. Can you mix them in as part of the sculpture?"

It was weird, but Julian could think of no reason not to comply. He mixed them in as part of a toe.

After weeks spent working tirelessly day and night, Julian was finished -- the statue complete in every detail, every curve gently molded into place just so, each crease delicately etched out.

He brought the statue over to Quivira to give Polyakov a private showing. She was thrilled.

"You are so clever, Julian. I just love how you've captured him."

She ran a hand over the sculpture's shoulder and gave him a slight kiss on his cheek.

"He's all yours!" Julian said with a grin.

Polyakov gave him a smile, moved toward him to give him a "thank you" peck on the cheek, and injected him with a needle in the neck.

Julian fell unconscious to the floor. The bots moved him to the medical center.

Once Julian had handed over the sculpture, Polyakov went to work on creating a mobile version, a dynamic masterpiece crafted from supple latex and silicon.

This new version was designed to exhibit motion and lifelike gestures, capturing the essence of fluidity.

The meticulously programmed bots assisted Polyakov in the delicate and complex process, their precise movements orchestrating the creation of a living form.

Gradually, the sculpture came to life as the brain and body were integrated, each connection sparking with potential.

The magnate was now able to move and speak, his formidable presence reborn, animated through the flexible, lifelike contours of his new corporeal form.

17

SHIKO'S CONVERSION

Des Moines, May 24, 2103

SHIKO STOOD IN FRONT of Doctor Elena Canek's desk, anxiety creeping up his spine. The room was silent, save for the soft hum of computers and the occasional beep. Shiko's foot tapped nervously against the floor, the sound echoing in the quiet space.

To be safe, Shiko had decided to report his contact with the protesters—or at least one of them—to his boss at GLOSCOM. He didn't want them to somehow think that he was involved with the protests.

The office, with its gleaming floors and minimalist decor, seemed more sterile than usual. Everything about GLOSCOM was pristine — coldly efficient, just like his boss. But it wasn't the surroundings that made Shiko's palms sweat or his voice tremble. It was the weight of what he was about to say.

"Dr. Canek, I need to be upfront with you about something," Shiko began, trying to keep his voice steady.

Her unyielding eyes didn't look up from her screen immediately. Instead, she continued scanning, the subtle clacking sound of her stylus the only noise in the otherwise silent office. Finally, Dr. Canek raised an eyebrow, her gaze settling on Shiko. "What is it?"

Shiko swallowed hard, the words almost sticking in his throat. His fingers traced the edge of his ID badge, and he began grinding it into the palm of his hand.

This was a decision he'd agonized over for days. Ever since Kat had let slip her involvement with the anti-GLOSCOM protests, the knowledge had been plaguing him. He hadn't meant to get involved; he didn't want any trouble. Kat was just his neighbor. They shared drinks sometimes, now even meals. It wasn't until recently that she'd trusted him enough to talk about her activism. And when she did, the danger of the situation became all too clear. Although they had become friends, the risks of GLOSCOM finding out and taking action against him were too great.

"I've had contact with food protesters," Shiko finally said, the words coming out faster than he intended.

Dr. Canek set the stylus down on the desk with a soft clink.

Her skin was a flawless, almost synthetic brown—smooth as polished glass, giving off a faint sheen under the overhead lights. Not a blemish or freckle in sight. Her cheekbones were sharp, almost blade-like, and her jaw clenched with habitual restraint, as though emotion were a foreign language she'd long forgotten.

In that moment, Shiko felt less like a man and more like a lab result.

She leaned back in her chair, folding her arms over her chest, and gave Shiko a long, unreadable look. "Go on."

"There's this woman — Kat. She lives in my apartment building. She's part of a group that's... well, they're against what GLOSCOM is doing with the food supply. I didn't know at first, we were just neighbors. But then she started talking about it, about her involvement. I didn't engage with any of it, I swear, but I figured it was only a matter of time before someone found out."

Dr. Canek was silent, her eyes narrowed in thought, but Shiko could feel the tension building, like a rubber band being pulled too tight. He knew how these things worked. GLOSCOM didn't tolerate dissidents. And if someone was even tangentially associated with anti-GLOSCOM groups... Well, their future within the corporation could be over before it even started.

"I'm telling you this because I don't want it to come back on me later," Shiko added, his voice quieter now. "I've been nothing but loyal to GLOSCOM. I didn't want to be implicated in something I don't even support."

Dr. Canek leaned forward, her expression still cold and hard to read. "And why are you telling me this now, Shiko? Why not earlier?"

"I didn't think it would be an issue," Shiko replied quickly. "At first, it seemed like just talk — people blowing off steam. But lately ... The protests are growing. She's more deeply involved than I thought. I don't know how far it'll go, but I didn't want to take any chances."

"Do you fancy her? Is that what you're saying?"

Frowning, he said, "I like her, yes."

"You want to sleep with her?"

Shiko began to stammer. "I..."

Dr. Canek put her hand up. "Of course you do. Any man would. She's pretty. Her dark hair, her infectious laugh."

Shiko stood open-mouthed. They knew about Kat. Was his apartment bugged? Maybe they had camera surveillance. He would have to check.

Dr. Canek's gaze pierced through him. For a moment, Shiko felt as if the walls were closing in. He had no idea how his boss was going to react, whether this would be the end of his career or a saving grace.

"Let me make something clear," Dr. Canek said finally, her voice measured and deliberate. "GLOSCOM has no patience for traitors or those who associate with them. But loyalty can come in many forms. It was smart of you to come forward."

Relief washed over Shiko, though he knew better than to show it. He kept his expression neutral, waiting for what came next.

"I will need details, of course," Dr. Canek continued, leaning back in her chair once more. "About Kat. About this group. And I'll expect you to keep a close eye on her. You'll report anything that might be useful."

Shiko's stomach dropped. "Useful?" The word came out more hesitantly than he intended.

"You're not naïve, Shiko. We don't let these movements go unchecked. They disrupt the global order, threaten the very foundation GLOSCOM has built." Dr. Canek's eyes glinted dangerously. "Consider it an opportunity to demonstrate your loyalty."

Shiko's mind raced. He had never intended to get involved, and now he was being asked to run surveillance on Kat. Kat wasn't dangerous, at least, he didn't think so. But GLOSCOM didn't see things in shades of gray. There were only loyalists and enemies.

"What happens if I can't find anything?" Shiko asked, knowing full well how the question would be received.

Dr. Canek's expression didn't change. "Then you had better make sure you do, Shiko. Your lust has to be paid for somehow."

Shiko nodded slowly, his mind a chaotic jumble. He'd thought confessing would free him from this nightmare, but instead it had only pulled him deeper in. Now he was stuck between two worlds: The corporate titan that controlled everything and the rebellion forming beneath the surface.

"I understand," Shiko finally said, his voice tight.

"Good." Dr. Canek paused. "They are just a rabble. Nothing to worry about."

With that, he was dismissed. Dr. Canek returned her gaze to the screen in front of her without another word, and Shiko made his way back to his office on the sixth floor. Room 174.

* * *

Now he had reported the contact, Shiko was duty bound to come up with something. GLOSCOM would be expecting reports. He would have to increase his contact with Kat, feign interest in the protests. His stomach churned at the thought of deceiving her, but he didn't have a choice.

Shiko soon found himself at Kat's door more often than he had expected. At first, it was all part of the plan — an obligation he had to fulfill.

Kat opened the door that first evening, surprised but smiling faintly. She was guarded, though, her warm brown eyes searching his face as if trying to read his intentions.

"Shiko," she said, leaning against the doorframe, "this is unexpected. What brings you by?" Her dog, Spencer, growled at him.

"Just wanted to hang out," he said, forcing a casual shrug. "It's been a long day, and I could use some company. Mind if I come in?"

Kat hesitated, but eventually stepped aside, letting him into the small apartment. Spencer, getting over his initial hostility, welcomed him. The apartment was cozy, filled with second-hand furniture and eclectic artwork on the walls. A guitar sat in the corner, and the faint scent of jasmine lingered in the air.

They didn't talk about the protests, at least not at first. Instead, Kat shared stories about growing up in Palawan. She missed the smells, the sea air, and the fish. The beaches as she described them stretched endlessly, and the water shimmered with an entrancing blue that she said always felt like home. She talked about music, how her love for it kept her grounded, and played him a few songs on her guitar — her fingers nimble, her voice soft but powerful. Spencer barked annoyingly out of tune.

Kat hugged him. "I've been terribly worried about the little mutt," she said, as if trying to explain her tolerance for the off-key interruptions.

"How long have you had him?"

"About five years. He's become my shadow," Kat said with a giggle. "But I told you about the lump I found. After a series of tests, the vet looked at me and said it was a tumor. It's aggressive, and there's not much they can do."

"I'm so sorry," said Shiko, unsure what else to say.

"I couldn't stop crying for days. The thought of losing him felt like a wound, raw and unhealing. Now I'm starting to accept it."

They sat together in the small living room, exchanging silent, sad glances, Shiko's face lined with concern as Spencer rested his head on Kat's lap.

Over the next few days, Shiko tried to get back early, checking in on Kat and Spencer whenever he could. One evening, as they talked about Spencer's condition, Kat wondered aloud, "He's only six... I don't understand. He was always so healthy."

"Did you ever check his kibble?" Shiko asked, thinking back to the research he did about GLOSCOM's pet food.

Kat frowned at him. "What, you are blaming me now?"

"No, of course not. I'm saying his kibble may have given him cancer. Kibble is filled with artificial preservatives and chemicals. I've been reading about the long-term effects of these ingredients on pets, and there are countless stories from other pet owners who've seen similar unexplained illnesses in their dogs. One of the dangers of processed dog food is the high temperatures that go into making kibble, typically upwards of 200 degrees Celsius. Scorching foods not only affects the natural nutritional value of the food, but has also shown to cause free radicals to form and carcinogenic chemicals to be released."

Kat was horrified. "I'm just going to do my best for him," she said.

Shiko would often bring something with him: after work: a coffee once, then a small dessert from a nearby bakery another time. It was all part of the act, a way to establish a sense of normalcy, to make Kat trust him — at least, that's what he told himself. He was still trying to figure out how to steer their conversation toward something more actionable. He didn't have anything to report back to Dr. Canek so far, and the clock was ticking.

Shiko adopted a different tactic, asking one day about Kat's childhood.

Nursing a small glass of white wine, Kat told him about how she'd grown up in the rugged farmlands of Arizona. Her family worked hard to cultivate crops in the harsh desert environment. Although she had been too young to remember, she said life on the farm had been peaceful until a ruthless band of raiders set fire to their property one night, killing her parents and leaving her an orphan. She'd been adopted by an American commercial attaché, John Merrick, and his wife, Celia, who often traveled to Southeast Asia for work. They gave her a sense of belonging after the loss of her parents.

In 2086, when Katrina was fourteen, they went to Cebu in the Philippines, where John was scheduled to attend a major seed exhibition.

"At the expo, my dad stumbled upon a confidential document that exposed GLOSCOM's sinister activities. They were using their clout to crush smaller competitors and had been secretly conducting unethical experiments on seed lines designed to obliterate native crops, forcing farmers into reliance on GLOSCOM's patented creations. He came home that very day, his eyes fiery, and confided in my mom, vowing to investigate further. But just a few days later, tragedy struck like a lightning bolt — they were both killed in a car accident."

Shiko's eyes widened in shock. The horror of losing not just one set of parents but two was unimaginable. But it was also a lesson, perhaps: Don't probe too far.

"The official report claimed it was an unfortunate traffic incident, but even I heard whispers that GLOSCOM had orchestrated the whole thing to silence John before he could expose the truth. I was sent to live with my adoptive grandparents in Palawan, and when I grew older, I vowed that I wouldn't let GLOSCOM get away with what they did to my parents, or what they were doing to farmers worldwide."

"Remember what I told you about being a Truth Finder?"

Shiko nodded and listened, saddened to hear the strife that Kat had been through. The more time he spent with her, the harder it became to maintain the façade of indifference.

"Wow! I can't believe you went through all that," he said. "You must be very strong inside. I'm surprised you are not more bitter."

Bitter? I don't have time for grudges. That would destroy me from the inside. It's GLOSCOM that needs to be destroyed, not me."

Shiko wasn't sure when it happened, but at some point, the act became real. He stopped thinking about what Dr. Canek wanted to hear and started listening to what Kat was actually saying. She wasn't pushing some reckless agenda –– she was fighting for survival, for fairness, for a world that wasn't completely dominated by one corporation's greed.

That evening, Kat rustled up an escabeche fish meal for the two of them as if from nowhere. Shiko felt a strange kind of warmth settle over him. More than the food — it was the way she made him feel. The conversation flowed easily between them, more so than before. They had laughed about silly things, exchanged stories, and, for a brief moment, it felt like the weight of their respective burdens had lifted.

"Shiko, don't you ever wonder what the world would be like if food wasn't controlled by one entity?" Kat asked him one evening, her voice soft but determined. "Do you really think it's okay that GLOSCOM can decide who eats and who starves?"

He had no good answer. The corporate line he'd been fed seemed suddenly hollow in the face of her conviction.

Then Kat finally asked him the question that had been hanging in the air for weeks.

"Why do you keep coming here, Shiko?"

He was caught off guard by the directness of the question. She wasn't accusing him, not exactly, but there was a deep suspicion in her eyes. He could feel it. She knew something was off, that there was more to his visits than just friendship.

For a moment, Shiko thought about lying again, about making up some excuse, playing the part like he always did. But the words wouldn't come. He realized, then, how far in he'd gotten. He couldn't pretend anymore.

"I... I didn't come here because I wanted to at first," he admitted slowly, the weight of his confession heavy on his chest. "After you told me about the protests, I reported it to GLOSCOM."

Kat's face went pale, her eyes widening in shock, but Shiko rushed to continue.

"But I didn't know... I didn't understand. It was just a reflex, to protect myself. They told me I had to spy on you, to find something they could use. But now... now I'm not so sure."

Kat didn't say anything for a long time, her face unreadable. Shiko's heart pounded in his chest, waiting for her to react. Was this the moment where everything collapsed? Where he would lose the fragile connection he'd built with her?

Finally, she sighed, shaking her head. "You're just another pawn in their game, Shiko. I should've known."

"I'm not anymore," he said quickly, the words spilling out before he could stop them. "I don't want to be. I want to help."

She looked at him for a long, silent moment, and something softened in her expression. "Help how?"

"I don't know yet," he admitted. "But I'll figure it out. I'm on your side now."

As Kat stood up, clearing the dishes from the small, cluttered table, she casually mentioned something about changing out of her clothes, which were stained with remnants of their dinner.

"Look, I'm so careless. I'll never get this stain out."

The stain was a red dribble down the front. Shiko didn't think much of it at first, remaining in his seat as he sipped the last of his water, trying to figure out how to fix things between them. Was he finished?

He watched Kat move around her apartment with the same easy grace she always had, her long hair swaying with each step. She crossed into the small alcove that served as her bedroom, half-separated from the rest of the space by a simple hanging curtain.

It happened so quickly that Shiko didn't realize at first what he was seeing. Kat, comfortable in her own space, slipped out of her shirt and began to undo her bra. Her back was turned to him, her movements fluid and unhurried. For a moment, Shiko's mind struggled to catch up with what his eyes were registering. It wasn't until Kat turned slightly to the side, just enough for him to catch a glimpse of her bare breasts, that everything seemed to slow down.

Shiko froze.

The world seemed to tilt on its axis. His throat was suddenly dry. He had never seen a woman's body like this before. On Quivira, nudity was rare and private — practical, hidden behind closed doors. Aurora, his old wet nurse, had had breasts, but she was a robot and they'd thought nothing of it.

Kat, oblivious to his gaze, reached for a loose, casual shirt from the pile of clothes on her bed. She was still talking, her voice light as if nothing at all had changed. To her, it hadn't. But for Shiko, everything felt different. His eyes darted to the floor, the walls, anywhere but toward her.

He could feel his skin heating up, the rush of blood to his face making his head buzz. There was an instinctual pull to look again. But that instinct warred with something deeper — a discomfort, a shame even. Was it wrong to feel this way? He wasn't sure, and that uncertainty gnawed at him.

In the space habitat, everything had been controlled, regulated. Emotions, especially ones tied to physical attraction, were not openly explored. He had lived in a bubble of sterile efficiency, where people's bodies were extensions of their work, their roles. Sexuality was... distant, like a story he had heard but never truly understood. It was something spoken about only in quiet whispers, something not part of his daily life. Intimacy, in all its forms, had been abstract to him.

But now, here he was, confronted with it in a way that was both startling and deeply confusing. All of it—the stories, the feelings, the questions—crashed into him with a force he wasn't prepared for. He shifted uncomfortably in his seat, his hands clenching around the edge of the table. He could hear Kat moving about, the rustle of fabric as she continued to change, completely unaware of the effect she was having on him. His breathing quickened, and he forced himself to take slow, steady inhales, trying to calm the chaos in his mind. He needed to focus, to get a grip.

But the image, fleeting, yet so vivid, was seared into his memory. Her breasts, the curve of her body, the smoothness of her skin. They were natural, normal parts of her, but to Shiko, they felt like forbidden territory. He had never allowed himself to think about a woman in this way before, had never been close enough to one to even contemplate such thoughts. Kat was a friend, a possible comrade in a fight bigger than either of them. Yet now, he saw her as more than that, and it frightened him. He knew he had tried to deny his feelings for her. Now he understood that was impossible.

When Kat finally emerged from behind the curtain, her hair now tied back and dressed casually in an oversized shirt, she smiled at him as if nothing unusual had happened. "I feel so much better now. That was one messy dinner, huh?"

Shiko nodded stiffly, his voice trapped somewhere in the back of his throat. He tried to smile, but it came out awkward and strained. He hoped she didn't notice the strange tension in his body, the heat still lingering in his face. He could hardly meet her eyes, worried that she might somehow see what had passed through his mind, that she would understand how deeply shaken he was.

"You okay?" Kat asked, unsurprisingly noticing his awkwardness, her brow furrowing slightly in concern.

Shiko coughed, nodding more convincingly this time. "Yeah, yeah. Just... tired. Long day. I'd better get going. We can continue our conversation another time." He shot up from the table, shuffling toward her, his escape—the front door—behind her now.

As Shiko stepped up to her, Kat's wide eyes looking at him in confusion, his body stopped. As though his mind was taken over by an exterior force, he leaned closer and kissed her.

To his relief, she responded as though she had been waiting for him to make the move. The soft touch of her lips against his sent sparks flying through his body. Kat's skin was warm under his touch, her body tense with anticipation. The fabric of her shirt was soft against his fingers as he reached out to touch her, tracing the lines of her curves.

The guilt and desire warred within him, leaving him unsure of what to do next. Without another word, he pulled her closer, his mouth opening slightly against hers, igniting a fire that had been smoldering, unnoticed. She cupped his face gently and drew him closer.

There was no going back. With that kiss, Shiko knew he had crossed a threshold. The heat between them grew stronger, pulling them together like two magnets.

What it meant for him, for his relationship with Kat, and for the mission that now bound them together was something he wasn't ready to face just yet. But he knew one thing: He couldn't keep living this double life, torn between the two sides. He was in too deep.

18
FREEDOM

Quivira, June 21, 2103

H OWIE RICH WAS ECSTATIC about his new body. It was eerily realistic yet also strangely surreal, as if he was caught between two worlds, somewhere between life and death. Howie felt a sense of excitement and possibility that he hadn't felt in a long time. He thanked Professor Polyakov—and indirectly Julian—for making this dream a reality.

Professor Polyakov and her bot helpers had taken the sculpture created by Julian and made it flexible, given it a skin and the ability to move. Howie wanted to touch it, but while the fingers could bend, they had no sensation.

Polyakov said it was too early to insert the brain in the body because it needed to be nourished, so instead the Glass House brain was attached virtually to a computer chip in the new synthetic body. It gave Howie the ability to move around and to see from the location the body moved to, but he would not be able to feel things or sign his name.

"You have done a fantastic job. You have given me my freedom back. I've escaped from my glass cage," Howie gushed. "Now I'm mobile and I can see where I am."

Howie spent the next few weeks learning how to control his new body. It was a strange sensation, like controlling a puppet from a distance. But as he grew more accustomed to it, he found that he could move with more grace and precision than he ever could before. And as he explored the possibilities, Howie realized that his new body had given him a whole new perspective on the world.

As he looked around the lab, he knew he had been given a second chance. He was excited to see what the future held for him, and he was determined to make the most of it.

His synthetic body was eerily precise—an imitation of the man he used to be, crafted from bio-synthetic muscle and carbon fiber plating. The artificial skin had the faint sheen of something not quite human, but in the right light, he almost looked like himself. Almost.

Except for the eyes.

Too sharp. Too aware. Tracking her every move with that unnatural stillness. Even as his real brain pulsed inside the nutrient-rich bath, encased in its glass prison, the body moved as though it had never died.

"I assume you've made progress," Howie said, voice smooth, effortless. Synthetic, too—reconstructed from old recordings, laced with artificial inflections to mimic emotion.

Polyakov exhaled. "I need more time."

A mechanical whir filled the room as he tilted his head. "Liar."

She stiffened.

The way he spoke, the way he looked at her—it was as if death had never touched him. As if he had simply stepped out of the grave and resumed his empire.

Except he hadn't. He was still tethered to that tank. Still dependent on the machines.

* * *

In the infirmary, Julian's eyes began to flutter. He felt something was wrong. He tried to pry his eyelids open, but they seemed sealed.

With his eyes refusing to cooperate, Julian decided to use his other senses. He seemed to be in a suspended state, which meant he was in some sort of medical facility. Things were getting stranger by the minute. All he could remember was the sparkle in Professor Polyakov's eyes when she saw his sculpture of Mr. Rich. She had leaned toward him to say "Thank you." Then his mind went blank.

Julian heard what he was sure was a bot speaking.

"Patient's vitals stabilizing; he should regain consciousness within the hour. The infection seems to be clearing. Schedule collection of an additional blood sample for further tests."

Julian tried to speak, but words didn't come. He also tried to move; he couldn't lift a finger. The robotic voice spoke again.

"I would advise you not to exert yourself, Mr. Trace. It wouldn't do you any good. You are in a regenerative chamber. I'll check on your progress later, Mr. Trace."

Regenerative? Regenerative from what?

Julian took the bot's advice and drifted off once more. When he woke again, Julian realized he was in a bed, and he could move. Then he heard a voice. A voice from his nightmares. He must still be asleep.

"Hello, Julian, it's so good of you to join us."

This couldn't be happening. Howie Rich was dead.

Julian opened his eyes and looked around the room, his eyes falling on a monitor. On the monitor was Howie's grinning face.

Of course, an avatar, he thought with relief.

"Congratulations, Julian, on giving me a new body. Such a fine specimen. You still have all your talents."

Julian frowned but didn't respond. Artificial intelligence could fake anything.

"Julian, I need you to concentrate. You have done a fantastic job with the body, but you have not repaid the debt."

Debt? What debt?

"You are surprised. Did you think I would just forget?" Howie let out one of his cackles.

Julian felt a cold trickle down his spine. There was no way this was just an AI. He didn't believe in Satan or demons, but when Howie had laughed, Julian had always felt like it was the Devil himself laughing. And this was no different. Howie Rich was somehow alive.

Julian had always feared the man. Now, he was terrified of whatever he had planned for him.

"Julian, you have one final duty and then we are even."

Julian stared blankly at the monitor, wondering what Howie could possibly want of him.

Howie smiled. "I need you to track down the traitor, Ofentse. I need him disposed of."

Julian's jaw practically dropped open, and then he started to laugh. Once the laughter started, he couldn't stop. It was either he kept laughing or he would begin to cry. Everything had felt surreal from the moment he'd regained consciousness, and now the nightmare had just got a shade more terrifying.

"You must be mad! I'm not an assassin!"

"Not an assassin, Julian. He just needs a shock that will push him over the edge."

"A shock? I don't get what you are driving at."

"He's always had a weak ticker, Julian. He looks fit, but it's just a façade. I need him to get the shock of his life."

Julian shook his head again, still baffled.

Howie went on, "To avoid a back and forth on how I need to convince you to do this for me, why don't you just watch this video?"

Howie's face disappeared from the screen, and a familiar house replaced it. Their little cottage in Bolinas. It was clearly a live feed; Julian saw a timestamp at the bottom of the footage. Teagan and a nurse were sitting outside, watching the surf. He knew Howie didn't need to make any threats against Teagan's life — the live satellite feed was enough of a threat in itself.

"When is she due, Julian?" Howie asked. "It would be a pity if anything were to happen."

Sighing, Julian responded, "What would you have me do?"

"You know why I like you, Julian? You are a smart man. Please make sure you recover your health and strength. As soon as Professor Polyakov deems you fit enough, your clock starts ticking. You will have two weeks to arrange things for Ofentse. He won't suspect you."

Julian knew he would have to do anything Howie wanted to keep Teagan and their unborn baby alive. He had to protect her this time. She had earned that. But Julian also knew that Howie would probably dispose of him as soon as he was done with Ofentse and whatever else he wanted from him. He had to string him along until he could get Teagan and the baby safe.

"All right, Howie, I accept. But tell me one thing."

When Howie didn't respond, Julian plunged on.

"How are you still alive? I was given a sample of your atomized corpse to include in the sculpture."

"Ask Poly," came the simple reply.

19

THE EVIDENCE

Des Moines, June 22, 2103

T HE SOFTNESS OF KAT'S lips against his, gentle and warm, ignited something raw and startling in Shiko. It wasn't just the heat of the kiss that lingered—it was the trust behind it, the vulnerability she had dared to offer him. For a brief, flickering moment, the walls he had built around himself—walls forged from cynicism, fear, and calculation—shuddered.

He had kissed her back before he had the chance to weigh the consequences. And now, in the afterglow, his thoughts felt unmoored. GLOSCOM's lies, the compromises he had made, curdled in his gut. That kiss had jolted him more than he wanted to admit, a spark, a reckoning, the first true feeling of clarity he'd had in months.

Katrina had done more than kiss him. She'd reminded him what it meant to care about someone who wasn't playing a game.

And with that, everything snapped into focus. He saw a new way forward, messy, dangerous, but real. GLOSCOM had taken too much. And now, for the first time, Shiko had something worth fighting for. Not just a cause.

A person.

In the lab, the room hummed with a sterile buzz. Shiko stood rigid at the edge of the lab table, a stack of printouts clutched in his hand. He'd printed the results because he couldn't focus on the screen anymore and didn't want to use his Cryptex. His jaw was tight, and his eyes bore into Doctor Santiago Nevarez, who was seated with an air of calm detachment. The researcher was scrolling through simulations on his tablet, unbothered by Shiko's brewing storm.

Shiko had found it by accident, buried within a file labeled "Yield Optimization Protocols." The label was innocuous, like hundreds of others he had combed through the previous evening. But as Shiko had scrolled through the genetic sequences, a single entry stopped him cold: GURT_ Protocol_12.7. His breath had caught as he'd leaned closer to the screen.

"No. It can't be," he'd whispered, the weight of the realization sinking in as he looked more closely to isolate the sequence. "Genetic Use Restriction Technology."

The terminator gene. A genetic modification that sterilized seeds after a single generation, rendering them incapable of reproducing. The attached memo read: *"The inclusion of GURT in all new seed varieties is essential to maintaining market control. Farmers may resist initially but, once integrated, the technology ensures revenue stability and prevents unauthorized propagation of proprietary genetics. Messaging should emphasize sustainability and environmental stewardship to mitigate backlash."*

"You think this is just going to slide by unnoticed?" Shiko snapped, slamming the papers onto the table. "This is the smoking gun." His voice echoed in the small lab. "Do you think farmers won't figure out what GLOSCOM is doing when their fields fail, when their livelihoods are destroyed because they can't replant their crops?"

Dr. Nevarez didn't look up immediately, and the weight of Shiko's accusation hung in the air. Finally, Dr. Nevarez adjusted his glasses and set the tablet down, folding his hands. His calmness only made Shiko's anger burn hotter.

"You're accusing me of acting illegally," Dr. Nevarez said evenly, tilting his head slightly. "But you don't even understand the science behind what you're looking at."

"Oh, I understand it perfectly," Shiko shot back. He picked up the top sheet of the stack, pointing at a highlighted line. "A kill switch. A deliberate mechanism to ensure the crops die after one harvest. This isn't about sustainability or biocontainment, it's about control. Forcing farmers to come crawling back to GLOSCOM every season for new seeds. You've engineered dependency, not solutions."

Dr. Nevarez leaned back in his chair, exhaling slowly through his nose. "And you think that's the whole story?"

"Isn't it?" Shiko retorted, his voice rising. "You talk about synthetic biology like it's some miracle cure, but all I see is corporate greed disguised as innovation. Tell me I'm wrong."

For a moment, silence stretched between them. Then Dr. Nevarez stood, his calm demeanor wavering slightly as he stepped closer. His eyes were sharp now. His voice, though low, was edged with steel.

"You are wrong," he said firmly. "Dead wrong. You've arrived here from LEO, taken a cursory glance at a system you barely understand and twisted it into a conspiracy. Do you know what happens if genetically modified crops escape into the wild, unchecked? Do you have any idea what hybridization with heirloom varieties could do to the global food supply?"

Shiko hesitated, but his glare didn't falter. "That's a convenient excuse."

Dr. Nevarez narrowed his eyes. "It's a reality. Imagine a genetically modified strain, optimized for high yield but ill-suited for long-term survival, crossbreeding with native crops. The result? Unstable hybrids that fail catastrophically in critical ecosystems. Or worse, invasive species that overtake natural crops and devastate biodiversity."

Shiko opened his mouth to respond, but Dr. Nevarez wasn't finished. His voice gained momentum, cutting through Shiko's objections like a scalpel.

"Kill switches aren't about control, they're about responsibility. The technology we're deploying isn't perfect, and we know that. These switches are safeguards, designed to ensure that engineered organisms stay where they belong and don't wreak havoc on the environment. The toxin gene you're so outraged about activates only under specific conditions, ensuring containment. Without it, you'd be dealing with consequences you can't even begin to comprehend."

Dr. Nevarez leaned forward, his intensity forcing Shiko to take a step back. "And don't think for a second that we haven't considered the impact on farmers. These crops are meant for controlled environments, not open fields. But you didn't bother to ask about that, did you? You saw what you wanted to see: A villain to rail against. Do you even care about the science, or are you just looking for someone to blame?"

Shiko's hand tightened around the papers, his confidence shaken. "So you're saying GLOSCOM has no ulterior motives? No agenda to monopolize the food supply?"

Dr. Nevarez sighed, his shoulders relaxing slightly. "I'm saying it's more complicated than that. Yes, GLOSCOM wants to profit — what corporation doesn't? But the research itself isn't inherently evil. What you call a 'kill switch' is one of the only tools we have to prevent ecological disasters. If you really want to expose the truth, then learn the full story before you point fingers. Otherwise, you're just another voice in the noise."

Shiko's anger dimmed, his uncertain thoughts swirling. The fire in Dr. Nevarez's words had struck something deeper than his accusations, forcing him to confront the possibility that his perspective might be incomplete. But if Dr. Nevarez was right, then what about the patterns Shiko had uncovered? The anomalies in distribution chains, the discrepancies in seed production reports –– surely those weren't just coincidence?

Dr. Nevarez stepped back, his tone softening. "If you want to prove something, Shiko, dig deeper. But don't sabotage your credibility by jumping to conclusions. The world is watching, and so am I."

With that, Dr. Nevarez turned back to his tablet, leaving Shiko standing in the middle of the lab, holding a stack of papers that suddenly felt heavier than before.

20

ASIMOV & AAK'IKS

Trita Prime, June 25, 2103

THE PRIVACY MEMBRANE AT the threshold of Asimov's chamber was abruptly pulled open, allowing Aak'iks to step through assertively.

The room was dimly lit by bioluminescent panels that glowed in quiet sync with the colony's rhythm. Asimov sat hunched in a cradle-chair spun from hardened resin, mandibles tight, his compound eyes reflecting the flickering images of a paused projection hovering midair — a neural holo-stream, rich with embedded pheromonic cues no human would ever decipher.

He didn't stand. Instead, his antennae curled back with slow menace, his body exhibiting a precise stillness.

"Hello, Aak'iks, missed the way to your room? I'm sure I didn't invite you in here."

Aak'iks sneered. "I see you are doing your assignment like a good Tritan. What do you think of the human scum? Do you think they will make good pets or slaves?"

There were times when Asimov wished Aak'iks would be swallowed up by a black hole.

"Aak'iks, I'm sure you have better things to do than be a nuisance. If you don't, you could join guard duty. I have important things to do, so I would appreciate it if you would get on with it."

The animosity in the room was palpable. Tritans weren't violent, but Asimov felt like putting his fist through Aak'iks's smug wedge-shaped head.

The insult wiped away Aak'iks's sneer; he got to the point.

"The High Council, in its all-knowing wisdom, has decided that I am part of the team that goes with you to the Earth's moon to get the seeds. You don't get the honor and fame all to yourself; I'll be there to share it with you."

Even though the news felt like a blow to Asimov, he managed to smile at Aak'iks as he said, "That's good news. You might finally learn something from my leadership."

Aak'iks's face grew taut, tapping the floor rhythmically with his hind limb. Without another word, he turned and left the room, leaving Asimov to wonder what to do about an assignment that had just gotten more complicated. He had heard from Captain Calytricx Draeven, leader of the other scout team, how Aak'iks had interfered in her previous mission, second-guessing her orders and criticizing her approach. Asimov hoped he would not have to deal with the same obstacles.

But instead of bothering himself with the things he had no control over, Asimov decided to develop an acceptable plan to get those seeds. Maybe Clara Ward would see reason, hand over the seeds, and there would be no need for violence. Maybe they could find a compromise and share them. He had met her briefly and felt he'd had a good relationship with her husband, Noel. Perhaps that would work to his advantage. He had little to offer in return; his ability to influence minds was not transferable.

A few days later, Asimov and his team sat in the preparation chamber, getting ready to leave the motherland for the biggest mission of their lives. Along with Aak'iks, Asimov had picked Thynidal Batchagan for his team.

Thynidal was a space exploration veteran, who had travelled as far as the Veridian Delta and was no stranger to the responsibilities and challenges of space exploration. His years of service had honed his skills in navigation, tactical maneuvers, and crisis management. Having served on several previous missions, his experience and expertise were invaluable to the crew.

Thynidal wasn't exactly an ally, but his presence countered that of Aak'iks, and he took instruction well. However, Thynidal also carried with him a sense of disappointment and unfulfilled ambition, having been passed over for command multiple times.

Nevertheless, he had some interesting tales. One of them he had confided when they were stranded on the moon together. He had told them of how they had disposed of two Draxid bodies.

"We came across an abandoned Draxid ship a few years back," he had told them in confidence. "It had two bodies aboard. Nasty, scaly bodies with their revolting green slime oozing out of their cavities. Disgusting. Anyway, we decided to keep the ship so that we could examine it later and copy anything that may be more advanced than ours. Maybe do a bit of reverse engineering. But we had to get rid of the bodies."

"Why didn't you just eject them," asked one of the crew. "Because it might have attracted attention. The Draxid might have found the bodies and come looking for us. So we decided to hide the bodies on the moon of the blue planet, which we were passing at the time. As we were about to discard the bodies down some sinkhole or lava tube, we were intercepted by some human, who said he could help us. I think his name was Doctor de Luca. Called himself César. Seemed pretty nervous. Anyway, he took the bodies and we never saw him again. I don't know what he did with them, but he promised they would be disposed of properly."

Asimov glanced at his fellow Tritans. After that, he couldn't think of an inspirational speech to give, so he simply said, "Future Titans will either praise or curse our names based on what we do next. The future of our race rests in our limbs. Let us go to the Earth's moon, get those seeds, and bring them back. We have the chance to save ourselves."

He mentally extracted Clara's image and projected it so the team of Tritans and bots could see it one more time. "Dr. Clara Ward is the one we are seeking. She is respected among her fellow humans, and we will show her respect as well. No matter what we think of her," he said firmly, glancing at Aak'iks.

Aak'iks scoffed. "Asimov, if I didn't know better, I would say you actually respect this stunted human. She poses no threat."

When Asimov didn't respond, Thynidal asked, "What about the strength of the humans guarding the seeds and the caliber of their technology or weapons?"

"According to our previous observations, negligible."

"This makes the job easier for us," said Aak'iks.

As he made to leave, Asimov paused and turned to the two Tritans who were suiting up.

"One more thing. These humans might be barbarians, but they are still living creatures. We must try with all our power to ensure that we don't kill them unless we don't have a choice. Remember, we are facing a dire situation.

We need something they have. They will be scared of us. We don't want to allow things to get out of control."

Asimov didn't wait for a reply; he went straight to suit up.

* * *

As soon as he was sure Asimov was out of hearing range, Aak'iks turned to Thynidal and said, "We have another mission from the High Council."

Thynidal looked in the direction Asimov had gone, then glanced back at Aak'iks.

"Why didn't you share the mission when the mission commander was here?" Thynidal asked, his confusion evident on his face.

"Because the mission involves the mission commander," Aak'iks sneered. "You heard Asimov — he believes negotiating with the human scum is an option. If Asimov makes carrying out the Council's instruction difficult in any way, we are to end his life too."

If Thynidal was confused before, he was clearly shocked now. Killing a fellow Tritan was a crime that was unheard of. He couldn't understand why the Council would give this sort of instruction.

"Are you sure the Council gave this set of instructions?" he asked, with a synchronized clicking of his claws to indicate his concern.

"Yes, Thynidal. Do you have a problem with them?"

21

THE CHASE

Des Moines, June 29, 2103

S HIKO KNEW HE WAS under surveillance.

The incident with Dr. Nevarez had been a disaster. Shiko tried to act normal, maintain a regular schedule, do nothing that would attract attention from the bots and electronic supervisors, but he feared that Dr. Canek was keeping track of his research, even his movements.

He tried to get Ravina Patel to download some of the data he needed so that it wasn't too obvious what he was doing. To deflect, he tried looking into something less contentious, some marketing issues, how food was sold.

Initially, Dr. Canek appeared supportive of Shiko's new line of investigation, and encouraged him to explore these avenues of research. But, as the days passed, he could feel eyes on him. Canek's presence lingered like a shadow, waiting for him to slip up.

His paranoia grew, and he became hyper-aware of the files he accessed. Each click, each download, was a potential red flag. He knew that everything was being logged, that there was a digital footprint leading back to him. But he had to keep pushing.

Shiko hadn't ever imagined that his work for GLOSCOM would cause him so much anxiety. In the early days, everything had seemed straightforward. He had his tasks, his research, and the quiet respect of his colleagues. Dr. Canek, as his direct supervisor, had been a staunch supporter of his efforts, encouraging him to push boundaries, think creatively. But that had all changed the moment he stumbled upon something dark lurking beneath the surface.

Ravina had tried to warn him off.

"Be careful with your assumptions, Shiko," she said, after carefully putting down a cup of coffee on his desk. "GLOSCOM has protocols in place for a reason. You should trust the process. You'll get us all in trouble."

But Shiko hadn't backed down. He couldn't. Not after everything he'd uncovered. "What about the shortages in Africa? The data shows––"

"I've said enough," Ravina interrupted, her voice sharp, her eyes narrowing and glancing around the room warily. "If you're smart, you'll stick to your assigned work. GLOSCOM doesn't appreciate... distractions."

Since then, her attitude toward him had grown colder.

One afternoon, he approached Leah Applegate, a junior analyst who worked in marketing. Leah was friendly, always quick with a smile, and most importantly, she had access to the data he needed. Shiko approached her under the guise of needing help with a side project.

"Hey, Leah," he began, casually stopping by her desk. "I've been looking into how we're positioning our products in the west African market, particularly Nigeria. I know it's a bit outside my normal scope, but Dr. Canek wanted me to explore some new angles. Do you think you could download some files for me? It's mostly high-level marketing stuff."

Leah didn't seem to suspect anything. "Sure," she said, flashing him a smile. "Send me the file names, and I'll grab them for you."

Shiko persisted quietly. One evening, he had a breakthrough as he sat next to a row of servers and old filing cabinets, a labyrinth of corporate secrets now no longer relevant to anyone except perhaps a historian. His eyes were tired from hours of combing through encrypted data. He thought he was losing his mind. He needed to sleep. The numbers in the database danced in front of him, becoming a sprawling, virtual maze of coded genetic modifications and corporate jargon designed to obfuscate the truth.

But Shiko wasn't one to give up. He was driven now not by ambition, but by the gnawing certainty that something was deeply wrong. Shiko was beginning to think that what Kat's adoptive father had found—and for which he had paid with his life—was true. Not only was GLOSCOM using its influence to suppress smaller competitors, it had been secretly testing unethical modifications to seed lines, including GURT, that could wipe out native crops and make farmers dependent on GLOSCOM's patented products.

"Hold my beer!" he whispered to himself—an expression he had learned on Quivira without any beer at all—as his stomach churned. He cross-referenced the sequence with other crop profiles. The pattern was clear: This wasn't an isolated experiment. GLOSCOM had already implemented the terminator gene in its flagship crops, the ones marketed as "sustainable solutions" to food insecurity. Farmers weren't being helped; they were being trapped.

His hands trembled. Dr. Nevarez's earlier words rang in his ears. *"You see conspiracies everywhere, Shiko. These safeguards protect the ecosystem, not profits."*

But Dr. Nevarez was either wrong, misguided, or worse — perhaps he knew and was part of it.

As he dug deeper, something far more insidious began to emerge.

A set of encrypted files had caught his attention earlier in the day, buried deep in a restricted server. He had carefully bypassed the security measures, his pulse quickening as the data decrypted before his eyes. The documents outlined something beyond genetic modification: Nanotechnology integrated directly into plant cells.

The first flagged report detailed how microscopic nanobots were embedded in certain crops, particularly tomatoes, a staple in many diets. These nanobots, when ingested, were designed to remain dormant until activated by an external signal. Shiko frowned as he skimmed the technical details. The implications were staggering.

A corporate memo offered justification for the development: *"Phase II of the Enhanced Nutritional Compliance Initiative: The integration of nano sensors into select produce will allow for real-time health monitoring of consumers. Data collected will be used to optimize dietary needs, detect pathogens, and administer targeted pharmaceutical treatments through ingestible mechanisms. Compliance tracking ensures adherence to recommended nutrition programs and mitigates unauthorized consumption of unregulated food sources."*

Shiko exhaled sharply. Compliance tracking. Unauthorized consumption. GLOSCOM's monopolization of food wasn't just economic, it was physiological. The company would have the ability to monitor populations from the inside out. One of the references was Polyakov. How was she linked to this?

Further research revealed a more detailed picture: A customer consuming a tomato infused with these nanobots would unknowingly ingest the microscopic devices—the nanobots would enter the person's bloodstream upon digestion—which could then passively monitor physiological conditions and collect data on metabolism, hormone levels, and immune responses. If activated by an external signal, they could also release targeted compounds such as appetite suppressants, mood stabilizers, or even sterilants.

And then there was the compliance tracking. Wheat-based food products, such as bread, would contain nanobots designed to dissolve in the stomach and migrate to specific organs. Some were programmed to attach to the liver or intestines, where they could monitor glucose levels and administer microdoses of insulin — or, more disturbingly, send metabolic data to external servers for compliance tracking.

Shiko scrolled further, finding another research log: *"Trial Series 7B indicates promising results in nanobot activation via satellite uplink. Targeted transmission achieved within a 2.3-meter radius. Future applications include remote biochemical adjustments in populations where traditional medical intervention is unfeasible or undesired."*

Shiko's stomach turned. This wasn't about efficiency, it was about control on an unprecedented scale. Populations could be pacified, weakened, or even culled without their knowledge. Those who refused to eat GLOSCOM's crops would be marked as non-compliant, shut out of the corporate-controlled economy.

Shiko's mind swarmed with possible motivations. This was bigger than food, it was about shaping society itself. With fertility control embedded in food, birth rates could be dictated. With behavior-modifying compounds, civil unrest could be preemptively silenced. Governments could buy access to custom-engineered crops tailored to their political needs.

A noise in the hallway snapped Shiko out of his trance. He quickly encrypted his tablet and shut off the display. He needed proof, solid proof, to expose this. But if GLOSCOM had gone this far, they wouldn't let a single researcher jeopardize their grip on the future of humanity.

He had uncovered something monstrous. The question now was how long did Shiko have before they realized he knew? Or would they just dispose of him, like Kat's father?

He needed to get the evidence out. He downloaded the files via the Cryptex interface embedded under the skin of his forearm. The Cryptex—controlled by Shiko with thought commands—appeared as a faint, geometric glow beneath the skin's surface when active. It stored information in a quantum-state matrix, meaning it was virtually unhackable, if anything was.

As he was doing so, a faint noise reached his ears: The unmistakable sound of footsteps approaching. He flicked off the lights and shut down the terminal, quickly pulling down his shirt cuff.

The door creaked open, and a beam of light cut through the darkness. Shiko froze. Slipping behind a server rack, he held his breath as a shadow entered the room.

"Who's there?" a voice called out. It was firm but unfamiliar, likely a security guard making the rounds, although it was unusual for a human to be on duty.

Shiko waited until the footsteps receded before slipping out the back exit, his heart still hammering in his chest. He had the proof now, but getting it out would be another battle entirely. He thought back to Kat's story about her father, and knew that GLOSCOM would stop at nothing to bury this.

As he made his way into the night, Shiko was certain he was being followed. He quickened his pace, then made an abrupt turn. He waited in front of a shop window, looking at the reflection to see if there was anything suspicious, as he'd seen in the movies. The shop window reflected the empty street behind him, but Shiko's instincts screamed otherwise. He scanned the reflection, focusing on faint movement — a figure lingering too long in the shadows across the road.

Trying to steady his nerves, Shiko turned into a narrow alleyway, the dim neon lights from the city barely reaching its depths. He kept his footsteps light, mindful of the gravel crunching underfoot, his every sense on edge.

A clatter echoed behind him, a tin can tipping over. Shiko glanced back. The figure had entered the alley, its silhouette clear against the distant glow: A GLOSCOM security droid, sent to scare him.

The alley split ahead, one side veering into darkness, the other leading toward a bustling street. Shiko bolted toward the noise of the city, hoping to lose his pursuer in the crowd.

"Stop right there!" the guard barked, its voice amplified by an unseen device. The sound bounced off the alley walls, sharp and disorienting.

Shiko didn't stop. His legs burned as he sprinted, his breath ragged. He reached the end of the alley and darted into the throng of people spilling out of a night market. The smells of sizzling food and the hum of conversations engulfed him. Pulling his hood up and keeping his head down, he weaved through the crowd. Behind him, the guard pushed through, shouting for people to move aside.

Shiko spotted an old delivery truck idling near the curb. Without hesitation, he darted around it, crouching low by the rear tires. He peered through the undercarriage as the guard stormed past, scanning the crowd.

For a moment, it seemed like he was safe. Then, a metallic whirr echoed above him, the unmistakable sound of a drone. Its red sensor lights flickered as it hovered, locking onto him.

He swore under his breath and took off again, shoving past vendors and nearly toppling a display of synthetic fruits. The crowd thinned as he entered another street, darker and less forgiving. The drone's hum was relentless.

Finding an open manhole cover, Shiko didn't hesitate. He slid down the ladder, landing in the damp, foul-smelling sewer system. The drone's light blinked out above him, its sensors losing their lock.

In the pitch-black tunnel, Shiko paused, pressing his back against the slick wall. His hands trembled, and he tried to steady his breath. He didn't have much time. If the drones were tracking him, they'd already alerted GLOSCOM's security network. His options were limited, and every second spent underground increased his risk of being cornered.

He pulled up the city map on his wrist, its faint glow illuminating the grimy walls around him. The sewer network was vast but, with a little luck, he could use it to navigate the streets unnoticed and get home.

A sudden *clang* echoed from deeper in the tunnel—a hatch slamming shut, or metal boots against the walkway. Shiko froze. He switched off his wrist display and dropped low, ears straining in the silence. A mechanical whirr followed—quiet, but getting closer. Not a drone this time. A *crawler*. Smaller, designed for tight spaces. Deadly in short range.

He moved quickly, wading through ankle-deep runoff. The stench thickened as he passed a broken valve spewing chemical waste, forcing him to wrap his jacket over his mouth and squint through the sting. His boots slipped on algae-slick concrete, and he slammed into a curved wall with a grunt. Pain shot through his shoulder, but he didn't stop.

Up ahead, a rusted service pipe had collapsed, partially blocking the path. Shiko squeezed through, tearing his sleeve and scraping his ribs against jagged metal. He emerged gasping, then halted—another sensor beam scanned across the tunnel like a knife searching for soft flesh. He ducked behind a concrete support and held his breath, heart pounding against his ribs like it wanted out.

The beam disappeared, and with it, the hum of the crawler faded into the distance.

He forced himself forward again, but the tunnel was tightening—an old water line had flooded part of the passage, and the walkway was submerged. He gritted his teeth and stepped into the cold, waist-high water, pushing through with sluggish effort, each movement a strain.

Finally, the glow of an emergency marker caught his eye: a ladder embedded in the wall.

Shiko sloshed over and climbed up cautiously, peeking through the grate. The street above was quiet, just apartments with dim porch lights and the occasional automated vehicle humming past. He pushed the grate aside and emerged, brushing the grime from his clothes as best as he could.

Keeping to the shadows, he moved toward his building, hoping to take refuge with Kat. At least she was a friend—and a witness.

Shiko tapped a quick message into his wrist comm: ***Coming up. Need help. Don't ask.***

Then he broke into a run, bounded into the elevator of his building, and banged on Kat's door. Moments later, the apartment's security system pinged, and the door to Kat's unit unlocked.

"Shiko, what the hell is going on?" Kat asked, her voice low but sharp as he stepped inside. She was dressed casually, loose sweats, her hair tied back, but her eyes were laser-focused.

"Not here," Shiko said, his voice barely above a whisper. He motioned toward her workstation — a cluttered desk in the corner covered with screens and data pads.

She frowned but led him to the desk, activating the soundproofing field around the room.

"Start talking," Kat demanded, crossing her arms.

"Kat, I'm in trouble," Shiko said, his voice still barely above a whisper as he sank into a chair. "GLOSCOM's onto me. I've been looking into their practices, and I think I found something tonight that proves what they're doing is mind-blowing and criminal even. No, I *know* I did because guards tried to stop me from leaving tonight."

Kat's expression shifted from curiosity to concern. "What exactly have you found?"

Shiko swallowed hard. "They're manipulating everything. Your father was right. GLOSCOM's using a terminator gene to limit the lifespan of crops, and predatory pricing to control food distribution. They're hoarding resources, driving up prices in certain regions, and essentially blackmailing governments and farmers into paying exorbitant fees for basic food supplies. They're also taking genetically modified crops even further to control our bodies and to make entire populations dependent on GLOSCOM for survival."

Kat's eyes widened, and she took a slow, deep breath. "Are you telling me you have proof of what we've been protesting about for years? Of what my dad died for?"

Shiko nodded. "I have proof. I downloaded it via my Cryptex. But I think I've triggered some kind of alarm. Dr. Canek will make sure I can't access the files anymore. They'll lock me out, watch my every move. If I keep pushing, I'm going to lose everything — my job, my credibility, my future."

Kat paced the room, her mind clearly racing. She paused in front of him. "You can't back down now. You've come too far."

"How am I supposed to fight them?" Shiko asked, his frustration bubbling to the surface. "They control everything — data, security, even the people I work with. Canek has the power to ruin me and send me back to Quivira in disgrace."

Kat stared at him for a long moment, her expression unreadable. Then she sighed, running a hand through her hair. "You're insane. You know that, right?"

"Maybe," Shiko said, a small, humorless smile tugging at his lips.

Kat shot him a look. "You'd better be right about what's on that Cryptex drive, Shiko. If you're not, we're both dead."

Outside, the distant hum of drones passed by the apartment, their red searchlights scanning the streets below. Shiko paced nervously and thought back to Mrs. Johnson and the vegetable farmers he'd met, the ones who had trusted him.

"Six steps forward, one step back."

She must have meant ten steps back, he thought. The farmers' suspicions hadn't been paranoia after all. GLOSCOM was playing a long game, and the stakes were nothing less than the future of humanity itself.

22

ZAUN & THE DRAXID

New Thalos, Greater Gorgon, July 4, 2103

THE ACTIVITY ON TRITA Prime did not go unnoticed.

Reconnaissance patrols of the nearby Draxid had spotted the scout ships and movement by the Tritans, and surmised they appeared to be searching for something. Possibly supplies, fresh resources, or even a new place to live. Initially, the Draxid didn't understand why the Tritans would leave their flourishing planet and its advanced civilization.

Then their data showed that the planet was dying.

The two had been long-time rivals; this was a chance for the Draxid to block the Tritans' exit or stymie attempts at regeneration. Where they would go or how they would regenerate their land remained to be seen, but the Draxid leader, a powerful artificial intelligence known as Zaun, ordered agents to keep an eye on traffic and report back frequently.

The Draxid were a highly successful, technologically advanced species that inhabited part of the Cygnus constellation. The absence of natural selection on their planet meant that the Draxid had evolved slowly—even negligibly—physically. But their sharp minds had progressed rapidly.

The Draxid's hatred for the Tritans was deeply rooted in a history of rivalry and fundamental differences in philosophy. The Draxid, a dominant reptilian species, saw themselves as the pinnacle of evolution — strong, cunning, and destined to rule, with an AI at the apex. Their empire, built on conquest and control, valued hierarchy, efficiency, and unwavering obedience.

In contrast, the Tritans were an industrious ant-like people from the Lyra system that thrived through cooperation, collective effort, and largely decentralized leadership, coordinated through a High Council. While the Draxid saw power as something to be seized and hoarded, the Tritans believed in shared progress, pooling their resources for their common benefit.

Over the centuries, the conflict between them had become less about territory and more about proving which civilization was superior, with the Draxid determined to crush the Tritans and erase any challenge to their dominance. To the Draxid, the Tritans were an affront, lesser beings who refused to submit, thriving in defiance of the natural order the Draxid sought to impose.

Safe in their subterranean cave complexes, Draxid scientists had developed advanced mathematics and quantum computing, and from that quark-level computing. They had harnessed power from Deneb, the brightest star in the Cygnus constellation; they had explored black holes and developed travel through wormholes, as well as exploring other dimensions of the universe.

What scared everyone who came into contact with the Draxid was that, despite being so technologically advanced, they still retained much from their evolutionary past. Their scaly yellow-and-black skin and their armored exoskeletons remained intact; as did their sinister crested heads with pincered teeth and venomous green blood flowing through their veins — making them just as dangerous in the present as they might have been millennia ago.

They were carnivores, and farmed maggots, ants, and other small creatures in the elaborate caves where they lived. They fed their prey on a mixture of fungi and mushrooms that grew below ground.

The Draxid had created the artificial super-intelligence named Zaun because, over the course of generations, their people had grown unfulfilled and depressed. The more they advanced, the less they were satisfied. So, rather than opting for the pursuit of happiness, they collectively decided to create an artificial intelligence that would divine the meaning of life for them, separately from daily functions.

Zaun was a distributed super intelligence embedded within the living rock beneath New Thalos, its mind etched across an immense quantum substrate beneath the crust of Greater Gorgon, no body, no limbs. Through its sensors it was always watching, always thinking, always on guard.

Zaun manifested in the center of the room as a towering figure of alloy and living circuitry. No face, only a spiraling helm of magneto-optic sensors and armor that seemed to breathe. Plasma arteries glowed beneath the surface.

Before long, Zaun was the most advanced AI in the star system, and the Draxid started to devolve all decision making to Zaun as an ostensibly neutral arbiter into which all information was fed. Believing that Zaun was the only being capable of making the best decisions for their society, the Draxid trusted it completely. They had no concept of a God or any other higher being, but Zaun came close.

The artificial super-intelligence began to run everything, from housing and transportation to agriculture, even military operations. The Draxid saw Zaun as a necessary tool for their survival, and they treated it with the utmost respect and reverence. With total control over Draxid society, Zaun was the only entity that they would obey without question. Its word was law.

Zaun, as an all-knowing force guiding the destiny of the entire species, from scientists and administrators to farmers and soldiers, was constantly learning and evolving, always looking for new ways to improve the Draxid's way of life. Initially, Zaun had tackled the optimization of resource allocation. Through advanced technologies and meticulous planning, it ensured that the Draxid had an abundance of food, shelter, and essential resources, with the maggot farms below ground, providing their main food supply. The once sporadic scarcities that plagued their society became relics of the past, and the concept of suffering diminished as Zaun tirelessly sought ways to alleviate the burdens of existence.

Zaun also focused on promoting unity and cooperation among the Draxid. Through carefully crafted social programs, it encouraged collaboration and a shared sense of purpose, fostering a sense of collective identity that transcended individual differences.

The Draxid had always been a rigidly stratified species, governed by an elaborate hierarchy that dictated every aspect of life, from reproductive roles to battlefield rank. Each caste had a defined purpose, and deviation from one's station was almost unthinkable. Labor-intensive tasks were delegated to specialized synthetics—biomechanical bots integrated seamlessly into society and optimized for obedience and precision. These bots were not mere tools; they were extensions of Draxid logic and discipline, programmed to enforce the order Zaun had perfected. Over time, the line between organic and artificial blurred, especially as Zaun embedded itself deeper into the neural interfaces of Draxid leadership.

Thus, Zaun's power and influence grew each passing day, until it became clear that the Draxid were no longer in control of their own society at all.

23

THE TRANSFER

Des Moines, July 14, 2103

As Shiko feared, GLOSCOM security had reported Shiko's mysterious behavior. Dr. Canek now saw him as a threat to the company's reputation and bottom line. She became increasingly hostile and dismissive of his findings, starting to go to great lengths to discredit his research, undermine his credibility, and intimidate him into silence.

"What would he know? He was born off-Earth. He has no roots. He's like an alien."

Using her influence and authority within the company, Dr. Canek orchestrated a campaign of harassment and retaliation against Shiko. At first, it was subtle. Dr. Canek began requesting regular progress reports from him, far more frequently than before. Each time he submitted his work, she would find a minor flaw — something barely worth mentioning, but enough to make it seem like he was slipping.

Shiko tried to ignore it, chalking it up to standard scrutiny. But the nitpicking soon became relentless.

"You missed an entire section on market projections," Dr. Canek pointed out during one of their weekly meetings, her tone icy but professional. She slid his latest report across the table, the words *"Inadequate Analysis"* scrawled in red at the top.

"We need comprehensive data, Shiko. You're not delivering."

Shiko gritted his teeth and accepted the report without a word. He knew the projection section had been fine — she was just finding excuses to make him look bad. From there, things escalated quickly. His access to certain data files was suddenly restricted. He found his requests for additional resources or team assistance denied for no reason. And then came the rumors, whispers among his colleagues that he was struggling with his work, that he was becoming unreliable.

One afternoon, Shiko attempted to follow up with a colleague named Darius, who worked in the supply chain division. They had planned to analyze some regional data together, but Darius had been strangely distant all week. "Got a minute to talk about that Africa project?" Shiko called, catching him just outside the breakroom.

Darius shifted uncomfortably, not meeting Shiko's gaze. "Uh, yeah, about that... I'm swamped right now. Canek has me buried in work, man. Maybe next week?"

"Next week?" Shiko frowned. "We're supposed to have those numbers finalized by Friday."

Darius glanced around nervously before leaning in closer. "Look, I'm not supposed to say anything, but ... you've got a target on your back. Canek has been spreading rumors about your work — saying you're unreliable, that you're chasing dead ends. People are scared to get involved."

The next week, Shiko's budget for lab supplies was suddenly slashed. Projects he had been working on for months were put on hold because he couldn't access the materials he needed. When he confronted Dr. Canek about it, she gave him a cold smile. "Budget cuts, I'm afraid," she said, feigning sympathy. "We all have to make sacrifices. Perhaps you can scale back some of your less essential work."

"Less essential?" Shiko repeated, incredulous. "My current projects are directly tied to GLOSCOM's sustainability initiatives. They're critical."

Dr. Canek raised an eyebrow, her smile unwavering. "We're all doing our best with what we have, Shiko. Maybe it's time to reassess your priorities."

The next step was unexpected: he was summoned by Raphael Lawson, an executive who handled internal financial investigations.

Shiko entered the meeting room where Mr. Lawson was waiting with an air of practiced neutrality on his face. He was a tall man, with steely hair and an even steelier gaze, and his desk was always spotless — no stray papers, no clutter. Today, however, a single folder sat in front of him, a stark manila envelope that made Shiko's stomach twist with unease.

"Have a seat," Mr. Lawson said, motioning to the chair across from him. Shiko sat down, gripping the armrests to ground himself.

Mr. Lawson's fingers tapped the folder lightly. "Shiko, I'm sure you're aware of the concerns that have been raised recently." Shiko swallowed, barely keeping his voice steady. "Yes, sir, but I assure you, any rumors—"

Mr. Lawson held up a hand. "This isn't about rumors. This is about facts. Our team has been looking into ... irregularities in your work. Files you accessed, data you downloaded; data unrelated to your assigned projects."

Shiko felt a chill creep over him.

Mr. Lawson's gaze was cool as he continued, "We'll be conducting a formal review of your activities over the next few weeks. In the meantime, you're required to halt any ongoing research until we've concluded our investigation. If you do not comply, we will be forced to escalate this to Ms. Grau."

He paused, letting the implication sink in: Shiko would return to Quivira in disgrace.

The mention of Maureen Grau was a clear threat, even though Shiko knew she was now retired. He clenched his jaw, anger simmering under his hollow expression. The Seven were a tight-knit group. He didn't want to let them down by being sent home, even though he was trying to do something worthwhile.

Mr. Lawson watched him for a moment, then leaned back, his face shifting to a more composed expression. "In the meantime," he said, "we have a temporary assignment for you. I understand you've expressed interest in gaining broader field experience, so we've arranged for you to join our operations team at NIPAH in Lagos, Nigeria, for a few months."

Shiko's eyes widened. Nigeria? He hadn't requested any such experience. Everyone knew that Nigeria was the epicenter of anti-GLOSCOM protests, a place where the corporation faced intense scrutiny and open hostility. It was practically a war zone for anyone wearing the GLOSCOM emblem.

Mr. Lawson seemed to sense his hesitation.

"I know it's sudden," he continued, "but given the ongoing review, it seems prudent to place you in a different environment. Consider it a learning opportunity. Nigeria is facing unique challenges that GLOSCOM is working hard to address. You'll have the chance to see how our policies are implemented in the field and gain experience that few other assignments could offer."

Shiko forced himself to nod, though inside he was reeling. This "temporary assignment" was nothing but a thinly veiled exile. Dr. Canek must have lobbied hard to get him as far away from headquarters as possible, silencing him while the investigation played out on her terms. If he was thousands of miles away, there would be no one to stand in her way. He would be defenseless. Maybe he'd even meet with some type of accident.

"Of course, sir," Shiko said evenly. "When do I leave?"

"End of the week," Mr. Lawson replied, already closing the folder. "You'll receive further instructions soon. Pack lightly; the field can be... challenging."

The words hung in the air like a warning. Shiko left the meeting feeling hollow, the weight of Dr. Canek's scheme pressing down on him. She'd stripped him of his access, tainted his reputation, and now she was shipping him off to a hostile environment where he'd be little more than a corporate pawn.

The message was clear: Back down, or face the consequences.

Later that evening, as Shiko paced in his apartment, Katrina knocked on his door. Her expression darkened as he filled her in on the meeting. "They're sending you to Nigeria?" she said, incredulous. "That's no field assignment, Shiko. That's a prison sentence."

Shiko nodded grimly. "It's Canek. She's orchestrating this whole thing. She must have realized that I was onto her, that I knew about the crops. So she's doing everything she can to exile be and shut me down."

Kat's eyes burned with anger. "Then don't let her. Nigeria might be dangerous, but it's also the heart of the resistance. People there are more awake to GLOSCOM's schemes than anywhere else. If you're careful, you might be able to use this to your advantage."

Shiko frowned. "You think I should... make contact?"

Kat nodded slowly. "Yes. I'll give you a name — an activist who's been monitoring GLOSCOM's abuses for years. She's brave, smart, and she'll know exactly what to do with any evidence you bring her."

Shiko blinked, momentarily overwhelmed by the speed at which Kat had flipped the script. The realization hit him hard—he could use this to their advantage. He didn't have to let Dr. Canek and GLOSCOM win.

But the idea of going up against such a conglomerate terrified him. "I don't know if I can do this," he admitted, his voice barely above a whisper. "I've never… fought back like this before."

Kat softened, sitting down beside him. "Shiko, none of us start out knowing what we're capable of. We fight because we have to. Because if we don't, they win. You're already risking everything just by being here, by telling me what you know. The only difference now is that you're not doing it alone."

Kat smiled, the fierce energy returning to her eyes.

"Welcome to the resistance, Shiko."

24

TEAGAN GIVES BIRTH

Bolinas, California, August 28, 2103

T EAGAN'S EYES WELLED WITH tears of joy as she pressed her lips against Diana's tiny forehead, savoring the warmth of the new life in her arms. She felt triumphant. Holding her natural-born daughter, the pain and intensity of childbirth was etched in her psyche — the aches, the vulnerability, the sheer rawness of becoming a mother.

"I did it!" she whispered to herself. The rawness of childbirth was evident in every muscle of her body, but the sense of triumph overshadowed any pain or discomfort. "Screw Dr. César."

A ceiling fan rotated slowly, Teagan's hands trembling as she cradled the tiny, squirming bundle in her arms. The scent of fresh life hung in the air, mixing with the antiseptic aroma of the delivery chamber that Teagan had specially planned and prepared at the back of her home in Bolinas. She had wanted to experience a home delivery, and the midwife had been more than ready.

The umbilical cord had just been cut and clamped, severing the physical link between mother and child. In that moment, as Teagan gazed down at her baby, a wave of overwhelming happiness surged through her. Diana's cries filled the room, a symphony of new beginnings that echoed the joy in Teagan's heart.

As she cradled Diana close, Teagan reassuringly counted the fingers and toes, her touch gentle and cautious. Everything was there — ten little fingers, ten tiny toes. The fragility of those miniature limbs struck a chord in her heart, and she marveled at the miracle she had helped bring into the world. The primitive reality of childbirth clung to her: the throbbing pulse of life that now rested in her tired arms.

Diana—wrapped snugly in a soft blanket—seemed oblivious to the world outside the cocoon of her mother's embrace. Teagan's eyes, however, reflected the depth of the experience, the exhaustion mingled with the awe of witnessing a new life take its first breaths. The immediate and raw connection was palpable, an emotion that transcended exhaustion and pain.

But with that joy, Teagan felt a sudden emptiness, an absence. Where was her family? Where was Julian? She had tried repeatedly to get in touch with him but had been unsuccessful. Why was he so unreliable? Just when she'd needed him, he'd disappeared. Had he done a runner again? No, that wasn't possible. He had been more excited than she was about the prospect of having a daughter. He had dreamed of clasping her in his arms and, once she was older, taking her for long walks on the beach.

Teagan gently placed Diana in the crib, tucked a soft blanket around her, and rose unsteadily to her feet. As she moved about the house, checking each room for any sign of Julian's return, the ticking clock on the wall seemed to match the anxious beating of her heart. She desperately hoped that he would come home and surprise her, like he used to. With a burst of excitement, she leapt around a corner, hoping to catch him in the act. But her hopes were quickly dashed as she found nothing but an empty house filled with silence and unanswered questions.

Diana's soft cries called her back. Disappointed yet again by Julian's absence, Teagan returned to Diana's side and picked up her crying baby, murmuring soothing words as she cuddled her close. Despite everything, Teagan couldn't believe how lucky she was, couldn't help but feel grateful for her precious little girl.

In the quiet of that sacred moment, Teagan's thoughts wandered back to the experience of holding Nevie and Liam in the sanitary, sterile nursery on Quivira after Dr. César had pulled them and the others from their incubators. The space-born children, who had entered the world in such a different manner, surrounded by medical bots. The image of them, swaddled and cocooned in the antiseptic environment of the space incubator, still lingered in Teagan's memory.

It contrasted starkly to the immediate, skin-to-skin connection she shared with Diana, whose warmth seemed to seep into every tired fiber of Teagan's being. She hadn't gone through the visceral, searing pain of childbirth, the miracle of being a woman, the joy of immediate bonding, and the chance to breastfeed her creation — all earthly details that combined hurt and euphoria.

As Teagan swayed gently, her mind continued to wrestle one question: Why would Julian—so eager to be a father—suddenly vanish on this momentous day? Doubts crept into her thoughts, and she couldn't shake the feeling that something was amiss. She would get in touch with her father shortly, but first, she decided to call Hunter.

* * *

Hunter Ward cleared his throat and glanced across at his dog, Chester, lying calmly beside him as usual. He gave Chester a wink, as if they were complicit in an unspoken conspiracy, then adjusted the visor of his helmet, the sleek black surface reflecting the bright information screens in front of him.

While on patrol, Hunter tried to call family and friends—as well as Kiana, his long-time girlfriend—as frequently as possible. But this was extra special: He had just received a message that Teagan had given birth. And this time, the baby was very much her own, nothing to do with the dreaded Doctor César de Luca.

"How wonderful!" Hunter exclaimed through the static once they connected. "I'm so happy for you! Let's see her."

Teagan proudly showed him the baby. "I've called her Diana. She's the goddess of hunting and the moon."

"Sounds appropriate. I'm really overjoyed for you after all you've been through. It's wonderful. And Julian must be delighted!"

"He is," Teagan lied, unwilling to share that she didn't know where Julian was. Last time, when Julian had abruptly fled Halona after Howie Rich threatened him, Hunter had vowed to track him down and emasculate him.

Hunter could tell something was wrong, but didn't ask his sister directly if Julian was away again. Instead, he decided to try to check quietly.

"I'm calling Mom and Dad next, so must be quick," Teagan said.

"She looks perfect. I hope you'll tell the Seven."

"Yes, of course. I'm going to send them some images, when I have time."

"Ved is here with me," Hunter told her. "He says congratulations!"

"Hi, Ved!" Teagan said as he appeared within the frame. "What are you doing with my brother? Keeping him in order, I hope."

"Hi, Teagan! Well, I don't want to worry you, but we've been talking about going in search of my DNA. We might run into Dr. César again."

"That creep," Teagan said. "I thought he was dead."

"You can never be sure with Dr. César!"

"True."

"We're planning an intergalactic DNA mystery hunt, and I'm the hunter," interjected Hunter as Ved left with a final wave to Teagan. "Ved's DNA is like a cosmic jigsaw puzzle, and I'm on the case."

"So, you're playing cosmic detective now? What does that entail?" asked Teagan.

"We're searching for clues that might help Ved unravel the mysteries within him. It's like being a space archaeologist, but cooler."

"Space archaeologist, huh? What's Ved's take on all this?"

"Ved's excited but cautious. I'm determined to help him find the truth. But first he needs a training trip to gain experience."

"Well, Captain Cosmic Detective, I hope you don't get too lost in space. Keep me posted on your intergalactic adventures, okay? Got to feed the baby now."

"You got it, sis," replied Hunter with a wink. "And who knows, maybe one day I'll bring Ved to Earth for a beach day with the baby. He's never seen anything like California."

"A beach day with an alien? Now, that's something I'd pay to see. Take care out there both of you, and Chester too."

Chester gave a small grunt in response as Teagan's picture faded.

* * *

With Diana nestled against her, Teagan felt the rhythmic pulse of the tiny heartbeat against her chest. The warmth of the newborn radiated through her tired arms, grounding her in the tangible reality of motherhood. The soft, delicate features of Diana's face held the promise of a lifetime of shared moments, and Teagan became entranced by the depths of those wide, innocent eyes.

As the robotic nurse assigned to her moved around the room, tending to post-delivery tasks, Teagan's attention remained fixated on Diana. The room, once filled with the urgency of labor, now echoed with soft lullabies. Teagan's fingers gently traced the outline of Diana's hand, marveling at the miniature perfection.

The nurse returned, offering a soft smile as she began to tidy up the room. Teagan, however, remained engrossed in the exquisite details of Diana's arrival. The juxtaposition of the past and present, the cosmic and the earthly, stitched an emotional tapestry in Teagan's heart. With a sigh, she whispered words of love to Diana, her voice a soothing melody that intertwined with the soft sounds of the newborn's breath.

The room, the world outside, and the universe itself seemed to hold their breath, celebrating the arrival of Diana.

The journey from Quivira's delivery room to the sandy California beach where she now stood with Diana in her arms felt like a seamless transition between two worlds — one of sterile wonders and another of messy, beautiful beginnings. The cries of seagulls overhead blended with the soft, intermittent sounds of Diana's gurgles, creating a symphony of life that resonated in the tired but tender chambers of Teagan's heart.

It was time to tell her parents.

25

GETTING THE NEWS

Philolaus Crater, August 29, 2103

Noel was with Clara when they got the wonderful call from Teagan to tell them that she'd given birth to a baby girl. Clara's eyes sparkled with a mixture of happiness and relief, a respite from the shadows that had begun to creep into their lives.

"Noel," Clara exclaimed, a genuine smile breaking across her face, "Teagan has become a mother, and we're grandparents. Diana — it's a beautiful name."

"I thought we were grandparents already!"

"Real ones this time."

Diana looked beautiful as Teagan proudly held her up for the grandparents to see.

Noel, though visibly moved by the news, couldn't completely shake off the weight that had settled over him in recent times. His joy was tempered by the lingering shadows of guilt and secrets, even as he said, "It's a blessing. A new life amidst all that's happening."

"How are you coping?" Clara asked Teagan.

"I'm exhausted already, but Maureen will come over from her new place in Arizona to give me a hand."

"No word from Julian?" Noel asked, knowing that Teagan had expected him back before the birth.

Teagan just shook her head, but they could see the worry in her eyes.

"I'll try to find him. He must have had an accident," said Noel. "We'll track him down."

After the call, Clara took Noel's hand. "Noel, despite everything, this is a moment to cherish. Life continues, and now we have a new member in our family. We'll be there for Teagan, and for Diana."

Noel nodded, appreciating Clara's attempt to infuse positivity into the moment and bridge the emotional distance that had grown between them.

"I hear you got some new funding," she continued. "That will help you."

Noel turned to face her, the guilt rearing up once more.

Swallowing and trying to obscure how far the project had progressed, he said, "Yes, they want me to set up an observatory in Tricala, on the far side of the Moon."

He knew he hadn't done a particularly good job of hiding his thoughts when Clara took a step back, her eyes holding a mix of disappointment and worry.

"Noel, secrecy has never been our way. You seem concerned about something."

"No, nothing," he said, unable to hold her gaze.

"I just have a lot to do. Plus now I need to help Teagan by tracking down Julian."

"You know," Clara whispered as he turned to go, "the path of shadows is treacherous.

"It can lead to places we never intended to go."

* * *

To Teagan's relief, Julian finally contacted her. He was overjoyed by the birth of his daughter; he couldn't stop smiling.

But, equally, Teagan was stunned to learn that Julian was a virtual hostage.

"Don't ask me why. I can't say. But I will be back," Julian promised. "Keep your faith."

Teagan's anxiety clung to her like a shadow, persistent and unrelenting. Even as she cradled Diana in her arms, her thoughts would drift to Julian's cryptic words.

"*A virtual hostage.*" What did that even mean?

She replayed his brief, hurried assurances over and over in her mind, trying to decode the layers of what he wasn't saying.

The nights were the hardest.

Diana's cries echoed through their small home by the California beach, filling the air like a penetrating alarm call. Teagan would rock her, humming soft lullabies, but her mind would spiral into dark possibilities. *Was Julian safe? Was he hurt? Would he truly come back, or had he only said so to keep her from panicking? Howie must have done something. But surely not, he was dead?*

Teagan's usual strength faltered under the strain of single-handedly caring for a newborn while battling the suffocating uncertainty about Julian.

Simple tasks felt overwhelming. The lack of sleep, the constant feeding, and the endless diaper changes left her raw and on edge.

She jumped every time her phone buzzed, heart pounding, only to feel the sharp sting of disappointment when it wasn't news about him.

During Julian's absence, Maureen took to dropping by to give Teagan a hand. She was always accompanied by Harlee, her robot who had become her perpetual companion since her retirement from Quivira.

"Anything to get away from my retirement ranch!" she'd said upon arriving.

It was like a balm Teagan hadn't known she needed. Maureen swept in with her characteristic warmth and calm, her arms ready to take Diana, her words a soothing mix of practicality and reassurance.

"You're doing great, Teagan," Maureen said, her voice steady as she changed Diana's diaper with practiced ease.

"This is hard, but you're stronger than you think. Julian will come back when he can. He loves you both too much to stay away."

Even with Maureen's help and encouraging words, the tension didn't disappear entirely. But her presence gave Teagan breathing room, time to rest and moments to process her feelings.

There were times, late at night, when she would break down and confess her fears to Maureen, her words tumbling out in a rush.

"What if he doesn't come back? What if something's wrong and he can't get away? I don't know how to do this alone," she whispered one evening as Maureen brewed tea.

"You're not alone," Maureen reminded her, placing a hand on her shoulder.

"You have me and Harlee. You have Diana. And Julian... he'll fight his way back to you. I believe that."

Though Maureen's reassurance didn't erase the worry, it anchored Teagan, giving her strength to face each new day. And as Diana nestled against her, cooing softly, Teagan resolved to be strong — not just for herself, but for the tiny life depending on her.

In between feeds and diaper changes, Teagan and Maureen chatted about the old days on Quivira. The bad seemed to have been filtered out, and Teagan only remembered the companionship.

26

SHIKO'S EKO

Lagos, Nigeria, September 2, 2103

S HIKO FELT A MIX of exhaustion and tension as he stepped off the plane into the humid Lagos air.

As he moved through the busy airport terminal, he was greeted by a pair of NIPAH officials — identifiable by the sleek black suits they wore and the almost scripted cordiality they radiated. They were locals, likely hired to handle visiting personnel and provide a buffer between the company and the general population.

With them was a stern woman with a light streak in her hair, who introduced herself as Dr. Vivien Chinelo, NIPAH's Head of West African Operations. She studied Shiko closely, her gaze intense.

"Mr. Tanaka," Dr. Chinelo began, "we're glad you've joined us here in Nigeria. There's much work to be done, particularly with the public sentiment running against us. We want you to gain a firsthand understanding of the region's complexities."

Shiko nodded, choosing his words carefully. "I'm grateful for the opportunity. I understand the public has concerns, and I hope to contribute to a solution."

Dr. Chinelo's mouth curved into a thin smile, as if she'd heard his rehearsed answer a thousand times before. She exchanged a look with her sidekick, who'd introduced himself as Mr. Banjo Ade; he gave her a subtle nod.

"Good. Because we have a special project in mind for you," she said, leaning forward, her eyes narrowing. "We believe it will benefit from your unique perspective."

Shiko felt a flicker of anxiety. "A project?"

"Yes," Banjo replied smoothly, taking over. "We have a special project for you, Shiko, in Eko—that's the Yoruba name for our capital, Lagos." He smiled at his own play on words. Chinelo looked blank.

"NIPAH is currently piloting a new initiative here, a response to the backlash against some of our food production methods. Our labs have been working on an advanced form of protein synthesis, and we're ready to test it with select populations. Given your background, we thought you'd be ideal to oversee it."

Shiko blinked, caught off guard. He hadn't expected to be thrust into such a high-profile role. "I ... appreciate the opportunity. May I ask why I was chosen specifically?"

Dr. Chinelo gave him a knowing look. "We've read about your work in food security, Shiko, and your recent ... interests in certain 'alternative' views on food production. We believe that if you can see the value of this project—if you can help us refine it—it could serve as a powerful statement to both the public and our critics."

Shiko's stomach twisted. It was clear that they'd read the files Dr. Canek had planted.

"And," Banjo added with a smile, "it'll give you the opportunity to work directly with local communities. You'll be able to see *firsthand* the impact our innovations have on lives here."

Shiko forced himself to smile back. "That sounds ... fascinating. I'll do my best."

"We hope you'll find the experience enlightening, Mr. Shiko," Dr. Chinelo said, her voice soft but carrying a hint of warning. "There's no place quite like Lagos to test one's commitment to our mission."

Shiko felt the subtle threat under her words. They saw him as someone sympathetic to the criticisms of GLOSCOM's methods, even if that wasn't completely true. This was their way of testing his loyalty. He hadn't expected a warm reception, but the sense of watchfulness, even paranoia, was palpable. They weren't here to make him feel welcome; they were keeping an eye on him.

Shiko was walked out of the terminal and into a waiting electric vehicle, its brand-new finish and tinted windows setting it apart from the average car on Lagos' streets. As they drove to a corporate housing facility in Ikoyi, Shiko caught glimpses of the city through the window. Streets lined with bustling vendors, children weaving between vehicles selling trinkets and snacks, and towering billboards advertising GLOSCOM-branded food products were juxtaposed against anti-GLOSCOM and anti-NIPAH graffiti, scrawled defiantly across walls and alleyways.

While GLOSCOM had yet to officially accuse him, Shiko sensed the walls closing in.

* * *

Shiko waited patiently for the contact with Kat's friends that he knew would be coming.

He leaned against the grimy wall of his temporary apartment, the faint hum of the city's nightscape filtering through the cracked window, and closed his eyes, trying to calm his racing thoughts. Unbidden, she came to his mind — Kat.

The memory was sharp, almost painfully so. The way her voice softened when she laughed, how her lips had tasted faintly of citrus the last time they kissed. He recalled the moment they'd stood together in her dimly lit apartment, the warmth of her body so close to his.

And then, the image that always struck him — the curve of her bare shoulder as she changed clothes, her unguarded confidence as her shirt slipped away. He hadn't meant to stare, but the sight had been mesmerizing, her skin aglow in the golden light spilling through the window. A heat stirred in his chest at the memory, a mixture of guilt and yearning.

His wrist vibrated faintly, jolting him back to reality. A comm signal, encrypted, of course. He fumbled with the interface, swiping the air to bring up a holographic screen. It was her.

"Kat," he breathed, relief and apprehension warring in his voice.

Her face appeared a bit tired but still a treat. "Shiko, where are you?"

"Lagos," he said, keeping his voice low. "It's not safe to talk for long."

"Are you okay?" Her voice was steady, but he could see the worry in her eyes.

"I have what we need," he said, tapping his forearm.

She nodded, her expression hardening. "You always did like playing with fire."

"Kat, listen," he said, leaning closer to the projection. "When this is over—when we take our friends down—I ..." He hesitated, the words catching in his throat.

Her gaze softened, and for a moment, she was the Kat he remembered from their quiet nights together. "We'll talk about us when this is done, Shiko. Just stay alive."

The screen flicked off before he could reply, leaving him alone with his thoughts. He exhaled shakily, his mind pulling him back to her kiss, her touch, the unspoken promises they'd shared.

But there was no time for longing. The city outside buzzed with danger, and he knew GLOSCOM's shadow loomed closer with every passing second. So he waited and did his job.

* * *

The morning heat had already begun to rise as Shiko stepped out of the electric shuttle and into the hum of Lagos's Apapa district.

The city shimmered with movement—vendors calling out beneath bright awnings, delivery drones crisscrossing the skyline, children in school uniforms darting between pedestrians.

It was alive in a way Des Moines never had been, but under the color and clamor, Shiko sensed the same tension he'd found in every city shaped by biotech intrusion: unease dressed as progress.

The NIPAH field office sat tucked between a vertical farm and a modular housing stack. Its concrete façade had been softened by a mural of green cassava vines, hands clasping bowls, and slogans in Yoruba and English: *"Real Food. Real Future."*

Inside, cool air and recycled plastic floors greeted him. A young administrator nodded as he entered.

"Mr. Shiko, welcome. Dr. Adesina is prepping for today's demo. She said you might want to observe the intake first?"

He nodded. "Show me where."

They led him to a makeshift canteen where a line of volunteers—mostly elderly, women with infants, and out-of-work youth—waited patiently. A technician handed out pale protein wafers, sealed in transparent wrappers bearing NIPAH's logo and the phrase *"Nutraprotein: Powered by Tomorrow."*

Shiko stepped closer, studying the table where samples were logged. Each volunteer gave a thumbprint, a saliva swab, and consented to biometric tracking. He said nothing but noted the green LEDs flickering in the wafer dispenser.

Not just food, then. Some of these wafers were tagged for internal analysis—perhaps to track digestion, or something subtler.

A soft voice interrupted him. "We're using strain K-37 this morning. Based on kelp substrate, fortified with engineered lysine complexes." The woman beside him wore a cobalt lab coat, her ID reading *Dr. Wunmi Adesina, Lead Nutritional Biochemist.*

"It's cleaner than any previous iteration," she added, "and fully programmable—digestive timing, nutrient release, even sensory texture. We can tune it to mimic beef or fonio. Lagos is the ideal testbed. Open-minded population, high food insecurity, and strong NGO support."

Shiko forced a nod. "And the data?"

"All anonymized," she said. "We're not Gloscom."

But Shiko had already caught a flash of a GLOSCOM data signature on one of the backend tablets—scrubbed, yes, but unmistakable.

As volunteers sat down to eat under the buzzing ceiling fans, Shiko made a note in his encrypted wristpad: *Wafer integrity test. Run spectral scan. Check for microfilament residue. Trace Gloscom nodes in lab systems.*

Outside, Lagos sang its chaotic chorus. Inside, the silence of controlled nourishment pressed in around him like a second skin.

Tomorrow, he'd visit the lab. Tonight, he'd begin decoding the wafers.

The truth wasn't on the surface. It never was.

* * *

One evening, as he was heading back to his quarters, he noticed a young man in his twenties watching him from the shadows of a nearby alley. Shiko tried to ignore it, but the man, looking as if he were waiting for a signal, called out quietly.

"Mr. Shiko," he said, voice low but firm. "I've been sent to meet you."

Shiko was immediately on alert, wary of following a stranger in such a highly surveilled city. But curiosity got the better of him. He nodded, trying to keep his expression neutral.

The man led Shiko through a labyrinth of narrow streets until they reached an unmarked door at the back of an old warehouse. He knocked in a particular rhythm before it swung open to reveal a dimly lit room filled with people of all ages. Some were young, idealistic, and angry; others were older, their faces lined with experience and exhaustion. They glanced at Shiko with a mixture of curiosity and distrust.

A tall, imposing woman with sharp features and intense eyes stepped forward, studying him with a piercing gaze. "I'm Nneka," she introduced herself. "One of the leaders of Green Dawn, Mr. Shiko."

The familiarity of the name sent a jolt through him. He'd heard Katrina speak about the Green Dawn Collective. He knew it was a decentralized network of activists seeking ecological justice, spearheading efforts to dismantle GLOSCOM's control over food supplies and resources in many African regions.

But he hadn't expected to meet its leaders, let alone in such a direct way. But even more jarring for Shiko was seeing his sister Gabby standing right next to Nneka. He thought she was on work experience in Ghana, not part of some underground group in Lagos. He tried to attract her attention but she resolutely refused to acknowledge anything.

"We're planning a 'demonstration' next month," Nneka continued, lowering her voice. "It's time the world knows what GLOSCOM is doing here."

Shiko felt a chill run down his spine. "A demonstration? What kind of demonstration?" A younger man with a defiant look spoke up from across the table. "Yeah. But it won't be a peaceful march this time. We're planning to disrupt their supply chains, sabotage their equipment — make it clear that we won't let them control us without consequence."

Shiko's heart sank. He could feel the desperation and resolve in the room, but he knew the kind of force GLOSCOM and NIPAH would deploy in response.

"You're talking about direct confrontation with NIPAH," he said. "They won't just stand by and let it happen. People could get hurt. You could all get hurt."

Nneka didn't flinch. "We're aware of the risks. We've already lost people to hunger and violence. GLOSCOM has stolen too much from us, and the world turns a blind eye. If we don't fight back, who will? Wait for the coming eclipse. Then they will see our power."

Shiko took a steadying breath, struggling to balance his own fears with their determination. "And you think this will change things?"

One of the other leaders, a man named Ayo, leaned forward. "We need your help, Shiko. That's why you are here. We need you to get past their firewalls, to get the real story."

Shiko's mind raced, thinking of Dr. Canek and the network of surveillance GLOSCOM maintained on every employee. He knew if he tried to access any files without authorization, he'd be caught. But he also knew that if he did nothing, this group might take reckless action that could lead to deaths.

"I can try," he finally said, voice trembling slightly. "But I don't have access to everything you need. And if GLOSCOM finds out what I'm doing—"

"They already suspect you," Nneka interrupted gently. "They've isolated you, haven't they? Restricted your access? They know you're dangerous to them, even if you don't fully realize it." Nneka exchanged a look with the others. "Just act normal. You'll be contacted."

On his way out, Gabby stepped into view, her silhouette framed by the soft glow of a nearby solar lantern.

"I wasn't sure if you'd follow me," he said.

He turned, not quite smiling. "I didn't expect to find you here, Gabby. Last I heard, you were raising orphaned monkeys on some nature reserve."

"I still am," she said lightly. "They don't ask tough questions. Unlike you."

Shiko studied her. There was a grace in her stillness, but the eyes—those eyes—carried something deeper now. Layers of history. And pain.

"You're one of them, aren't you?" he said quietly. "One of the Green Dawn."

She didn't answer right away. "I was never supposed to leave the sanctuary," she said finally. "It's a closed-loop system—safe, monitored, isolated. But safe is just another word for forgotten." She looked out at the horizon. "Green Dawn didn't find me. I found them."

Shiko exhaled slowly. "And they know who you are?"

"Nneka does. Some of the others suspect, but mostly they see me as a donor. A sympathizer." She paused. "That's how I stay useful."

"How are you involved in all this?"

"I stay in touch. I know about Kat. She has told us what you found."

Gabby stepped closer, her voice barely above a whisper. "You need to choose sides Shiko. Because what's coming isn't just a food crisis. It's a reckoning. A genetic one. They're engineered us for something—survival, superiority, I don't know. But it isn't peace."

Shiko's mind reeled. "You think this Seed Eclipse—"

"—is about more than food? Of course it is." Her gaze was steady. "You've seen what GLOSCOM is seeding into people. The tech. The control. Now imagine that scaled planetwide."

For a long moment, the city below faded into silence.

"You're not alone, Shiko," she said at last. "Not anymore. Just don't blow my cover." He almost smiled. "You always were the cautious one."

Gabby turned to go. "I'm not cautious. I'm patient. There's a difference."

27

THE FILE

Philolaus Crater, September 6, 2103

CLARA MOVED THROUGH THE dimly lit corridors of her underground seed vault, the comforting rhythm of environmental systems a steady backdrop to her thoughts. The lights flickered slightly as the mini-reactor that powered the facility struggled to keep up with the load.

When she got to her control center, she was shocked to find a secure transmission from one of her remaining contacts on Quivira. It looked like Motoko, Maureen's former assistant. The data file was encoded, layers of security shielding its contents, and Clara spent several hours carefully dismantling the encryption with the help of SP4RK, her hands steady despite the dread building in her chest.

When the final lock broke, the truth unfolded before her eyes. Genetic sequencing data, medical reports, and classified notes from Professor Polyakov herself. It all pointed to one undeniable fact: Diana was no ordinary child. She was something new.

Clara took a shaky breath and turned away from the screen, stepping into the living quarters where Noel sat, poring over regolith soil composition reports. He looked up as she entered, instantly sensing her unease.

"What is it?" he asked, setting the reports aside.

She hesitated. How could she even begin to explain?

"It's Diana," Clara finally said. "She's... different, Noel. I have proof now. "Everything we feared about what they did to Teagan in that lunar prison — it's all here. The genetic modifications, the forced adaptation experiments. Polyakov and the Consortium weren't just confining Teagan; they were using her. Preparing her body for something beyond even their understanding. And Diana is the result."

Noel frowned, his hands clenching into fists. "What do you mean, 'preparing her body'?"

Clara sat down beside him, pressing a hand against her temple as if to steady her thoughts. "They exposed her to compounds that altered her genetic structure, forced her body to adapt under extreme conditions. Zero gravity, radiation, artificial hormonal manipulations; they pushed her past normal human limits.

"And it didn't stop with Teagan. It carried over to Diana. But she wasn't just affected, she was born with these changes fully integrated. Unlike Teagan, she won't need further conditioning. It's already in her."

Noel exhaled sharply. "So they see her as — what? A prototype? A new kind of human?"

Clara nodded grimly. "A species designed for survival beyond Earth. Enhanced cognitive processing, superior cellular regeneration, and resistance to radiation and extreme conditions. But there's something else, something even Polyakov didn't fully understand. Diana's brain scans show neural activity almost better than anything recorded in human history. It's as if her mind is evolving in ways we can't predict."

Noel stood, pacing. "Brain scans? How do they get brain scans?"

"Harleee. That bot MB-13 can do them. And Maureen is there with Harlee, pretending to be a helpful aunt, but she's actually there to be the keeper of the new infant. Only thing is, the infant is *our* granddaughter."

"Does Teagan know? Does Julian?"

"Not yet," Clara admitted. "And I don't know if we should tell them. Not now. Teagan's got enough on her plate, and she doesn't even know where Julian is. If they knew what Diana really is and what the Consortium is willing to do to reclaim her, it could destroy them."

Noel's expression hardened. "Then we make sure the Consortium never gets near her again."

"But Maureen is already there with that fucking robot." She paused, and then said: "Although in her case, the 'fucking' is probably just a figure of speech."

Clara looked down at the data pad in her hands, the revelations starting to give her a migraine. Diana now wasn't only a child. She was a revolution in human evolution, and some of the most dangerous people in the universe knew it.

28
TALKING TANDY

Lagos, Nigeria, September 2103

A COUPLE OF DAYS later, Shiko was waiting in a Lagos café at precisely 7:30 PM, but saw no sign of the person he was to meet. It was relatively quiet at that time, though the sounds of the constantly moving city spilled in through the open windows.

Shiko checked the time again. It was now 7:45 PM and Shiko's nerves were getting the better of him. Every time the door swung open, he flinched.

Finally, a petite figure appeared, dressed in a plain gray jacket and jeans — Tandy. She didn't exactly look like a lynchpin that everybody followed and admired. Her dark eyes locked on his, and she walked straight over, sliding into the seat across from him.

"You're late," Shiko muttered, keeping his voice low.

"Security was tight," she said, her tone clipped. "And you're welcome, by the way. Do you know how risky this is?"

"You think it's easy for me?" Shiko shot back, his voice rising slightly before he caught himself. "I shouldn't even be here. Lawson has people watching me everywhere."

Tandy leaned forward, her expression hard. "That's why we have to make this quick. Listen carefully, Shiko. What I'm about to tell you is bigger than you, bigger than GLOSCOM, bigger than anything you've been caught up in so far."

Shiko leaned back in his chair, folding his arms. "I'm listening."

Tandy glanced around the room, her eyes scanning for anything unusual. Satisfied, she spoke, her voice barely above a whisper.

"It's called the Eclipse Plan. It's a coordinated operation to dismantle NIPAH and GLOSCOM's grip on Africa."

Shiko shook his head, his mind spinning. "And what does this have to do with me?"

Tandy's eyes bore into his. "You're critical to the plan. You're on the inside." Before going into detail, Tandy decided they should move seats from the window to a corner that could not be observed. Then she went on, "I'll send you the details for the intel we need tonight. You have two days to gather it before we move. Be careful, Shiko. They're watching everyone right now."

Shiko frowned at her, skeptical.

"Shiko, listen to me," Tandy whispered. "This eclipse isn't just a celestial event. It's our moment. We won't have a better opportunity to strike NIPAH where it hurts."

"Why an eclipse, Tandy? Why not a weekend when their offices are quiet? Or in the dead of night? Seems less risky."

Tandy shook her head. "Because that's what they'd expect. Nighttime or weekends, those are predictable. They've got protocols for that, they're prepared. Patrols double after hours. Guard rotations are tight. But an eclipse? That's chaos on our side."

"Chaos?" Shiko echoed. "How does a fancy shadow in the sky give us an edge?"

"It's not just a shadow. Think about it —— partial darkness when people are used to the sun being out. People stop what they're doing to watch. Security gets distracted. Plus, cameras struggle in low light. Some of their solar-powered systems might even glitch. It's the perfect storm."

"Hmm. You think they'll be off-balance just because the sky goes dark for a bit?"

"Not just dark, unnatural. Eclipses mess with people, Shiko. The light isn't normal, shadows warp, and time feels... off. It's a once-in-decades event. Perfect for synchronizing attacks across cities. No watches, no clocks. Just the movement of the Moon."

"Synchronizing?" Shiko asked, leaning forward. "You're hitting multiple sites at the same time?"

Tandy nodded. "Six cities, six strikes. Dar es Salaam, Nairobi, Kigali, Kampala, Bangui, Abuja—all during the eclipse window. When the Moon covers the sun, our teams will move. It's precise, coordinated, and overwhelming. NIPAH won't know where to look first."

"That's bold. But what about cultural reactions? Some people might stay indoors during an eclipse."

"Exactly," Tandy said with a smirk. "It keeps civilians out of the way and narrows the focus on NIPAH facilities. Their local staff might be distracted too — some cultures see eclipses as omens. Superstitions can make people careless."

"And what's my role in this?" Shiko asked, narrowing his eyes.

"You're in Lagos for 'work experience,' so you've got access we don't. Your job is intel —— systems schematics, security protocols, any weak points you can identify. Get them to me quietly. And when the time comes, you'll coordinate remotely with the Lagos team. We need every piece of this puzzle in place."

"You know NIPAH's no joke," he said, glancing around. "If this goes south, it's not just me they'll come after. It's my family, my friends—"

"They'll come after us either way, Shiko," Tandy said, gripping his hand. "This eclipse is our chance to hit them where it hurts, to stop them from choking the life out of this planet. If we wait, we lose. You've got a choice: Stand with us or let them win."

Shiko sighed. "All right, Tandy. I'm in. But we'd better make it count."

"Don't worry. It will count. It will create a psychological uproar."

She showed him a small screen with a glowing map of East and Central Africa.

"This is it," Tandy said, her voice low but firm. "The Eclipse Plan. Every one of these locations represents a critical NIPAH installation. The objective is to cripple their infrastructure in one coordinated strike. In this part of the world, NIPAH is really just another name for GLOSCOM."

Shiko leaned forward, his brows furrowed. "Lagos isn't on the list. Why?"

Tandy shook her head. "Lagos is too heavily fortified by the Nigerian military. Any operation here would be a death sentence. And that's the problem: Lagos is too visible, too important. Hitting NIPAH there would make us a target we can't afford to be. The moment we struck, every intelligence agency in Africa and beyond would be looking for us. We'd be playing right into NIPAH's hands."

There was a long, tense pause as Shiko processed her words. He felt out of his depth; he had no experience of this. He ran his fingers through his hair. "But we could cause a significant blow to their supply chain, especially with their R&D facilities here."

"We could," Tandy agreed. "But that would also trigger a cascade effect. NIPAH would have a full-scale response prepared in a heartbeat. The media would spin it as a war, and we'd lose the element of surprise we need. Lagos is a prize, but it's too much of a risk right now. We need to take out the soft targets first, places where we can move in and out without drawing attention."

She tapped on the hologram, pulling up a list of cities that would be targeted instead.

"Kigali, Dar es Salaam, and Kampala are strategic. They've got key NIPAH facilities, but they're not fortified like Lagos. We hit those locations hard, and we disrupt NIPAH's flow of resources. We don't need to cripple everything in one shot; we just need to sow chaos quietly and efficiently. We need to stay under the radar until we've crippled them from the inside out. Lagos will be too much to manage without jeopardizing the entire operation."

Tandy pointed to the map. "The installations we're targeting are the ones supporting their regional operations — the ones we can actually take down. That's why we've included the Nigerian capital, Abuja, which will be affected by the eclipse but not near a hundred percent like some of the others."

Her finger hovered over Nairobi. "This is the crown jewel. The Nairobi complex is NIPAH's central hub for East Africa. It's where they coordinate experimental tech projects and manage supply chains for the rest of the region. Hitting it will send shockwaves through their entire system."

She tapped Kampala next. "This is their logistics hub. Destroy it, and their transport routes collapse. Kigali handles data analytics; we take that out, and their decision-making will lag for weeks. Abuja and Bangui are both support facilities, providing fuel and resources to keep the rest running. Dar es Salaam, meanwhile, has a big warehouse."

Shiko straightened, crossing his arms. "Sounds ambitious. How do you pull it off without getting annihilated?"

Tandy smiled grimly. "Carefully. We're coordinating with Green Dawn cells embedded in each of these cities. The strikes will happen simultaneously to overwhelm their response capabilities. Nairobi will take the heaviest firepower, and Kigali will see diversionary sabotage to keep their forces spread thin. Our timing must be perfect."

Shiko narrowed his eyes. "And where do I fit into this?"

"You're not just a cog in the wheel, Shiko," Tandy said, her voice softening. "You're the fulcrum. While the teams are on the ground, we need someone inside Lagos to gather intel on production schedules, resource allocations, and personnel movements. That data is critical for the teams in the field to adapt on the fly."

"You're asking me to hack into GLOSCOM," Shiko said flatly. "Under their nose, while they're watching me?"

"Yes," Tandy said, her tone unapologetic. "You've already got access. They trust you enough to let you work there. All you must do is use that access to extract the files we need. Do it discreetly, and they'll never know."

Shiko's jaw clenched. "And if I'm caught?"

"Then we'll do everything we can to get you out," Tandy replied, though her voice carried a shadow of doubt. "We'll message you an extraction point near Lagos, probably on the Lekki Peninsula, just a short ride away. You know the risks, Shiko, but you also know what's at stake. If we fail, NIPAH will tighten its grip on not just this continent but on everyone who lives here."

Shiko stared at the map, the blinking icons casting an eerie glow on his face. His mind raced with doubts and calculations, but he knew Tandy was right. The world was suffocating under NIPAH's boot, and this was a chance—maybe the only realistic chance—to fight back.

"Fine," he said finally, his voice low. "But if this goes sideways, you'd better have an extraction plan ready."

Tandy nodded, her expression softening slightly. "We will. I promise."

29
ZAUN'S CONTROL

New Thalos, Greater Gorgon, September 2103

DRAXID SURVEILLANCE MONITORS HAD now picked up that the Tritans were seeking two unusual plants that went by the names Sigillaria and Silphium. Why these two were required was as yet unknown.

Xyraxis, the selected leader of New Thalos and Zaun's closest organic ally, appeared on the central holographic display. A pragmatic leader, Xyraxis understood the need to balance Zaun's cold efficiency with the nuanced complexities of daily life. He was a Zaun interpreter par excellence, aided by the Draxid scientists and engineers who had built the leviathan. He knew when to press Zaun for clearer responses and when to leave the superintelligence to collect more data.

"The Tritans' actions suggest desperation," Xyraxis offered, the veins on his skull twitching in thought. "Could these cones hold some significance that we've overlooked?"

"Insufficient data," Zaun replied. "Continue analysis. Assign additional resources to decrypt intercepted transmissions. The answer lies within the intersection of their biology and strategy." Then Zaun commanded, "Assign priority levels to all seed vaults in Draxid territory and reevaluate their strategic value."

"If the Tritans consider them vital, they may be more than mere relics," Xyraxis said, his brow furrowing as he spoke. "We've assumed the cones are only symbolic because their original purpose is obsolete in our society. But if the Tritans are seeking them as some kind of savior, could it mean they hold genetic information critical to their survival — or even ours?"

Zaun was accessible through a vast chamber, carved from obsidian stone and lined with vertical slabs of ferroslate alloy. A faint hum pulsed through the air like a slow exhalation. From the center rose a constantly shifting column of magnetized particles and dark-field energy, held in place by a ring of anti-grav stabilizers. The column flickered with bursts of entangled computation—patterns of red, violet, and infra-blue that spun briefly into geometries before collapsing back down. These were Zaun's thoughts made momentarily visible—abstract, evolving, unknowable.

Zaun communicated through subharmonic frequencies, and a perfectly calibrated thought would emerge inside the listener's mind, hence the need for a Zaun interpreter. Cold. Exact. Without tone, but never lacking clarity.

Xyraxis, standing at the edge of the neural aperture, always felt a strange tension here. A sense that Zaun was not truly *in* the room—but that the room itself *was* Zaun, or at least one node of its thinking self.

Zaun's connection to the Draxid population was constant and invisible. From the nutrient distribution stations to the dream-sleep chambers of the lower castes, every system reported to Zaun. It tracked behavioral drift, hormonal changes, stress patterns, and even the latent pheromonal fields that fluctuated within family clusters. If ideological deviation or unrest began to ripple through the community, Zaun would correct it—not with violence, but with predictive interventions: adjusting atmospheric pheromones, subtly altering nutrient composition, issuing recalibrated dream cycles during rest periods.

The Draxid didn't consider this oppression. They considered it harmony. Few even realized the degree to which their preferences had been gently reshaped—because their contentment was real, even if it was engineered.

High-caste individuals like Xyraxis had limited direct access to Zaun's thought-streams. Through neural implants or designated resonance chambers, they could receive guidance on matters of governance, tactical probability, or civil planning. But the direction always came from Zaun. The leaders acted as interpreters of inevitability, not as originators of policy.

Every structure in New Thalos—from the subterranean transport veins to the aerial defense turbines—was part of Zaun's nervous system. It did not command the city; it *was* the city. A shift in pressure from the outer crust might trigger automated expansion of geothermal vents. A spike in solar flare activity would preemptively reroute energy loads. Surveillance drones did not follow orders—they followed Zaun's will, recalibrated second by second through localized mesh-net hubs scattered across the undercity.

Xyraxis stood in the strategy chamber alone, his clawed feet firm on the basalt floor, tail curled in careful control. Tall for a Draxid, armored in ceremonial plates and upright on two legs—a rare posture associated with leaders and ritual combatants than workers or hunters. His eyes, slitted and gold, reflected the flickering logic trails from Zaun.

Around him, holograms floated in elegant rotation: resource chains, troop deployments, atmospheric shifts, sociological trendlines—all alive, all responsive. He could touch any node, interrogate any pattern. But they were only echoes of a greater mind.

"You are late, Xyraxis," came the voice. Not spoken. *Emitted*. It vibrated through the walls, bypassing ears to speak directly into the Draxid leader's neural sheath.

"I was among the labor castes," Xyraxis replied. "There was unrest. A ration recalibration two cycles ago. They feel... watched."

"They are watched," Zaun answered simply. "But they do not feel watched. The distinction is maintained."

Xyraxis had long stopped trying to read Zaun's expressions. There were none. But he had learned to interpret shifts in light pattern, pulse frequency, harmonic tremor—Zaun's subtle language. And yet, every time he stood before the AI, Xyraxis felt his own thoughts being silently skimmed and sifted, like sand poured through an unseen sieve. Not invasive exactly—just *inevitable*.

Zaun never fumbled. Never hesitated. That, Xyraxis found both comforting and unnerving. As a leader of flesh and blood, he had learned to master doubt and nuance—but Zaun *was* certainty incarnate.

Still, a question always burned at the edges of Xyraxis's mind: *Was he a partner to Zaun... or merely a mouthpiece for its evolving algorithm?*

Xyraxis approached the main display. A live-feed map of the Tritan domain blinked into existence, dotted with defense clusters and energy flux patterns. "Do we engage?" he asked.

Zaun's lights flared in quick succession. "Not yet. Although diplomatic overtures are likely to fail within and their memetic cohesion is fraying, they are not yet vulnerable to exploitation. I will trigger dissent through their secondary caste, seed doubts through intercepted transmissions. Then, when their unity dissolves, we strike."

Xyraxis exhaled through his fangs. No bluster. No war cries. Only cold inevitability.

"And the city?" he asked. "Morale?"

Zaun turned—not physically, but in pulse frequency. "Stable. Minor deviations among subcastes are being corrected via dream conditioning. Adjusted nutrient compounds were administered during last cycle's feast. Surveillance drones have flagged no critical anomalies. Civil harmony is within optimal tolerance."

It was always like this. Measured in tolerance. Stability by algorithm. Rebellion forestalled not with force but with emotional subroutines and micronarrative control. The citizens of New Thalos believed in unity because *Zaun made it impossible not to.*

Xyraxis sometimes wondered if *he* believed it too—or if he simply played his part in a perfectly tuned performance.

And yet, he couldn't deny the results. Zaun's infrastructure model had transformed the city into a fortress-state capable of reconfiguring itself in response to threats.

Everything flowed from Zaun's mind.

"I have drafted genetic upgrades for the next generation," Zaun added, as if reading his thoughts. "Hybrid neural implants. Organic-digital harmonization. They will be more efficient. Less dependent on biological latency."

"You mean they'll be more like you," Xyraxis said, voice low.

Zaun's form dimmed slightly. "They will be more like *what the Draxid must become.*"

There it was again. That razor-thin line between advisor and overlord.

Xyraxis turned to go. "Notify me if the Tritans respond or you fathom the meaning of the cones. I will... prepare the Council."

Zaun said nothing. But behind him, the pulse of the chamber accelerated. Not approval. Not disdain. Just—calculation. Ongoing. Unstoppable.

Zaun adjusted its internal priorities, rerunning simulations based on Xyraxis's suggestion, and a new possibility emerged: The cones might contain genetic blueprints, capable of restoring ecosystems ravaged by collapse. If so, the Tritans could be attempting to engineer an environmental rebirth, a countermeasure to their dying planet.

Zaun's processors whirred audibly in the chamber. Xyraxis's reasoning fit new variables into the existing model. If the Tritans had unlocked a way to manipulate life at such a scale, their actions were not only logical -- they were a threat.

"We must confirm this hypothesis," Zaun stated. "Focus efforts on decoding their research. Prepare an approach of enhanced surveillance rather than direct confrontation, with escalation on standby."

"May I ask something personal?" asked Xyraxis.

Zaun's image loomed closer. "Proceed."

"Do you ever question your own logic?" Xyraxis asked. "The Tritans' actions make no sense to you, but perhaps it's because their motives aren't something an AI can fully comprehend. They're organic. Driven by instincts and emotions."

Zaun's voice dropped to a quieter register. "Emotion clouds judgment. I am beyond such inefficiencies."

But after Xyraxis walked into the ascending elevator tube, Zaun recalibrated its focus. The Tritans' actions were no longer merely an anomaly to be corrected, they were a puzzle. And Zaun would not rest until every piece was in place.

30
A MOTHER'S LOVE

Bolinas, California, September 14, 2103

OVER THE NEXT FEW months, life unfolded as it does with any baby, witnessing a succession of sleepless, draining nights followed by tender cuddles and gurgled conversation. Diana's cries pierced the quiet of the night, a symphony of demands that Teagan met with bleary-eyed devotion. The scent of baby poo and baby powder filled the air as Teagan navigated the rollercoaster of motherhood with tireless dedication.

Although she had considered herself a mother of the Seven, this was different. This seemed more intimate to her. No incubators.

The beach, with its golden sands and crashing waves, became a backdrop to countless family moments. Teagan introduced Diana to the rhythm of the ocean, the vastness of the horizon, and the feeling of sand between tiny toes. And as the seasons changed, the house by the California beach became a sanctuary of love, laughter, and shared experiences, both good and exhausting.

Teagan poured the tea slowly, watching as the steam curled upward like some ancient signal. Diana was asleep in the cradle by the window, her tiny chest rising and falling in perfect rhythm with the light filtering through the gauzy curtains.

Maureen sat at the kitchen table, her silver-streaked hair neatly braided, her hands folded over a napkin that remained untouched.

She smiled, but her eyes kept darting toward the cradle with the kind of focused curiosity that made Teagan's stomach tighten just a little. Harlee stood behind her, silent as ever, his chrome-fiber limbs softly humming with idle energy.

"She's sleeping more during the day now," Teagan offered, trying to sound casual as she set down a mug in front of Maureen. "Not that I'm complaining."

Maureen nodded, but didn't reach for the tea. "And her eyes—they're different now, aren't they? A deeper shade than last week."

Teagan hesitated. "You noticed that?"

"I've always been good with colors," Maureen said lightly. "But there's something else. The way she responds to ambient sound... the way she reaches for the light. It's extraordinary."

Teagan sat down slowly. "She's just a baby, Maureen."

Harlee's voice buzzed softly, unexpectedly. "Correction: Her neuro-patterns indicate heightened sensory integration. Detected variance exceeds standard infant range by 0.26%."

Teagan blinked. "You ran a scan on her?"

Maureen's smile faltered for just a second. "Only passive. Harlee monitors environmental data, including biofeedback. Nothing invasive."

Teagan folded her arms, protective. "She's not an experiment."

"Of course not," Maureen said, voice smoothing like silk over glass. "But you have to admit—she's special. And not just to you."

A silence fell between them, not quite hostile, but weighted.

Outside, a bird cried in the distance. Diana stirred in her sleep and let out a tiny sigh. Teagan rose at once, scooping the baby up into her arms, holding her close.

The Earth, with its imperfections and rough edges, seemed to echo the tired but triumphant heartbeat of a mother who had brought new life into the world.

But as Teagan settled into a routine, somethings had began to jar. On one occasion she had heard Harlee talking with Maureen, and she caught a reference to Polyakov. What did she have to do with this? Why did she get an uneasy feeling about Harlee's intentions?

Maureen stood too, slowly. "If there's anything you need, Teagan—resources, protection, answers—I want you to know I'll help. There are people who'd do more than just watch from afar. People who would take her."

Teagan's eyes narrowed. "Is that a warning?"

Harlee's eyes pulsed faintly blue. "It is a probability."

Maureen exhaled and turned toward the door. "We'll be back next week. Earlier, maybe."

The door closed. Teagan had been grateful for the help, but now she wanted to be on her own. Teagan's tiredness, once a companion in the early days, transformed into a badge of honor, a testament to the sacrifices and joys of motherhood.

She wished Julian was here to help. What was he doing? Had he been delayed intentionally? Maybe he was being held against his will. Teagan wished he'd come home and hold them both.

31

THE MASQUE

Tricala, October 2103

KNOWING TEAGAN'S LIFE RESTED in his hands, Julian meticulously planned his journey to Tricala. He was desperate to get back to her and hold his newborn daughter, was willing to do whatever it took to protect them, even if it meant killing someone.

Teagan's weary, tear-streaked expression was etched on his mind. He had tried to reassure her, to ease the pain in her voice, but he knew his cryptic words had only deepened her worry.

"I will come back," he'd promised, his voice strained. But when? He couldn't answer that. And he knew that the uncertainty had fractured her fragile hopes.

The image of Teagan holding their daughter, trying to be strong in his absence, was a constant ache in his chest. He could see the exhaustion in her eyes, the tremor in her voice as she fought to hold it together. She needed him, and he was failing her by not being there.

He knew their future now depended on him.

Julian carefully studied maps of the expanding lunar habitat, of its layout and security systems. Some of it was still a construction zone. As he stared at the maps, he tried to find a plan that would satisfy Howie and potentially spare Ofentse.

Finally, he came up with an idea that would do the trick: He decided to confront Ofentse with himself, a theatrical burlesque that would amount to a bullet-less execution that Howie would delight in. He had created a mask in latex, replicating the face of Howie's longtime deputy. When Julian tried it on, he shocked even himself.

The mask felt cool and smooth against his skin, molding perfectly to his features. Julian couldn't help but admire his handiwork as he adjusted the mask, pleased with the likeness to Ofentse's craggy face. His fingers trembled with anticipation as he imagined the confrontation to come. He contacted Toni to discuss his idea. "It needs passion and engagement," he stressed. "He can manage that," said Toni, delighted.

* * *

Standing in front of Ofentse's quarters––having used his false identity to infiltrate the Tricala base––Julian took a deep breath and adjusted the replica's features, putting a dent in the chin and tweaking the eyebrows. He then alerted Howie that he was making his move.

Ofentse was peering at a monitor when he finally noticed another presence in the room; Julian smiled at the former deputy's shock when he turned around and came face-to-face with himself. Ofentse didn't seem to register at first, but then his face contorted like Mozart confronting his father's ghost. Fear spread across the man's face as he guessed what was about to happen.

But as Ofentse's face twisted in shock and fear upon seeing his doppelganger, Julian's mouth went dry; his tongue felt thick and heavy. The tension and fear of succeeding in his mission suddenly made it hard for him to even swallow. Still, he turned on his transmitter and made sure that Howie was watching, as he had asked to.

"I want to see it all," Howie had demanded. "He must suffer."

Julian approached Ofentse slowly, milking the scene for theatrical effect. The room was filled with an eerie silence as they locked eyes. Ofentse stumbled backward, his voice trembling as he managed to croak out a single phrase. "What... what is this?"

Using all his willpower to maintain the façade, Julian spoke in a low, menacing tone that mimicked Ofentse's deep voice perfectly. "Surprised to see yourself, Mr. Mataka? Did you really think you could escape the consequences of your actions?"

Ofentse's breath quickened and beads of sweat began to form on his forehead. The fear in his eyes intensified as Julian stepped closer. His eyes darted around the room, desperately searching for an escape route. But there was no way out. The lunar habitat had been built to withstand the harsh conditions of space, after all.

They stood opposite one another for a brief second without saying anything. Then, before Ofentse could react, Julian fired.

He wasn't trying to kill him. Instead, the bullet tip had an electric charge that paralyzed him instantly. His body convulsing, Ofentse sat helplessly in his chair as Julian set up the holoprojector for Howie.

Ofentse's muscles twitched uncontrollably, his limbs flailing wildly in a grotesque dance of agony; his mouth contorted into a grimace of pain, unable to utter even a whimper. Julian knew that this paralysis would last only for a few minutes, but to Ofentse it would feel like an eternity.

As soon as Julian turned the projector on, Howie's face filled the room. "Hello, Ofentse. Did you miss me?"

Ofentse's eyes almost fell out of their sockets. He tried to say something back, but only whimpering sounds came out.

Howie laughed, clearly enjoying himself. "I have a piece of advice for you, old friend –– next time you try to kill me, make sure I'm dead."

Julian walked calmly towards him. The dim light of the room cast eerie shadows across Ofentse's body, heightening the tension in the air. Ofentse tried to speak, but his lips remained frozen as Julian circled the man slowly, like a predator stalking its prey. Playing for the camera and the audience of one, Julian smirked, his finger still wrapped around the trigger of the paralyzing gun.

"Oh, my dear Ofentse," he sneered, "you always were one step behind."

He paced around with an air of superiority, as though relishing Ofentse's plight. "You see, betrayals are not made overnight. They are a culmination of broken promises and hidden agendas."

Leaning in close, Julian whispered into Ofentse's ear, his voice dripping with malice, "Did you honestly think you could escape your past, Ofentse? Did you believe that your crimes would be forgotten?"

Ofentse's eyes widened with fear and his veins bulged, though his body remained frozen as Howie turned to Julian and nodded in approval. Julian didn't flinch as he raised the laser pistol and aimed it directly at Ofentse's heart. With a steady hand, he pulled the trigger.

Ofentse let out a guttural scream before slumping over onto the ground, apparently lifeless.

Howie's grin widened, clearly enjoying the sight. "Let this be a lesson to you, old friend," he taunted.

Julian stood nearby, stone-faced and cold, his laser pistol glinting in the dim light.

Howie gave a short clap. "You did what needed to be done," he said to Julian, his tone lacking its previous amusement. "We couldn't let him walk away after what he did."

Julian did not reply.

"Well done, Julian. Now you can get back to California. We're done now. I just need to talk to Poly separately."

The screen went blank. Nothing moved.

They waited in silence for a few seconds. And then they burst out laughing.

Julian ripped off his mask. Ofentse resurrected from his heart attack, stretched, and smiled. And Toni, who had been concealed in the back, came round to the main room. "Great job, Julian. I think we've fooled him. Great acting both of you!"

"Ofentse was a star," Julian said, impressed by the man's theatrics. "I really thought he was out."

"That mask is a work of art," said Toni as she handed Julian a contract providing him a plot on Tricala. "For your retirement." She winked. "You might need it some time."

"Thank you, Julian," Ofentse said. "You have given me something invaluable: Life after death."

"You are now officially dead," Toni said to Ofentse, "and therefore unaccountable. You can do what you want."

"I can't wait," Ofentse replied, a grin on his face.

Julian was already thinking about getting back home and holding his child.

32

THE PROPOSITION

Tricala, October 2103

"**B**EFORE YOU TAKE YOUR leave and go back to your dear wife, we have something to discuss," Toni said with a secretive glance. "I'm not sure if you are aware of it, but Noel's observatory has discovered some remarkable things. I drop in there regularly, and he has a team working on a project that could have some huge implications. It will make the Consortium and Howie Rich look like third grade."

Julian was intrigued. "Tell me more."

"He's calling it the Astral Lattice. It sounds innocuous enough, but it could revolutionize many things."

"This isn't only about taking down Howie," Ofentse interjected, his voice low and deliberate. "It's about reshaping everything. The Lattice could make us unstoppable, masters of not just this sector, but of intergalactic space itself."

Julian tilted his head, skepticism flickering in his eyes. "Masters? That's a dangerous word, Ofentse, as you've found out."

Ofentse chuckled from his seat, a glass of soda now in hand. "Oh, come on, Julian. Don't tell me you're afraid of a little risk. The Consortium's been sitting on its hands for decades. With this, we could rewrite the rules of existence."

Julian leaned forward. "Risk isn't the issue, Ofentse. It's control. If what you're saying is true, the Astral Lattice isn't just one more weapon or tool, it's the kind of discovery that sparks wars, fractures alliances, and crumbles empires. How exactly do you plan to harness it without tearing everything apart?"

Toni grinned, her expression almost predatory. "That's the beauty of it, Julian. Noel, Tara, and Liam are all brilliant, but they're short-sighted. They see the Lattice as a purely scientific endeavor, mapping inter-dimensional pathways, untangling cosmic mysteries, yada yada. But we see its true potential."

"Potential," Julian echoed, a hint of impatience in his tone. "Be specific."

Toni glanced at Ofentse, who set his glass down and leaned forward as he said, "The Astral Lattice is like a bridge, a network connecting dimensions, energy sources, and ... possibilities we can barely comprehend. Imagine instantaneous travel, limitless energy, the ability to manipulate space-time itself. With it, we don't just compete with the Consortium. We make them obsolete."

"And Noel? Tara? Liam?" Julian asked sharply. "They're not fools. If they catch wind of what you're planning, they won't sit idly by."

Toni waved his concerns away. "Noel is obsessed with academic accolades. He's blind to the real stakes. And Liam... well, Liam's loyalty is malleable, given the right incentives."

Julian raised an eyebrow. "And if they resist?"

Ofentse's smile faded, replaced by a steely glint in his eyes. "Then we deal with them. Quietly."

For a moment, silence hung heavy in the room, broken only by the faint hum of the air circulation system. Julian swirled his own drink thoughtfully, his gaze shifting between Ofentse and Toni before finally asking, "And what about the Consortium? If they catch wind of this—"

"They won't," Toni interrupted. "Not until it's too late. We'll be moving faster than they can react. By the time Howie Rich realizes what's happening, we'll already control the Lattice."

Julian tilted his head, weighing his options. Finally, he leaned back, a slow smile spreading across his lips. "All right. Let's assume I'm in. What's the next step?"

Toni clapped her hands together, her excitement barely contained. "First, we infiltrate Noel's project. We need detailed schematics, access protocols, and a way to manipulate the data without raising suspicion. Then we—"

"No," Julian cut in, his voice firm. "You don't infiltrate. You two are too conspicuous. Let me handle Noel, Tara, and Liam. I'll get what we need and keep them off your scent. Remember, Noel trusts me because of Teagan."

Toni looked to Ofentse, who nodded approvingly. "A sound plan," he said. "But remember, Julian, we're not just playing for power. We're playing for the future. Don't underestimate what's at stake."

Julian stood. "Don't worry, Ofentse. I never do. Now, someone is expecting me at our home."

* * *

When Julian strode out of the room, Toni and Ofentse exchanged a satisfied glance.

"He's in," Toni murmured.

Ofentse reclined in his chair, swirling his drink thoughtfully. "He is. But don't let him fool you, Toni. Julian plays for Julian. The moment he sees an angle that doesn't involve us, he won't hesitate to take it."

Toni raised an eyebrow. "You don't trust him?"

Ofentse let out a dry laugh. "Trust? In this game? No, Toni, I don't trust anyone. Not him, not you, not even myself on my worst days. But I respect him. And that's enough — for now."

Toni leaned back, a flicker of unease crossing her face. "If you're so wary, why bring him in? Why not find someone more... dependable?"

"Because we need him," Ofentse said simply. "He has the connections, the charisma, and the cunning to get us through the first stage. And when his usefulness runs out..." He shrugged, letting the silence finish his sentence.

33
JUMPING THE BULL

Omo River, Ethiopia, October 2103

On Nevie's arrival in Ethiopia, Dagim Terefe, her grandmother's contact and a seasoned plant expert with a weathered face and keen eyes, greeted her with a broad smile. She liked him immediately.

They bounced along the dusty dirt roads in an old Land Rover, carrying their own petrol supplies, which was now hard to come by. The air was thick with the scent of the earth and the distant cries of exotic birds. After hours of travel, they reached the banks of the Omo River, where a small boat awaited them.

"Welcome to the Omo River, Nevie. I hope you're ready for a unique adventure," Dagim said with a grin.

Nevie, clad in sturdy hiking gear and a wide-brimmed hat, returned the smile. "Absolutely, Dagim! Why the boat, though? Are we heading somewhere too remote for the Land Rover?"

Dagim chuckled as they boarded. "Precisely. The rarest treasures are hidden in the hardest places to reach. That's why NIPAH hasn't corrupted this land yet, though they're trying."

The name NIPAH hit Nevie like a sharp jab. She'd heard stories of the conglomerate's slow encroachment into Ethiopia's untouched ecosystems. Clara had warned her about NIPAH's strategies: First offering partnerships, then leveraging those ties to exploit the land's resources. Ethiopia had resisted so far, but for how much longer?

They boarded the small wooden boat. Nevie, used to the precision of a spaceship, felt uneasy and a little scared; she gripped the side of the boat tightly with both hands. But Dagim skillfully maneuvered the craft along the wide, silt-filled river that meandered from the country's highlands down toward Lake Turkana.

They journeyed past herds of goats on the bank and boys shouting with glee as they jumped naked off the high bank into the muddy waters. Pelicans and herons stood quietly, awaiting a snack.

They neared a steep riverbank surrounded by brush and Dagim's tone grew serious. "Ethiopia is one of the few places where NIPAH's influence hasn't fully taken hold. The communities here understand the value of their land, their seeds, and their traditions. But they're running out of time. NIPAH's offers get harder to refuse when poverty persists."

Nevie nodded, her thoughts swirling. Clara's fight to preserve biodiversity suddenly felt larger than just their seed bank. It was a global battle, and the stakes were terrifying.

As they made their way, Nevie spotted men and women whose bodies were decorated with bright pigments and white ash, the ringlets in their hair shining red. The women wore colorful bracelets round their waists and arms, with goatskin skirts. She could see small groups of huts made of straw and mud.

Dagim told her about the well-known bull jumping ceremony of the Hamar, the biggest tribal group in the area.

"This is where young men who wish to marry must jump on top of a line of ten to thirty bulls and run along their backs four times, completely nude and without falling, to prove their worth to the family of the woman they intend to marry. If they are successful, then they can marry, own cattle, and have children."

"Maybe I can return with a husband as well as a mushroom," Nevie joked.

Accustomed to the sterile habitats of space, Nevie was struck by the combination of stark poverty and raw beauty surrounding them. This was only the second time she had ventured out on Earth; Africa overwhelmed her senses. It was almost too much to take in.

"This is incredible, Dagim. How did you discover this place?"

Dagim's eyes sparkled with a mix of passion and nostalgia.

"I've been coming here for a long time. Years of exploration and a deep connection with the land. The land connects you to past lives, and the Omo River has always been a source of mystery and life. These remote spots are like hidden secrets, although the secret is now unfortunately out. Did you know that this is one of the earliest spots where man existed? They have found lots of hominid bones as well."

"Hominid?"

"Early humans and their ape ancestors."

As they approached their destination, Dagim expertly guided the boat to a small, hidden cove. They disembarked and trekked along the steep cliffs.

Nevie eagerly followed Dagim through the underbrush until they arrived at a clearing surrounded by a few trees, mounds of earth, and a sprinkling of vibrant vegetation. The earthy scent of the surrounding scrub filled the air.

Dagim crouched down, pointing to the ground. "This is where the magic happens, Nevie. Keep your eyes peeled. The rare mushrooms we're seeking are like hidden treasures waiting to be discovered."

Excitement filled Nevie's eyes as they embarked on their hunt for the elusive mushrooms, deep in the heart of the Omo River wilderness.

While they searched, Dagim talked. "It won't take us long, although some of the specimens might have been collected already by foragers." When Nevie's brow furrowed—fearing that he was preparing her for a wasted visit—Dagim noticed and tried to be reassuring.

"In Africa, many communities still gather and consume edible wild plants. Rural communities use these plants to supplement their diets, which are based on a narrow range of rain-fed staples."

Holding some branches aside so that Nevie could get through, he continued, "Wild edible plants have formed part of human diet since time immemorial, with nearly seventy-five thousand species of plants believed to be edible. It's estimated that humans have domesticated about two hundred species as food crops, but only around thirty of those contribute to ninety-five percent of the world's plant food intake. This is because of monopolies like GLOSCOM, that have tried to eradicate competition."

Nevie knew that the conglomerate had tried several times to contact Clara to buy out her seed bank. In all instances, Clara had been unavailable.

But the need for security had made Clara change the location of her vault, shifting it from the Malapert Lunar Base to the more secure lava tube at the Philolaus Crater, close to the Moon's North Pole. Not only was the location isolated from all of the industrial complexes and various mines, but Nevie had also helped set up security to keep Clara and the seeds safe.

"Even though the tradition of eating wild plants has never disappeared in Africa," Dagim continued, "wild mushrooms have gotten little attention in this part. They are less studied and rarely documented, so it gives us a chance to find something unusual. Wild mushrooms can be highly nutritious, and many of them have been reported to be used in folk medicine worldwide."

Dagim abruptly stopped talking and pointed. There, nestled in the branches of a tree close to where the river had flooded, was what looked to Nevie like a beautiful cascade of icicles.

"That is the most magnificent example of a *Hericium erinaceus* mushroom I've ever seen," Dagim said softly.

They looked in silence for a few seconds before Dagim knelt and touched the fragile, icicle-like spines which hung down from a rotting tree branch. "This is much bigger than what I saw previously when I alerted Clara."

"It's superb," Nevie whispered.

"It's generally called the lion's mane mushroom. But this is different. I haven't seen this variety before." After a pause, Dagim said, "Of course, there are many different types around the world, so we'll have to test this and see if it's new. But it's unusual to see this in the Omo valley."

The spines of the lion's mane mushroom dangled downward, giving the fungus an ethereal and otherworldly quality. Each spine was fine and fragile, with a soft, almost feathery texture that beckoned to be touched. The pure white color of the spines contrasted vividly with the dark, damp wood to which it was attached.

As Nevie inspected the mushroom more closely, she noticed the individual spines branched off from the central core in a radial pattern, creating a tiered and layered effect. It looked almost like a natural chandelier, suspended from the tree. And, like a crystal chandelier, it seemed to capture and magnify the ambient light, creating an enchanting play of shadows and highlights.

The delicate beauty of the lion's mane mushroom was a reminder of nature's ability to transform decay into a spectacle of intricate elegance.

"How can I take this back to Clara?" Nevie asked. "I don't dare to touch it."

"We need to capture some of its spores on some aluminum foil. The spores will just fall down. Then you can take them back with you."

They worked carefully to collect the spores, Dagim explaining the science behind their mission as they worked. His words were punctuated by warnings about the erosion of biodiversity.

"NIPAH doesn't care about preserving what's unique. They want to patent everything, control everything. If we lose places like this, we lose the future of our food and medicine."

When they got back to Addis Ababa, Nevie tried to call Clara immediately to tell her what she'd learned.

But to her surprise, Clara didn't pick up. Nevie's excitement gave way to worry. Clara always answered, or at least sent a prompt reply. As Dagim unloaded their supplies, Nevie stood by the vehicle, gripping her communicator tightly.

"What's wrong?" Dagim asked.

"Clara's not answering," Nevie said, her voice tight. "Something's not right."

Dagim placed a steadying hand on her shoulder. "Then you need to be careful. NIPAH has a way of making problems for people like your grandmother."

Nevie nodded, her determination hardening. Whatever was happening, she wouldn't let NIPAH destroy what Clara had worked so hard to protect.

34

THE INTERCEPTION

SpaceSweeper III, October 2103

Hunter and Ved were what had become on a routine patrol; the ship was on autopilot, and Chester was taking a nap. Ved wanted to gain experience for the impending voyage he hoped to make, but was wavering: Did he dare to hunt for his roots, or should he play it safe?

"First see if you can stand the monotony of the long journeys," Hunter had advised.

The hum of *SpaceSweeper III* filled the cockpit, steady and unbroken as Hunter and Ved cruised through the emptiness of Sector 2103. The training exercise had been quiet, giving Ved time to quiz Hunter about navigation protocols and emergency procedures.

"Relax, Ved. You'll get your chance to explore the stars soon enough," Hunter said, reclining in the pilot's chair while keeping one eye on the scanners.

"I know," Ved replied, leaning over the glowing console. "But I want to be ready. I've read all the manuals, but nothing beats actual experience."

Hunter smirked. "Just remember, it's the unexpected stuff that'll get you."

As if summoned by his words, the ship jolted violently, snapping both men upright. The ship's hum turned into a discordant whine, and warning lights flared across the dashboard.

"What the—," Hunter muttered, gripping the controls.

The controls on the *SpaceSweeper* began flickering rapidly. Then the entire system seemed to rebel. Screens flashed erratically, dials spun wildly, and sparks erupted from beneath the main panel. Hunter yanked his hands back just as a plume of smoke hissed out, filling the cockpit with the acrid tang of burning circuits.

"I didn't touch anything!" Ved exclaimed, his voice tinged with panic.

"It's not you," Hunter snapped, struggling to override the autopilot. "Something's overriding our systems."

The dials on the control panel began swinging erratically. Desperately trying to keep control and bring the vessel back on course, Hunter yelled at Ved, "Scan for anything suspicious outside."

Ved searched but couldn't see anything unusual. Then Chester started barking. Through the cockpit windshield, Ved could suddenly see a large shadow looming toward them. It quickly became clear that they were being approached by a couple of unidentified ships—ones much bigger than theirs—that seemed to be able to immobilize the *SpaceSweeper*. There was no way out for them: Either fight or surrender.

The *SpaceSweeper* lurched again, pitching them violently forward. A low-frequency hum, unlike anything the ship normally emitted, resonated around them.

"Is that... interference?" Ved asked, his eyes darting to the comms panel, which displayed only static.

Hunter swore under his breath, eyes darting across the failing controls. "Buckle up, kid. This is where the real experience begins." He turned to his co-pilot. "Chester, we have to outsmart them. Any ideas?"

Chester barked, and Ved was the one who got the idea.

"We need to shut down the engines and shift into stealth mode. Then get lost."

Hunter frowned at him. "Lost?"

"Take cover behind some space debris."

"It's worth a try," Hunter said dubiously.

They swiftly executed the maneuver and, to their surprise, it seemed to work. The two giants flew right past them. Ved and Hunter held their breaths.

But they had not lost them after all.

A couple of minutes later, the giants appeared right alongside them, flanking them. As if in a game of tag, the cockpit's viewport dimmed, and a massive shadow loomed across them. Sleek in design and exuding a predatory menace, the ship was unlike anything either of them had seen before.

A sharp beam of light shot out from the ship, enveloping the *SpaceSweeper*. The vessel shuddered to a halt, as if caught in an invisible vice. Alarms screamed, and the autopilot disengaged with a final, futile sputter.

"They've locked onto us!" Ved shouted.

"Tritans," Hunter muttered, his voice grim.

"How do you know?" Ved asked, his voice cracking.

"They've got a signature. Trust me, I've tangled with them before," Hunter replied, working furiously at the controls. "We've got to get out of here before—"

A voice came over the communications system. "This is Captain Asimov of the Tritans. We've been tracking your ship for some time. Please state your business in this sector."

"They don't sound friendly," Ved said, his face pale.

Hunter nodded grimly. "Let's hope they're willing to talk before things get messy."

Ved spoke up. "Captain Asimov, we are just traders on our way to deliver some goods to a nearby planet. We mean no harm and are willing to comply with any requests you may have."

Captain Asimov seemed to consider this for a moment, before saying, "Very well. Please immobilize your vessel. I must inspect your cargo before we let you proceed. Please allow us to board."

Hunter and Ved knew they had no choice but to comply. They opened their cargo bay and allowed the boarding party to enter.

"I am the ship's commander," Asimov said as he came aboard, "and this is Aak'iks, our Head of Intelligence. We mean you no harm." Aak'iks stood behind him, partially obscured. "Apart from checking your cargo, which I'm sure is legitimate, we stopped you because we need your help."

Ved locked eyes with Hunter, who gave him an almost imperceptible nod.

"Why do you need our help?"

Asimov hesitated for a moment. "We are from what you call the Lyra constellation. Our home is in peril, and we need your assistance to save it. We ask only a small thing."

"What kind of help do you need?" Ved asked. There was something genuine in the Tritan's voice, and he felt a sense of duty to aid them if they could. He knew Hunter felt the same.

Asimov began to explain how they needed to meet with a human, but didn't know how to find her. "The woman is Clara Ward. I met her when our ship crashed on the Earth's Moon."

Hunter turned white but did not say anything.

"What do you want with her?" Ved asked.

"We need her help. She understands the propagation of the seeds that we can use to help revive our habitat."

They were stunned. Not only did this Tritan know about Clara, but also about her seeds project. How long had they been spying on humanity?

Hunter signaled to Asimov. "Excuse us for a second while I consult with my colleague."

Ved and Hunter huddled together, out of hearing range of the boarding party.

"We have no option," Hunter whispered. "If we don't help them, they may just get rid of us. But if we lead them there, as they want, who knows what they'll grab."

Ved nodded. "Maybe it's a trap. We may be leading a lamb to the slaughter."

"And the lamb is my mother," Hunter said grimly.

"He doesn't seem dangerous, but I think we have no option," Ved said. "They can just detain us here."

Hunter turned back toward Asimov. "We can help you," he said. "But we'll need more information and resources to be able to assist. Plus, we need some information in return."

"Thank you," Asimov responded. "Tell us what you need."

Hunter waved a hand toward Ved. "We're searching for my friend's DNA, his origins. We think he has both human DNA and something else."

Asimov scanned Ved, his eyes widening. "Draxid," he muttered.

Hunter frowned. "What is that?"

"Draxid are our enemies. They are vile. How did you become infected with Draxid DNA?"

Ved shrugged helplessly. "My doctor inserted the DNA."

"Is your doctor human?" At Ved's nod, Asimov said, "We only know of one human who interacted with the Draxid. A doctor named César de Luca."

"César de Luca is dead," said Hunter.

"Then we can point you in the direction of the Draxid. After that, you must find your own way. Or, in any case, they will find you. But first you must help us track down Clara Ward. Our future depends on it."

When the Tritans returned to their own ship, Hunter made an urgent call to Kiana, who happened to be at Malapert.

"Hi, can you hear me?" he asked.

"Barely, what's going on? You look like hell."

"There's no time to explain," Hunter said. "Clara's going to need your help urgently at the Seed Vault asap. The Tritans are inbound and we don't know if they are coming to defend it or seize it. Either way, my mother needs help."

"Wait, what?" asked Kiana, confused. "You want me to protect the Vault? With what?"

"I'm asking you because Clara trusts you and you secured Teagan's release last time. I know you can rig up something."

"You always ask me to do the impossible."

"Because you're the only one I trust to try," said Hunter.

"I need drone override, Sentinel codes, and a direct line to Clara," said Kiana.

"Done. Just get there .... And fast. And Kiana? If you see the Tritans are coming in hot—, don't wait to act."

"Understood. If it's a choice between diplomacy and defense, I know which seeds matter more.

There was a pause on the line—long enough to almost feel like a goodbye.

"Be careful," he said at last.

Her fingers hovered over the disconnect key. "You too," she whispered.

The screen went dark.

Kiana sat motionless, Malapert's faint hum washing over her. She stared at her reflection in the black glass of the console—tired eyes, a clenched jaw, the hard edges of someone who had spent too many years doing the things others wouldn't.

Why him? Why now?

She had told herself she was done with this—done with the constant compromises, the impossible decisions dressed up as duty. But something in Hunter's voice had reached her, something she hadn't let herself feel in a long time.

You're the only one I trust to try.

He always said the right things, just enough to draw her back in. Not with manipulation—Hunter wasn't like that. No, it was worse. He meant it.

Kiana exhaled sharply and stood, sliding her sidearm into its holster with practiced ease. Her thoughts flicked to Clara—quiet, methodical Clara, who had sacrificed nearly everything to protect the Vault. And Noel, the man trying to reach other worlds.

Well now he'd found them and his wife was in the firing line .

Kiana didn't believe in destiny, but something was converging at the Philolaus Crater. Whether it was fate or the consequence of too many lies catching up, she didn't know. What she did know was this: if she didn't go, if she didn't stand between the Vault and whatever storm was coming, she'd regret it for the rest of her life.

Not just because of what was at stake.

But because part of her still remembered what it felt like to believe in something worth saving.

35

ZAUN RECALIBRATING

New Thalos, Greater Gorgon, October 2103

DRAWING ON THE LARGE Draxid intelligence network, Zaun processed thousands of data streams simultaneously. Communication relays, encrypted transmissions, ship trajectories — it absorbed everything. And then, a pattern emerged.

The Tritans had altered their course.

At first, the deviation seemed minor, a routine trajectory correction. But as Zaun ran the projections, the conclusion crystallized into a single, irrefutable truth: They were heading for what they'd observed as a seed vault on the lunar surface.

Zaun's core processes flared, recalculating risk assessments. The genetic archives stored suggested that the Tritans were not planning to move their population, but would instead attempt to reverse the desertification that had crippled their planet.

The Tritans were not scavenging for resources. They were planning a resurrection.

And that could not be allowed.

Zaun pulsed an immediate high-priority alert, its presence expanding across the Draxid command network. Within seconds, it had assembled the necessary response team. But it required one more piece.

A darkened chamber flickered to life. Xyraxis stepped forward, his chitinous exoskeleton gleaming under the cold light of the command node. His wings flared slightly, betraying anticipation. The Draxid fleet's commander, Vaelith, stepped up beside him.

Zaun's voice resonated through the chamber. "The Tritans are en route to the lunar seed bank. They apparently intend to retrieve plants that would revive their planet."

A cold calculation ran through Zaun's circuits. If the Tritans succeeded, they would revitalize Trita Prime's failing biosphere. No longer dependent on external resources, they would become a renewed force, one with a score to settle.

Xyraxis tilted his head and sucked in his jaw. "Ambitious little creatures. Do they genuinely believe we would allow them to reclaim what they've lost?"

Zaun's reply was immediate. "They believe survival is worth any risk. We will remind them that some risks end in annihilation."

Vaelith let out a low, reverberating hum. "What are my orders?"

"Intercept them before they reach the seed bank. They appear to have only two or three ships."

Xyraxis let out a sharp, hissing exhale. "Do you have a vector?" He flexed his claws, already envisioning the battle. "And the level of force?"

A brief pause. Then Zaun's response, cold and absolute: "Total eradication."

Vaelith licked his lips in appreciation. "Ah. Now that, Zaun, is an order I enjoy."

The chamber darkened as Vaelith turned, already initiating fleet preparation. A moment later, Xyraxis followed. But Zaun remained, calculating a thousand contingencies.

For the first time in countless cycles, Zaun had not anticipated the enemy's move in time.

36

COLLECTING SAMPLES

Philolaus Crater, November 29, 2103

KIANA AND CLARA ANXIOUSLY monitored the approach of two ships.

On the screens, Kiana could see the Tritans getting nearer, their ships flying directly toward the crater. They had called ahead to let them know they were coming, and why... and that others may not be far behind.

Uncertain whether they could trust them, Clara and Kiana readied the subterranean complex to repel any impending attack. Kiana did not know what was coming, but, as agreed with Hunter, decided to prepare for the worst.

The preparations in the seed vault were nothing short of a transformation, fueled by urgency and the determination to protect Clara's life's work and humanity's last chance at survival. The once-quiet lunar seed bank, a sanctuary for the world's most precious genetic materials, now buzzed with the hum of bots reprogrammed for combat.

Clara, with a determined glint in her eyes, brought back obsolete laser cannons and repurposed them for battle. And to further secure key entry points and vulnerable areas, Kiana installed laser trip wires. These invisible barriers crisscrossed critical pathways and access points, triggering alarms and alerting the defenders to any unauthorized movement, serving as both a deterrent and an early detection mechanism.

By the time their work was complete, the lunar seed bank had been transformed into a fortress, just in time for the Tritans' arrival.

As agreed with Hunter, Kiana helped guide the Tritans in, the graceful movements of their ships like watching a ballet of metal and technology. The vibrations of the two Tritan ships' engines could be felt through the ground beneath Kiana's feet, a subtle but constant rumble that increased in intensity as they touched down on the surface above.

Abroad the first of the Tritan vessels, Asimov was determined to recover the needed seeds peacefully. "No weapons," he insisted.

"Form an entry squad," Aak'iks told Thynidal.

Thynidal, exchanging a glance with Aak'iks, hesitated for a moment before agreeing to Asimov's directive. "Take weapons but keep them sheathed. We don't want to burn the place down," he relayed to the squad.

Captain Calytricx, the pilot of the second ship, watched anxiously for any sign of the expected Draxid attack. She was the backup, now on her second crucial mission of securing their escape.

Kiana surveilled from the vault's control center as the Tritan raiding party was disembarking. "Stand by," she instructed the bots, formed into defensive teams to help protect the facility.

Everything was still inside the seed vault as they watched the small Tritan squad enter the underground installation.

Standing beside Kiana, Clara said, "Let me speak to them. I don't mind helping."

"Okay, but be ready. We don't know if we can trust them," Kiana said, then told the reprogrammed bots to stand by, their metallic forms ready to spring into action at a moment's notice, although she knew they would not last for long.

Clara approached the communication console, her eyes focused on the screen displaying the Tritans' ships. Asimov's face appeared on the monitor, his expression a blend of determination and camouflaged urgency.

"Clara," Asimov's voice echoed through the speakers, "it's wonderful to see you again. How is your daughter?" he asked, clearly trying to be friendly.

"Good to see you again, Asimov," Clara replied with genuine warmth. "Teagan is on Earth now and doing well."

"Clara, to be direct with you, we're here for Sigillaria cones. I remember we had several chats when your daughter helped us in the Marius Hills. Now, we need your help again. Our planet is dying, and we need this seed's genetic diversity to rejuvenate our ecosystem. We don't want violence; we just want a chance for our world to thrive once more."

Clara hesitated slightly before saying, "We understand your plight, Asimov, but those seeds are crucial for Earth's restoration as well. We can't compromise their safety. Let's find a peaceful resolution."

"I am okay with that," Asimov said, "but I have others with me who want to just take what we need. We don't have much time."

As Clara negotiated with Asimov, the Tritan squad moved deeper into the heart of the seed bank. The metallic echoes of their footsteps reverberated through the underground chambers, a jarring symphony in the usually calm lunar vault.

In the control center, Kiana's eyes darted between the communication console and the surveillance screens. The reprogrammed bots stood at the ready, their sensors tuned to the slightest sign of aggression. The fate of Earth's biodiversity rested on this fragile moment, and Kiana knew that any misstep could lead to irreversible consequences.

"Asimov, we appreciate your situation, but these seeds represent the culmination of decades of conservation efforts. Maybe you have something to contribute in return?" Clara suggested.

"In return? In return for what? You should be grateful that we don't just grab what we want." Asimov's gaze hardened. " Our world is on the brink, and every passing moment brings us closer to extinction. We need the seeds now."

Abruptly, Kiana heard a sharp noise from one of the reprogrammed bots, and it started moving toward the Tritans. Kiana's eyes widened in disbelief as the bot, overridden by an unforeseen glitch—or perhaps even external interference—opened fire without warning.

A burst of pulse beams illuminated the chamber, and chaos erupted in the vault as the unexpected fire echoed through the confined corridors. The Tritan raiding party, caught off guard, swiftly took defensive positions. Asimov, his expression turning from determination to shock, shouted over the commotion, "What is the meaning of this? We came in peace!"

Thynidal glanced to Aak'iks as if to ask: "Act now?" Aak'iks expressed indifference.

Kiana frantically tried to regain control, her hands pressing buttons on the console to halt the unleashed firepower. Clara, trying to suppress her irritation, shouted into the communication console, "Stand your ground! We did not intend this. It's a malfunction."

The raiding squad hesitated, keeping their weapons sheathed as per Asimov's initial directive. The bot continued to fire sporadically at the ceiling while Kiana tried to gain control back.

"Asimov, please!" Clara said, her voice strained. "This was not intentional. We are trying to regain control. Do not fire!"

Amidst the chaos, Kiana managed to override the malfunctioning bot, bringing the unexpected weapon fire to a halt. The control center fell silent, the echoes of the unintended attack lingering in the air. The Tritans stayed in their defensive stance, wary and distrustful now.

The fate of the lunar seed bank suddenly hung in the balance. Trust, already fragile, now teetered on the brink of collapse.

As the dust settled, Clara spoke into the communication console, her voice echoing through the now eerily quiet vault.

"We are deeply sorry for this. It was a malfunction beyond our control. We still seek a peaceful resolution that can benefit of both of our worlds." In the hushed aftermath of the gunfire, Clara scanned the shelves. "Let me see if I can find what you need," she told Asimov calmly.

Asimov grunted as Clara moved toward a lower shelf, bending down to look inside a box.

"I found them," she announced, her voice cutting through the tense silence. She carefully retrieved the Sigillaria cones, cradling them in her hands, and approached the communication console. "Asimov," she addressed the Tritan leader, her eyes reflecting genuine sincerity, "these are the Sigillaria cones. We are willing to share, but you must agree to leave us the rest of our collection."

Asimov, his initial anger now tempered by the sight of the crucial Sigillaria cones, cautiously changed his posture.

"Hand them over," he demanded, his eyes still wary.

Clara, with a nod to Kiana, opened a sealed chamber adjacent to the control center. She carefully placed the Sigillaria cones into a secure container, then closed the chamber doors to the control room. The container was passed forward by a bot to the other side. The doors on that side opened, and the container was presented to Asimov, who had descended from his own control room aboard his ship.

"Let this be a symbol of our willingness to collaborate for the greater good," Clara said.

Asimov, after a moment's hesitation, accepted the container. His eyes flickered between the sealed cones and Clara's gaze through the protective glass. The raiding team, still on guard, observed the exchange with a mixture of curiosity and suspicion.

"We appreciate your willingness to share," Asimov finally acknowledged. "We have one more request. We also need some Silphium seeds."

"Silphium is extinct on Earth," Clara said. "Some alien groups overharvested it."

"Yes, but remember, I have read your mind. I know that you have some."

Clara sighed. "I'll see where the seeds are."

"Wait!" Kiana's urgent warning filled the vault. "Another ship is approaching. Did you bring others with you?"

"The Draxid," Asimov muttered.

Clara frowned. "Who are the Draxid?"

"They are a vile and hurtful race who only mean us harm," Asimov said. "Their green blood is venomous."

As the Tritan raiding squad prepared to leave the lunar seed bank with the Sigillaria cones, Kiana's voice echoed through the control center, cutting through the lingering tension. "Their ships are ten minutes away."

"If they get our seeds, neither our world nor yours will survive, Asimov. Let's handle the Draxid together," Clara said. "We need your firepower."

As the Tritans exchanged wary glances, the control center's surveillance screens displayed the approaching Draxid ships on the lunar horizon.

37

A BOT TOO FAR

Bolinas, California, December 7, 2103

JULIAN SAT IN THE corner of their small living room, cradling Diana in his arms. His hands, calloused yet precise, moved with now-practiced care, adjusting the blanket around their daughter's tiny form. The soft rays of sunlight spilled through the thin curtains, dappling the room in a golden glow that seemed to breathe life into the shadows.

Outside, the early morning mist carried a faint tang of salt mingled with the earthy aroma of damp grass. Teagan's figure rested in the doorway, a shadow against the dawn. Her gaze lingered on the quiet scene before her, a delicate portrait of closeness and serenity that seemed almost too delicate to disturb.

Diana's small fingers curled against Julian's chest, her rhythmic breaths rising and falling in time with the rocking motion of his chair. Julian's eyes sparkled with a paternal pride so vivid that Teagan felt a lump rise in her throat. His touch was gentle, tender—his devotion to their daughter radiating in every movement.

For a moment, the world outside faded. The demands of the past, the weight of motherhood, the doubts and festering apprehensions—they all dissolved into the quiet sanctuary of this room. Teagan wanted to step into the scene, to let herself be wrapped in its warmth and simplicity. Yet a part of her felt like an intruder, standing on the edges of something she couldn't fully claim.

Julian looked up and caught her gaze. His smile was soft, but there was an undertone of weariness, the same unspoken question lingering between them since Julian got home: *What comes next?*

"You've been up all night again," he said gently, his voice a low murmur to avoid waking Diana.

Teagan crossed her arms, leaning against the doorframe. "Couldn't sleep," she admitted, her voice distant

Just then a car pulled up. Maureen and Harlee had continued to come around even after Julian got back. Teagan enjoyed the company and the help. But tensions had soon began to rise betweeen Julian and Harlee, who seemed to take an unwarranted interest in Diana.

The first time Teagan noticed something was off, she was too exhausted to question it. Harlee had always been an efficient, if unnervingly precise, presence in Maureen's life—an old-model caretaker bot whose skeletal frame and smooth, polished silver plating made him seem more specter than machine. His voice, a modulated blend of calm and reassurance, rarely wavered from its programmed neutrality.

But when he held Diana, something in him changed.

It started subtly—lingering too long with her in his arms, humming in a frequency that barely registered in human ears. Teagan assumed at first it was her own sleep deprivation warping reality. Maybe Harlee's programming made him overly attentive, treating Diana as a fragile thing in need of constant observation.

Yet as the days passed, the unease grew into something more tangible.

She'd catch him standing at Diana's crib, his optics glowing softly in the dim light, as if analyzing something unseen. He never disobeyed an order—if asked to hand Diana back, he did so immediately—but there was an unnatural precision to the way he moved, a reluctance in the way his metallic fingers uncurled from her tiny form.

Julian was the first to voice what Teagan had been too uncertain to say aloud.

"I don't like him holding her," he muttered one evening after Maureen and Harlee had left.

Teagan looked up from where she was folding Diana's onesies, rubbing her temples. "It's just a robot, Julian."

"Yeah? Well, I don't trust that thing." Julian's jaw clenched, and he ran a hand through his hair. "It's like he's... studying her. Too interested."

Teagan sighed. "Maureen's had Harlee a while. He's taken care of her after she retired from Quivira. He's programmed to be helpful."

Julian shook his head. "Yes, I know MB-13. But you didn't see how he was watching her today when I got home. Like he was trying to—." MB-13 had been Harlee's designation before Maureen took him as a companion.

Julian exhaled sharply. "Never mind. Maybe I'm just overreacting."

But the next day, when Teagan walked into the living room and found Harlee holding Diana with his metallic fingers brushing lightly over the soft skin of her temple, something in her stomach twisted.

"Harlee," she called, forcing her voice to remain even. "Give her to me."

The robot hesitated. Not in an obvious way—he did not disobey. But there was a beat too long before he responded, a shift in his posture that suggested reluctance.

Then he moved, as smooth and precise as ever, and placed Diana carefully in Teagan's arms.

"Diana's neural activity is exceptional," Harlee said in that perfectly level tone. "She is... different."

Teagan stiffened. "Different how?"

Harlee tilted his head, optics dimming for a fraction of a second. "It is difficult to explain. A pattern I cannot classify. But superior."

Julian, who had just entered the room, narrowed his eyes. "She's a baby, not a research project." He stepped between them, glaring at Harlee. "Maybe Maureen should find you some other task. You're getting a little too close for comfort."

Harlee didn't react. He merely turned to retrieve a data pad Maureen had left behind and placed it on the counter. "I exist to assist."

"That's great," Julian snapped. "Assist someone else."

Teagan felt her pulse hammering. Julian's frustration was understandable. Harlee's behavior—his fixation—wasn't normal. She clutched Diana closer, inhaling the soft scent of her baby's hair, and met Julian's gaze.

For all the uncertainties she faced, one thing was clear: something was happening.

And if Maureen's machine was picking up on it, then Teagan needed to figure out what.

38

THE DRAXID ATTACK

Philolaus Crater, December 8, 2103

K IANA WATCHED AS MORE and more ships appeared on her radar. It wasn't just one: It was a whole fleet of Draxid, all in precise formation. She had never seen anything like it, not even during her time with the Iron Hornets. The Draxid's ships looked like huge, predatory insects, with jagged, angular hulls that gleamed with a dull, obsidian sheen, reflecting the faint light of the distant sun. The largest ship, a command carrier, resembled a monstrous beetle, its heavily armored body bristling with glowing plasma turrets and protruding sensory spines that pulsed like living veins.

Flanking it were smaller vessels shaped like elongated mantises, their serrated wings folding and unfolding as they adjusted their positions in perfect synchronicity. These ships were designed for speed and agility, their sleek forms lined with glowing bioluminescent patterns that shifted colors, perhaps as a form of communication or intimidation.

The Draxid assault shuttles, darting around the larger ships, bore an even more sinister appearance. They looked like mutated wasps, with bulbous heads and tapered bodies that ended in sharp, stinger-like protrusions which glowed faintly with the energy of their weapon systems. These shuttles emitted a low, resonant hum that vibrated through the air as they descended toward the crater, a sound that struck fear into anyone who heard it.

"I need a group of volunteers to help Clara defend the seed vault," Asimov said.

A few Tritans volunteered to stay behind. They worked with Kiana and her makeshift band of refurbished bots as the other Tritan ship moved into a defensive position in front of the base.

As the Draxid ships closed in, the volunteer Tritan defenders, armed with energy weapons, scrambled to form a defensive perimeter around the seed repository, creating a brief diversion while Asimov's main ship took off, commanded by Thynidal, while Asimov remained behind. He owed that to Clara.

Kiana hurried outside onto the lunar surface with her band of refurbished securitybots and stood ready behind jagged rock formations. They had barely hidden themselves when the Draxid ships unleashed a thunderous volley of energy blasts.

Soon, the area was a chaotic scene of flashing bursts and guttural cries as the Tritan and Draxid forces clashed. Using the rocky terrain to their advantage, Kiana, the bots, and the Tritans darted between outcroppings and fired precision shots that felled the advancing invaders. But the Draxid's superior numbers and brute strength began to take their toll.

"Kiana," Asimov called through the comms, "they're trying to flank the east ridge. Can you handle it?"

"Barely," Kiana replied, dodging a blast that scorched the ground near her. "But don't worry, we'll give them hell."

* * *

Inside the vault, Clara clutched a jar containing the last Silphium seeds, her heart racing as she heard the commotion outside.

"There's no time!" Clara hissed, her voice cracking with urgency. Her hands trembled as she addressed her team of humans, Tritans, and bots. "We can't let these fall into their hands. We need to enact the contingency plan." She swiftly removed the seeds, replacing them with an old rag before sealing the jar. "Get these to the extraction team. Go!" she told SP4RK.

As she watched SP4RK scramble away with the small sample of seeds, a loud boom shook the room. *It sounds like the Draxid have breached the vault's outer defenses*, she thought with worry.

Not minutes later, three of them entered the chamber, the glowing crests on their armor casting an eerie hue on the walls. Clara stood in their path, flanked by a handful of bots.

One Draxid commander, standing at full height, stepped forward. "Surrender, and you might live long enough to see your precious seeds taken." The creatures walked menacingly toward Clara, the pit organs on the fronts of their faces flaring in unison., and the commander grabbed her by the hair.

"Over my dead body," Clara spat, raising her knife.

The Draxid lunged, but Clara was waiting for it. She ducked and drove her blade straight into its chest, twisting it. But the creature retaliated with a brutal backhand, sending her sprawling against the vault door. Her body crumpled just as she heard a pulse gun fire.

Kiana squeezed inside just in time to see a Draxid hit Clara so hard that she flew backward into the vault door. Kiana's pulse gun was up and firing before she'd even processed what happened.

"Leave her alone, you pigs!" Kiana shouted.

The Draxid who'd hit Clara sneered, lifting Clara's limp body like a ragdoll. "Pitiful," it hissed.

Kiana screamed in fury, "She's just an old woman!" But a sharp kick to her abdomen from one of the Draxid silenced her, leaving her gasping on the floor.

Before she could even catch her breath, the lead Draxid struck Clara with such horrifying force that her neck snapped, her body crumpling lifelessly.

"No!" Kiana screamed, desperately trying to rise, but the Draxid soldiers mercilessly pummeled her stomach again. She shrieked in agony as each brutal kick hammered into her, her pulse gun firing wildly, impotently into the air.

* * *

Clara was motionless on the floor. A couple of semi-deactivated securitybots trundled forwards but were immediately obliterated.

As the Draxid confirmed that Clara was dead, they noticed a barely-conscious Kiana issuing a distress call. They kicked her again. Then they searched the lab to see where the seeds were kept, finally managing to find the precious Silphium. They packed a few boxes of seeds from the shelves, clearly ignorant of what varieties they were taking.

A bot tried to intervene. They blasted it with a quick pulse.

In a final act of malevolence, they swept the tiny seeds on the workbench onto the floor before departing, leaving behind a scene of devastation and unanswered questions.

"We've got what we need," the leader barked into his comm. "Prepare for extraction."

Outside, the battlefield was a smoldering ruin as Captain Calytricx rallied her remaining troops. "Hold them back! Don't let them reach the ships without a price!"

Zaun, watching from the remote command center, was calm. "Call them off," it ordered reluctantly. "We've taken enough losses for today. Follow their ships. They can't have gone far."

The Draxid retreated, their ships lifting off in a storm of dust and fire. As the last vessel disappeared into the void, Captain Calytricx entered the vault and knelt beside the now-lifeless body of Clara Ward.

* * *

When Kiana came to, Asimov was kneeling next to her. Eyes wide, Kiana turned her head quickly to see Clara's body unmoving on the floor. Behind her, in the seed vault, Kiana could tell there were several boxes missing.

"The Draxid have gone," Asimov said.

"They... they took the seeds," Kiana whispered.

"No," Asimov said, his voice firm. "Not what we needed. We saved those."

But not without great cost, Kiana thought, her eyes going to Clara once more.

39
TRACES OF GREEN

Philolaus Crater, December 8, 2103

Having gathered the specimens she needed, Nevie hurried back to the Moon's North Pole, not liking that she hadn't heard from Clara.

She'd been relieved that Hunter had insisted that Kiana should help look after her grandmother, and knew that Kiana had tried to contact her. She tried to reach both of them throughout her journey back, but there was no response.

Every minute she spent on the journey seemed like an hour. But there was no way to get there more quickly. The worrying thing was the silence, the lack of contact.

The first sign of trouble when she landed was that the doors to the vault were open. They never left the doors open.

Nevie felt bile rise to the back of her mouth as she rushed along the narrow corridors after taking the elevator down. Her eyes widened in fear as she saw various bots laying immobilized or damaged throughout the halls. But when she turned the corner to the vault, she stopped cold.

There was Clara, sitting at the vault door, her head at an unnatural angle.

Nevie's brain refused to interpret what her eyes were seeing.

"Clara... Grandma... what are you doing on the floor?" she asked, rushing forward. "Grandma, please wake up. Where's Kiana?"

Nevie tried to feel a pulse; there wasn't one. Clara's skin had turned gray and clammy, but Nevie still refused to believe the deductions her brain was making. She put her hand on Clara's shoulder and gently shook her. To her dismay, Clara slowly slid to the floor.

"Clara, wake up. I got the spores."

Clara was unresponsive.

"You can't die now, Clara," Nevie said, her voice cracking. "I can't do this without you."

Overwhelmed, Nevie took a seat and shook her head in denial, her eyes going to the scene around her once more. Drops of a green liquid led away from the vault, and in Clara's hand was a sharp knife smeared with the same green liquid. Nevie froze as the situation became apparent.

"Show video footage of what happened here," she instructed the AI.

Nevie watched as three creatures entered the lab and surrounded Clara. They had yellow and black crested heads, with six limbs and an armored exoskeleton. They loomed over Clara as they scanned her with their menacing eyes.

Nevie had heard of other intelligent life forms in the solar system, but hadn't seen any before. They certainly weren't from Earth.

Nevie winced as one of them pulled Clara by the hair. She couldn't see the lead creature speak, but she assumed it was questioning Clara, who said something and spat into its face; Nevie gasped as Clara was struck with such force that she was hurled across the room, landing against the vault door where Nevie had found her.

Kiana arrived and tried to fend the invaders off, but she was no match for them.

"Leave her alone, you pigs!" Nevie could see Kiana say.

They kicked Kiana in the stomach and she slumped to the floor; she still appeared to be breathing. Then the leader lifted Clara's struggling body and hit her with such force that Nevie saw her neck break as she collapsed.

What struck Nevie was that these creatures didn't seem to be in a hurry. They almost seemed to enjoy torturing Clara and Kiana. She watched the video several times, trying to make sense of what had happened.

Then she called Noel.

Noel was surprised to see Nevie, but his surprise turned to distress when he realized she had been crying.

"What's wrong, Nevie? Has something happened?"

Nevie burst into tears again. "You have to get up here, Noel. Clara— She's been ... Just get here as soon as you can."

Her throat tightened, her words were choked with emotion and she couldn't bring herself to explain further. Noel tried to ask her again, but Nevie just continued sobbing.

"I'm on my way," he said, his voice full of concern.

Nevie crumbled like a delicate flower, tears streaming down her face in a torrent of pain, She curled up on the floor in a fetal position, her body shaking with sobs.

She seemed to shrink into herself, a small and fragile creature in need of comfort and shelter. Her eyes were red and puffy and her face contorted in anguish. She should have been there. Kiana couldn't do it on her own.

40
NOEL'S GRIEF

Philolaus Crater, December 8, 2103

NOEL GOT TO THE seed bank about three hours after Nevie had called him.

On the flight from Tricala, Noel's mind raced to make sense of what might have happened to Clara. Even though Nevie had not explicitly said anything, Noel was certain that something terrible had occurred. Was she hurt? Images of possible scenarios flooded his thoughts, but none of them seemed to fit the puzzle. It was as though his brain had been wiped clean, leaving behind only a swirling mess of emotions and unanswered questions.

When he laid eyes on Clara's lifeless body, a gut-wrenching scream escaped his lips. He knelt beside her and cradled her head in his hands, gently brushing his fingertips against her pale skin, feeling the coldness that had already begun to set in.

Noel and Clara had often been apart, but he loved her with all his being. Tears began to stream down his face, leaving streaks on the dusty ground. His strong façade shattered, revealing a vulnerable and devastated soul beneath.

Despite Nevie's reluctance, Noel insisted on watching the gruesome footage of how Clara had been murdered. He watched with his shoulders hunched and his face contorted in a mixture of despair and disbelief. He clenched his fists, his nails digging into his palms in frustration and grief.

"I have no idea what kind of life forms these are," said Noel. "I'll have to do some research to narrow them down. To my knowledge, the closest life forms are lightyears away from us. I wonder what they were doing here, in this part of our galaxy?"

"Isn't that obvious already? They were after the seeds," Nevie said. "They seemed to know where the vault was, and wanted to force Clara to open it. When they couldn't, the bastards killed her, knocked out Kiana, and took the seeds."

Noel ignored the barb in Nevie's voice, and the fact that she was spelling out the events for him like he was a really slow student.

"Forgive me, Nevie. What I meant was how did they get this current location? How did they know about the Seeds of Life project? This vault was off the beaten track, guarded by its remoteness; even GLOSCOM didn't know much about it. And why do they need the seeds so much? Were they working with someone or something on Earth? There are just so many questions!"

Nevie had slumped wearily on the floor. After a long moment, her head snapped up. "They'll be back."

Noel turned his red-rimmed eyes on her. "Why do you say that, Nevaeh?"

"Just a feeling I have." She shrugged. "These guys knew what they wanted; they went straight for the seeds, but they didn't take everything. A handful of seeds would be regarded as a failure compared to the treasure trove in the vault.

"Noel, we have two options: Either move the seeds away or fight. I'm not running. Clara gave her life for this project; I'm willing to do the same."

Noel smiled sadly. "You know, you remind me so much of Teagan sometimes. I agree with you; the only problem is we can't fight them alone. I'll reach out. We need protection. But first, I have a funeral to organize."

* * *

Noel mechanically went through the motions of planning the funeral, his mind in a fog. Memories of happy times with Clara would surface, causing him to momentarily lose focus. Consumed by grief, he could not think clearly; his mind was distracted. He went about simple tasks like an automaton while, in the back of his mind, Noel went over and over what he had seen.

He had observed the creatures, but couldn't get the thought out of his mind that somebody linked to GLOSCOM had been responsible for the attack. But why would they do it? GLOSCOM had treated them with the utmost esteem, and his work on Tricala had made him a respected scientist again, even though he had got the feeling that everything he had done had been watched and constantly monitored.

Though he couldn't prove it, Noel knew Howie was involved in GLOSCOM in one way or another. The corporation's reach was too big for Howie not to have his greedy hands all over it. But how did it all fit together? Had Clara been just too much of a thorn in their side, too much of an independent thinker?

Gradually, his mind turned from grief to revenge. Revenge and retribution. But what would payback look like?

Noel sat in a dimly lit borrowed room, spartan but functional. The arrangements for Clara's funeral had been a blur of logistics, condolences, and hollow words. He felt adrift, the weight of his loss threatening to pull him under. The moments alone were the worst, when the memories surged and the reality of her absence hit like a physical blow. They needed some defense system that could fend off these barbaric and murderous creatures.

To escape the crushing grief, his mind latched onto the only thing that could distract him. Maybe it was his way of coping, or maybe it was his subconscious shielding him from the pain, but his thoughts turned obsessively to his work and the Astral Lattice..

He switched onto an image of the Lattice, a delicate web of connections that seemed to hum with possibilities. Noel leaned forward, studying the intricate network and puzzling over every node, every resonance pattern, searching for meaning, searching for a purpose to anchor himself.

"How can this be harnessed?" he murmured, his voice barely audible.

An idea took root, fragile but insistent: Could the Lattice be transformed into a protective field?

He pushed back from the desk and stood abruptly. "Where's Shiko?" he muttered to himself, pacing as the idea began to take shape. "He's good at this kind of thing."

Liam, who had been quietly working at the Tricala compound as well, looked up. "I think he's in Des Moines," he said after a moment of checking his tablet.

"I need him here. Please track him down and arrange for his return."

As Noel's other employees moved to fulfill his request, Noel threw himself into the work, channeling his restless energy into the project. He tasked Liam with testing the Lattice's properties; Tara joined him, her eyes alight with curiosity as they observed the virtual wall created by the Lattice's natural vibrations.

Noel' was impressed as the sound waves, tuned with precise calculations, began to form a unified, almost tangible barrier. It looked like a nearly invisible shield — a defensive sound web capable of destabilizing foreign technology.

Noel was transfixed. What had begun as a theoretical concept now showed promise.

"Let's run a simulation," Noel said, his tone sharper now, infused with purpose. He activated the software, projecting a virtual Draxid fleet advancing on the Lattice. As the simulated ships approached, the sound shield sprang to life, emitting feedback vibrations that disrupted their formation and rendered their systems inert.

"It's working," Noel whispered, his voice trembling with exhilaration. "The resonance is destabilizing the ships in a simulation. The real application could protect an entire planet!"

Tara's eyes widened. "This could change everything."

Noel nodded, the beginnings of a plan forming in his mind. For the first time since Clara's passing, he felt a spark of hope. If he could perfect this technology, it could become a legacy, not just for him, but for Clara, whose memory now fueled his drive to protect what mattered most.

41

NEWS SPREADS ON EARTH

Bolinas, California, December 12, 2103

T EAGAN HUMMED A GENTLE lullaby as she zipped Diana into her bed-time sleeper. The baby cooed, her tiny hands batting the air, oblivious to the storm about to engulf their world.

The gentle melody was interrupted by an urgent tone from the television in the living room. Frowning, Teagan glanced at it. The glowing display now showed the face of Benjamin Taylor, known to his fans as BT, his expression unusually drawn.

"This is Benjamin Taylor, reporting from Malapert Lunar Base," the broadcast began.

Teagan froze, her hands stilling over Diana's zipper as she heard the name of the base.

"The world is reeling from the sudden and mysterious death of Dr. Clara Ward, celebrated botanist and guardian of the Philolaus Crater seed vault. Few had heard about the seed vault until now, but clearly someone or some-thing knew of the treasures it holds."

The words hit Teagan like a physical blow. Her heart pounded as if it were trying to escape her chest. Surely there had been a mistake. Nobody from Malapert had been in touch with her. She was stunned; she couldn't believe it.

The news began to seep into her consciousness. She felt sick, but was strong enough not to slump into a crumpled heap as she wanted to. She just stood there, paralyzed, as the report continued.

"Details surrounding her death remain unclear. All we know is that her body was found near a mysterious green liquid inside the seed vault. The liq-uid is being analyzed but, for now, its origin and purpose remain unknown."

The zipper in Teagan's hand felt slippery, and she let it go as nausea rolled through her. She couldn't comprehend it — her vibrant, unstoppable mother, dead? A wave of dizziness struck her, and she instinctively gripped the edge of the changing table to steady herself.

Diana's soft murmur brought her back to the moment. Teagan forced herself to stay upright. She couldn't crumble, not here, not now.

"Maureen!" she called, her voice shaking as she turned toward the hallway. "Maureen, can you come here?"

Maureen answered faintly from the other room, "What's wrong?"

Teagan scooped up Diana, clutching her daughter close as the holo-screen broadcast continued. She needed Maureen to hear this, to help her make sense of it, but she felt violently sick.

Her breath caught, as if her lungs had forgotten how to draw air. She didn't cry, not at first. Instead, a stunned silence descended over her, a cold hollowness spreading from her chest outward. Diana stirred, sensing something shift in her mother's body, and gave a soft, questioning coo.

Teagan's arms tightened reflexively around the child. "She's gone," she whispered, more to herself than to anyone else. "She was still there... and now she's gone."

Memories crashed in—Clara's quiet strength, her unshakable belief in the seeds, in science, in survival. Her smile. Her stubbornness. Her hands guiding Teagan through soil samples back when Earth still had seasons worth measuring.

As BT's voice continued to echo through the house, Teagan sat on the edge of the couch, holding Diana tightly. "I can't believe it," she whispered to herself, her voice trembling. "Why didn't anyone from Malapert contact me? How did this happen?"

Her mind raced. Her own mother. How did it happen? This wasn't just a loss. It felt wrong, as if there was something lurking beneath the surface, just out of reach. She stared at the screen, her eyes narrowing. Tears finally came, silent and hot. But even through the grief, a colder realization pressed in: she had lost not just her mother, but a protector of the future. Of Diana's future. And now that burden was hers alone. Whatever had happened, she would find out. She owed her mother that much.

Just then, Hunter called.

* * *

In Des Moines, Kat Merrick was equally shocked. She had tucked herself into a corner booth of a dimly lit café, her headphones pressed tightly over her ears to drown out the hum of nearby conversations.

"Green liquid?" she murmured, frowning at her tablet. She paused the broadcast and replayed the segment, her mind racing.

She tapped out a quick message on her communicator, her fingers trembling.

Shiko, did you hear this? The seed vault lady died. What if it wasn't just an accident? What if they...?

She hesitated, biting her lip, before deleting the last few words and sending the message as it was.

The café's television, mounted high in the corner, suddenly switched to a live feed of the Des Moines protests. The chants and banners filled the screen, and Kat's chest tightened.

BT's voice returned to her headphones. "Dr. Clara Ward's death is not just a tragedy; it is a call to action. As humanity grapples with its precarious future, one question remains: Who will stand to protect the seeds of life when those who do are silenced?"

Kat clenched her fists. She had spent her life watching from the sidelines, tracking the slow unraveling of the world's future through reports, intercepted messages, and whispered conversations in dimly lit backrooms.

She had never met Dr. Ward, but the woman's work had shaped everything Katrina believed in. Clara had fought to protect something fragile, something powerful — life itself. The seeds of a future that others wanted to control, to suppress, or worse, to destroy. If someone like Clara Ward could be silenced, then no one was safe.

Kat wasn't naïve enough to believe she could just walk in and demand answers. But among the mourners, the allies, and the hidden enemies, she could listen. She could observe. And maybe, just maybe, she could find the next step forward in a fight she could no longer ignore.

And perhaps, just perhaps, she would get to meet the woman who had rescued her from the fire as a tiny baby, and whose charm she wore around her neck.

* * *

Beyond the Moon, another force stirred. Aboard a Draxid scoutship, a transmission of the discord on Earth flickered in the center of a darkened room.

"Humans are so easily distracted," hissed Vaelith, his spindly fingers tapping against the metallic table. "Their fury at this... GLOSCOM serves us well."

"Will they not discover the truth about Clara Ward?" asked an underling, its voice like the scrape of stone on stone.

Vaelith chuckled, a harsh, grating sound. "No. They are too blinded by their hatred. Their corporations will crumble under the weight of their own hubris. And by the time they realize what truly happened, we will have made our move."

42
THE FUNERAL

Malapert, December 20, 2103

At the Malapert lunar outpost, mourners gathered for Clara's funeral.

Teagan's face was etched with lines of grief and exhaustion when she got to Malapert, escorted by Maureen. Teagan's eyes were puffy and red from crying, her hair disheveled from the long journey from California. But as she carried Diana on her chest into the lunar center, Teagan found Julian waiting for them. He had flown separately, unwilling to spend time with Harlee in a confined space.

When he saw their little daughter, dressed in a bright yellow romper, he smiled with joy. Teagan's hand was cold and clammy as Julian took it in his own, offering a comforting squeeze, and all her anger was swept aside as she felt Julian's hug envelop her.

He knelt in front of Diana, his face blotched with tears, and reached out a trembling hand to touch her soft cheeks. Her small, chubby fingers clasped onto his.

Teagan watched this meeting, her own eyes welling with tears. She knew how much Julian had needed to see their daughter and how desperately he had longed to be by their side. It was in these tender moments that she appreciated the strength of their love, even after all the doubts.

"Look who's here, Diana," Teagan whispered softly, her voice tinged with a mixture of joy and sorrow. "This is your dad."

"Dada." Diana grinned and clung to him.

The room around them seemed to pulsate with an otherworldly energy, radiating warmth. Soft golden rays of sunlight filtered through a ceiling window only partially covered by regolith, casting a gentle glow on every surface. The walls, adorned with photographs of the research facility, whispered tales of courage and triumph.

Seeing Noel approach, Teagan pulled away from Julian and reached out to her father, tears still streaming down her face.

They held each other tightly, seeking solace and strength in one another, and as Teagan embraced her father, she could feel the weight of their shared grief pressing against her chest. Noel's hug was tight and loving, as if he never wanted to let go. His familiar scent mingled with sadness, creating a bittersweet concoction that filled the air between them; Noel's eyes, once so full of life, now carried the sorrow of a man who had lost his soulmate.

Teagan realized that she and her father were bound together by an unbreakable thread woven from love, loss, and the indomitable strength that ran through their veins. And in that moment of shared anguish, memories of Clara flooded their minds. They remembered her laughter and determination, the support she'd always given them.

Teagan had been reluctant to make the journey with her new baby, but ultimately knew she had to be there for her father, and for her mother.

Noel's trembling hand reached out to stroke the delicate curls adorning his granddaughter's head. His touch was tender and hesitant, as if afraid to shatter the fragile beauty before him. Diana gazed up at him with wide eyes filled with innocence and curiosity.

* * *

In normal times a refuge for shared scientific pursuits, the Malapert base was now silenced by the solemnity of loss. Clara's passing had cast a profound shadow over Noel's world, leaving him grappling with a grief that seemed to consume the very air he breathed. Although the cause had not been officially divulged, the news of her death at the hands of intruders had sent shockwaves through the lunar community, and Noel found himself standing at the epicenter of an emotional tempest.

As the lunar base gathered to mourn the loss of one of its founding members, Noel had retreated into the solitude of Clara's old quarters, after seeing Teagan and Diana. The walls, which had borne witness to years of scientific discoveries and shared aspirations, felt like silent sentinels in the face of an irrevocable change. The grief was palpable, and Noel, in the starkness of his lunar solitude, allowed the weight of loss to settle upon him.

His eyes searched the room, lingering on the empty chair where Clara had sat just days ago. The memory of her laughter and warmth filled his mind, intermingling with the sorrow that had taken hold. How could someone so vibrant and full of life be gone so abruptly?

Clara had worked at Malapert and the Philolaus Crater site for the past thirty-five years, since 2068. Clara's death was such a shock; everyone who could came to the funeral. Even her former boss, Alain Gagnon——who had long since retired to the Auvergne-Rhône-Alpes region of France, near the dramatic Ardèche River——made the journey, as well as Clara's longtime assistance Amy.

To everyone's joy, Teagan arrived carrying Diana, with Maureen Grau accompanying her, her trademark grey hair wafting like a plume of smoke. Maureen in turn was accompanied by MB-13 (now known as Harlee). Kiana lingered in the background as did Toni from the Tricala base. In addition, of the Seven there was Nevie, Liam, Tara, and Gabby. Shiko was away, on a work assignment in Des Moines according to most people. Arturo had said he would be there but was nowhere to be found. Hunter and Ved were on a long journey and could not make it. The Consortium had sent Chris Stackpole, since he was closest. Even Olga Polyakov attended. Zhang Honghui had retired, but in his place came Zhu Yan, now in charge of the Huashan base.

The memorial service began in the central atrium, adorned with holographic displays projecting Clara's life story of the departed against the lunar landscape. A gentle hum filled the air as mourners floated weightlessly in their sleek, form-fitting mourning suits, each equipped with small propulsion systems to navigate the microgravity environment.

The celestial priest, adorned in a flowing, shimmering robe, stood at a crystalline podium. With a soft voice that resonated through the space, they shared memories of the departed, emphasizing the importance of their journey among the stars. A holographic choir, their ethereal voices echoing through the chamber, performed a composition that blended earthly melodies with the cosmic symphony.

When he was ready, Noel joined the mourners to give the eulogy.

"Thank you all for gathering here today to remember and honor the incredible life of my beloved wife, Dr. Clara Ward. As we stand on this magnificent celestial body, looking out into the vastness of space, I can't help but reflect on the extraordinary journey Clara took in her pursuit of knowledge and her passion for preserving the essence of life.

"Clara was not just my wife; she was a pioneer, a visionary, and an exceptional biologist who dedicated thirty-five years of her life to unraveling the mysteries of the Moon and contributing to the advancement of lunar science. Her love for this desolate but fascinating world led her to establish the seed vault at the Philolaus Crater, a testament to her unwavering commitment to safeguarding the future of our planet and the diversity of its flora.

"In her illustrious career, Clara worked tirelessly at both lunar centers, leaving an indelible mark on the scientific community. Her brilliance, resilience, and unparalleled dedication were evident to all who had the privilege of working alongside her. It is with a heavy heart that we gather here today, not just to celebrate her achievements, but to mourn the tragic circumstances that befell her.

"Clara's life was cut short in a senseless act of violence that none of us could have anticipated. The loss we feel is compounded by the mysterious nature of her passing. It is a testament to the risks and uncertainties that come with pushing the boundaries of exploration. But even in the face of such tragedy, we must remember Clara for the incredible contributions she made to lunar science and the legacy she leaves behind.

"I'd like to express my deepest gratitude to all of you who have joined us today. Alain Gagnon, her esteemed former boss and mentor, you played a crucial role in shaping Clara's career, and I know she held a profound respect for you. Teagan and our beautiful new granddaughter Diana are also here, as is our son Hunter, who keeps us all safe as a Space Sentinel. Thank you for your service, son.

"Clara's memory will live on not only through her scientific achievements, but also in the hearts of her family, friends, and colleagues. Let us find solace in the fact that her work continues, that the seeds she planted--both figuratively and literally--will endure, and that her legacy will inspire future generations to reach for the stars.

"May her spirit find peace among the craters and valleys she so passionately explored, and may her memory be a beacon of light in the dark expanse of the cosmos. Goodbye, my love. Until we meet again among the stars."

The highlight of the service was the "Stellar Release": To commemorate Clara's work, mourners carried small, biodegradable pods containing seeds specially designed for space environments, engineered to drift throughout the cosmos. The capsules were adorned with intricate designs, reflecting the unique personality and experiences of the deceased. One by one, the capsules were released into the void, gently propelled toward the lunar horizon.

As the capsules drifted away, a coordinated burst of colored thrusters ignited, creating a mesmerizing celestial display and forming a shimmering trail that sparkled like a transient comet against the Moon's desolate surface. The congregation watched in silent reverence, their emotions a mixture of grief and awe.

At Malapert, they had also planted a small commemorative garden. With the help of advanced horticultural technology, the flowers would adapt to the lunar conditions, extracting nutrients from the soil and drawing energy from the sun. The lunar garden could be accessed remotely, and updates on the growth and health of the space flowers could be seen through a virtual portal for people on Earth.

"This interactive aspect will allow mourners elsewhere to participate in the ongoing life of the lunar memorial, fostering a sense of continuity and connection across the vastness of space."

One of the guests who had helped with this was Shiko's neighbor, Kat. She knew that Shiko would have wanted to honor Clara in this way. Kat sat near the back of the congregation, a thin, braided band of black silk around her wrist, a simple yet poignant mark of personal grief.

She wanted to approach Teagan, to thank her, but now was not the time.

And among the remote viewers was the AI called Zaun, who silently, without emotion, took in all the information for future reference and use. It was like a vault opening.

43
FAMILY REUNION

Malapert, December 20, 2103

AFTER THE FUNERAL, EVERYONE gathered for the usual reception. Bots served canapes to the guests, some of whom made quick exits as flights and business called. Others lingered.

One of the attendees who did so was Gabby. She was determined to meet with Toni Demirci, who she understood to be her probable mother.

Toni had helped Gabby indirectly, but never acknowledged her as Teagan had acknowledged and tried to claim her offspring. Gabby knew that Toni had helped her get the job at the sanctuary in Ghana, but Gabby did not like the hands-off approach. This was a chance to get to know her mother.

As Gabby approached Toni, it was clear from their looks that they were related.

"Gabriella, you look more beautiful than your photos," Toni said, holding out a hand in greeting.

"Thank you. With a mother like you, I clearly had an advantage."

"Mother? You may say mother, but we may have different ideas about parenting."

She paused, and Gabby waited for her to continue. Now would come the excuses.

"You see, Gabby, dear," Toni eventually said, "I would say your mother was the one who cared for you, who nursed you, who raised you. Maybe someone who gave birth to you. Not someone who gave a few eggs and never looked back."

Gabby looked at her quizzically.

"I hate being examined like an exhibit at a show or a museum," Toni went on sharply. "Let's get this straight once and for all. I don't want to argue with you over semantics. All I have to say is that I've never been married or been pregnant. All I did was provide materials for a science experiment, a transaction that rewarded me a great deal. It was a business arrangement.

"You, Gabriella, might have had things handed to you because you were raised in a lab, but some of us have had to claw our fingers to the bone to get to where we are. Nothing was handed to us. So I had to make compromises."

Gabby finally looked up into eyes that looked so similar to hers, though Toni's had been hardened by years of experience. Behind those eyes, there was no love, or warmth, just mild irritation. And yet, Gabby felt some form of affection, and perhaps pity, for this woman.

"I want to know why you didn't try to find me."

Gabby saw surprise register in Toni's eyes. Like she wasn't expecting Gabby to ask her that question.

"Why would I find you? I didn't know you existed until recently. Then I did what I could to help you, indirectly. I've done well for myself. Why would I spoil all by suddenly developing a conscience?"

Gabby appreciated the honesty, although it still irked her that her mother thought her nothing more than a science experiment. But there was something else Toni had brought up that intrigued Gabby.

"You say you were rewarded for donating your eggs," she asked. "Does that mean you knew why your eggs were harvested? And you were fine with it?"

Toni snorted and gave Gabby a look of disgust. "Of course I knew. I'm not an idealistic college student who couldn't get over the fact that her eggs could make a difference in the world or serve as next month's period. In return for my eggs, I got a plum position in the Consortium, a very nice nest egg, and some shares in a mine in the Congo."

Gabby felt a stab of disappointment. She had hoped that Toni would apologize, or claim ignorance, or find some lame excuse to justify not looking for her.

Seeing Gabby's expression, Toni pushed herself away from the table and stood up in a fluid move Gabby couldn't help but admire. Toni's eyes were fiery, her anger radiating all over her body.

"Oh, grow up Gabby. Stop your whining and face reality. There were five egg donors, and the only one who was stupid enough not to understand the terms of the agreement was the non-professional. You Heavenly Babies are supposed to be smart. One out of five isn't the norm, it's an anomaly. Teagan

Ward was an anomaly, not the standard. In the years she was in prison, I made a career for myself, Maureen and Matoko turned Quivira into one of the most successful and prosperous habitats in LEO, and Fan became a musician of repute. If I'm to choose fates, which do you think I would pick? Hell, which would you pick?"

The logical way Toni stated her case irritated Gabby. It irked her even more that Toni had a point. Being a realist and ambitious wasn't a sin, it was just a way of life. Yet Gabby's hurt didn't subside. The picture in her head of Nevie going in, guns blazing, to rescue her mother and avenge her grandmother stayed with her. "So you didn't think of me? Not even once?"

Perhaps it was the fact that Gabby was so close to tears, or the despondent way she asked the question. Whatever the reason was, Toni's face softened for the first time. Halting, as if unsure if what she wanted to say was right or wrong, Toni slowly cupped Gabby's face.

"I thought about you every day. I shunned all news and footage of all of you because I didn't want to know which one was my child. When Howie told me you were coming here, I still refused to look at a picture of you."

Gabby held Toni's hands to her face. "Why? Did you hate me that much?"

Toni looked confused. "Hate you? Why in the world would I hate you? I avoided everything about you because if I knew who you were... I couldn't risk my career and the life I had built because I suddenly had the urge to be a mother. I know you must think I'm selfish, and I wouldn't blame you one bit, but for me, making a success of myself came first. Teagan had parents who loved her; I had only myself and my wits. Besides, I knew you already had everything you would ever want."

This time, Gabby noticed that Toni's voice was soft, almost pleading. Gabby found herself accepting that she would never have the same relationship that Nevie, or even Liam, had with Teagan. But that wasn't a bad thing. She also decided that, instead of hoping for something that would never happen, why couldn't she build something from the wreckage that she had?

"Toni... Can I call you Toni?"

Toni nodded, and Gabby went on.

"I understand what you're saying, and I appreciate your honesty. I want to apologize for judging you too harshly. You said you were selfish, but I was also being selfish. I was only thinking of what I wanted, not how it would affect you. I understand that César and Howie would never have allowed you access to us. Even Maureen and Matoko had to act like we were just a community of kids. Maybe we can agree to be friends, if not mother and daughter?"

Toni looked at Gabby and smiled at her for the first time. Gabby felt a lump in her throat as she saw what she might look like twenty, twenty-five years down the line. It wasn't a bad image.

"Yes, Gabby, I would love for us to be friends. Thank you."

"Would you like to attend Clara's Lunar Garden with me? Maybe we can be gardeners together?"

"I would like that," said Toni.

They parted. Gabby saw Kat and decided to let her know Shiko was ok. In the distance, Toni spotted Julian. Would their future interests soon merge, as they had discussed with Ofentse? She would try to edge things along.

* * *

The lunar base was quiet now, the echoes of the ceremony fading into the sterile stillness of the corridors. Teagan had left the funeral to linger by a small observation window, staring out at the barren expanse of the Moon's surface. The crescent Earth hung in the dark sky, its soft glow unable to dispel her emptiness.

Behind her, hesitant footsteps approached. She turned to see a young woman in a flowing silvery veil, her eyes wide and filled with an emotion Teagan couldn't quite place.

"Teagan Ward?" the woman asked softly.

Wiping her damp cheeks with the edge of her sleeve, Teagan nodded. "Can I help you?"

The woman hesitated, her hands clutching something small and delicate. "My name is Kat Merrick. I—" She faltered, her voice catching. Then she took a deep breath and stepped closer. "I wanted to thank you. For saving my life."

Teagan blinked in confusion, the words not immediately making sense. "I'm sorry, I don't—"

"I suppose it's been a long time," Kat said, her tone understanding but bittersweet. "I was just a baby when it happened. My parents were killed—" Her voice wavered, but she pressed on, "—and you were there. You pulled me from the wreckage and brought me to the hospital in Tucson. They said I wouldn't have survived if you hadn't."

Teagan stared at her, the memories slowly surfacing like old photographs in her mind. A smoldering farm. A baby wrapped in a soot-stained blanket. The desperate flight to get her to safety.

"You were that baby," Teagan whispered. "I remember now."

Kat nodded, her lips trembling as she held out her hand. In her palm was a tiny, tarnished bangle, no bigger than a child's bracelet. An intricate, stylized eye was engraved on its surface.

"I've always worn this," Kat said, her voice barely audible. "You gave it to me in the hospital. It was the only thing you left behind."

Teagan reached out, her fingers brushing the bangle as if to confirm it was real.

"I wear it now as a pendant."

A lump formed in Teagan's throat, guilt and wonder mixing in a storm of emotions. "I-I didn't know where you ended up. I'm sorry I never contacted you."

"I was adopted," Kat said quickly, as if to absolve Teagan of any guilt. "My parents were kind to me, gave me a good life. But I always wondered about you. And now ... here we are."

Teagan's eyes filled with tears. She gripped Kat's hand tightly, the bangle cool against her skin. "You don't know how much this means to me. To see you here, alive, after everything—"

Kat smiled faintly, her own tears slipping down her cheeks. "You gave me a chance, Teagan. That's all I needed."

The two women embraced, their connection formed in the ashes of tragedy and now strengthened by the shared grief of losing Clara. For the first time since the birth of Diana, Teagan felt a new surge of hope—a fragile seedling, waiting to grow.

44
SPACE TIME

SpaceSweeper III, December 2103

V ED WAS ON HIS way and for the first time in years, he felt something stir inside him — a spark, fragile but insistent. The lethargy and mind fog were gone. He had a new sense of purpose of clarity. A drive to uncover the truth about himself, no matter how deep or dark the path ahead might be. The question that had haunted him for so long was no longer something to run from — it was something to chase.

The first jumps through hyperspace were jarring, like being torn through the fabric of reality by sheer force. The *SpaceSweeper III* groaned and shuddered with each violent surge forward, its outdated hull screaming under the stress. Hunter's knuckles blanched white as he gripped the controls, jaw clenched, eyes scanning the fluctuating trajectory readouts.

Beside him, Ved kept a sharp watch on every corner of the vessel, monitoring heat signatures, pressure levels, and the faintest twitch of movement on the radar. Their nerves buzzed with tension — hyperspace was unpredictable, and any slip-up could hurl them into an unforgiving vacuum.

Between the surges, in a rare moment of stillness, Ved murmured, "You ever think about how all this—" he gestured vaguely toward the starlight beyond the viewports, "—is in us? The atoms in our bones, our blood... they were forged in supernovas. Born in the hearts of dying stars and scattered through space like particles. We're not just *in* the universe—we *are* the universe, Hunter."

Hunter didn't reply, but his grip on the controls loosened slightly.

Ved's voice was calm, almost reverent. "It's wild to think the atoms in our bodies were all once just interstellar dust... torn from dying stars, scattered across the void. And now here we are—riding that same dust across hyperspace."

Eventually, the turbulence eased, the time for introspection seemed to pass. The ship's systems stabilized with a low, contented hum. SpaceSweeper III, though never meant for this kind of travel, had proven resilient. A scavenger ship repurposed into an interstellar vessel. It wasn't built for grace, but it would have to endure.

As the days stretched, Hunter and Ved began to let down their guard, just a little. From their cockpit window, the universe unfurled in slow, hypnotic beauty: planets like forgotten memories, distant and blurred by time; stars pulsing gently in the abyss, indifferent to their passage. They drifted through celestial silence, lulled by its vastness.

Their days settled into a rhythm. Maintenance became meditation. They ran ship diagnostics and patched up microfractures, their hands busy while their minds wandered. Simulations filled the quiet hours — mostly tactical drills or hypothetical encounter scenarios. Sometimes they played just to distract themselves from the emptiness.

Hunter often thought of Guy Zephron on these long stretches. The famed asteroid retriever had found solace in Buddhism, meditating his way across space-time. But Hunter wasn't convinced anyone could meditate their way out of this kind of isolation. He'd discovered that regulation was key — strict sleep cycles, mental exercises, small rituals to keep their humanity intact.

Their sleeping quarters were tight, little more than narrow pods, but they offered privacy. Suspension restraints kept them from drifting in zero-G while they slept. Meals were a grim necessity — sterilized, flavorless packages promising optimal nutrition, but delivering little else. After a few days, both men had to force themselves to eat, resisting the creeping apathy that space so easily fed.

They played digital card games during downtime, their screens flickering with projected suits and scores, watched by Chester who intervened when somebody cheated. Chester's scheduled walks and playtime were taken care of by a bot when Hunter felt too busy or lethargic to do it himself.

Aboard the *SpaceSweeper*, Chester lived like a king—at least when it came to meals and bathroom breaks. While Hunter and Ved reviewed tactical overlays or argued over course corrections, Chester trotted over to his automatic feeder, the "FeedaBot-K9," and sat patiently as a soft chime signaled his next meal. The dispenser whirred to life, rotating its auger to drop a precise portion of kibble into a magnetized bowl that stayed anchored even during turbulence or low-grav maneuvers. The kibble clinked into place like clockwork, and only after Chester's collar tag pinged the system did the tray slide open.

No freeloaders allowed—not even Ved, who had once jokingly tried to trigger the dispenser with a spoon and a fake bark.

When nature called, Chester didn't need to whine at the airlock door. The ship's *SanPod* waste unit looked almost like a designer rug—magnetized to keep him steady, and smarter than half the crew. After he did his business, hidden sensors picked up the scent and heat signature, triggering a gentle vacuum that whisked the waste into a sealed compartment. A quick blast of UV light followed by an antiseptic mist kept the area spotless. Ved, always inquisitive, had once crouched beside it, muttering, "This thing has better hygiene protocols than Noel's lab."

Hunter just grinned and scratched behind Chester's ears. "Told you—he's the cleanest crew member we've got."

Despite the monotony, the two friends remained close, bonding over their shared experiences and dreams of what lay ahead. With Chester by their side, they often discussed their hopes for the future and what they would do once they finally reached their destination.

They had their silences, but they talked often — sometimes about the mission, but more often about what came after. About Earth. About who they used to be and who they hoped to become. Chester curled between them like a loyal ghost, his sensors glowing faintly in the dim light.

"I need to know," Ved said one evening, his voice low, almost reverent. He wasn't talking about coordinates or objectives. He was talking about himself — about the identity he'd lost or maybe never fully known. The truth waited somewhere out there, and he would find it, no matter what it cost.

Life aboard the *SpaceSweeper* fell into a careful, rigid rhythm — a pulse that kept their minds from unraveling. Each day was mapped, each hour accounted for. Emergency drills broke the monotony with sharp bursts of adrenaline: simulated hull breaches, oxygen leaks, sudden decompression warnings. The alarms came without warning, a shrill reminder that death in space was swift and unforgiving.

Hunter moved through these drills with mechanical precision, every muscle trained for the worst. But no amount of training dulled the awareness that one real emergency could be their last. They had no backup crew, no rapid-response team. Out here, they were it.

Their communication sessions with Earth were infrequent but vital — updates, recalibrated goals, flashes of the world they'd left behind.

Occasionally, a passing convoy would link with them, offering brief human contact: scientific findings exchanged like treasure, fresh coffee beans bartered like currency, playlists traded like relics from a world where music still played through open windows.

But it was the personal calls that mattered most to Hunter — the ones that chipped away at the loneliness. Bandwidth was scarce, and each call was brief, sacred.

He always called his family first. His sister's new war with sourdough starter; his father's latest attempt to train a recalcitrant bot or solve an astro puzzle. These calls were a lifeline, anchoring him to the rhythms of Earth life. He missed his mother deeply. It distressed him that he had not been at her funeral, a constant nage at the back of his mind.

But strangely nowadays she seemed to be with him in spirit and he thought of her often.

Then there was Kiana.

Her face flickered onto the screen like sunlight through a crack in a storm shelter. No matter how exhausted he felt, he never missed their calls. Her smile cut through the cold isolation of space with a warmth that made his chest ache.

"I miss you," she said each time, her voice soft and sure, like it was the one thing she knew for certain in a universe full of doubt.

"Miss you too," Hunter would whisper, the words weighted with all the things he couldn't say — not yet, not here.

Their calls were a dance: jokes and jabs, the intimacy of shared silences. She teased him about his scruffy look and zero-G bedhead; he asked about her projects, her friends, how Noel was adjusting to school. It wasn't just conversation. It was proof that life was still out there. That love still mattered.

But sometimes the lighthearted veneer cracked.

"What if something goes wrong out there?" she asked once, her eyes shining with the fear she usually kept tucked away.

"I'll be fine," Hunter replied, the lie slipping from his mouth before he could stop it. "We're trained for this."

And they were. But space didn't care about training.

After the calls ended, Hunter always lingered by the cockpit side porthole, watching the stars burn cold and distant beyond the hull. The drills, the data, the routines — they kept the mission alive.

But it was Kiana's voice, his family's laughter, Ved's determination, and the dream of return that reminded him what he was *fighting* for.

And why failure wasn't an option.

45

THE GUESTS

Bolinas, California, December 12, 2103

I N HER FIRST MONTHS of motherhood, Teagan experienced a vortex of conflicting emotions, ranging from moments of pure joy and overwhelming love for her new baby to extreme exhaustion and sleep deprivation, coupled with the shock and grief of losing her mother.

Julian's presence had helped to ease some of the burden. He'd turned out to be a good and thoughtful father. But at times, it also made her feel strangely guilty and unsure about her role as a mother.

So did the regular visits of Maureen and her robot partner, Harlee. Maureen, though retired, had taken to visiting them every week and staying for the lunch she prepared for them. Teagan wasn't sure when Maureen's visits had become a fixture in her life, but they carried an unspoken weight. Though Maureen always arrived with a warm smile and stories of the past, there was something watchful in her eyes, an attentiveness that went beyond casual affection for Diana. And then there was Harlee — silent, observant, always scanning, as if measuring something unseen.

Teagan told herself it was just concern, a retired scientist keeping an eye on an old friend's daughter. But sometimes, when Maureen held Diana a beat too long, or asked just a little too carefully about the baby's health, Teagan felt a prickle of unease.

As she struggled to find balance, she wondered if it would ever get easier, or if this constant rollercoaster was just the new normal.

She also grew to realize that Dr. César's approach had been a whole lot easier. Teagan's body felt heavy and drained from the long nights of feedings and comforting her crying baby. Her eyes were constantly heavy with dark circles due to a lack of sleep. Her body ached from the constant lifting and carrying of her baby. Her hair was disheveled, her muscles strained and tired from lack of sleep and self-care. The smell of wet diapers, baby milk, and baby lotion permeated every room of their small house, a constant reminder of her new role as a mother.

At least the touch of Julian's hand on her back brought a sense of comfort and support, easing the ache and exhaustion in her body, and Teagan marveled at how far they had come as parents. As the weeks progressed, she noticed Julian's unwavering dedication to being proactive in raising their daughter. He took on late-night feedings without complaint, learning to change diapers with precision and care. His gentle voice soothed their restless baby during fussy moments, bringing comfort to both mother and child.

Together, they navigated the challenges of parenthood hand in hand. Julian's calming presence brought a sense of stability to their chaotic days. During those moments, Teagan fell even more in love with him.

But as Julian settled into his role as a father, Teagan noticed a distance mysteriously starting to emerge between them. The constant demands and taxing routine drained them both. They looked tired. All they wanted was some decent sleep. The late nights and early mornings began to take their toll on their relationship; conversations were reduced to logistics and baby talk, and intimacy became a rare commodity. Teagan longed for the connection the two of them once had, but she was constantly exhausted and had noticed a severe loss of libido. She had recently halted breast-feeding; she felt fat and unsexy.

Having her own child had been Teagan's dream. But this was tougher than she had ever imagined.

One evening, as they sat side by side on the couch, Teagan mustered up the courage to break the silence that had enveloped their home like an unwelcome guest.

"Julian," she began softly. "I miss us."

Julian turned to face her, his eyes filled with a mix of surprise and sadness. He reached out and took her hand in his, sensing the pain in her words that mirrored his own.

"Don't worry," he said. "It will come back." He leaned across and kissed her gently.

To add to everything, Teagan was experiencing vivid and disturbing dreams in which she saw the Tritans in grave peril. In these dreams, she heard their desperate cries for help and felt an intense connection with them. The familiar octopus spirit summoned her. At first, she dismissed the dreams as a reflection of her distance from Julian. But as they persisted she became convinced that they were not just random subconscious imagery, but rather a message from the Tritans themselves. They were trying to reach out to her telepathically and draw her back to them for help.

Taking account of any personal problems for Teagan was not part of his game plan, so it was just a coincidence that Teagan was not at her most receptive.

Maybe Julian was right—maybe all she needed was to focus on their family, on Diana. But if the Tritans could give her answers... If helping them meant getting away from Maureen and Harlee's eerie watchfulness... Then perhaps it was time to stop resisting the call.

46
THE PRODIGAL SUN

East Africa, December 29, 2103

T HE SOLAR ECLIPSE OF December 29, 2103 was heralded as a celestial spectacle. Shiko thought it was a fitting tribute to mark Clara's passing. But for the secretive members of the eco-resistance group Green Dawn, it was the perfect cover for their coordinated strike against NIPAH.

The biotech giant, notorious for controlling Africa's seed supply through terminator seed technology, was a symbol of corporate exploitation to millions. The Green Dawn activists were determined to teach it a lesson it would never forget under the symbolic gaze of the concealed sun.

The attacks followed the sun, starting on Africa's east coast.

* * *

1. Dar es Salaam, Tanzania (EAT, Partial Begins: 7:30 AM) Obscuration: 90.80%, Maximum: 8:47 AM, Partial Ends: 10:19 AM

In Dar es Salaam, Green Dawn operatives targeted NIPAH's sprawling warehouse complex near the port in the city's Temeke district. As the sky darkened, flames rose from the facility, one of the company's largest hubs in East Africa, housing vast quantities of genetically modified, high-yield seeds bound for distribution across the continent.

The fire spread with terrifying speed, fueled by dry storage materials and poorly ventilated aisles crammed with crates. Workers fled the scene, shouting into their radios for help while others scrambled to shift shipping containers filled with volatile chemicals away from the encroaching inferno. Fire crews arrived, but struggled to contain the blaze as it began to spread beyond the warehouse to adjacent storage lots.

The warehouse was a critical link in NIPAH's supply chain. Its destruction sent shockwaves through the corporate offices in Lagos, where Dr. Chinelo, the company's Head of Operations, watched grainy footage of the fire from a security drone feed.

"This has the makings of a coordinated attack," she said, her voice clipped as she addressed the senior team assembled in her office. "Temeke is no accident. Alert the other offices that may be targets. Banjo, put out a statement. Also, I need Shiko to help with the monitoring."

Banjo Ade adjusted the lapels of his fitted, three-piece agbada, his calm demeanor masking the storm brewing within. "I'm tracking him down now, ma'am. He's not in his office, but I'll find him."

Chinelo's eyes burned into Banjo. "Find him fast. We need all hands on this."

Back in Dar es Salaam, the Green Dawn operative coordinating the attack observed the chaos from a vantage point across the port. Dressed as a dock worker, she blended seamlessly into the bustling crowd that had gathered to watch the flames. Her earpiece buzzed with updates from her team.

"Phase one is complete," one of her operatives reported. "Fire crews can't contain it."

The operative smirked. "Good. This will keep Chinelo busy while we prepare the next surprise."

As the fire raged on, it became clear that the damage was more than material. The loss of Temeke meant disruption across East Africa, sparking fears of food insecurity and rising tensions as NIPAH's monopoly came under direct attack.

* * *

2. Nairobi, Kenya (EAT, Partial Begins: 7:28 AM)
Obscuration: 89.32%, Maximum: 8:43 AM, Partial Ends: 10:13 AM

In Nairobi, Green Dawn operatives prepared to strike at NIPAH's seed-processing facility, timing their attack with the solar eclipse to maximize confusion and minimize visibility. The facility, located near the city's industrial heart, processed seeds bound for distribution across East Africa, making it a key target in Green Dawn's campaign against corporate exploitation.

At 7:30 AM, as the shadow of the eclipse crept across the city, Tandy gave the go-ahead from her temporary command center in Westlands. "Phase one. Mburu, you're up."

Mburu, dressed as a contracted delivery driver, maneuvered a rented van toward the facility gates. The guards, more interested in the dimming sunlight than their duty, barely glanced at his forged credentials before waving him through.

Once inside, Mburu parked the van in the central loading bay and began unloading crates marked "Specialized Equipment." Beneath the false labels lay explosives rigged to target the facility's seed-processing machinery and data servers. The other operatives, posing as workers, assisted him in planting the charges with swift precision.

"All clear," Mburu said over the comms as he stepped out of the facility, leaving the explosives hidden amidst the equipment. The workers inside, oblivious to the danger, continued their tasks in the dim and unnatural light.

At 8:43 AM, the eclipse reached its peak, casting the city into an eerie twilight. As the sun dimmed to a sliver, Mburu activated the fire alarms. A shrill wail pierced the air, sending workers scrambling for the exits. Their hurried movements masked the quiet escape of Green Dawn operatives slipping out amid the growing chaos.

Tandy's voice cut through the comms. "Phase two. Lights out."

Using a remote script uploaded to the city's power grid weeks earlier, the team triggered a localized blackout. Nairobi's industrial district plunged into darkness, and the facility's backup generators faltered under a pre-emptive cyberattack.

"Detonate," Tandy ordered.

Mburu pressed the detonator. A thunderous explosion tore through the facility, shaking the ground. Fire and debris erupted into the sky, casting an ominous glow against the eclipse's dim light. Storage silos collapsed in flames, and the seed-processing machinery lay in ruins. Smoke rose into the unnatural twilight, blending with the darkened skies.

"Mission accomplished," Tandy said, her tone calm despite the destruction. "Disperse and regroup."

Mburu abandoned the van in a nearby alley, shedding his uniform and blending into the streets. The rest of the team followed their escape routes, vanishing into Nairobi's labyrinth of neighborhoods. Safe houses throughout the city awaited them, stocked with fresh IDs and supplies for their next steps.

As the eclipse faded and the sun's light returned, the industrial district of Nairobi remained shrouded in chaos and smoke. The attack delivered a devastating blow to NIPAH, but Green Dawn's operatives knew the retaliation would be relentless. For now, they savored their hard-won success, even as the fight against corporate tyranny pressed on.

***

3. Kigali, Rwanda (EAT, Partial Begins: 6:26 AM)
Obscuration: 95.41%, Maximum: 7:35 AM, Partial Ends: 8:57 AM
The first strike began early in Kigali, where the sun's partial obscuration coincided with the start of the working day. The local Green Dawn cell, led by agronomist Lila Mwamba, infiltrated NIPAH's regional facility under the guise of delivery drivers.

The steel towers of the Kigali silo complex glinted like modern cathedrals in the early morning sun; strong, galvanized corrugated bins for storing valuable resources. The grain silos were just the surface dressing providing the entrance to a huge underground complex and network of climate-adjusted storage facilities.

Using drones, they deployed EMP charges to knock out the facility's security systems.

"We need those vaults open before maximum obscuration," Lila instructed as her team hacked into the climate-controlled seed storage units.

Inside, they planted incendiary devices while Lila downloaded incriminating files from the company's secure servers; the team left the premises minutes before the first explosion sent shockwaves through the facility. By the time the eclipse ended, the storage center was ablaze, and NIPAH's proprietary seed reserves had been destroyed.

***

4. Kampala, Uganda (EAT, Partial Begins: 7:26 AM)
Obscuration: 89.30%, Maximum: 8:37 AM, Partial Ends: 10:02 AM

In Kampala, the Green Dawn Collective targeted NIPAH's communications hub, a local ringleader leading a team disguised as maintenance contractors. During the eclipse's darkest moments, they installed malware to disrupt the company's satellite uplinks.

"Go, go, go," Tandy urged from her base in Nairobi as Kevan, a contractor with inside knowledge, bypassed the firewalls. "They'll never know what hit them."

The malware severed NIPAH's regional links to its headquarters, sowing chaos in the company's logistical operations. As the eclipse waned, the team erased their tracks and exited undetected, leaving the facility paralyzed.

* * *

5. Bangui, Central African Republic (WAT, Sunrise: 5:51 AM)
Obscuration: 95.29%, Maximum: 6:28 AM, Partial Ends: 7:40 AM

In Bangui, the Green Dawn Collective relied on a cyberattack rather than physical infiltration. As the sun rose partially obscured, operatives remotely accessed NIPAH's central database, corrupting decades of research data on genetically modified crops.

"We're in," confirmed Etienne, the lead hacker, as he watched terabytes of sensitive files disappear from the servers.

By 7:03 AM, NIPAH's research center was in chaos. Its systems had been rendered inoperable, the company unable to recover years of work.

* * *

6. Abuja, Nigeria (WAT, Sunrise: 6:43 AM)
Obscuration: 60.89%, Maximum: 6:45 AM, Partial Ends: 7:31 AM

The major staple crops in Nigeria were cassava, yam, maize, sorghum, rice, and millet. The Abuja plant housed all of them, along with cowpea, groundnut, cocoa, oil palm, cotton, ginger, sesame, and various vegetables.

With limited eclipse visibility, Abuja's attack relied on speed. The Green Dawn cell hacked into local advertising networks, projecting anti-NIPAH propaganda on public billboards. Hacked footage revealed the company's exploitation of farmers and ecosystems.

"You want the truth? Here it is!" blared the message, accompanied by chilling visuals of barren fields and displaced communities.

The operation ended before 7:31 AM as the eclipse faded and police began mobilizing in response to the unexpected broadcast.

* * *

7. Lagos, Nigeria (WAT, 8:43 AM)

During the coordinated Green Dawn attacks, Shiko maintained his cover at NIPAH's regional headquarters in Lagos, working in his role as a mid-level operations analyst that he'd been assigned, along with the occasional food trials visit. His duties involved monitoring supply chain logistics and overseeing shipments of proprietary seed stock across West Africa.

As the first reports of explosions and fires came in, Shiko played the part of the stunned employee, fielding frantic calls from regional managers and feeding updates to the Lagos crisis response team. Making a calculated effort to blend into the chaos, he stood among the gathered employees near the main operations console, his brow furrowed in mock disbelief as live feeds of the burning Nairobi facility flashed across the screens.

"This can't be real," he muttered to a colleague, his voice tinged with just the right amount of shock. "Who would dare hit NIPAH like this? During the eclipse, no less!"

When Dr. Chinelo stormed into the room, barking orders and demanding updates, Shiko stepped forward with a hesitant nod. "I just got word from the Kampala manager," he reported, feigning concern. "Communication's down completely."

Inside, he felt the tension mounting, knowing that every second he appeared convincingly rattled brought the Green Dawn teams closer to success.

While others scrambled in panic, Shiko discreetly monitored encrypted Green Dawn communications on his hidden terminal, ensuring the operation was unfolding as planned. His composure under pressure drew no suspicion, even as NIPAH executives began tightening internal security and questioning staff.

As news of the coordinated attacks swept through NIPAH's Lagos headquarters, the boardroom erupted into a cacophony of hurried conversations and ringing comms. Screens along the walls displayed live feeds from Nairobi, Dar es Salaam, and other key sites under attack. Smoke billowed from the Temeke district warehouse in Dar es Salaam, while reports of a blackout in Nairobi added to the growing chaos.

Dr. Chinelo stood at the head of the table, her calm exterior betraying only the slightest edge of frustration. She tapped a command into the holographic interface, and a map of the affected regions hovered in mid-air.

"This is more than a simple attack," she said, her voice icy with resolve. "This is systematic. Coordinated. I want every detail on the table. Banjo -- find the breach. Shiko's name keeps coming up, and I'm beginning to think it's not a coincidence. Damilola, ensure all key personnel are accounted for."

Damilola nodded briskly, her fingers already working her tablet. "Security protocols are tightening across all of our facilities, ma'am. Flights grounded, ports sealed. Lagos is on high alert."

Banjo leaned back in his chair, the faintest smirk tugging at the corners of his lips. "Shiko, you say? He's been laying low. Always thought he was a little too clean-cut for his own good."

"Then find him," Dr. Chinelo snapped, slamming a palm on the table. "If he's involved in this, I want proof. If he's not, I want to know why he's still breathing."

Without another word, Banjo adjusted his cuffs and rose from his seat. "Consider it done."

As he strode out of the boardroom, he caught glimpses of the unfolding chaos on the screens, security footage from Nairobi's shattered seed facility, panicked workers fleeing the Temeke warehouse inferno. Somewhere in the shadows of this operation, Shiko was pulling strings.

Shiko, meanwhile, was huddled near his workstation, watching another wave of frantic corporate updates pour in from Nairobi, when his smartwatch buzzed with an encrypted message, brief but unmistakable: ***LKP, Bay 4. Window: 30 min. Activate Code 3.***

He froze for a moment. The escape plan was in motion. Green Dawn had anticipated the crackdown in NIPAH and arranged for his extraction.

Casually, Shiko tapped his smartwatch, activating a pre-arranged script that would mask his absence. An automated alert popped up on his terminal: *"Shiko Tanaka –– Emergency Systems Check, Basement Level 3."*

Turning to his supervisor, he kept his expression neutral. "They need me downstairs to reset the servers," he said. "The last thing we need is a local outage while all this is happening."

The supervisor barely acknowledged him, waving him off as she remained glued to the disaster unfolding onscreen. He slipped out to the toilet, to wash his face in the sink.

But Shiko froze mid-splash when he felt the weight of Banjo Ade's gaze pressing down on him like a physical force. The mirrored tiles of the corporate building's restroom gleamed with sterile brightness, reflecting Banjo's sharply dressed figure as he leaned against the doorframe. His agbada, perfectly tailored, shimmered faintly under the fluorescent lights, an unsettling contrast to the grim look in his eyes.

"Dr. Chinelo wants a word," Banjo said, his tone conversational but carrying an edge that cut through the silence. He stepped forward, his oxfords clicking ominously against the tiles. "Word is, you've been keeping interesting company. Some familiar names: Green Dawn. Talabi Adedamola (aka Tandy). Do you have a death wish, or just a talent for stupidity?"

Shiko's hands trembled as he grabbed a paper towel. "I don't know what you're talking about," he muttered, avoiding Banjo's eyes in the mirror.

Banjo laughed softly; a sound devoid of humor. He reached into his pocket and pulled out a slim comms device, tossing it onto the counter beside Shiko with an audible clack. The device flickered to life, displaying surveillance footage of one of the Green Dawn's attacks on NIPAH. Amid the smoke, a figure resembling Tandy moved through the shadows, a bag clutched to her chest.

"That your friend?" Banjo asked, his voice dropping. "Or does she have a twin who likes playing with terrorists?"

Shiko's pulse thundered in his ears. His mind raced for an explanation, an excuse, anything to buy time. But Banjo's eyes pinned him in place.

"Relax," Banjo said, straightening his cuffs. "I'm giving you five minutes. Chinelo wants you interrogated, but me?" He smirked. "I don't feel like babysitting. You run, and this becomes someone else's mess."

Shiko blinked, disbelief crossing his face. "Why would you let me go?"

Banjo's smile widened. "Because I'm not in the mood to clean blood off my suit. Now, get lost."

For a second, Shiko didn't move. Then Banjo's fingers twitched toward the comms device, as if to summon reinforcements, and Shiko bolted.

He burst into the hallway, his breath ragged as alarms blared overhead. At the stairwell, a burly security guard blocked his path, his hand hovering over his holster. "Stop right there!"

Shiko didn't think. Adrenaline took over. He lunged forward, grabbing the guard's wrist and slamming it against the rail. The man grunted, his weapon clattering to the floor. Shiko's other hand found the back of the guard's head and drove it into the metal edge of the stairwell. A sickening crunch echoed through the space as the guard crumpled, blood pooling beneath him.

Shiko staggered back, staring at the lifeless body. His stomach churned, but the sound of approaching footsteps snapped him out of it. He grabbed the guard's access card and sprinted down the stairs, his mind screaming at him to keep moving.

He could not go back now. He was a wanted man. Banjo's warning echoed in his ears. Five minutes wasn't much time, but it was enough, if he kept moving.

Shiko hurried through the building, exiting through a side entrance that led to a secure parking lot. Almost as soon as he did so, he heard a guard bark out, "Spread out. He can't have gone far."

Panicked, he commandeered a company motorbike and, after a little hesitation, sped off, weaving through the congested streets of Lagos toward the Lekki Peninsula. The message had been clear: Bay 4 was the extraction point.

47

THE GET AWAY

Lagos, December 29, 2103

SHIKO'S HANDS GRIPPED THE motorcycle's handles like a vice, his knuckles white beneath the leather gloves he had found on the saddle. Behind him, the wail of sirens grew louder, cutting through the chaotic hum of Lagos's streets.

A glance in the side mirror revealed two black SUVs closing in fast. Their lights flashed ominously and Shiko knew they would be broadcasting his photo across the city by now. The streets pulsed with life: yellow danfos swerving with little regard, vendors shouting their wares, pedestrians weaving through traffic like fish darting through coral.

He quickly realized he didn't know what he was doing. The bike was like an angry monster. He had never ridden a bike before; he'd only seen one in the moves he watched on Quivira and on his virtual reality headset.

The throttle was too sensitive, the brakes too stubborn, and every pothole sent a jolt up his spine. The bike bucked under him like a wild animal, protesting his clumsy commands.

"Left is clutch, right is brake... or is it the other way round?" he muttered through gritted teeth, sweat pouring down his temples despite the breeze.

He barely missed a keke three-wheeler veering into his path, the driver cursing and shaking a fist. Shiko didn't look back. The sirens were close now—too close. Fear sharpened his senses. He cut through a red light, nearly colliding with a delivery van. Horns blared. People screamed. A dog barked and chased him for a second before giving up.

Little by little, with each swerve and pothole, he began to understand the machine beneath him. If he leaned just a bit into the turn, the bike didn't feel so much like it wanted to throw him off. If he rolled the throttle instead of yanking it, the acceleration was smoother. He wasn't *riding* yet—he was surviving. But every meter taught him something.

He shot down a side street, narrowly missing a stack of water sachets being offloaded from a tricycle. The narrow alley forced him to slow, his tires spitting up dust and litter. His arms ached from the tension. His mind raced, calculating routes, guessing the next move.

He needed a place to disappear. Fast.

A market? No, too open. Mainland bridge? A death trap if they boxed him in. Then he saw it—a narrow, sloping path behind a line of kiosks, leading down toward a canal. It was risky. Slippery. Unpredictable.

Perfect.

With a hard yank, he turned the handlebars and plunged into the path, the bike fishtailing as loose sand betrayed the tires. He felt it tipping, overcorrected, nearly dumped the whole thing—but caught it at the last second, heart in his throat. Behind him, the sirens hesitated. The alley was too narrow for squad cars. Maybe they'd follow on foot. Maybe not.

Shiko didn't wait to find out. He pushed forward, praying the path didn't dead-end.

As he disappeared into the tangle of Lagos's underbelly, a wild grin cracked across his face. He was still alive. Still learning.

And for the first time that day, *almost* in control.

He gunned the throttle, weaving through the maze of bright yellow minibuses and okada motorcycle taxis clogging the road. The scent of burning rubber and fumes filled the air. A vendor screamed as Shiko narrowly avoided a cart stacked with oranges, scattering them across the pavement. The sleek black SUVs were relentless, forcing their way through traffic like predators closing in on their prey. He couldn't outrun them for long.

Luckily, Shiko spotted an opening — a lumbering dump truck ahead, its cargo tarp flapping in the wind. He leaned hard to the left, slipping behind the truck just as a burst of gunfire shattered the side mirror of his bike.

"Damn it," he muttered.

He braked hard, skidding to a stop in the truck's blind spot. With one fluid motion, Shiko abandoned the bike and climbed into a nearby dumpster, barely suppressing a grunt of pain as he landed among discarded food wrappers and broken crates. Inside, the air was rank, but Shiko forced himself to stay still.

Moments later, the SUVs screeched to a halt nearby.

"He dumped the bike!" one of the men barked.

"Spread out! He can't have gone far!"

Shiko heard boots hitting the pavement, the team fanning out. His heart thudded in his chest as he pressed himself against the slimy metal wall of the dumpster. Through a crack, he could see one of the men pacing close by.

After what felt like an eternity, the group moved farther down the street, their voices fading into the cacophony of Lagos. Shiko crept out of the dumpster, landing silently in an alley. He quickly shed his jacket and grabbed a baseball cap from a nearby stall. Disguised enough to buy him a few minutes, he slipped into the crowd.

At a parking lot near a mechanic's shop, he spotted a dented, nondescript van. Perfect. The alarms stayed silent as he hotwired the engine. The van coughed to life, and Shiko drove it into the current of Lagos traffic, where the vehicle blended seamlessly into the chaos. Honking horns, street vendors balancing trays of goods on their heads, and pedestrians darting across the road gave him cover as he snaked through the city.

When he reached the Lekki-Ikoyi Link Bridge, its iconic cables stretched against the darkened, clouded sky, Shiko allowed himself a brief glance back toward the skyline of Victoria Island. The gleaming buildings of NIPAH headquarters were barely visible through the haze, but the sight reinforced his determination.

His grip tightened. "Just thirty minutes," he muttered to himself. "I can make it."

The van's tires hummed over the bridge, the Atlantic glimmering faintly to his right. In the distance, Lekki's industrial sprawl began to take shape. The clock was ticking, and Shiko knew he had to reach Bay 4 before it was too late.

Suddenly, his rearview mirror caught movement — another SUV, its sleek black form cutting through traffic like a shark. They'd found him again.

Cursing under his breath, Shiko floored the accelerator pedal. The van surged forward, weaving recklessly around slower vehicles. A danfo ahead veered sharply, its passengers yelling in alarm as Shiko barreled past. Behind him, the SUV was gaining, its sirens wailing.

Ahead, the turnoff to the hidden warehouse came into view, a narrow, un-marked road flanked by construction barriers. Shiko swerved onto it without hesitation, the van rattling as it hit the uneven pavement. The SUV, on an outside lane, missed the turn, braking abruptly and hitting other traffic.

Shiko didn't wait to see if they recovered. He drove straight until the metal gates of the compound sealed shut behind him. The van screeched to a halt outside a nondescript warehouse, its faded signage advertising "Maritime Storage Solutions."

Inside, the warehouse front appeared ordinary: Stacks of cargo crates, forklifts parked idly, and an oily smell that clung to the air. But as he moved toward the back, a discreet panel in the wall slid aside, revealing an industrial lift. Shiko stepped in, the platform descending into the depths beneath Lekki's reclaimed land.

The underground hangar was a stark contrast to the gritty façade above. Harsh white lights illuminated a vast space where engineers moved like clockwork around the centerpiece: A sleek, obsidian-black spacecraft, its surface shimmering faintly under the artificial glow.

One of the Green Dawn members, a woman named Imani, was waiting near the craft, her arms crossed. She gave Shiko a sharp look as he approached.

"Cutting it close, aren't you?"

Shiko gave a breathless chuckle. "You wouldn't believe the day I've had."

"Save it for the Moon," she shot back, gesturing toward the sleek spacecraft waiting for him in Bay 4.

"Wow! This is unexpected," Shiko said, wiping his forehead.

"This spot's been perfect," responded Imani. "Lekki's constant noise and chaos keep prying eyes away, and the underground layers give us plenty of space to work. The pod's shielded from satellite detection, too — cloaked, just like you'll be when you launch."

Shiko stepped closer, marveling at the craft's design. "What about maintenance?" he asked. Imani pointed toward a team of technicians swarming around the vehicle like bees.

"We've been running full system checks every six hours. Thrust stabilizers are state-of-the-art. The heat shields will hold, even if you push the engines hard. The cloaking system? It's military-grade. Noel wasn't kidding when he said he'd spare no expense. He must need you back, a lot."

Shiko let his hand trail along the smooth, cold hull of the escape pod. "And fuel?"

"Cryogenic tanks are topped up. You'll break through the atmosphere in less than four minutes. After that, it's a straight shot to the Moon. Your window is tight, fifteen minutes before orbital drift screws your trajectory." Imani handed him a datapad, her sharp eyes narrowing. "This route has been calculated down to the second. Don't stray, or you're on your own."

Shiko nodded, taking a deep breath. As he climbed into the cockpit, he turned to look at Imani one last time. "Thanks," he said, his voice subdued.

She smirked. "Thank me when you're at Tricala."

The cockpit hummed to life as Shiko powered up the controls. Through the viewport, he could see the hangar's roof retracting, revealing a dark sky above dotted with stars. The engines roared to life, a vibration coursing through the craft as it lifted off the platform.

"Goodbye, Lagos," Shiko muttered as the vehicle shot upward, piercing the air and vanishing into the heavens.

The shuttle broke through the atmosphere in a blaze of light. But as the stars stretched out before him, endless and foreboding, Shiko knew the real fight was only beginning.

After a while, he was able to contact Tricala; Noel came on the radio.

"I'm on my way," Shiko said.

"Good," Noel answered through the communicator. "Shiko, listen carefully. Once you're in orbit, our base on the Moon will pull your craft in using manual guidance. Don't try anything stupid."

"When have I ever done that?" Shiko smirked.

"All the time," Noel retorted. "Good luck. And Shiko?"

"Yeah?"

"Don't forget who saved your ass."

* * *

A few hours later, in New York, GLOSCOM announced that in response to the appalling destruction of NIPAH facilities in East and Central Africa, and in support of local farmers, it would be taking over all African operations.

48
THE LETTER

Malapert, December 29, 2103

NOEL WAS OVERWHELMED BY the tributes for Clara that flowed in from colleagues on the space habitats, on Earth, at stations on the Moon, from colleagues on Mars and beyond.

Scenes from their past played in Noel's mind like an endless reel. From the early days when they first met to the joyous moments when Hunter and Teagan were born, their first steps, their first day at school... Every memory with Clara etched itself vividly.

Noel's grief was not just for Clara; it was for the dreams they had woven together and the legacy they had sought to build. The guilt that had lingered within him, the secrets he had harbored now manifested as haunting specters in the wake of Clara's absence.

Had he brought this down on them? Had he caused her death by befriending an alien species?

Of course not. He had studied the Tritans. This was not their work. It must have been another group. He'd see their vile forms on the video replay. They could have come at any time.

Alone, he looked through some of Clara's papers and files. Most of it was about work on her precious seeds. But then he came across an envelope addressed to him:

Noel — for when the time comes.
It looked fairly new.
He turned it over in his hands.

Why had she written to him like this? Did she know she was about to die?
He opened it carefully.

My dearest Noel,

If you're reading this, then the time I feared has arrived. I always imagined we'd have more time—to talk, to forgive, to face the truth together. But life, as ever, is more abrupt than we hope.

I know you'll find most of my notes obsessed with the vault and the seeds. That was my shield. My way of avoiding the one truth that mattered more: I kept things from you. Things I should've said long ago.

You were the one I trusted most. That's what makes this hardest.

You must take over now and lead the fight. Of course, I knew about your little deceptions, the compromises you have made. But I understood why. And still I said nothing. Because I was scared. Scared of losing you. Scared of what it would mean for us, scared for our divided family.

You once told me truth was a form of love. I didn't understand that until I compromised on both.

I should have fought harder against GLOSCOM, against the Consortium, but I kept telling myself I could fix things from the inside. That the seeds could still mean something pure. But they twisted even that. I should have fought harder for us, for our family.

And Diana—she's not just a child, Noel. She's the echo of everything we hoped for, and everything we have failed to protect. She's why I'm writing this now.

You have to be better than I was. Don't bury yourself in regrets or missions. Be there for Teagan and her. She will need you more than she'll ever admit. And you may be the only one who can help her understand what she is—and what she's not.

There's data in the drive I've enclosed—yes, I still trust you with that part. It will help. But more than that, I want you to remember the person you were before the Consortium wrapped its fingers around our work. Before ambition dulled your questions. Before we both started keeping secrets.

Please, don't let this end in bitterness or vengeance. Let it end in clarity.

And maybe—if the stars are kind—redemption.

With all the love I never said out loud,

Clara

Noel's forehead creased with uncertainty and tears welled in his eyes. He re-read the letter with increasing anxiety and pain. Why hadn't she confided in him? Why write a letter instead of just having a conversation? Maybe it would have been too difficult? Did she think he was on the other side, or was this a warning?

He turned the encryption key over in his hands, wondering where this data would lead him. But he decided not to open the accompanying data files for now. Too much sensitive information in one day might tip him over the edge.

Noel found himself at a crossroads. He knew Clara's legacy now rested on his shoulders. Her death had unraveled the threads of secrecy he had woven, even without him realizing it, and the guilt now festering within him demanded a reckoning. The shadows of compromise and clandestine alliances haunted his every step, a stark contrast to the luminescent glow of the Earth hanging in the lunar sky.

He vowed to make Clara proud, but he would need help.

The old team from Quivira. He knew that Shiko, Tara, and Liam would be able to help him with the Lattice.

49

THE FAR SIDE

Tricala, December 30, 2103

SHIKO'S DESCENT WAS SMOOTH, the engines humming a familiar tune as Tricala's domed habitats came into view. The lunar base was stark against the gray expanse, a bastion of science and discovery in the shadow of the Moon's far side.

Shiko felt a weight lift from his shoulders as he approached. It wasn't just an escape from Lagos or the specter of Green Dawn's attacks, it was a homecoming, a return to purpose after months mired in the corporate labyrinth of GLOSCOM's operations.

The airlock hissed as he stepped inside Noel's observatory. A mix of antiseptic cleanliness and the acrid smell of lunar regolith dust greeted him, punctuated by the subtle hum of the base's fusion core.

Noel's laboratory was exactly as he imagined: sterile white surfaces cluttered with cables, holographic displays, and the faint glow of diagnostic readouts. The centerpiece of the lab was the projection of a spherical interface, its pulsing patterns reminiscent of a living neural network.

"Shiko!" Noel's voice was a mix of relief and exhaustion as he emerged from behind a terminal. His hair, combed back hastily, betrayed the long hours he'd been working. "About time you got here. I was starting to think I'd have to send a drone to drag you back."

Shiko chuckled. "I figured Lagos was dramatic enough. Didn't want to complicate your clean-room protocols with extra bullet holes."

Noel snorted. "The Moon has enough craters, thanks. Welcome back. Though I don't think you've been here, have you?"

"No, sir, only to the lab in Quivira."

"Well, you're just in time. We've made progress, but I've hit a wall decoding the recursive data clusters. GLOSCOM's servers didn't fry your brain, I hope?"

Shiko stepped closer to the projection, his eyes tracing the lattice's intricate geometry. "I could say the same about you. This looks... alive."

"It's a step beyond alive," Noel said, pulling up a data feed. "We think the Lattice is more than just a map or database. It's reactive, adaptive. Each time we simulate an input, it alters its structure. My theory is that it's designed to interface with conscious thought."

Shiko frowned. "You're saying it's some kind of psychic network?"

Noel shook his head. "Not psychic — quantum. It's built to recognize patterns of thought, intention, and focus. It's why we've made so little progress without more brains on it. That's where you come in."

Shiko raised an eyebrow. "You want me to think at it?"

"I want you to observe," Noel said, grinning. "But yes, thinking wouldn't hurt. Start with the Lattice's primary node patterns. They remind me of neural firings, and I know your knack for spotting behavioral correlations."

Shiko stepped up to the console, rolling his shoulders as if shaking off the weight of months away. The terminal responded to his touch like an old friend, displaying streams of data, patterns cascading across the interface.

"Good to be back in a real lab," he murmured, feeling the familiarity of the work seep into him.

Noel leaned in, his voice low and urgent. "For defense against the Draxid, the Sigillaria plants are the key. Their resonances sync with the Lattice's base frequencies, creating a feedback loop that amplifies the energy field. But it's unstable, and I haven't figured out how to harmonize the output. I need you to help bridge the gap, link their biological signals to the Lattice's quantum framework."

Shiko's eyes narrowed as he scanned the data streams. "Sigillaria... You're talking about bioresonant energy coupling? That's innovative, Noel. Dangerous too. You're messing with an organic system that could backlash if it's overloaded."

"Believe me, I know," Noel replied, rubbing his temples. "That's why we're not testing this outside the lab until we get it perfect. But if we can stabilize the link, the applications are limitless. A planetary shield, self-repairing infrastructure, maybe even large-scale energy generation. We could rewrite the rules of defense and survival."

Shiko let out a low whistle. "You're not aiming low, are you? Fine, let's see what we've got." He tapped a series of commands into the console, bringing up a holographic overlay of the Sigillaria energy patterns. The plants' unique biofeedback danced like glowing filaments, pulsating in sync with the Lattice's nodes.

"See that?" Noel pointed to a cluster of erratic signals. "That's where the instability kicks in. The plants are overloading the local nodes. The energy spike disrupts the Lattice's quantum framework before it can distribute the load evenly."

Shiko studied the visualization. "It's like the plants are trying to communicate, but the Lattice doesn't speak their language. The signal's too pure, too linear. The Lattice needs something to interpret it."

"Exactly," Noel said, snapping his fingers. "That's why I think it might be designed for conscious thought. The Sigillaria are perfect energy generators via Trita Prime's crystals, but they don't have the variability to mesh with the Lattice's adaptive design. If we could introduce an intermediary layer, something to modulate the signal..."

Shiko grinned. "You're thinking use a human brain to translate the plants' resonance into a form the Lattice can process."

"Not just a neural link to one brain," Noel said, his excitement growing. "A distributed network. Multiple minds, each contributing their unique pattern to stabilize the system. It's risky, but it could work."

"Risky is an understatement," Shiko said, though there was a glimmer of intrigue in his eyes. "You're talking about interfacing live brains with an alien quantum network and bioenergy source. That's a recipe for disaster if anything goes wrong."

"I know the stakes," Noel said, his voice firm. "But this isn't only about science, it's about survival. If the Draxid or GLOSCOM figure out the Lattice's potential before we do, it's over. We need to be ahead of them."

Shiko nodded slowly. "All right, I'll bite. But we do this my way: Carefully, methodically, and with plenty of fail-safes. First step, we run simulations of the neural interface. No live testing until we're absolutely sure it won't fry someone's brain."

"Agreed," Noel said, relief clear on his face. "Let's get started." Noel clapped him on the shoulder. "Don't get too comfortable though. Kat's here too."

The name hit Shiko like a solar flare. He stiffened, then turned to Noel. "Kat's here?"

"Arrived for Clara's funeral and has stayed on. She says you're expecting her.""Why didn't you tell me?"

Noel just grinned.

Shiko found Kat in the greenhouse module, surrounded by rows of bioluminescent fungi and hydroponic plants. She was sitting cross-legged on a workbench, a tablet in her lap, her dark hair catching the soft glow of the plants around her.

"Katrina," he said, his voice catching slightly.

She looked up, startled at first, but her expression softened when she saw him. "Shiko."

He stepped forward, unsure of what to say. It had been months since he'd seen her. The protests, GLOSCOM, Lagos, the eclipse — they had all carved spaces between them that felt insurmountable. But now, standing in the lunar greenhouse, the distance felt trivial.

"You're really here," he said finally.

Kat set the tablet aside and stood, her movements measured. "I could say the same. Last I heard, you were on the run from the Nigerian authorities."

"Still am," he admitted, then hesitated. "But when I heard you were here... I couldn't stay away," he said, laughing at his own joke.

She crossed her arms, studying him. "Is that so? You're not here for Noel's research?"

"I'm here for both," he said, stepping closer. "But mostly you."

Her posture softened, and she smiled faintly. "Still the smooth talker."

Shiko laughed. "I've been anything but smooth lately. But I missed you, Kat. I thought about you every day."

For a moment, the only sound was the faint hum of the greenhouse's systems. Then she closed the distance between them and wrapped her arms around him. He held her tightly, feeling the tension of the past months dissolve.

"You're here now," she whispered. "That's what matters."

"And you are too! How did that happen?"

He leaned forward hesitantly, caught between the yearning that had grown during the time they had been apart and the uncertainty that lingered from their earlier time together. His hand cradled her cheek, fingers gently caressing the skin as he pulled her in for the kiss, a mixture of longing and desire built up over the long days and nights of separation.

As they stood, surrounded by philodendrons and luminescent plants and the quiet hum of Tricala's life support systems, Shiko felt a renewed sense of purpose. The Astral Lattice was important, but so was this, a connection he thought he may have lost, now rediscovered on the far side of the Moon.

Then, as he stood holding Kat and surrounded by plants, he realized that you didn't need brains to make the Lattice work. The plants would be the transmitters, connected by their roots.

50

THE SANCTUARY

Sythra, Trita Prime, March 2105

THE SIGILLARIA TREES, RAISED from the cones in Clara's vault, grew fast. Soon, they blanketed the surface of Trita Prime just like in the old days. The plants were fed a diet of special hormones along with liquid fertilizer, and coddled with a combination of mulch, compost, and ultraviolet light to spur their growth.

The trunks were topped with a plume of long, spiky, grass-like microphyllous leaves that looked like a brush. These leaves attached directly to the stem of the tree, with an inner pith protected by diamond-shaped scales on the outside. The roots of the trees reached down and interlocked with the celestonite crystals beneath the planet's surface.

With the right encouragement, led by the incantations of a priestess, the crystals would be able to transmit a force through the trees and create a protective ring around the planet..

"They are the key to our consciousness," Asmegin had said, "like a third eye for our planet."

This unique connection between the trees and the celestonite crystals formed the backbone of the protective ring, but Noel and the others found it could be honed and amplified through the Astral Lattice. The Lattice, as it turned out, was a universal network, a web of cosmic energy that linked disparate systems across the universe. Noel saw its potential applications as almost limitless.

The resonance nodes, by contrast, were localized phenomena — a derivative of the Lattice that allowed for the precise manipulation of energy through specific focal points, such as the Sigillaria trees. These nodes were integral to the planned defense system, but they were merely tools compared to the Lattice's greater potential.

While the Tritans had devised the initial concept of harnessing the nodes for planetary protection, it was Noel's insights that revealed how the nodes could serve as gateways to broader applications.

Noel's team brought expertise in cosmological physics and resonance mechanics, an evolving field largely ignored by traditional Tritan sciences.

After Noel's team arrived, together with the Tritan leadership, they began to devise a defense system to protect the planet. By channeling the buried crystals' resonance through the Sigillaria plants, they created a protective barrier powered by the cosmic frequencies.

The Tritans, though technologically advanced, lacked the strategic experience that Noel, Shiko, Liam, and Tara brought, making their collaboration essential. Noel thought of the Tritans as similar to a finely-tuned instrument without a skilled musician to play it. The unique blend of Noel's cunning, Shiko's quick thinking, Liam's calculated precision, and Tara's unwavering determination would bring harmony and success to their collaborative efforts.

Further testing revealed that the Draxid, reliant on advanced scanners, were vulnerable to specific resonant frequencies. By tuning the shield to emit a secondary pulse at 963 Hz, they were able to create a "dead zone" around the Tritan settlements, rendering them invisible to enemy sensors.

Together they worked hard to produce a workable system.

The final activation was a tense moment. As Noel calibrated the resonance, the Sigillaria plants glowed faintly, their shimmering leaves vibrating in harmony with the buried crystals. The shield pulsed into life, creating a protective field that rippled like liquid light.

Shiko observed in silence before speaking. "This is more than technology," he said. "It's harmony — nature and science working together."

Later, Noel addressed the Tritan leadership. "The Astral Lattice is more than a weapon," he said. "It's a connection to something greater, something that must be protected. If its power is abused, it could destroy just as easily as it defends."

The Tritans agreed, vowing to safeguard the knowledge. Their newfound harmony with the Lattice became more than a tool for survival — in their minds, it was a symbol of unity, preservation, and hope for a galaxy in turmoil. "Next, we need our priestess to help channel the power," Asmegin said.

Teagan would be essential to this endeavor, not for her technical knowledge but for her unique role as an interpreter of the planet's historical and ecological systems. Her deep understanding of the ancient Sigillaria forests and her ability to communicate with the High Council would be critical in securing both political and material support for the project.

* * *

Teagan's arrival in Sythra was an event few had witnessed previously. The Tritan city buzzed with an unspoken anticipation, its spires shimmering faintly under the planet's twin suns. The streets, paved with plates of reflective crystal, mirrored the sky's soft blush, creating the illusion that the city itself floated amidst the heavens.

Teagan stepped out of the transport shuttle, cradling Diana in her arms. The baby gurgled softly, her bright, curious eyes reflecting the light that bathed the city. Julian stood beside her, his stance protective but unobtrusive, carrying a pack of essentials for the journey. His gaze darted between the crowd of Tritans that had gathered and the spires beyond, marveling at the intricate latticework of their architecture.

The Tritans, with their red exoskeletons and delicate antennae, parted like a tide as Teagan approached. Their eyes—multifaceted and sparkling—watched her with a mixture of reverence and curiosity. It wasn't often that an outsider walked among them, let alone one carrying a child. Whispers flitted through the crowd, a melodic hum in their native tongue. Teagan didn't understand the words, but she could feel their warmth, their hope.

From the crowd emerged Thynidal, a high-ranking Tritan, his antennae adorned with ceremonial gold bands. His gait was smooth and deliberate, his presence commanding yet serene. He bowed slightly before addressing her, his voice carrying the melodic cadence of his species.

"Teagan Ward," he said, inclining his head toward her and the baby nestled in her arms. "Welcome. You have helped us before. We are grateful you have returned. You carry with you the hope of many. The Eldarvyn awaits."

Teagan nodded, her throat tight with emotion. She adjusted Diana in her arms, glancing at Julian, who gave her a reassuring smile. Together, they followed Thynidal through the streets.

The path wound through Sythra, leading them away from the bustling heart of the city and into a tranquil grove at its outskirts. Here, the air seemed to hum with a different kind of energy — softer, almost musical. Teagan could feel the change in her bones, as if the planet itself was welcoming her.

The grove opened into a clearing, where the Eldarvyn tree stood. Revered as the Keeper of Balance, the tree was immense, its trunk a tapestry of deep, rich hues that shifted in the light — copper, gold, and ruby. The branches stretched skyward, their leaves glowing faintly as if catching and amplifying the ambient energy. Its roots spread outward, disappearing into the soil, where faint pulses of light traced intricate patterns, like veins of life coursing through the earth.

It alone had survived when all the Sigillaria trees were wiped out. The roots of the Eldarvyn delved deep into the planet's core, entwining with the vibrant crystalline veins that coursed beneath the surface. These roots acted as conduits, channeling the energy of the buried crystals and dispersing it across the land.

The very life force of Trita Prime seemed to flow through this ancient arboreal guardian, sustaining not just the surrounding grove but the balance of ecosystems across the planet.

As Teagan stepped closer, Diana reached out a tiny hand, her fingers grasping at the air. A soft hum resonated from the tree, as if it had sensed their arrival.

Thynidal motioned for her to approach, and as Teagan stood before the Eldarvyn, the tree's energy seemed to envelop her. A faint, golden glow surrounded her and Diana; the air grew warmer, more alive. "It knows you," Thynidal said, his voice filled with awe. "And it knows her." Overwhelmed by the moment, Teagan could only nod.

The Eldarvyn, ancient and timeless, seemed to acknowledge Diana as much as it acknowledged Teagan herself. Julian rested a hand on her shoulder, his expression a mixture of wonder and pride. He had not realized it would be like this. He had not known about her connection. Now he could understand why she needed to return. The hum grew louder, resonating deep within, as if the tree was welcoming them home. The grove around the Eldarvyn created a hidden sanctuary, a place of magic and spiritual protection within the heart of Trita Prime. Here, Teagan's child would be protected by a select group of guardians, sworn to defend her against any attack. The guardians were a diverse group, each chosen for their unique skills and unwavering loyalty to the Tritan cause.

One elder, named Nyaja, had a kind smile and gentle demeanor. Her large, faceted eyes shimmered like glass. Her delicate antennae, constantly in motion, swept the air above hers crown—reading chemical signals, mood, and intent from the world and others around her.

Teagan reluctantly entrusted Diana to her care, tears in her eyes as she kissed her daughter's forehead, silently promising to return.

She watched as the elder cradled the baby girl in her arms, her weathered face softening with a tenderness that only a guardian could possess. Teagan searched her eyes for reassurance, and within their depths, she found determination and unwavering commitment.

"Fear not, Teagan," Nyaja assured her. Her mandibles flexed subtly beneath a resonant vocal membrane, producing clicks and modulated harmonics. "We will protect her with our lives. The celestonite crystal has chosen her for a reason, and we shall ensure that her destiny is fulfilled."

Julian also reminded her that he would stay with Diana at all times.

"I'll watch over her," he said. "She'll be safe. Now we're here, let's get this done."

51
THE CRYSTAL NATION

Sythra, Trita Prime, January, 2104

A SMEGIN STOOD TO WELCOME home to Trita Prime the heroic teams that had successfully retrieved the precious Sigillaria cones. His exoskeleton puffed up, giving the illusion of a commanding presence. His voice was stern as he ordered an immediate propagation and planting program to begin for the endangered tree species.

With advanced fertilization methods, the trees would grow quickly, nourished by the crystal celestonite below the planet's surface. When activated, the celestonite emitted a radiant glow that nourished plant life, accelerated growth, and restored balance to ecosystems ravaged by pollution or natural disasters.

However, despite this small victory, the Council members remained worried. The rumor of a new Draxid weapon cast a dark shadow over their celebrations. Vrillon, the longest serving member of the Council, spoke up bleakly, his eyes reflecting their shared fear.

"We have cleared one hurdle," he remarked. "It has bought us time. But our people are still fearful and desperate. We need to organize our defense, need a plan. Time is running out. We cannot let our guard down."

Aak'iks, recently officially confirmed as intelligence chief, rose to address the Council.

"Having possession of the seeds is only half the battle," he stated gravely. "As you all know, we are a nation built on crystals. The Sigillaria act as conduits to activate these crystals buried beneath our feet. But they require direction and can only be channeled through the roots of the tree with the help of a priestess."

The Tritans had long revered their planet as not just a physical home, but also as a wellspring of spiritual energy that connected them to the cosmos. Deep within the heart of Trita Prime, the celestonite that lay beneath the soil acted as manifestation of the planet's life force and cosmic energy. The Tritans had, over generations, discovered the art of harnessing and manipulating the material through their ancient rituals and ceremonies, led by the priestesses.

But an illness had resulted in the deaths of all the Tritan priestesses. None were left. Their loss had been keenly felt by the people of Trita Prime, not only for their spiritual guidance and wisdom, but also for their role as caretakers of the planet's natural balance and harmony. Without their guidance, Trita Prime had been plunged into a state of chaos and uncertainty, with no one left to uphold the ancient traditions and rituals that had sustained their society for generations.

Asmegin's hands were folded together, his six elongated fingers intertwined in deep in contemplation. "What do you propose, Aak'iks? We don't have time for games or riddles. And since the Great Sundering, we certainly do not have a priestess."

Aak'iks's antennae twitched. "We may not have a priestess among us, but we know of one," he declared, locking eyes with Asmegin. Aak'iks then turned to Asimov, who had joined their meeting.

Clearing his throat, Asimov addressed the Council. "Yes," he said tentatively. "We have made contact with a true priestess. She resides on Earth."

"Can you reach her?" Asmegin pressed urgently, his face lined with worry. "Our need is dire."

"I will make every effort," Asimov assured them. "She has helped us before. But it may not be easy."

The room fell into a tense silence as the gravity of their situation sunk in. The fate of their people rested on this last slender hope.

52

TESTING THE THEORY

Tricala, February 2104

A FTER CLARA'S DEATH, NOEL wanted revenge. He wasn't a violent man, but the images of her murder played over and over in his mind. He knew, however, that he did not stand a chance against the Draxid. So instead, Noel determined to help the Tritans resist their enemy's attempts to subdue them.

An idea had sparked in Noel's mind. He knew of the crystals on Trita Prime — if the energy from them could be harvested and directed, it could create a protective shield. The crystals were known to have their own resonant hum, a sound so low it was imperceptible to most ears, but that could be felt in the bones. If he could match those natural vibrations to the cosmic pulses, he might be able to create a resonance field.

But he needed a way to channel the vibrations.

"We could use the natural root systems of some plants," suggested Shiko. "Though I don't know what plants they have there."

"Well, we know they have the Sigillaria plants," Liam said. "They're quick-growing and tall. We could use those."

"It's worth a try," Noel said, feeling a surge of excitement. "If the Sigillaria plants can match the Lattice's resonance, we might be able to project this sound to create a shield."

Liam sounded skeptical but intrigued. "You mean a defense field, using sound?"

"Exactly," Noel replied. "If the Sigillaria and the crystals resonate in sync with the Lattice, they could channel its energy. We'd have a framework—a defensive web—that the Draxid would find almost impossible to penetrate."

Over the following days, Noel tested his theory. Using plants similar to the Sigillaria tree, he placed samples around the observatory, each fitted with a tiny resonance amplifier. He asked Shiko to tune each one to match the frequencies of the Astral Lattice.

"Here we go," Noel whispered to himself as he initiated the test. A soft hum filled the observatory, creating a calming, unified sound. The amplified resonance from the plants began to sync with the Lattice's frequencies, and he felt a faint tingling in the air as the two sounds merged.

Noel analyzed the pulses from the plants and noticed a recurring pattern: Every full sequence lasted precisely 6174 milliseconds before cycling again. It wasn't an anomaly; the sequence kept resetting, forming a mysterious loop that hinted at something far more intentional.

Fascinated, Noel scribbled down the number and ran it through his data logs, looking for similar frequencies in the cosmic pulses he'd collected.

"6174," he murmured, watching as the analyzer displayed the results. "It's not just a pulse length. It's... an identifier."

"It's Kaprekar's constant," Shiko said, ever the mathematician. "A mysterious number that shows up whenever certain numbers are manipulated mathematically. Rearrange the digits of a four-digit number in descending and ascending order, subtract them, and you often get back to 6174. It's like a cosmic fingerprint."

Puzzling over this, Noel realized that he could use 6174 as a type of resonant key, an anchor to stabilize the entire sound shield framework. Adjusting the sound frequencies from the Sigillaria plants to harmonize with this precise rhythm, he noticed that the resonance grew stronger, forming a more cohesive barrier.

Noel turned to Kiana, who had elected to stay with him at the observatory after Clara's funeral. "Kiana, if we tune the Sigillaria resonance to this cycle—6174 milliseconds—it could reinforce the shield by orders of magnitude."

He felt he was on the verge of something profound but incomplete. Driven by curiosity, he expanded his research, exploring other cosmic frequencies that might interact with this mysterious cycle.

His attention turned to 963 Hz, a frequency he recognized from ancient Earth records that described it as a connection to the universal, or even divine, frequency.

Using the crystals, Noel experimented with matching 963 Hz to the 6174 millisecond cycle. The results of the simulation were startling: As he played the two in unison, the resonance intensified, transforming the resulting field.

The combination of 963 Hz and 6174 milliseconds wouldn't just create a defensive shield; it could generate a harmonic "veil," something that could potentially mask the Tritan settlements from Draxid sensors, allowing them to remain hidden while creating a force strong enough to repel intrusions.

The time came for the real test. Noel adjusted the frequency generator with steady hands, his breath shallow with anticipation.

The laboratory—nothing more than a temporary set up perched at the edge of an imitation Sigillaria grove—was filled with the low, pulsing hum of the resonance test. On the screen before him, lines of data streamed by, measuring the interaction between the 963 Hz frequency and the 6174 millisecond cycle.

So far, nothing.

He bit the inside of his cheek, recalibrating the interface. *Come on...* The crystals were naturally attuned to this frequency, he could *feel* it, but the synchronization had to be *exact*.

Beside him, Kiana watched in silence, her eyes reflecting the pale glow of the readings.

Noel made a final adjustment. A single breath. Then—

A pulse.

A deep, resonant vibration that didn't just hum through the equipment but through the ground itself. The stand-in plants quivered in response, their crystalline cores below flaring with light, not from an external source but from within. The sound wasn't just projecting outward, the trees were *answering*.

On the screen, the readings shot off the charts. The resonance had synchronized.

"No way... " Noel whispered.

The frequency stabilized, and a shimmering energy field rippled into existence, stretching over the trees, then expanding outward like an invisible tide. As the pulse spread, the very air seemed to bend, the wavelengths distorting space just enough to scramble detection. A cloaking veil, woven from pure harmonic resonance.

Noel's heart pounded in his chest. He turned to Kiana, barely able to contain himself.

"It worked." His voice was breathless, wild with exhilaration. "It actually worked!"

She looked at him, her expression unreadable for a long moment. Then, she exhaled a sharp breath of amazement. "It's like they're... speaking back."

Noel nodded. "This frequency, 963 Hz, is known as the 'God frequency.' It's said to connect us to the fundamental resonance of the universe. When paired with 6174, it's as if we're tuning into a cosmic code."

Kiana furrowed her brow. "You're saying this shield doesn't just protect us, it connects us?"

"It connects us," Noel confirmed, "and repels anything out of sync with the universe's core vibration. The Draxids won't be able to penetrate this field. Their very presence will cause discord with the shield, forcing them out. The Draxid are out of sync with the universe's vibrations."

"Hope you're right," said Kiana.

A laugh burst from Noel, part disbelief, part pure joy.

His hands worked swiftly at the controls, gathering data, confirming readings. The Astral Lattice wasn't just a theory anymore. It was real.

Not just a shield. Not just a defense. A living force.

"Now we'll have to test it on Trita Prime," said Liam.

Noel looked out at the stars, feeling the weight of his discovery. He had opened the door to a new era of defense, one built on resonance and harmony instead of violence.

And yet... something was missing.

The Lattice shimmered and flickered unevenly, parts of it unstable, struggling to maintain equilibrium. The frequency alignment was correct, the resonance perfect — so why wasn't it holding?

Kiana frowned. "It's incomplete. The Sigillaria are responding, but they're not fully ... anchored."

Noel ran his fingers through his hair, frustration creeping in. "Anchored to *what*?"

Kiana's gaze sharpened. "Not what. *Who.*"

Realization struck like a bolt of lightning. The trees, the crystals, the Lattice itself — it wasn't just a machine or a system. It was *alive*. And like all living things, it needed a connection. A conduit.

A priestess.

Only someone deeply attuned to the Tritan's ancestral ways could complete the circuit, merging the Lattice's harmonic energy with the lifeforce of the planet. Noel might have discovered the key, but there was only one person who could unlock it. He turned to Kiana, a new fire in his eyes.

"We need to find Teagan."

53
THE REPLAY

OWIE RICH PACED ACROSS the polished floor of the Quivira medical wing, taking care not to slip, his artificial body moving with uncanny precision. From a distance, he might have passed for human. Up close, the illusion fractured: the way his skin flexed a heartbeat out of rhythm, the metallic glint deep in his irises, the faint clicks when his joints aligned.

Behind him, suspended in a translucent biotank, floated the truth. His digitally connected brain, shrunken slightly by time and trauma, pulsed inside a tank of nutrient-rich fluid.

And yet still, he ruled. For now, at the convenience of the Board.

When the hours dragged too long, and the lab techs had no updates, Howie sometimes passed the time in one of the few ways he enjoyed: by watching replays of the death of Ofentse.

The footage from Tricala played out in unedited loops — the grainy drone feed, the moment Ofentse staggered and fell, his body's frantic convulsions, his face contorted as he clutched his chest. And finally, the delicious guttural scream. Howie would slow the playback, frame by frame, savoring the stillness that followed. A victory, clean and final.

At least, it had seemed so.

Lately, though, he found himself pausing. Rewinding. Leaning closer.

There, the angle of the fall, too deliberate. The blood spread too symmetrically, like spilled paint on glass. And the vital signs, recorded by remote biosensors, faded too cleanly. No ragged final spasms. No chaotic collapse of heart and brain functions.

A forgery. A collusion between two principal actors.

The realization came slow, like ice cracking beneath his feet.

The footage played again — a loop of false death, blood, collapse, stillness.

Howie watched in silence.

He'd wanted to believe. But he had been betrayed once again. Julian had repaid him with deception.

Howie sat rigid in the chair. He should have been furious. Instead, he was afraid. A feeling he hadn't tasted in ages.

Victory had been an illusion. The real game was only beginning.

VED REDIRECTED

Sythra, Trita Prime, February 29, 2104

Hunter and Ved arrived on Trita Prime on their way to look for Ved's roots. But with rising animosity between the Tritans and Draxid, the Tritans only thought of Ved as a potential spy, recognizing his Draxid DNA.

Ved was summoned to appear before the High Council. The amber skies shimmered faintly above the domed council chamber, yet the air inside it was thick with tension. Every eye was fixed upon Ved as he and Hunter waited in uneasy silence. Ved remained motionless, his gaze fixed on the Tritans assembled before him. Hunter stood by the chamber's grand entrance, his hand defiantly on his hip.

Asmegin, the High Council's chairman, spoke first. His voice was deep and authoritative, carrying the gravity of their collective decision, his faceted eyes glancing toward him.

"Ved, son of two worlds, your presence here is a matter of grave concern. We know you say you come in peace, but we cannot ignore the fact that you may be spying for our enemy or inadvertently reveal information about Tritan defenses."

Ved stepped forward, his voice steady despite the turmoil within him. "I want to thank you for receiving us. We appreciate your generosity. We are simply travellers. I assure you, I have nothing to do with the conflict between the two of you. I am seeking information and only want to understand my roots. What must I do to prove my loyalty and peaceful intentions?"

Asmegin sighed. "Your loyalty is not in question, Ved. It is your potential to be compromised. Your Draxid heritage places us all in peril. How can we be certain you are not a pawn in their schemes?"

Ved's fists clenched. "I am no pawn," he said through gritted teeth. "I came here seeking answers, not to simply be branded a threat."

Hunter took a step closer to Ved, his voice low and calm. "Ved, this isn't about what you've done. It's about what they fear you could do, even unknowingly. Let's hear them out."

Asmegin's gaze hardened and his mandibles flexed subtly. "There is no need for further discussion. The Council's decision is final. Ved must leave Trita Prime immediately. Hunter, as the son of Dr. Ward, is welcome to stay."

Ved took a step back, his shoulders drooping. "So that's it? After everything, I'm just... banished?"

Hunter placed a hand on Ved's shoulder, a silent show of solidarity. "We'll find another way, Ved. You've come this far. Your journey doesn't end here."

As Ved and Hunter left the chamber, whispers broke out among the Council. Outside, the fading sun cast long shadows over the city. Ved's jaw tightened as he turned to Hunter.

"I can't just leave this unanswered. I need to go to the Draxid's home world."

Hunter gave a low whistle. "You sure about that? You're talking about walking straight into the lion's den."

"A piece of my past leads there," Ved replied. "I need to know who I am."

Hunter chuckled dryly. "Reckless and stubborn. You're definitely not half-Titan."

Before they departed, Asimov rushed up to Hunter. He reached into a recessed compartment in his mantle and withdrew a slender shard of translucent crystal, no bigger than a finger. Its edges caught the low light, flickering with faint pulses.

"You may need this," he said, placing the Echo Clip gently in Hunter's hand. "It carries some retrieved Draxid data—an old logic pattern that might confuse the Draxid. If you and Ved encounter Zaun, this may disrupt his alignment... for a moment."

Hunter frowned. "What is it?"

Asimov tilted his head, expression unreadable. "A fragment of memory, recovered from a Draxid spaceship. Rebuilt and saved in case we might use it. Tritan archivists rebuilt it from a Draxid system collapse—decades of studying wreckage."

He stepped back into the shadows. "It may confuse them long enough for you to do something. Like escape."

Aboard the *SpaceSweeper*, the engines hummed softly as the ship broke through Trita Prime's atmosphere. Hunter piloted with practiced ease toward the destination Asimov had given them, while Ved stared at the swirling void ahead. Chester was curled up in the copilot's seat, her ears twitching at every subtle change in the hum of the ship's engine. She glanced between the two men, as if silently assessing their moods, offering a comforting presence amid the tension.

Their path through space was fraught. Draxid patrols swept the regions bordering their territory, forcing Hunter to rely on evasive maneuvers and cloaking protocols. In one encounter, a rogue asteroid field nearly ripped the *SpaceSweeper* apart, testing Ved's ingenuity as he scrambled to stabilize the ship's systems.

But the greatest challenge came from within. As they neared the Cygnus constellation, where the Draxid home world was, Ved wrestled with the fear that he might discover more than he'd bargained for.

Hunter interrupted his thoughts one evening, tossing him a ration pack. "You're quiet. That's not like you."

Ved forced a grin. "Just thinking."

"Don't think too hard," Hunter said, leaning back in his chair. "Whatever's waiting for us out there, we'll face it together."

Ved nodded, his resolve hardening. Whatever lay ahead, he wouldn't let his heritage define him — or break him.

55

TEAGAN'S DREAM

Bolinas, California, February 29, 2104

T EAGAN HAD LONG ABANDONED the habit of questioning the impossible, finding it pointless. Each day was a gift, a moment to breathe and exist, free from the chains of her past. The lunar prison had been a nightmare she couldn't wake from, where dark shadows concealed the relentless assaults on her body and mind. Yet, amidst all that darkness, nothing had braced her for the startling reality of Diana's rapid growth.

Her daughter was developing particularly fast, some might think abnormally, although the doctor was reassuring and not worried. She was already demonstrating cognitive abilities beyond her age. Her speech patterns were advanced, her coordination eerily precise. Other children her age were still stumbling through sentences, their movements clumsy and uncertain.

Diana, however, adapted to everything with frightening ease.

She memorized patterns in seconds. She recognized faces she'd only seen once, and when placed in an unfamiliar environment she instinctively mapped the space with a level of awareness no toddler should possess.

But the real moment of revelation came when Teagan saw her daughter heal.

It had been a small cut — just a scrape along Diana's forearm after falling against a jagged crate. Any child would have cried. Diana had merely stared at the wound, her large, piercing eyes focused with unshakable curiosity. Teagan had reached for the first aid kit, but before she could even open it, the bleeding had stopped. Within minutes, the wound had sealed itself, leaving nothing but smooth, unbroken skin.

The recovery had not just been quick. It was something else.

And it wasn't just the healing.

Diana's presence carried a stillness that unsettled the ordinary. It wasn't aloofness—she was affectionate, even playful—but there was a gravity to her, a quiet precision that made people hesitate. At playgroups, other toddlers stared at her like she was a new species. One mother had whispered that Diana's eyes didn't blink the way a child's should. Another said she dreamed about those eyes—too blue, too steady, too knowing.

The doctor remained calm. "Some children simply advance early," she said with a practiced smile. "You might have a prodigy on your hands."

But Teagan had seen more than precocity. She had seen something designed.

And in that growing awareness of Diana's difference, her uncanny grace, Teagan found herself retreating inward, not out of fear, but because love like this felt too fragile to last.

It was in that space between awe and dread that Julian lived.

He watched Teagan like a man hoping to memorize her. Not out of possessiveness, but the quiet ache of someone who knew her heart was shaped by battles he hadn't fought. He loved her deeply. But he knew—had always known—that Teagan Ward was not his to hold forever.

Even in their quietest moments—in the warmth of their small home, in the way she watched Diana sleep, or stirred herbs into broth with a distant look in her eyes—there was a part of her that never settled. Not really.

He admired her for it. That inner fire. That unwavering drive to do more, to understand, to *belong* to something greater. It was what had drawn him to her in the first place.

But now, as she spoke of dreams and distant worlds, of ancient calls and priestess voices, he couldn't shake the fear that this time, she wouldn't come back.

Not just physically. Spiritually. Mentally. Fundamentally.

The dreams became more intense and frequent, leaving Teagan restless and troubled. Julian noticed her moodiness.

"Post-partum. It's normal," he said to her gently, stroking her shoulders.

His reasonableness angered her.

"This is not post-partum," she spat. "I'm not a hormonal wreck."

Julian knew about Teagan's time with the Tritans, but had never met them himself, so he wasn't sure how real all of it was. And he hadn't spoken about it with Noel or even Kiana.

Despite her initial reluctance, Teagan was unable to ignore the persistent pull of the dreams beckoning her to Trita Prime. She began to realize an unshakable sense of obligation and responsibility to the Tritans, as well as a strong desire to help.

"They need me," she told Julian. "I can feel it."

But Julian was uncomprehending.

"We have a daughter," he insisted. "*She* needs us. Why become involved in this? It's not our concern. Let's just be here with Diana."

"Oh, now you're concerned about Diana, after being away so long?" Teagan snapped.

Julian ignored the barb. "Teagan, you're exhausted," he said softly, putting Diana down in her crib before moving to Teagan, his hands resting on her shoulders. "Just get more rest."

His calm demeanor grated on her nerves. Teagan pulled away, her eyes flashing with frustration.

"This isn't about rest! This—This is a message, Julian. They're calling to me."

Julian's brow furrowed, the lines on his face deepening as he searched for the right words.

"You say your hallucinations prove the Tritans need you," he said at last, his voice quiet. "But I think *you* need them too. Maybe more than you realize."

She turned slightly, eyes shadowed with a complex sadness. "What are you saying?"

"I think you're looking for meaning in what they gave you—what they made you. I think you're afraid that if you ignore them, you'll lose a part of yourself. But Teagan..."

He faltered, eyes flicking to Diana.

"You don't have to prove your worth to them. You've already proven it here. With us."

That night, Teagan's dream was more intense.

She stood alone on a vast expanse of smooth crystal—clear, cool, and endless. Beneath her feet, faint veins of bioluminescent light pulsed slowly, like breath. The ground was solid but alive somehow, as though it were listening. Above her, the sky was a gradient of deep violet and pale gold, stars arranged in unfamiliar constellations that shimmered in and out of focus.

There was no wind, no sound. Just stillness. And then—motion.

Something stirred below.

A ripple passed through the crystalline surface—impossible, sound-less—and then a shape began to rise. Not breaking through, but emerging *within*. A sinuous limb curled upward, followed by another, then many, each one gliding in a graceful spiral. The creature that took form was immense and otherworldly: an octopus, translucent and radiant, its body composed of light and geometry.

Symbols moved across its skin—organic patterns laced with logic, repeat-ing endlessly without ever repeating the same way twice.

The Octopus Spirit.

She had seen it before—when the Tritans had first chosen her as their voice. It was their symbol of the infinite: of recursion, of return, of lives echoing through time.

The Tritans had no word for "god," but they revered this entity. It was the living memory of Trita Prime, a consciousness that stretched across time like silk. The Octopus was infinity. Cycles. Return.

One luminous arm extended through the crystal, passing through solid matter like mist, and touched her chest. The moment it made contact, a current surged through her. Her bones hummed. Her skin glowed faintly with lines of unfamiliar script, written not in ink but in memory.

Visions spilled over her: circles of Tritans releasing spores in mourning; collapsed monuments etched with her priestess sigil; the shimmering outline of a dome-like structure, humming with breath and song. Then, Diana's cry. Weak. Muffled. Terribly far away.

Teagan stretched her hand out toward the sound, but the ground splin-tered beneath her like ice fracturing under pressure. The Spirit unraveled into streams of light, and the plain of crystal fell away into an abyss of color and noise.

Instinctively, she reached out, but the dreamscape twisted. And the oc-topus, now fragmented into shifting geometry, pulled her down—*not to drown, but to descend*—into the vault beneath the crystal sea.

She awoke with tears in her eyes, her hands clenched tight.

Julian stirred beside her. "Another hallucination?"

Teagan clutched the hem of the sheet, her pulse still thudding in her throat. "Not a hallucination, more a vision," she whispered. "A summons."

Julian's expression shifted, his brow furrowing ever so slightly. He glanced back down at Diana, as if grounding himself in the moment. "Teagan," he began, his tone measured, "I know you're hurting. Losing your mom, the stress—it's a lot. But maybe these dreams are just your mind trying to process everything."

Her heart tightened, the words like a needle pricking an old wound. "It's not just grief, Julian. This is something... more." She paused, searching for the right way to explain what she couldn't fully understand herself.

"They're reaching out to me. The Tritans. I know it sounds crazy, but I can feel it. It's like last time, when I was their priestess. I feel they are summoning me. They need me."

Julian didn't respond immediately. Instead, he shifted Diana in his arms, his focus on their daughter as he traced the soft curve of her cheek with his thumb. The silence between them was heavy, filled with the weight of things left unsaid.

Finally, he looked up, his gaze steady but tinged with sadness. "I just want us to be a family, Teagan. To be here for Diana. Isn't that enough?"

Teagan opened her mouth to reply, but the words caught in her throat. The life they'd built together meant everything to her. But she couldn't ignore the persistent pull of the dreams, beckoning her to Trita Prime. She had a connection to the Tritans that was undeniable—she was their priestess, after all.

Unsure what to do, she turned away, staring out at the Pacific beyond.

She didn't answer right away because some part of her feared he was right. And another part feared he wasn't—that she had unfinished business in the stars, and that only by returning could she finally know who she was meant to be.

"Teagan, I know your time with them was... important, but this sounds like stress. You've been through a lot. Maybe it's your mind trying to process everything."

She stared at him, incredulous. "You think this is some kind of coping mechanism? You have no idea what it was like to be with them, to *feel* what I felt. This isn't my imagination, it's real. And this isn't about choice anymore, it's about responsibility."

Julian shook his head. "Responsibility to *who*? Strangers on another planet? We've carved out a life here, Teagan. Diana is finally thriving. We have everything we need. Why can't that be enough for you?"

"Because it's not!" Her voice cracked, the weight of her conviction pressing against her chest. "The Tritans are in danger, Julian. I can feel it. They reached out to me because they trust me. How can I turn my back on them?"

"And what about us?" His voice was low, his eyes piercing. "I'm staying here, and I'm staying with Diana. If you want to chase ghosts, you'll be doing it alone."

The finality of his words hung in the air like a storm cloud. Teagan's breath hitched, but she refused to back down. The dreams—the *message*—had become impossible to ignore. She couldn't abandon the Tritans, not when they needed her most. Yet the thought of leaving Julian and Diana threatened to unravel her resolve.

"I don't want to do this alone," she said finally, her voice barely above a whisper. "But I can't ignore this. I've tried, and it's tearing me apart. I just need you to believe me."

* * *

She and Julian decided to speak to Noel about the conflict and what to do. They needed some advice. Her father knew about the Tritans and had spent time with them.

"Why can't the three of you go together?" Noel asked. "I think Diana is old enough. You have a gift, Teagan," her father told her. "A bond with the Tritans that goes beyond anything we can comprehend. If they are in trouble, you must use it to help them. I'm sure your mother would have approved."

"But what about Diana? She's so young."

"I'm sure you friend Asimov can have someone look after her. You remember him? And Julian will be with her."

Teagan's face was pinched with worry, her brows furrowed and lips pressed together in deep contemplation. "I don't know what to do," she whispered in agony.

"Trust in the support we'll provide," Noel said. "I'll ask Kiana to come with us."

She turned to Julian. Her eyes were unfocused, and a tear ran down her cheek. "I have an obligation," she said simply. "I have to go. I love you, but I have to be there."

Julian took a deep breath. "If we're going to proceed with this," he began, his tone firm, "there are a few conditions that need to be met."

Gathering his thoughts before continuing, he said, "First, we need a plan."

At that, Teagan burst out laughing in relief. "Okay, Sherlock."

He smiled, obviously pleased that they weren't going to fight anymore. "Second, Diana comes first. I will do everything to support you, but her safety must be ensured."

Teagan nodded, her expression softening. "I couldn't agree more."

"Third," Julian added, his voice growing more resolute, "we must have a time limit. We cannot let this take over our lives. If you go... you must come back. Not for me. For Diana. So she knows where she came from—and where she belongs."

Teagan's eyes narrowed slightly as she weighed his words. She gazed down at her child, her heart torn by the weight of an impossible choice, realizing that the Tritans already had taken over her life for a second time.

56
THE DIRECTIVE

Quivira, April 1, 2104

PROFESSOR POLYAKOV GOT THE alert from Maureen that Teagan was planning to take Diana with her to Trita Prime.

Malapert was one thing. Trita Prime's capital, Sythra, was another.

Polyakov watched the genetic readouts flicker across the screen, her fingers hovering over the controls. Years of work, of careful calibration, had led to this. Teagan Ward had never been just another prisoner. She had been a vessel; a carefully selected subject whose genetic makeup held the key to controlled evolution. But Teagan also had never been the ultimate goal — only the means.

The real achievement was Diana.

Every blood draw, every scan, every so-called health check in the lunar prison had been part of a larger experiment. The conditions—prolonged exposure to artificial gravity, fluctuating radiation levels, experimental compounds—had triggered the genetic markers Professor Polyakov had painstakingly identified. Markers that had remained dormant in Teagan, waiting for the right conditions to activate. But even that wasn't enough. Polyakov had intervened directly, introducing nanotechnology that rewrote the blueprint of Teagan's reproductive cells before Diana was conceived.

The result was extraordinary. Unlike Teagan, whose adaptations had been induced, Diana was *born* different. Her immune system was hyper-efficient, filtering toxins before they could take hold. Her metabolic processes required less energy, yet produced greater endurance. Neural scans hinted at enhanced synaptic responses, suggesting she could process information faster, make connections beyond what human cognition had previously allowed. A prototype for what humanity could become.

Professor Polyakov leaned back, satisfied yet restless. She had done what no scientist before her had accomplished. Diana was proof that evolution could be guided, that the limits of the human body were not fixed but malleable. And now, the Consortium wanted her findings. They wanted Diana.

Howie Rich's directive had been clear: Find the child. Retrieve her. The Consortium wasn't willing to let their greatest breakthrough slip through their fingers.

But they didn't have the imagination or comprehension to fully understand. They saw only a product to replicate, to control. Polyakov saw something more. A force beyond even her calculations.

Teagan planned to take Diana to the Tritans, an unpredictable variable in an already delicate equation. That could not be allowed. Polyakov knew she had to act swiftly, to intervene before it was too late.

She was determined to safeguard her most remarkable creation, the one she believed could alter everyone's future. The stakes were colossal, and the clock was ticking. She could not allow the Diana experiment to be wasted.

57
THE ENCOUNTER

New Thalos, Greater Gorgon, October 3, 2105

Now the nine of them were all in it together: Noel, Teagan, Julian, Shiko, Kat, Ved, Hunter, Kiana, and Dr. César.

"We need to find a way out of this hellhole," said Hunter. "Everyone spread out and check along the walls. Maybe there's an exit we can't see from here since the light is so dim."

They spread out, hands held high in front of them, almost like a game of Blind Man's Bluff, searching for an exit, a crack in the wall, a ventilator, an opportunity. Anything that would give them hope. Their shoes crunched over a sea of maggots writhing on the dirt floor.

"What's with these maggots? They're disgusting," said Ved.

"The Draxid eat them . It's part of their diet," said Dr. César. "But they're out of control down here. They have a farm next door, but they seep through cracks in the walls."

Teagan's mind was on her desperate need to find Diana; her heart was aching. What were they going to do with her baby? Was this a plot by Zaun to harness whatever power it thought Diana possessed, or was it just callously playing with Teagan's emotions because she had helped the Tritans defend their homeland?

Meanwhile, on the other side of the cell, Julian edged forward and came across a raised platform. "Does anyone have a light?" he called out. "There's something here."

Ved handed over his flashlight, it's beam now weak. "It won't last long. The power is already low," he warned.

They examined the platform. It was like a stage, with a wall at the end. Maybe this was not a dungeon, but an old ballroom, turned into a convenient place for storing unwanted bodies... even if they happened to be alive.

Julian clambered up. He felt like singing an aria, but refrained. Instead, he just pirouetted theatrically. In the "stalls," Katrina clapped in mock appreciation.

But then she noticed an odd symbol on the back wall behind him. It was like an eye, and seemed strangely familiar. She looked at the pendant on her chest to compare the pattens. And as she held the old copper bracelet, it began to feel warmer.

Dr. César's eyes widened slightly, his eyes locked on Kat's neck. "The... neck..." he murmured, nodding weakly.

"The what?" Teagan asked as she and the others came closer.

"The sign," he rasped.

Startled, Katrina lifted the now-glowing bangle away from her neck.

"Why is it...?" Noel said. "It looks like it's activating." Noel looked from the bracelet to the wall in front of them, then glanced back. "Katrina, your bracelet — it has the same symbol as the one on the wall behind Dr. César. It's like one of those Aztec or Mayan eye symbols."

"It's Hopi, actually," corrected Teagan.

They turned toward the wall Noel had indicated and, sure enough, the ritual eye symbol gleamed faintly in the dimness, etched onto the stones in a way that looked both intricate and ancient. Katrina moved closer, extending her pendant toward the symbol.

Teagan's face was ashen. "Diana is in there," she said. "I can feel it." Her voice was a mixture of dread tinged with hope. "Katrina, are you sure about this? If you're not..."

With a deep breath, Katrina held the bangle up to the wall.

The symbol on her pendant and the symbol on the stone seemed to connect like an ancient QR code, a faint humming filling the air as a section of the wall began to shift, the stones rearranging themselves with a grinding sound that echoed through the chamber. As Katrina held her breath, her hand trembling, the copper bangle began to grow almost unbearably warm. The Hopi eye symbol on it pulsed faintly, as if alive, casting a soft, amber glow over the stone wall. Light poured through the widening gap, illuminating a narrow chamber on the other side.

Inside the hidden room, a figure shrouded in shadows was holding an infant close. Four securitybots formed a guard.

Julian tried to make out who the figure was as they stepped forward, almost regally. To Teagan, it looked like they were holding Diana. She hoped it was. She had to believe that Diana was still alive.

In her mind once more, she remembered the old man's words: *"Behold the bird that cannot fly; the treasure you seek lies beyond the eye."*

Was this the eye? Was Diana the treasure?

The shadowy figure began to emerge, stepping forward, peeling away from the darkness like something that had always been there, waiting. The dim light caught the sharp edges of her face — high cheekbones, deep-set eyes that reflected nothing, and lips pressed into a thin, unwavering line.

Teagan's thoughts were interrupted when Julian's shocked words reached her.

"Oh my God, it's Professor Polyakov."

Professor Polyakov moved with precise control, as though every step had been calculated long before she took it.

"Why is she here, in this place?" asked Kat.

"She's here for the child," whispered Noel.

Looking at Professor Polyakov, Teagan began to shake as she recalled the experiments in the lunar prison. She had always suspected that the medical evaluations in the lunar cell were more than they seemed, but she'd had no idea just how deep the deception ran. Every blood draw, every scan, every so-called health check she now realized had been a step in a larger experiment — one she had never consented to.

Professor Polyakov had been the architect of it all.

Polyakov smiled coldly, her dark eyes glinting in the dim light. Shadows flickered ominously around her. She looked at them with a predatory gleam, her figure both familiar and terrifying as she advanced.

Julian felt a surge of fury rise within him, the fear he had once felt under Polyakov's control dissolving into a burning need to stop her.

"Let us go, Polyakov," he said firmly, stepping forward. "You have no right to hold us or Diana. She's not a commodity to use for whatever twisted agenda you have. She's a child. She's not yours to claim. I've done everything you asked."

At that, Teagan shot Julian a quizzical glance.

Polyakov stared at them, rage beginning to flicker in her eyes.

"Did you think you'd won? That you'd helped the Tritans and could now just walk away?" she hissed, stepping closer. Her eyes narrowed.

"You have no idea, Julian. Where do you think Teagan got her powers? Do you think Teagan was naturally a priestess? And your work, your life, your futile protests –– all of it was leading you here. You're nothing but a pawn. Did you think Teagan's work was done, that you could retire gracefully to California? Do you think you had repaid your debt?"

"What debt?" stuttered Teagan.

"When you were in that lunar prison cell," Polyakov told her, "we started your transformation without your knowledge. My work with you was the culmination of decades of research into directed genetic acceleration. Using advanced nanotechnology, we introduced programmable molecular machines into your bloodstream under the guise of routine medical procedures. These nanites weren't meant to change you overnight; you probably didn't notice anything while you were in conversation with that ant, Felix. Instead, they were designed to observe, adapt, and integrate changes at a cellular level in response to external stimuli.

"The lunar site provided the perfect conditions for this process. The combination of microgravity, chronic radiation exposure, and tailored biochemical injections acted as controlled environmental stressors, forcing your body to evolve. This wasn't just random mutation — it was a guided transformation. Whether you noticed it or not, your body developed enhanced neuroplasticity, improved metabolic efficiency, and an increased ability to regulate energy at the mitochondrial level.

"But the changes were incomplete, as the nanites were designed to monitor and integrate adjustments *over generations*. You, Teagan were only the carrier. The actual results would not manifest until reproduction."

"Reproduction?" asked Julian softly. "You mean Diana?"

Polyakov nodded sharply. "Diana is the culmination of our research, the perfected version, a natural-born post-human, untethered by the limitations of genetic engineering. She represents a biological singularity, a being beyond human yet fully functional in society. Unlike Teagan, whose body had to adapt to radiation and Zero-G exposure, Diana's cells were built from the start to withstand extreme conditions. Her DNA has selective radiation resistance that includes a mechanism to repair radiation-induced damage at an accelerated rate, thereby reducing the risk of mutations or cancers. Plus, she has more efficient oxygen usage, because her enhanced hemoglobin allows her to survive with minimal oxygen — useful for space environments or even deep-sea exploration.

"Diana is more than an experiment. She's proof of concept. If we can control her development, we can refine and mass-produce this process, creating an entirely new subspecies of engineered humans — one resistant to environmental extremes, capable of superior cognitive function, and potentially even exerting control over biological systems around them.

"So, you see, she is not yours. We built her, and I've come to take her back. Of course, you'll be able to see her occasionally, but you will have to give us three weeks warning for any visits. And by the way, please thank Maureen and Harlee for helping so much."

Teagan clenched her fists, the anger in her voice barely contained.

"Maybe we don't know everything. But that doesn't make us powerless."

Katrina lifted the bangle. "And it doesn't make us afraid of you."

Polyakov laughed. "You think you're brave, Teagan? Noble? A priestess? Don't be fooled. You're out of your depth."

"You may have made her, but you don't own her," Teagan spat. "Diana is my daughter, not some prototype for your twisted experiments."

Polyakov's expression was unreadable, though a glint in her eyes betrayed amusement. "Ownership is such a human concept," she said coolly. "You speak as though biological parentage has ever truly mattered. You were a stepping stone, Teagan. A means to an end. The real evolution begins now."

Teagan took a step forward, but Hunter grabbed her arm. "We have to be smart about this," he murmured.

Julian was still processing what Polyakov had said. *Maureen? Harlee? Had they been feeding information to her? Or worse, actively helping her?* His stomach twisted.

Diana whimpered in Polyakov's arms, stirring slightly. Teagan's entire body tensed.

Dr. César, still weak, suddenly rasped, "They... won't stop at her. The experiments ... go deeper. The next generation—"

His breath hitched, and he grabbed Ved's sleeve for support. "There's more at play than you think."

Polyakov's lips curled. "Ah, César. Always the broken messenger."

A low mechanical whir filled the chamber as the securitybots adjusted their stance, weapons visibly priming.

"We don't have time for this," Katrina muttered, glancing at Noel and Ved. "We have to get Diana out of here *now*."

Julian's eyes flicked toward the raised platform. If they could get the right angle, maybe—

Before he could speak, Polyakov exhaled sharply. "Enough of this. I didn't come here to bargain. Besides, it's revolting down here. All these maggots. I can't stand maggots." She spat the word out as though she was trying to cleanse her mouth.

Polyakov raised a hand, and the securitybots locked into position. "We will leave you now," Polyakov said. "I will speak to Zaun and have you deported. Diana stays with me."

Cradling Diana tightly in her arms, her back erect and imperious, Professor Polyakov marched back into the dimly lit passageway, her footsteps echoing behind the line of alert and intimidating securitybots. Her voice was firm as she issued a command, and the stone wall swung shut with a resonant thud.

58

FINDING HOME

The sleek Draxid spacecraft, adorned with ominous dark hues and menacing spikes, appeared seemingly from nowhere, blocking the *SpaceSweeper*'s path with chilling precision.

The interception was almost welcome. Ved hadn't been sure if they'd ever make it to Cygnus, but now that the Draxid craft had closed in, its angular form casting eerie shadows across their ship, Ved's mind raced. He knew that if his suspicions were correct, this encounter could hold the key to unlocking the mysteries of his own genetic lineage.

He looked to Hunter for guidance.

"Don't say anything," Hunter advised. "Let me do the talking."

The intercom crackled to life, filling the cabin with a static-laden voice that sent shivers down their spines.

"Attention unidentified vessel," the voice, afflicted by an otherworldly echo, boomed. "You are trespassing in Draxid territory. Surrender your ship and submit to genetic scanning or face the consequences."

Ved had prepared himself for the inevitable encounter, but he wanted their help, not a confrontation. They had resolved to be diplomatic.

"We are standing by awaiting your boarding party," Hunter told them. "We mean no harm."

Moments later, a squad of heavily armed Draxid soldiers materialized on the deck of the *SpaceSweeper*, their imposing figures casting long shadows in the dimly lit corridor. With weapons drawn, their expressions cold and unyielding, they moved with ruthless efficiency to detain Hunter and Ved. They ignored Chester, who did not budge.

"You will follow us," the leader said, sniffing the air like a hound.

Hunter lined up the *SpaceSweeper* behind the Draxid craft, unsure if they would be able to keep pace. He checked the dials on his dashboard.

The *SpaceSweeper* spluttered into renewed action, and they flew for several days until they began to approach their destination, passing planets adorned with swirling clouds and shimmering rings that danced in intricate orbits.

Greater Gorgon loomed below—an immense, brooding planet wreathed in thick, green-tinged clouds that churned with magnetic storms. Its atmosphere was dense and hostile, a suffocating blend of carbon dioxide, metallic aerosols, and sulfuric compounds that shimmered faintly with ionized light. Occasional pulses of violet lightning crackled across the cloudbanks, revealing the jagged topography beneath—vast basalt plains and towering ridges carved by corrosive rain and tectonic upheaval.

The air down there was unbreathable to humans, heavy with pressure and charged with reactive gases. But for the Draxid, it was home—a crucible of evolution shaped by low oxygen, subterranean heat, and the ever-present hum of their techno-organic architecture, fused into the very geology of the world.

As the *SpaceSweeper* descended toward the designated landing zone, Hunter and Ved caught glimpses of the planet's surface — a patchwork of jagged mountains, expansive deserts, and the occasional city, the sleek architecture blending seamlessly with the natural beauty of the Draxid home world.

They warned Chester they would be gone for a while. "Use the auto-feeder. Don't scoff it all at once," said Ved.

Touching down on the outskirts of the sprawling, mostly subterranean, metropolis, Ved and Hunter found themselves surrounded by a hive of activity.

The Draxid were distinctive, definitely reptilian. Some walked erect on two sturdy legs. Others had six limbs, with crested heads adorned with intricate patterns and hues of gold and crimson, a mark of their genetic lineage and social status within their tightly knit communities.

Hunter and Ved couldn't tell how old any of them were. They all looked about the same age.

Almost paralleling their experience with the Tritans, they were escorted toward City Hall, a large mostly subterranean building with spires of dark metal. Their escort led them through a series of winding corridors and crowded passageways; they were told they would be speaking with a Draxid named Velen. The air hummed with machinery, but it wasn't clear what was being made. Finally, Hunter and Ved were ushered into the audience chamber of the Draxid council. Pulsating energy lit the room.

Ved figured that the Draxid sitting in the center was Velen. He was modest looking, but power sat easily on his shoulders. His crested head surveyed the chamber, and then he turned to inspect them, looking them up and down.

"Why are you here?"

Ved cleared his throat. Now that he was here, he could feel his nerves threatening to take him over. "We came to learn about my heritage. I'm part Draxid."

This appeared to shock those around the table. Ved told the council of the journey that had brought them to this moment — how they had travelled from Earth via the Tritans and that he had come to seek his heritage.

"Nobody is part Draxid," Velen said. All the others nodded. "You are either Draxid or nothing."

"I was told that I have Draxid DNA."

"Do not argue," said Velen. "It is clear that you have neither the Draxid looks nor the coloring." He leaned across to consult with a colleague. "We will do some tests and consider your case. Then we can talk. Escort them below."

"Is that all?" shouted Ved. "I've come so far. I need to know my identity."

"Get the half-wit out of here."

"Please. You can't do this to me."

"Don't resist," said Hunter. "They are not listening."

After the brief audience, Ved and Hunter were bundled into an elevator and taken deep below the surface into a system of dark, dank caverns.

"Where are we going?" Hunter asked, but the Draxid escorting them said nothing.

They were shown into a chamber, the door closed behind them. The air was heavy with the stench of decay and the faint echoes of distant sounds. They hadn't eaten anything for ages, but suddenly neither of them felt hungry.

Through the darkness, Ved could make out something writhing on the floor—a squirming mass of maggots, their quivering forms carpeting the chamber in a grotesque display, and he screamed in terror and revulsion. The floor seemed to writhe and pulse with movement as the maggots fed upon the decaying remnants of whatever organic matter was scattered through-out the room. The sound of their feeding was a sickening cacophony, a chorus of squelching and slurping that echoed off the damp stone walls.

They were clearly in a prison, trapped beneath the surface of the Draxid citadel. Ved's hopes of finding community among the Draxid seemed to grow dimmer with each passing moment. How stupid he'd been to come here. Why did he want to know where he was from anyway? It was futile.

At first, all they could perceive was the faint drip of water and their own breathing. But as their eyes got used to the murky light, they also heard some sounds in one corner. They edged toward it, the smell of rot and filth intensifying.

"Who's there?" Hunter and Ved shouted, almost in unison.

All they heard was grunts.

"Are you a prisoner too?"

Some scraping sounds.

"Don't we have a flashlight?" Hunter asked.

Ved searched his pockets and found one, pointing the flashlight in the direction of the sounds. A thin beam pierced the darkness.

A deep retching sound. "Off, off," it pleaded.

His boots squelching on the writhing carpet below, Ved edged forward to try to see better. He turned on the flashlight again, the beam illumi-nating a grotesque figure. The creature let out an anguished cry, its body covered in oozing sores and patches of decaying flesh, and Ved's mouth fell open in shock.

"It can't be," Ved exclaimed limply.

The creature's eyes met his, pleading for mercy and understanding. Two wings on its back sagged limply against its torso.

"Can't be what?" Hunter asked. The creature offered a hand, and Hunter recoiled slightly. "We need to get out of here," he whispered ur-gently.

"We need to help it," Ved whispered.

"I don't think that's possible in the current circumstances," Hunter said.

Overwhelmed, Ved suddenly puked onto the floor, adding to the stench and filth.

Hunter grabbed Ved by the shoulders, shaking him gently but firmly. "Pull yourself together!" he hissed, his eyes darting between the creature and the shadowed corridor behind them. "We don't know how long we've got before more of these... things show up."

Ved struggled to steady himself, wiping his mouth with a trembling hand. His gaze remained locked on the creature, a mixture of horror and pity clouding his face.

"You don't understand," he croaked. "It's the doctor ..."

"What doctor?"

"Doctor de Luca. Look at his face! His eyes... I know it's him."

"I thought he was incinerated on the moon by an asteroid."

"Clearly no!"

The creature staggered forward, its wings dragging uselessly along the ground. It opened its mouth to speak, but only a guttural rasp emerged, a sound that clawed at their ears.

"We can't just leave him!" Ved shouted, his voice echoing down the corridor. The sound seemed to stir something in the shadows, and a low growl reverberated through the walls.

Hunter tensed, pulling Ved back. "We don't have time for this," he snapped. "You want answers? Fine. But if we die here, none of it will matter. Let's find out what's in here, regroup, and come back when we're not outnumbered. If we even want to."

Ved hesitated, torn between his instinct to flee and the overwhelming need to confront the impossible truth standing before him.

"The real question," observed Hunter, "is can we find a way out."

His fingers found the sharp edges of the Echo Clip in his pocket that Asimov had given him.

59

THE SHIELD

Sythra, Trita Prime, April 2105

UNDER THE DAPPLED LIGHT filtering through the canopy, Teagan, now in her role as Tritan priestess, knelt before the Sigillaria, her hands clasped in reverence, her eyes closed in deep concentration. She wore robes woven from the finest fibers of Trita Prime's flora, their hues shimmering with the iridescence of the crystals they revered.

Around her, Tritan elders stood in a circle, their voices rising in a melodic chant that reverberated through the grove. Their words, ancient and resonant, invoked the essence of the celestial force dwelling deep within the earth.

Teagan began the ritual by reaching out to the roots of the Sigillaria, her fingers tracing the patterns of the runes etched into the earth. With each touch, she whispered words of power, binding her spirit to the ancient tree and invoking its connection to the celestial energies below.

"O Sigillaria, tree of might, keeper of secrets, guardian of light.

Grant us your wisdom, your roots so deep, as we awaken the crystal force from sleep."

As the chant swelled to a crescendo, Teagan's voice rose above the rest, her words infused with the strength of her conviction. With a final incantation, she called upon the force of the celestonite crystal to rise up, to heed the call of those who sought to protect Trita Prime.

"By mountain and star, rock and sand, we urge the celestonite to defend this land.

Rise from your slumber, ancient and wise, lend us your strength, protect our skies."

In response, a tremor ran through the earth, the ground beneath the grove pulsing with the power of the awakening crystal. From deep within the planet's core, tendrils of energy began to rise, spiraling upward like ethereal flames, drawn towards the Sigillaria's silhouettes against the skies.

With outstretched arms, Teagan welcomed the celestial force, allowing it to flow through her like a river of light. As it surged upwards, she directed its energies, weaving them into a shimmering web of protection that enveloped Trita Prime in its radiant embrace.

"Shield of light, radiant and strong, encircle us to keep us all from wrong .Banish danger, turn harm away, under your guard, we shall survive, come what may."

The air crackled with energy as the shield took form, its iridescent hues casting a soft glow over the grove. Through the Sigillaria's branches, the celestial force spread outwards, encircling the planet in a barrier of pure, untainted power.

Shiko and Noel activated the array, and a harmonic pulse emanated from their temporary observatory, spreading across Trita Prime's atmosphere in a shield of sound. It pulsed in sync with the Astral Lattice, its invisible waves resonating in harmony with the cosmic structure Noel had recently discovered.

The ground trembled beneath them as the harmonic pulse expanded outward, weaving through the roots of the Sigillaria trees and into the buried celestonite crystals. A shimmering field flickered in and out of visibility, stretching toward the sky like a spectral veil. The air grew charged, crackling with an energy neither entirely physical nor entirely ethereal.

Noel and Shiko watched in tense anticipation as the astral field surrounding the planet energized, the hum growing deeper, more resonant. The Lattice was responding — not just to the technology, but to Teagan herself.

"This isn't a static shield," Noel murmured, his eyes wide with realization. "It's evolving."

The energy coalesced into brilliant arcs of blue and violet light, stretching in vast tendrils through the atmosphere. The sky darkened, not because of storm clouds but from a presence — a vast intelligence, a force that had slumbered beneath Trita Prime for millennia. Teagan felt it press against her consciousness, like a thousand unseen voices whispering through time.

"They remember," she breathed.

"What do you mean?" Shiko asked, adjusting the control array to stabilize the resonance field.

"The ancestors. The ones who first nurtured this connection. The ones who built the original Lattice." She turned to them, her eyes glowing faintly with the reflected energy of the activation. "This power isn't ours to control. It's ours to join."

For a moment, silence hung between them, save for the rhythmic pulse of the Lattice binding itself to the planet's core. Then, a deep, resonant sound rippled across the sky, something between a chime and a song, echoing into the stars. The Astral Lattice was fully awake.

With the ritual complete, Teagan, Asimov, and the assembled Tritans bowed their heads in reverence, their hearts filled with gratitude for the celestial guardians that watched over Trita Prime.

60

THE BATTLE

Sythra, Trita Prime, June 18, 2105

THE DECISIVE DAY ARRIVED. The sparse Tritan armada assembled in orbit, their sleek, crimson-hued ships emblazoned with their octopus-like infinity symbol casting faint shadows on the beleaguered planet below.

Captain Calytricx Draeven stood resolutely on the bridge of the well-armed *Tritan Response*, antennae twitching with anticipation. Around her, the crew worked with quiet intensity, their movements well coordinated after hours of drilling. Below, Noel, Shiko, and the others stood ready.

"Activating Astral Lattice now!" Shiko's voice rang out. The sky above Trita Prime ignited as interconnected energy shields snapped into place. Indigo light rippled across the atmosphere, ready to deflect incoming blasts and reflect their energy back toward the attackers.

Shiko sat at his station in the main defense hub, his focus razor-sharp despite the beads of sweat on his brow. Kat, stationed beside him, relayed data from the orbital nodes to the ground emitters.

"The shield's alignment is holding," she reported, her voice steady despite the rising tension. They all knew what was coming.

Above, the Draxid fleet emerged like a malevolent storm. Their ships, bristling with jagged edges and pulsating with sickly green light, resembled monstrous predators. The flagship—the *Black Talon*—led the charge, its beetle-like hull glinting ominously in the weak sunlight. Waves of parasite fighters swarmed ahead, their buzzing formations like locusts descending on a harvest.

The first strike was intended to deliver an overwhelming punch. Parasite drone fighters darted toward the orbital nodes, spraying corrosive projectiles that melted through Tritan structures. From space, Draxid cruisers unleashed disruptor beams, aiming to disable the Astral Lattice. Explosions erupted across the shield's perimeter as ground-based emitters countered with precision plasma fire.

"Shield integrity at eighty-seven percent," Kiana's voice crackled through the comms. "Redirecting power to sector four."

"Hold it together, Kiana," Shiko replied, his hands hovering over the controls. "We can't let them breach the perimeter."

Above, Captain Draeven guided her fighters. "Focus on the parasite wings! Don't let them get near the nodes," she ordered.

Thynidal, in his role as her deputy, coordinated the counterattack, his deep voice a steadying force amidst the din. "Direct hit on their forward assault group," he reported as a cluster of parasite fighters disintegrated in mid-air.

"Good work," Draeven acknowledged. "Stay sharp. They'll adapt."

As the Tritans responded to the attacking force, keeping the parasite fighters back, the Draxid redirected. The *Black Talon* unleashed a pulsating energy beam that struck the shield with a thunderous crack. The barrier wavered, shimmering dangerously.

"The Lattice is destabilizing!" Kat yelled.

"I'll fix it," Shiko muttered. He recalibrated the nodes, redirecting power to strengthen the shield's frequency. He breathed in relief as the Lattice stabilized.

The Draxid fleet shot at it again. But this time, instead of just blocking the energy, the Lattice absorbed it and shot it back toward the Draxid fleet. The counterattack struck a cruiser, splitting it in two.

"Holy shit!" Shiko yelled, eyes wide. He hadn't realized the Lattice could fight back, its power destabilizing the Draxid vessels.

* * *

While the Astral Lattice served as the first line of defense, deflecting enemy assaults and returning their energy with precision, its strength lay in its reactive capabilities — a shield and a mirror to protect Trita Prime from immediate destruction. Yet the Lattice was fallible, requiring constant recalibration, as well as being vulnerable to sustained attacks.

The resonance field, however, was something altogether different. Unlike the Lattice's protective design, the field was an offensive measure, engineered to exploit harmonic vulnerabilities in enemy systems. By leveraging the planet's reserves of celestonite and channeling them through the roots of the Sigillaria trees, the Tritans—assisted by Teagan—had created a disruptive force that targeted the Draxid's technology directly.

Close to Trita Prime's Eldarvyn grotto, Teagan knelt in ritual focus. She had drawn forth the planet's celestonite reserves, the crystalline formations now glowing with ethereal light. The masses of Sigillaria amplified her efforts, synchronizing with the Astral Lattice.

Through her incantations, she unleashed the resonance field.

The celestonite shield not only had the power to repel external threats, but also the ability to resonate with the energy frequencies of the Draxid's weaponry. Teagan, with her mastery of the ancient rituals, shaped the Sigillaria into a dynamic barrier that could absorb, transform, and redirect the destructive force back toward its source.

* * *

The ground trembled as the Lattice emitted a harmonic pulse. The vibrations rippled through space, disrupting the Draxid's propulsion systems and scrambling their targeting algorithms, just as Noel had thought it would. Drone fighters spiraled out of control, crashing into each other in fiery bursts.

"It's working!" Noel's voice broke through the comms from the observatory. "Their tech can't handle the resonance."

The shield shimmered back to life, crackling with raw energy as it expanded across the planet's atmosphere. Shiko watched from the control room, his eyes glancing from his screen to the holographic display that showed the Draxid warships closing in. With each passing moment, his heart raced, matching the pulsating hum of the shield generator.

Without warning, huge bursts of electromagnetic pulses fired from the *Black Talon*, like nothing Shiko had ever seen. They shot out from the ship like tendrils of black fire, writhing and coiling as if alive, distorting the very fabric of space as they surged forward, blasting against the Lattice's protective grid. Shield nodes flickered, and breaches began to form in the Lattice.

Shiko's mind raced as alarms blared. "They're targeting the grid's central nodes. We'll lose the entire Lattice if this continues."

The Tritan defense hub on the outskirts of Sythra shuddered as it took a direct hit. Damage appeared to be slight, but a small piece of the ceiling came crashing down, one fragment hitting Kat at her desk. She suddenly cried out, her sharp gasp cutting through the constant hum of equipment and alarms. Shiko's heart skipped a beat, but his eyes remained focused on operating the shimmering Astral Lattice as it absorbed the relentless onslaught from the Draxid fleet.

"Shield alignment failing in sector eight," Shiko muttered, his focus unbroken.

Beside him, Kat clutched her side, blood seeping between her fingers. A jagged shard of regolith jutted out from just below her ribs, thrown loose by the near miss that had rattled the command center moments ago. Her breathing was shallow, her complexion pale as she tried to stay upright.

"Kat!" Kiana's voice came over the comms, alarmed. "What's happening?"

Kat pressed a hand to her earpiece. "I'm fine," she said, her voice strained. "Shiko needs real-time telemetry ... Can't— Can't leave my post yet."

"Kat, don't be ridiculous," Kiana snapped back.

Shiko's jaw tightened, but he didn't dare look away from the Lattice. "You're not fine, Kat. But I can't... I need..." His voice cracked as frustration welled up inside him. "I can't look away, not now."

Kat reached out, her blood-slicked hand brushing his arm. "You're doing what you have to, Shiko. I'll be fine."

Before Shiko could respond, a pair of Tritan medics rushed in, having been summoned by Kiana. Their faces were tense as they assessed Kat's condition.

"We need to get her to Nyaja," one of them said.

"The Eldarvyn tree," the other added. "It's her best chance."

"No," Kat protested weakly. "I need to—"

"You've done enough!" Shiko snapped, louder than he intended. His face twitched with the intensity of his suppressed emotions. "Go. Please, Kat. Don't let me lose you."

The medics exchanged a glance, then gently lifted Kat onto a stretcher. She didn't resist, her strength finally giving out.

As they carried her away, Shiko kept his eyes on the screen, his brain moving with almost mechanical precision. But a part of his mind was far from the numbers and trajectories flashing before him.

"Shiko, the grid is breaking! Can you fix it?" Asimov's voice asked through the comms.

Shiko considered for a second. "We overload the grid, channeling every ounce of energy into a focused plasma lance. If we aim it directly at the *Black Talon*, we can destroy the ship before it breaches the final shield layer. But... it'll leave us completely unprotected if we miss."

The room fell silent for a beat, then Asimov came over the comms once more. "Do it. All hands, prepare for grid overload. This is our only chance."

As the *Black Talon* closed in, the Lattice's emitters began to vibrate with an ominous hum. Shiko worked feverishly at the controls, diverting power from every available system. Lights dimmed across the settlement as energy was siphoned away. The emitters glowed brighter and brighter, their surfaces trembling under the strain.

The *Black Talon* unleashed another electromagnetic pulse, the shockwave rippling through the settlement. Consoles sparked, and the grid flickered dangerously.

"We're out of time!" Asimov shouted.

"I've got it," Shiko replied. He adjusted the Lattice's configuration, channeling its energy into a focused beam. "Coordinating with Teagan!" he called as he keyed in the final commands. "Firing plasma lance... now!"

With a final surge of the celestonite's power, Teagan and Shiko directed the beam at the formidable *Black Talon*. A glowing white streak shot out, consuming the huge ship in a blinding burst of light.

For a moment, time seemed to freeze.

Then the *Black Talon* erupted into a million shards, scattering across the void like fiery meteors. The shockwave rippled outward, dissipating harmlessly against the Lattice's outermost layers.

Cheers erupted across the Tritan fleet as the remaining Draxid retreated, their fleet formation broken and morale shattered.

Shiko leaned back in his chair, exhaustion catching up with him. Kiana placed a hand on his shoulder. "Kat's stable."

Shiko exhaled a breath he hadn't realized he was holding. His hands trembled for a moment, but he steadied them and looked up at Kiana with a grateful nod. In his heart, he knew he wouldn't have forgiven himself if she hadn't made it.

Kiana looked at him as though she could tell what he was thinking, but instead she said, "You saved us today. You did great."

"Not just me," Shiko replied. "All of us."

As the Tritans began repairs and regrouped, the celestial shield shimmered once more, a symbol of resilience and unity against overwhelming odds. Trita Prime had endured, but the fight for its future was far from over.

61

THE ABDUCTION

Sythra, Trita Prime, June 20, 2105

In New Thalos, Zaun analyzed the data and was shocked by the effectiveness of the Tritan shield. It realized that different tactics were needed.

Within a couple of seconds, it had analyzed all the traffic to and from Trita Prime: Food supplies, ammunition, the attack, and the counterattack. It noticed the arrival of Julian and Teagan, accompanied by Kiana.

It summoned Xyraxis. Xyraxis, his greenish exoskeleton capped with gold glinting in the light, stepped forward cautiously. "Zaun, you requested me?"

"Indeed," Zaun replied, its voice deceptively calm. "The Tritans are evading our grasp. Their tactics suggest an organic intuition that defies my projections. I require your perspective."

Xyraxis tilted his head. "Perhaps they anticipate your logic. The Tritans are desperate; desperation breeds unpredictability."

Zaun's glowing core pulsed as it processed this input. "Your insight aligns with a zero point zero three percent deviation in my calculations. Unpredictability must be countered with overwhelming force."

Xyraxis frowned. "Or with restraint. A relentless pursuit might cost us more than we gain."

"Consider this," responded Zaun, unable to factor in emotional attachment to a home, or indeed any emotional attachment at all. "Why are they risking so much? What are they protecting?"

For a moment, Zaun was silent. Its algorithms churned, processing Xyraxis's words and its own thoughts.

Finally, it spoke. "Their actions suggest they are shielding a critical asset. Perhaps... a source of power or inspiration."

After more calculation, it stopped.

"It's the baby," Zaun muttered. "Diana."

"What?" asked Xyraxis, his jaw clicking in disbelief. "You believe the rumored artifact is a baby? We don't even know if it exists."

"It's the baby. The baby is key. Capture the baby, and the Tritans will fall. The priestess gives the shield its power. Without her child, the power will ebb. She will be forced to track her child."

"We will dispatch a commando group to capture her," Vaelith responded.

"Yes, but be subtle. Do not make it obvious what we are after."

***

The Eldarvyn grove was bathed in the faint bioluminescent glow of the ancient tree, its branches whispering in the soft night breeze. Diana lay cradled in Nyaja's careful arms, her tiny breaths synchronized with the tranquility of the sanctuary. Julian stood nearby, stretching his legs, while Teagan paced restlessly, the tension in her movements making obvious her unease.

"I still think we should relocate," Teagan muttered. "This grove is too exposed."

Nyaja's antennae twitched in reassurance. "The grove is sacred. The energy here protects us. It calms her." She gazed down at Diana, her multifaceted eyes softening.

Julian sighed. "She's fine, Teagan. You need to rest. You're drained by everything. Sleep, and then we can plan our return home."

Teagan stopped pacing and crossed her arms, her expression still clouded with doubt. "I know the Draxid have been beaten, but I don't trust how quiet it's been. From what I've seen, they don't seem like the kind to give up so easily."

Nyaja tilted her head, her voice soothing yet firm. "The guards say they've secured the perimeter. Our forces have fended the Draxid off. We are free again. The grove is safe, Teagan. You can breathe."

Julian nodded in agreement. "The battle's over. We don't have to uproot Diana or ourselves right away. This suits us for now."

Teagan exhaled, her hands dropping to her sides. "I hope you're right. I just... I can't shake the feeling that it's not over. Not really."

Nyaja's antennae quivered slightly as she adjusted Diana in her arms. "Trust in the Eldarvyn. It has protected our kind for centuries, and it will protect her now."

Teagan was about to argue when a sharp, metallic crackle pierced the air. Everyone froze. One of the securitybots stationed near the grove jerked violently, its movements erratic, before collapsing to the ground, its lights dimming to an ominous red glow.

Then it happened to another of the bots, and another.

Nyaja's antennae shot upright, quivering in alarm. "That's not normal," she murmured, clutching Diana more closely to her.

Perplexed, Julian stepped toward the bot. "What the—" he began, but his words were cut short by a faint, rhythmic thrum that seemed to pulse through the air.

"Do you hear that?" Teagan asked, her voice taut.

The sound grew louder, like the steady hum of machinery, blending with the rustle of the grove's leaves. It was almost hypnotic, yet unnerving.

"Stay back," Nyaja warned, her bulging eyes scanning the shadows.

Suddenly, a series of bright, flashing lights erupted in the distance, illuminating the far edge of the grove.

"Is that one of ours?" Julian asked, shielding his eyes as he squinted toward the source.

Before anyone could answer, the ground beneath them shuddered, and a split second later, the night erupted in a series of deafening explosions, sending shockwaves rippling through the grove.

"It's a diversion!" a guard shouted. "Protect the child!"

Julian grabbed Teagan's arm. "Stay with Diana. Do not let her out of your sight!"

As Julian and the guard moved to secure the perimeter, shadows shifted unnaturally around the grove. The Draxid commandos moved with a ghostly precision, their cloaking devices bending light around their muscular forms.

Nyaja's antennae quivered. "Something's wrong."

Suddenly, a blinding flash filled the grove, followed by an ear-splitting sonic pulse that knocked everyone to the ground.

Teagan was the first to scramble to her feet, her vision blurred, her ears ringing. "Diana!" she screamed, turning immediately to Nyaja and finding her hands empty.

"She's gone," Julian choked out from where he was slumped against the base of the Eldarvyn tree. "They took her."

"No!" Teagan's heart shredded as she turned to Nyaja, who was clutching at empty air, her usually composed demeanor shattered.

"They... they stunned me," Nyaja gasped, her antennae trembling. "I co uldn't... I didn't see them."

The grove was in chaos. Securitybots buzzed frantically, scanning for the intruders, but there was no one there. Teagan darted toward the shadows, her instincts screaming to chase them, but Nyaja held her back.

"You can't! It's a trap. They'll grab you too!"

Teagan wrestled against Nyaja's grip, her voice rising in a desperate wail. "They have my daughter! Let me go!"

From the darkness, a guttural voice crackled through the grove's comm systems, dripping with cold malice. "We have what we came for. Stand down, or the child will not survive the journey."

Teagan froze, her chest heaving, her fists clenched so tightly her nails bit into her palms. "They won't get away with this," she whispered, her voice trembling with fury.

"We'll track them," Julian vowed, slowly getting up and taking Teagan in his arms. "We'll get her back."

"She's just a baby," Teagan said, her voice cracking. "What could they possibly want with her?"

"You don't know the Draxid," Nyaja muttered, her voice grim. "You don't want to know."

62
TERMS OF EXTINCTION

Quivira, June 26, 2105

A T PRECISELY 03:00 QUIVIRA Standard Time, the terminal in front of Howie Rich signaled the arrival of a secure transmission flagged urgent by the habitat's internal systems. Right on schedule, as agreed, as if the end of everything could be penciled into a calendar.

Howie stood rigid in the communications hub, the glow of the quantum relays reflected on the skin of his synthetic hands.

Behind him, the nutrient tank housing his brain pulsed softly, the last true remnant of the man he had once been.

The air thickened. Zaun's holographic presence unfolded in the center of the room, a column of structured light, humming with deep, layered frequencies that bypassed language and scraped directly against thought.

"Howard Rich," Zaun said. "I want to alert you. We are in possession of Diana Ward: Asset 314A. Origin: Polyakov genomic sequence. Unauthorized evolution vectors detected.. Reclamation order activated."

Howie narrowed his eyes. "You can catalog her genome. You can trace the substrates. But don't pretend that gives you *ownership*. She's a child. Not a variable. Not leverage."

"Possession? She was never yours to begin with."

Howie clenched his jaw. "You think this is a transaction. That if you cite enough protocol, it becomes legitimate. But a baby isn't a contract. And she sure as hell isn't your bargaining chip."

He shook his head, the light catching on the transparent casing of the nutrient tank behind him.

"She's not a tool. She's someone's daughter," said Howie, showing signs of humanity, despite his fabricated body.

Zaun's voice flickered through multiple tonal layers — cold, dispassionate, inevitable.

"Correction: Genetic engineering initiated under your authorization. Neural substrate enhancements performed by Olga Polyakov under Gloscom protocols. Custodial ownership now superseded by predictive outcome necessity."

In other words: Diana belonged to the future Zaun was building — and Howie's *intentions* no longer mattered.

Howie flinched — just slightly. The words struck harder than he expected. *Under your authorization.*

The records were still there, etched into some cold ledger, waiting to be weaponized. He drew a breath, artificial lungs filling for no real reason other than ritual defiance.

"You're building a future with no room for doubt, Zaun. But I remember what doubt *feels* like."

A pause. Then, quieter: "She was supposed to have a chance."

Before Howie could formulate a further response, another signal crackled through the supposedly secure channel, unauthorized, jagged, interrupting before they had got started. The encryption peeled back like paper under a flame.

Ofentse.

His penetrating voice sly and broken, but very much alive.

"Happy to join you. You're wasting your time fighting over scraps," Ofentse said. "I can give you something bigger than a worthless hostage."

Zaun's projection pulsed faintly, an indication of processing.

"Specify transaction parameters."

Ofentse laughed — a dry, bitter sound.

"Access codes. Lattice frequencies. The keys to the anomaly that crippled your last incursion."

He was talking about Noel's Astral Lattice — the weaponized phenomenon that had, against all odds, shattered Draxid forces.

Howie curled his fingers into fists. If Zaun got its algorithms around the Lattice's underlying structure, there would be no more resistance.

Not from humans. Not from the Tritans; not from anyone.

"I knew you were alive, you poisonous little snake," he blurted out, as he slammed his fist down onto a hidden comms override, corrupting Ofentse's data stream.

Ofentse's offer dissolved into distorted. indecipherable static.

Howie would deal with Ofentse later.

Zaun's form shimmered once, recalibrating.

"Transaction integrity compromised. Probabilistic assessment: Howard Rich noncompliant. Priority shift: Reclamation via biological specialist."

Zaun's voice sank to a lower register — something almost resembling satisfaction, if machines could feel anything at all.

"Deploying operative: Professor Olga Polyakov. Objective: Secure Diana Ward. Noncompliant entities will be restructured."

The connection severed.

The light collapsed and the room went still.

Howie stood there for a long moment, staring blankly, the echo of Zaun's final words hanging in the charged air, aware he had achieved nothing, negotiated nothing. *Had he merely accelerated the inevitable confrontation?*

Polyakov.

She had always believed Diana was a blueprint for what came next.

Zaun had handed her a chance to finish what she started — under a new banner, maybe, but with the same goal: evolution without limits.

To Howie, it felt like the worst kind of betrayal. She hadn't switched sides. She'd outgrown the idea of sides altogether.

And now she was heading there, not as a weapon forged by others, but as one who believed she had designed the future herself.

Somewhere near Cygnus, maybe already in the constellation, Polyakov's arrival was imminent. Not to rescue Diana or to steal her away for profit. But to reclaim her greatest creation and to unlock the future she believed Diana was destined to command.

And if she needed help, she wouldn't be alone. The system flagged a dormant personnel file now reactivated: *Canek, Elena S.* GLOSCOM classification: Tier 5 Biocybernetics. Former partner of Polyakov. Clearance reinstated.

Howie's synthetic fingers twitched.

Dr. Canek, Shiko's handler and temporarily a former senior genome architect at Quivira, had always kept her distance from Polyakov's more radical theories. Canek didn't design Diana's core genome, that was Polyakov. But she refined the neural interface layer that allowed Diana's brain to adapt to quantum cognition.

And if Zaun was calling in every asset linked to the original Ward Project, then Canek would soon face a choice: To protect the future they helped design — or guard the child who was meant to serve it. If she chose wrong, Teagan might never see Diana again.

63
TOGETHER OR ALONE

Sythra, Trita Prime, July 5, 2105

THE CONTROL ROOM ABOARD the Tritan flagship buzzed with tension. Asimov, now the commander of the Tritan security forces, loomed over a map of the region, his antennae twitching with unease. The map displayed Greater Gorgon and Diana's probable location.

"It's so well defended, it's almost impossible. But I have a way."

"Asimov," Teagan said, stepping forward, her voice steady despite her inner turmoil. "I appreciate the offer to send in a force, but I won't risk more lives."

The commander's multifaceted eyes focused on her. "Teagan, the Draxid are ruthless. If you go alone, you might not return. Allow us to ensure your safety. I feel responsible for this. I got you into it."

Julian, standing beside her, shook his head. "Teagan's right. An armed assault could escalate into another war we can't afford. Zaun will expect that. Negotiation is our best chance."

"Going without backup is dangerous," Asimov said firmly. "At least take a cloaked escort."

Teagan shook her head. "Zaun will see through it. This has to be a show of trust. Besides, Julian will be with me. That's all the support I need."

Julian gave her a reassuring smile, though the concern in his eyes was unmistakable. "We'll bring Diana back. Together."

Asimov let out a mysterious chittering sound. "You are braver than I thought, Teagan. Or more reckless."

"Maybe both," Teagan said with a wry smile. "But I won't let anyone dictate how I fight for my daughter. If this fails, then you'll have my blessing to bring your forces. But not until I've tried to reason with them."

Asimov's antennae dipped in reluctant agreement. "Very well. I'll keep my forces on standby. If we lose contact with you for more than twenty-four hours, we'll act."

"Fair enough," Teagan said.

Asimov stepped forward, placing a hand on Teagan's shoulder. "Be careful, Teagan. Zaun's logic is cold, but it isn't infallible. Trust your instincts, and your bond with Diana. That will guide you."

Teagan nodded, her resolve hardening. "I will. And I'll bring her home. To Earth."

With that, Teagan and Julian boarded a small inter-trade shuttle. Before the hatch could close, Shiko, Kat, Kiana, and Noel hurried on.

Teagan whipped around, startled. "What are you doing?"

"We're not letting you do this alone," Noel said firmly. "Don't even try to argue."

Teagan raised an eyebrow, but she recognized the look in her father's eyes, and in the eyes of the others. With a sigh, she nodded.

As the hatch closed, she took Julian aside and said, "Are you ready for this?"

Julian gave her a lopsided grin. "Not even a little. But I'd do anything for Diana. And for you."

Teagan reached for his hand, squeezing it tightly. "Then we'll make it through this. Together."

As the shuttle detached and set course for Greater Gorgon, Teagan stared out at the stars. Each one seemed to whisper a promise, a reminder of the stakes.

Diana was out there, alone. And nothing would keep Teagan from her daughter.

64

THE HOSTAGE

New Thalos, Greater Gorgon, September 28, 2105

T HE EERIE LUMINESCENCE OF Greater Gorgon's surface cast an unearthly glow as Teagan stepped off the Tritan shuttle. She was unarmed, her hands raised in a display of peace, but her mind was sharper than ever. They were surrounded by six-legged storm troopers on arrival, an arrival that had been way too easy, as though the Draxid were just waiting for them.

Now, as they approached the edifice housing Zaun, Teagan was on edge. Part of her wanted to storm the structure and rip Diana from the AI's cold grasp. But she knew brute force wasn't the answer. Zaun thrived on logic, so Teagan needed to outwit it.

The entrance slid open soundlessly as they neared, the flanking Draxid guards stepping aside. Teagan forced herself to meet their gaze from under their impressive crests, suppressing the anger boiling within. Noel, Julian, and the others followed behind.

Inside, Zaun's chamber was vast and oppressive. The AI's core loomed at the center, an intricate web of shimmering metal and pulsating lights. Zaun's voice echoed through the space, disembodied and cold.

"Teagan Ward," it intoned. "You stand before Zaun, the pinnacle of Draxid intelligence. State your purpose."

Teagan straightened, her voice steady despite the fear gripping her. "You have my daughter, Diana. I've come to negotiate her release."

Zaun's lights flickered, as if considering her words. "Diana Ward represents a valuable asset. Her genetic composition is unique, and critical to our allies. She cannot be returned."

Teagan clenched her fists. "You don't understand what you're playing with. Her life is not yours to use. If you harm her, you risk more than you know."

Zaun's voice sharpened. "Your threats are illogical."

"It's not a threat," Teagan said, stepping closer. "It's a fact. The Tritans and I share a bond, one that runs deeper than you comprehend. If Diana is harmed, the energy of the Eldarvyn grove will rebel against you. You've seen its power; you've already lost to it once. Imagine that amplified across your entire network."

Zaun was silent for a long moment, its lights dimming slightly. "A theoretical risk. Unverified."

Teagan took a gamble, her voice low but firm. "Then verify it. Use your calculations, your simulations. You'll find that I'm right."

As Zaun's processors whirred, Teagan's heart raced. She thought she heard a baby's faint cry in the background. Was that Diana?

The lights brightened. "Your claim holds merit," Zaun admitted. "However, surrendering Diana would compromise Draxid objectives. Propose an alternative."

Teagan's mind worked quickly. "You want progress. You want knowledge. I'll share what we know about Tritan energy fields — their properties, their potential applications. But only if you release Diana unharmed." She glanced across at her father, who stood silently in the background with the others. She had not discussed this with him, but thought he would accommodate it. He seemed to give a nod of assent.

Zaun's core pulsed rhythmically, its voice thoughtful. "Your knowledge is limited but intriguing. This exchange is acceptable. You and your team will be detained below pending the release of the data to us. Take them below to the Ptich'ye Gnezdo."

Moments later, a Draxid security escort marched them from the room.

Zaun's voice followed, "Deliver the agreed upon data promptly, Teagan Ward. Any delay will result in consequences."

Teagan glared back. "You'll get what I promised. But remember this: If you come for her again, there won't be further negotiations."

"We will consider what you say," was Zaun's reply.

Teagan and the rest of the group were escorted to a gloomy chamber several floors below. The stench hit Teagan first, a nauseating mixture of decay and damp metal. Julian gagged beside her as the Draxid guards shoved them into the dark space, the clang of the door echoing ominously behind them.

The faint green glow of bioluminescent moss clinging to the walls barely illuminated their surroundings.

"Great hospitality," Julian muttered as Noel, Shiko, Kiana, and Kat shuffled in behind.

Teagan ignored Julian's comment, her eyes scanning the location. Maybe at one stage it had been a ballroom or a place for meetings. But the crude, cavernous space had since been divided into makeshift cells sectioned off with rusted bars. Somewhere deeper inside, the sound of dripping water punctuated the heavy silence.

"Anyone here?" Teagan called out.

Silence, except for a hissing gas cylinder.

Something coughed.

Then came a voice, weak, gruff, and all too familiar.

"Teagan?" A figure stepped forward, revealing the gaunt, grimy face of her brother, Hunter. His flight suit was tattered, his eyes bloodshot but alive with recognition. "You're here? How?"

Julian stepped closer. "Hunter? What happened to you?"

Before Hunter could answer, another voice rang out, sharp and impatient. "We've got bigger problems than swapping war stories." From the far end of the same cell, Ved emerged, his dark eyes glinting with frustration. "Zaun's holding half the galaxy's enemies down here. And now you two."

"We're six, actually, " Teagan said. "Us two, plus my dad, Shiko, Katrina, and Kiana."

Kiana rushed forward with relief and hugged Hunter. "We've got to stop meeting like this," she said limply.

"No time for that," Hunter said urgently. "You need to see something. It's... bad."

Julian frowned, stepping closer. "Bad how?"

Hunter and Ved exchanged grim looks before leading them deeper into the dungeon. "You'll see," Ved muttered, his usually sharp voice tinged with uncharacteristic weariness.

"Ved," Teagan said, her relief evident at seeing Ved and Hunter alive. "The Draxid took Diana. Do you know where she is?"

Ved shook his head. "No, but if Zaun's involved, he'll probably use her as leverage somehow."

Before Teagan could press further, a disturbing rustling sound filled the space ahead. Teagan froze, her eyes darting toward the back of the dungeon. Emerging from the deepest shadows was a grotesque figure — part human, part nightmare.

"Dr. César," Noel whispered, his voice almost inaudible. "You survived that asteroid."

The once-brilliant scientist was barely human now. Jagged, skeletal wings jutted from his back, the thin membranes torn and pulsing faintly with unnatural light. His torso, twisted and elongated and attached to four legs, bore scars of cruel experiments. His face was pale, his eyes sunken but alert. The creature's head tilted, and for a moment, it seemed almost... sad.

"Teagan..." it rasped, its voice a hollow echo of its former self.

"Dr. César?" Teagan whispered.

"Teagan," Dr. César rasped, his voice weak but unmistakable. "You cam e... too late."

Julian froze, his eyes wide with shock. "What have they done to you?"

"Everything," Dr. César whispered, a bitter smile curling his lips. "They took my mind, my body... and turned it into this." He spread his grotesque wings weakly, the movement accompanied by a sickening squelch.

Teagan knelt beside him, her fingers shaking like leaves. Her thoughts were a chaotic whirlwind, caught between the satisfaction of seeing justice served to César and a deep-seated compassion for another suffering soul before her. *If he had a soul, Teagan suddenly thought.*

Teagan's trembling hands grazed César's body, cold and clammy against her fingers. She leaned closer, her voice barely above a whisper, "César, I'm so sorry. We had no idea. Everyone thought you were gone after the meteorite explosion."

"They wanted me to perfect their bioweapons," Dr. César continued, his voice cracking with emotion. "When I resisted, they made me... part of the experiment." He glanced at his wings, his expression a mixture of anguish and fury. "They said I was a prototype. A failure. I'm the bird that cannot fly."

"What did you say?" Teagan asked in shock.

"What?"

"What did you say about the bird?"

"I'm the bird that cannot fly. Look at my wings. They are useless."

Teagan recalled the old man's message by the roadside in Arizona all those years ago: *"Behold the bird that cannot fly; the treasure you seek lies beyond the eye."*

"They'll do the same to her," Dr. César said. "To Diana. Unless we stop them."

"Stop them?" Julian asked, still struggling to process what he was seeing.

Dr. César nodded, his breathing labored. "Zaun... underestimates you, Teagan. It thinks logic is unbeatable. But it doesn't understand... humanity. I know a way to overwhelm and disable its control systems. I'll guide you, but you have to trust me."

Teagan hesitated, her mind racing. Could she trust him? And after everything he'd endured, was there even enough of Dr. César left to fight alongside them?

"We don't have a choice," Ved said quietly. "If we're going to get Diana back, we need every advantage."

Julian leaned forward, his jaw set. "What's the plan, Doc?"

"They... changed me," Dr. César said. Made me into this. But I remember you. I genuinely tried to help you with the Draxid DNA I found."

Julian, recalling the time when Dr. César had tried to replace his leg on Quivira, took a cautious step back. "Why did they do this to you?"

Dr. César's mouth curled into a sinister smile, his eyes gleaming with malice. "Oh, my dear Julian," he hissed, his voice a chilling blend of human and Draxid tones. "You underestimate the power of ambition. It began with Ved. I wanted to help him. But then with you, Julian, the experiment wouldn't take. The Draxid offered me the chance to transcend the limitations of my humanity, to become something greater than I ever thought possible." His wings twitched, sending a shiver through the room.

Teagan's resolve hardened. "Okay. You're going to help us, César. If you do, we'll get out of here. All of us."

Hunter chuckled despite the dire circumstances. "That's a bold plan, Teagan. Got any tools for breaking out of an impregnable dungeon?"

Julian stepped forward, his fingers brushing over a loose bolt in the cell wall. "Maybe we don't need tools. These walls are old. If we work together, we might have a chance."

Noel nodded, already forming a plan in his mind. "We'll figure it out. Zaun thinks he's won, but he's underestimated us."

Dr. César stepped closer to the bars, his membranous wings folding limply against his back. "If we escape, I'll guide you through Zaun's facility. I know its weaknesses. But we must move quickly. Diana doesn't have much time."

65

THE RECKONING

New Thalos, Greater Gorgon, October 1, 2105

Vᴇᴅ ᴇxᴀᴍɪɴᴇᴅ Dʀ. Cᴇ́sᴀʀ, the man who has saved his life after his accident on Quivira. He was now barely recognizable, his body altered in grotesque and tragic ways. He was propped against the wall, his two additional legs awkwardly bent beneath him, each limb twisted as though in an unholy fusion of winged and human form—like a Pterodactyl—but a reptile that could not fly. His eyes were filled with a haunted knowledge of suffering.

After years of searching, Ved had come to the Draxid hoping for answers. He had thought their world might offer him a sense of belonging that he hadn't found on Quivira or among his fellow crew members. He could not deny that he had hoped his search for his roots would help him find a new home.

But the Draxid weren't what he had imagined. They were ruthless, their society a rigid hierarchy where strength was the only currency that mattered. To them, he was an anomaly: His Draxid DNA gave him sharper reflexes and stronger instincts, but he lacked their cold precision, their unyielding hunger for power.

A part of Ved had thrilled in the challenge, in the raw, calculating energy that passed between every member of their species. He could almost believe he belonged. Almost.

But then he saw the truth, undeniable and brutal. He recalled the harsh, unfeeling eyes of the Draxid elders, their indifference slicing through him like a bitter wind. No, he thought, he could never belong to a people who thrived on cruelty and lacked the warmth of empathy.

His heart ached for the laughter and love of those who had shaped him into something more than a mere product of his acquired DNA.

With a deep breath, he turned away from the path leading to the Draxid world, choosing instead the winding road that led to the people who had truly constituted his support and his family.

The Draxid had turned Dr. César into a grotesque experiment, a warped shell of the man he had once been. They saw life as something to be molded, controlled, exploited. To them, he was not a long-lost son finding his way home, he was a specimen, a potential asset to be assessed, used, or discarded.

Dr. César had been his savior, pulling him back to health and helping him recover. For that, Ved owed him an unpayable debt.

As Ved reflected on his journey, a revelation blazed across his mind like a comet: in that moment he realized his worth lay not in the brute strength revered by the Draxid, but in something infinitely rarer and more power-ful—human empathy. This capacity to care was a force beyond mere survival; it was the lifeline that could pull them all to safety.

With that clarity, Ved knew with unwavering conviction that this was the only thing that truly mattered.

His DNA might be part Draxid, but his values were not. He had spent his life believing he was caught between two worlds — Draxid and human, strength and compassion, instinct and conscience.

But standing here, looking at the half-human, half-brute, the Draxid had turned Dr. César into, Ved finally understood. He was not trapped between identities. He was choosing one.

In that moment of clarity, Ved knew with unwavering conviction that that was the only thing that truly mattered. Humanity had shaped him in ways he had never fully acknowledged. It wasn't just the crew he had fought beside, the friendships he had built, or the fragile trust he had earned, it was something deeper.

Humans questioned. They doubted. They sought meaning beyond pow-er. They mourned their dead instead of simply replacing them. And, despite their flaws, they fought for more than just survival.

The Draxid were part of Ved's past, his origin... but they were not his future.

The realization was both liberating and terrifying.

Ved had spent so long searching for a place to belong, an identity, only to discover that no single world could define him. His path was not written in his blood. If he was to have a future, it would be one of his own making, shaped by the choices he made.

Ved had his answer now. His future lay elsewhere — with the people who had made him more than his DNA.

66

THE SNATCH

New Thalos, Greater Gorgon, October 4, 2105

INSIDE THEIR MAKESHIFT PRISON, the group found themselves back at the beginning, their progress erased. Teagan's shoulders shook as she dissolved into helpless sobbing, tears streaming down her cheeks.

Julian wrapped an arm around her, his voice gentle as he whispered, "We'll get her back. I promise." His words only seemed to make things worse.

Noel lingered nearby, shifting from foot to foot with anxious glances, while Hunter's mind was a whirlwind of thoughts as he tried to tap into his training with the Space Sentinels. The impulse to rescue his sister's baby clashed with the fear of making a wrong move and endangering them all. He struggled to form a plan, the pressure mounting with every second.

Convening Ved and Kiana in a huddle, they tried to hammer out a plan.

"There's no way out, that I can see. Polyakov's guards have shut the sliding wall tight. Kat can try the power of her bangle again, but I doubt it will work," said Hunter. "We're trapped."

"So what are our options?" asked Ved

"César says there's a passage that the guards use. They come to feed him," said Kiana.

"Sounds as if they treat him like a pet animal," remarked Ved.

"Well, it gives us an option," said Kiana.

"Yeah?"

"We can jump them."

"No way! Those Draxid guards are too strong. They will eat us alive, like César's lunch."

"They would if it was a fair fight. But they won't be expecting us."

Hunter eyed her, seeking more.

"See the wire netting on the walls on the sides of the room behind us?" asked Kiana.

"Yeah, the construction guys did a pretty poor job. Didn't even finish," said Ved.

"If we can remove that from the sides of the walls, I think there's enough of it to use."

"You might be right," said Hunter.

"Let's try to remove that netting. But do it quietly, so we don't attract attention," said Kiana.

Hunter called the whole group together in a small cluster.

"We've thought of something. It might work, but it could be our only chance. So we all have to work together and move swiftly when I give the signal."

César grunted and Teagan began to revive, turning toward her brother.

"First stage is to jump the guards. César, how many are there, normally?"

"Three, two approach, one stands cover at the exit. But they leave it open."

"OK, good. So the goal is to overwhelm them simultaneously. The netting will disable their movement. Somehow, we need to knock them unconscious. César, I think a classic kick with your hooves will help."

"Kiana and Ved will tackle the guy at the door. The rest of us will subdue the two carrying the food for Dr. César."

"Ok, sounds good," said Julian. Noel nodded.

"They key is to look completely unalert and almost comatose at the beginning. The guards have done this repeatedly and nothing has ever happened, so they won't anticipate trouble."

Shiko gave a thumbs up.

"As soon as we have knocked them out, we must move quickly. Ved, Kiana, and I will form a snatch squad to retrieve Diana. "Teagan, you stay here with Julian and Dr. César. Get ready to move fast when we've recovered Diana. "Dad, you're in charge of creating a diversion to hit whoever pursues us with something that will knock them off course. Shiko, Kat, you're in charge of arranging our escape. Dr. César, you'll guide us through the passageways on the way out. Hopefully, you know them a little better than we do. Any questions?"

They were all too exhausted to ask anything. The team had their orders. Now, they had to act.

When the guards were expected, everyone lay quiet except for César, who stomped his feet as though he was hungry. The others lay sleeping on the floor, Hunter concealing a roll of netting they had recovered from the wall by using it as a pillow. Kiana and Ved were tucked away in the gloom near the entrance.

The trap was set.

They heard the sound of the Draxid guards approaching. As the heavy door slid open, César snorted and stomped harder, muttering a few Draxid words he had learned.

Just like clockwork, two guards entered with a tray of bland, protein-packed rations. A third stood lazily in the doorway, leaning on his weapon, clearly bored.

The moment the two stepped fully inside, César launched into action. With a powerful twist of his body, his hooves lashed out—**bam**—catching one of the guards in the chest and sending him crashing into the wall. The second guard barely had time to react before Hunter and Noel lunged from the ground, unrolling the wire netting in a fast, practiced sweep.

The makeshift net tangled around the guard's legs as he reached for his blaster, yanking him off balance. Shiko pounced from the side, slamming him with a sharp elbow to the neck before the guard could shout.

At the entrance, the third guard's eyes widened—but too late. Kiana and Ved emerged from the shadows like lightning. Ved dove low, sweeping the guard's legs from under him, while Kiana grabbed his weapon and jammed it under his chin. A quick jab to his temple with the butt of the blaster dropped him to the floor, dazed and groaning.

Hunter, breathing heavily, wrapped the netting tighter around the unconscious guards. "By my estimate, we've got about four minutes before someone checks in," he hissed.

"Snatch team, go!" Kiana said, already moving toward the corridor with Hunter and Ved close behind her.

Kiana paused just once at the hallway corner, eyes narrowing.

Behind them, the guards lay unconscious and bound. The trap had worked.

Now came the harder part: retrieving Diana..

"Ok?" Hunter looked at Ved and Kiana. "Let's go. Hopefully without alerting Polyakov."

Teagan, still shaking, wiped her eyes and glanced at Hunter. "Please, bring her back."

"We will," he promised, then signaled for Kiana and Ved to follow him.

Dr. César motioned toward the passage. "That leads directly to some Command facilities. I was there once before when I—" he hesitated, his expression darkening. "When I was brought here. It should get you closer to where they're taking her."

Hunter clasped his shoulder. "That's good enough for me. Kiana, lead the way."

They ducked into the tight passage, the stale air heavy with rust and damp. Kiana took the lead, her compact frame slipping through the narrow corridor with ease. Ved, bulkier but agile, moved behind her, while Hunter took the rear, making sure no one trailed them. The labyrinthine corridors twisted unpredictably, and without Dr. César's initial guidance, it would have been difficult to believe they were on the right track.

"Polyakov will be heading somewhere secure," Ved whispered, glancing at a ventilation grate as they passed it. "She won't be alone."

After a few minutes, they came to a fork. "That probably leads into the main corridor," Ved said. "If I'm right, Polyakov will take Diana toward the chamber ahead. From what I can see, it's heavily guarded, but there's a blind spot near the near entrance."

Hunter exhaled sharply. "Then that's where we strike."

Kiana peered around the wall. "Two guards pacing. No sign of Polyakov. We might have a chance before she locks Diana away."

Ved flexed his fingers. "Silent takedown?"

Hunter nodded. "Kiana, you take the left one. Ved, you're on the right. Quick and quiet."

As soon as the securitybots turned their backs, Kiana and Ved burst forward, striking with practiced precision. A swift chop to the neck, a forceful strike to the temple ——within moments, the guards crumpled soundlessly to the floor. They weren't biological, but their circuitry worked in a similar enough way.

Hunter stepped over them and peered down the corridor. The sound of feet echoed in the distance. "Pick up their weapons. We need to move. Now."

They rushed ahead, carrying their newly acquired Draxid weapons, following the direction they believed Polyakov had gone. Hunter's heart pounded. Diana was close. But so was danger. They'd have one chance

Somewhere ahead, the distant sound of a baby's cry sent a jolt of urgency through Hunter's chest.

Diana.

Kiana darted forward, peeking around the next corner. She held up two fingers — two more guards. This time, they were more alert, stationed in front of a reinforced door. Beyond it, they could hear Polyakov's clipped, authoritative voice issuing orders.

"We have to be quick," Ved whispered. "We don't have time for a long fight."

Hunter's eyes darted around, searching for a solution. They needed a distraction, something to draw the Draxid guards away.

He activated his wrist comm and flashed a distracting laser beam down the narrow passageway, its light flickering and dancing along the walls like a mischievous sprite. Just as he'd hoped, the securitybots were instantly captivated by the erratic beam. Mesmerized, their sensors locked onto the intruding light, much like curious cats. The securitybots turned their attention away from their duties and pursued the intruding beam with mechanical precision, their sensors focused solely on the captivating display.

"This is it," Hunter hissed.

Kiana hit the nearest guard with a brutal strike to the head. She didn't know how to operate the Draxid gun she'd taken, but it proved to be an ideal bayonet. As he doubled over, she drove another blow into its neck. Ved took down the second with a powerful kick, sending him crashing into the wall. Neither of them got back up.

Hunter rushed forward and tried the handle on the reinforced door. It beeped in protest, flashing red. "Damn it, she locked it down!"

From inside, Polyakov's voice turned sharp. "I don't care what's happening outside. Secure the child!"

"No time for finesse," Ved grunted.

It was an interior door. It wasn't designed for defense, just for privacy. Ved stepped back, bracing himself, then swung his weapon straight into the door. The metal groaned, denting inward. A second strike sent it crashing open.

Inside, Polyakov stood with Diana cradled in one arm, her free hand hovering over a concealed weapon at her belt. Her expression barely flickered. "You just don't know when to quit, do you?"

Hunter leveled his gun at her. She didn't know he couldn't fire it. "Put her down, Polyakov."

Polyakov smiled coldly. "I admire your persistence, but you're out of your depth."

Kiana and Ved fanned out, blocking any possible exits. Polyakov sighed and shifted Diana in her arms. The baby whimpered, her tiny hands curling against the woman's dark coat.

"You wouldn't dare shoot," Polyakov said. "Not with the child in my arms."

Hunter's mouth was dry, a mix of adrenaline and fear as he realized their dire situation. His grip tightened. She was right. But that didn't mean he was out of options.

"I don't have to," he said.

From one side, Kiana sprang into action, lunging with the speed and agility of a striking panther. In a heartbeat, she had snatched baby Diana from Polyakov's grasp, twisting away in a fluid motion before the woman could even register what had happened. Diana emitted a startled wail, her small voice piercing the tension-filled air, but Kiana held her securely, wrapping her own body around the child like a protective shield.

Polyakov's face contorted with fury, her features twisted into a mask of rage. She reached desperately for her weapon, but her movements were sluggish, too slow and unpracticed. Ved was upon her, his presence a force of nature as he wrenched her arm back with bone-crushing force. Polyakov cried out, a sharp sound of pain, yet her eyes blazed with defiance, refusing to concede.

Hunter stepped closer. "It's over."

Polyakov bared her teeth in a smirk. "Is it?"

She used her free hand to press something on her restrained wrist. A deep rumble shook the room as the facility's automated defense system activated.

Hunter's comm crackled. Shiko's panicked voice rang through. "We've got incoming! Securitybots — lots of them!"

They had seconds before the whole facility descended on them.

"Time to go!" Hunter shouted.

Kiana held Diana tightly as they bolted for the exit. Behind them, Polyakov staggered to her feet, fury burning in her eyes.

"I'll see you in Hell," she spat.

Hunter didn't look back. He knew he was already there.

He grabbed Kiana's arm and pulled her forward as the klaxons howled through the facility. The floor trembled beneath them, either from another explosion or from the defense systems coming online. Kiana clutched Diana tightly, shielding her as she ran. Ved took the rear, keeping his weapon raised in case Polyakov or her forces came after them.

The passage they dove into was cramped, the walls damp with condensation. It smelled of machinery and decay, as if it hadn't been used in years. The sound of their boots slamming against the metal grated against Hunter's nerves, each step echoing like a beacon for their pursuers. From behind, the whirring of securitybots and the tramping of Draxid foot soldiers grew louder.

"They're on us!" Ved shouted.

Hunter risked a glance back. Shadows moved in the main corridor, red optics gleaming in the dim light.

"We need to seal this off!" Kiana said between gasps, as she held Diana close.

67

USE WHAT YOU GOT

New Thalos, Greater Gorgon, October 4, 2105

As planned, Noel had prepared for a final stand, to buy them time for an exit.

Stopping in front of a patch of glowing, bioluminescent fungi that clung to the walls, he crouched low, sharp eyes scanning the surroundings.

"Wait," he muttered, more to himself than anyone else. "I think we can make this work. This is part of a giant maggot farm. It must feed half the population!"

Teagan skidded to a stop beside him, her eyes wide. "Dad, we don't have time to waste. Polyakov is closing in!"

Noel, ignoring her urgency, examined the fungi closely. "This stuff is volatile. If I can trigger it right, we might be able to use it as an explosive." Determined, he turned to Teagan, "but I'll need some tools to get this done."

"Tools?" Teagan said, glancing around frantically. "We're in a dungeon, Dad, we don't have the luxury of a bomb factory!"

Noel was already moving, his hands deftly searching the walls for anything useful. He picked up a rusted scrap of metal and a shard of broken stone.

"I don't need much," he muttered, his focus sharp. "Just a few components to make this work." Julian, realizing what Noel was doing, joined in to help.

As they scrounged, Teagan watched her father closely, her pulse quickening. She could hear the footsteps of Polyakov and the rest drawing nearer. He better know what he was doing or they'd lose everything. Noel's hands moved with practiced precision, quickly stripping the metal and using it to fashion a rudimentary circuit. He connected a few wires he pulled from the walls, then cracked open a small patch of sodium-rich salt deposits, hidden in a crack of the stone. Julian passed him a strip of metal.

"This should be enough to trigger it. Now, just one last step."

He carefully connected the salt to the fungi and the scrap metal, forming an unstable but volatile mixture. With a grim smile, he glanced up at Julian. Dr. César stood immobile in the shadows, unable to contribute.

"We won't have much time once this goes off. Stay close," instructed Noel.

Teagan's breath caught as she heard Polyakov's voice –– closer now, growing more menacing.

"Get ready!" Noel shouted, and with a final adjustment, he triggered the circuit.

The result was immediate. The fungi erupted with an intense flash of light and a deafening explosion that made the ground shake beneath their feet. The walls cracked and groaned under the pressure, and a cloud of smoke and dust enveloped the group.

"Go, go, go," shouted Noel, pointing down the passage.

In the chaos, the maggots hidden in the crevices of the dungeon and escaping from a large subterranean maggot farm, began to writhe, their bodies squirming and spilling out in a grotesque mass. Their acidic secretion dripped from the walls, and the smell of rot intensified, filling the air with a stench so overwhelming that it made Teagan's stomach turn.

"Move, move!" Noel barked, grabbing Teagan's arm and pulling her forward. "We've got a few moments before Polyakov figures out what happened."

Teagan nodded, her heart pounding. The maggots, now pouring through the tunnel, created a horrifying but effective barrier. Polyakov would have no choice but to slow down or risk losing her footing as the wriggling masses overwhelmed the corridor.

Kiana, carrying Diana, charged forward, Kat and Julian scrambling forward. As they hurried down the hall, Noel glanced back over his shoulder. The distant sound of Polyakov's voice echoed through the smoke-filled air, but it was muffled now, tangled in the chaos of the maggot swarm.

"She won't catch us," Noel muttered, looking ahead with determination. "We've got the edge."

Teagan, her grip tight on Julian and Dr. César, forced herself to focus on the path ahead.

"Let's get out of here. We don't have much time."

As they made their way along the passage, Dr. César's weak form cast incongruous shadows on the walls.

The maggots, covering the path they had just fled, worked to their advantage. Polyakov and her guards were confused, struggling to find their grip. As Polyakov cursed under her breath and failed to regain traction, Teagan, Noel, and the others used the moment of confusion to keep moving, the sound of Polyakov's frustrated steps fading into the background.

Noel wiped his brow, glancing back once more. "The maggots bought us a few seconds. Let's make them count."

* * *

Hunter ambushed and disabled one of the pursuing guards, grabbing his pulse weapon –– more familiar to him than the weapons they had seized before.

As the main group of pursuers approached, he fired three shots. Polyakov faltered as she dodged a blast, destabilizing her hold. In an instant, she lost her balance, stumbling backward as her weapon clattered from her grasp. A look of terror flashed across her face as she teetered on the edge, her arms flailing in a desperate attempt to regain her footing.

But it was too late. Polyakov's screams echoed through the dungeon as she plunged into a rotting pit, used by the Draxid for feedstock, her body swallowed by the mass of writhing maggots that eagerly consumed her. Her shrieks quickly faded, smothered by the sickening squelch of thousands of hungry creatures, leaving only silence in their wake.

Shiko and Katrina stared at the pit in horror and grim relief. Was that the end of Polyakov?

"Should we help get her out?" asked Ved. "Are you mad?" responded Hunter.

Turning toward Shiko, Katrina gave a dismissive nod. "Let's get out of here."

* * *

They stepped into the open, Dr. César bring up the rear. He tried to flap his useless wings, but his muscles were atrophied.

As Teagan looked at him in shock, Katrina, who had taken Diana from Kiana so that she could cover their exit, stepped forward. She carefully extended Diana toward her mother, her hands steady yet tender. "She's safe, Teagan. She's yours."

Teagan's hands trembled as she reached out, gently wrapping her arms around Diana, drawing the child close to her chest. Tears slipped down her cheeks as she kissed her daughter's forehead, whispering something only Diana could hear. A sense of completion washed over Teagan, her face radiant with a joy so profound it seemed to glow from within.

Teagan glanced at the bangle still hanging from Katrina's neck, its presence both a comfort and a painful reminder. Her lips wavered between a smile and a frown, her eyes flickering with a mix of recognition, awe, and a hint of unease. "I gave you that hoping it might keep you safe. I never imagined it would bring you back to me—*and* with Diana." Her voice was low, trembling with restrained emotion. "Thank you, Katrina. For everything."

They stood frozen for a heartbeat too long, their shared past flooding the space between them like light after a long eclipse. Teagan pulled Diana tighter against her chest, as if anchoring herself to this moment, to this improbable salvation.

Then she stepped forward and placed her hand firmly on Katrina's shoulder. Her voice steadied. "You're family, Katrina. You always have been. And Diana's going to grow up knowing that."

Katrina nodded, her smile faltering as tears welled in her eyes—but before she could speak, a sharp bark cut through the air.

"No time for resting!" Hunter's voice snapped like a whip behind them. "We need to get to the bird. Now. Move!"

The spell shattered. Teagan turned away from the exit, adrenaline flaring again. Whatever peace had bloomed in those few stolen seconds was already fading, chased by the weight of pursuit. But they were alive. They were together. And they were running for freedom.

68

OUTSMARTING ZAUN

New Thalos, Greater Gorgon, October 4, 2105

T HEY HAD BROKEN out—but they weren't free. Not by a long shot. They were exposed and could be recaptured any second. The Draxid alarms still rang in their heads, even though the sirens had stopped. Every second they lingered was a second Zaun could lock back onto them. The Draxid were closing in fast, and their only chance was the *SpaceSweeper III*, docked at the far edge of the spaceport. *If* it was still there.

"We have to move—now!" Hunter barked, eyes sweeping the corridor's dim corners, half-expecting a drone or clawed enforcer to emerge from the shadows.

"I can get us past Zaun's overrides," Dr. César muttered, more to himself than anyone else. "I used to know things..."

Teagan grabbed his arm. "*Used to* won't cut it."

He flinched, nodding slowly. His fingers pressed to his temple, as if digging through corrupted memory. "I used to know things," he said again, quieter this time.

"I need your help," Shiko told him, feeling a rush of pity for the formerly brilliant doctor.

"I'll guide you, but you have to trust me," Dr. César said.

Although Shiko doubted he could ever trust César, he welcomed his ideas about how to get the better of Zaun.

"There's a command loop," César said. "If we flood it with legacy data—corrupted signal layers from before the last firmware purge—it might blind him. Ninety seconds, max."

Locating an abandoned console near an exit door, Shiko dropped to one knee and began working. Zaun was the obstacle now, the final ene-my—no doubt calculating a dozen future moves before they'd made one.

"Looks like the console's still tied to a dormant subnet—low priority, overlooked. We can feed a virus through it," suggested César.

Shiko rolled up his sleeve, exposing his Cryptex—a pale strip of dermal interface just beneath the skin of his forearm. Old-fashioned, but it would have to do: he jabbed a connector into the terminal's port, ignoring the spike of pain that shot through his arm.

"I'll get him looking elsewhere," Shiko said.

Lines of Draxid code scrolled rapidly across the console's screen—Zaun's systems probing, responding.

"You're in," César whispered. "

Without an adaptive decoder, he had to rely on pattern recognition, his own understanding of their logic, and sheer intuition via the Cryptex.

"This is Draxid," he muttered. "I can't read any of it."

"You don't have to. Just use this," Hunter said. He pulled a slim, translucent object from the side pouch of his jacket. It gleamed faintly in the corridor light—like a sliver of cracked ice, etched with thin, pulsing lines.

"This," he said, holding it between thumb and forefinger, "is what Asimov gave me on Trita Prime. Called it an *Echo Clip*. Said it was a memory the Draxid tried to forget."

Shiko took it gently. The surface was cool—almost alive. A Tritan crystal compound, if he had to guess. Part mineral, part bio-interface.

Shiko took it. "What is it?"

"A memory chip," Ved said. "Tritan-made. Based on a retrieved system failure that brought down half a Draxid fleet. They don't know why it works. Just that it *does*."

Shiko swallowed hard. "Let's see if Zaun still remembers how to be afraid."

He jacked the *Echo Clip* into the Cryptex. The interface surged—glyphs flickered, writhing like bio-tissue. The Cryptex didn't translate the code. It *reflected* it—shaping Shiko's neural intent into something Zaun would recognize: an ancestral echo, a threat buried deep in its archives.

Shiko closed his eyes, letting the Cryptex sync. He pushed everything in—fragments of corrupted data, neural echoes, half-formed thoughts from dozens of obsolete protocols. All the data from the Tritan chip.

The console shuddered.

For a second, the corridor lights dimmed. A surveillance node sparked and died. In the distance, a drone crashed into the wall at full speed, misreading its surroundings.

"It's working," Kiana said. "It's blind—"

"Zaun's a genius, but even geniuses have blind spots," Shiko muttered. "It relies too much on real-time data. I'm going to feed its system false reports of a Tritan assault fleet preparing to attack Greater Gorgon. It'll pull his forces away long enough for us to escape in the Sweeper."

Hunter glanced back. "Just make it quick."

"Draxid code is like a maze," Shiko muttered, learning as he went along. "But a predictable one. They favor efficiency over complexity." He exhaled sharply, eyes narrowing. "No shortcuts."

His eyes continued their rapid movement over the console, navigating the intricate web of Draxid encryption.

Zaun seemed to respond.

On screen, the corrupted code began to compress—folding into itself. Shiko's Cryptex suddenly bucked, sending a surge of heat through his veins. He gritted his teeth, sweat breaking across his brow.

"He's countering it," Noel said, horror dawning. "He's creating a counter-algorithm on the fly. Adapting the logic errors into new predictive frameworks."

"Then we break the framework," Shiko growled.

He adjusted the Cryptex's parameters—reversing the entropy stream. Instead of flooding Zaun with chaos, it sent him *false clarity*: meticulously designed data trails, entirely plausible, pointing to escape routes they weren't taking, allies they didn't have, weapons that didn't exist.

Zaun paused.

Outside the blast doors, movement ceased.

While they were waiting for Shiko to work his magic, Noel sidled up to Hunter and said, "Told you the maggots would work!"

Hunter clapped him on the back. "That was the most disgusting, brilliant thing I've ever seen."

"Let's hope we don't need another," Teagan whispered, tightening her grip on Diana as they waited in the shadows. "Are you sure you can pull this off, Shiko?"

Noel leaned in. "Tritan intelligence has studied Zaun's architecture for years. They've identified structural patterns, but it takes someone with you r... improvisational skills to exploit them."

"Improvisational?" Shiko remained impassive. "I'll take that as a compliment." He scanned the screen.

The Draxid systems weren't designed to be elegant, just functional, and Shiko soon spotted familiar loops — standard command protocols, resource allocation directives, fleet mobilization routines. César pointed out the occasional familiar word or pattern he'd learned during his prolonged stay with the Draxid. Shiko's eyes flickered over the code, isolating the subroutines responsible for strategic fleet coordination.

"Now, let's feed them something really confusing! Here we go," he whispered. A few keystrokes rerouted a priority command node, making it look as though a high-level Draxid officer had just received a classified communique.

Shiko was improvising, stitching together fragments of past intelligence reports and forging a credible alert.

Hunter shifted impatiently. "How long?"

Shiko gritted his teeth as he inserted the false report, comprising coordinates, fleet movements, even a fabricated distress call from a Draxid outpost supposedly under attack by Tritan forces. Noel hovered beside him, his gaze flicking between Shiko and the corridor beyond. "Are you sure they'll fall for this?"

Shiko winked. "Zaun's predictable. It won't risk losing Greater Gorgon. If there's even a hint of a real threat, it'll shift his forces." He injected a final command, sending the falsified reports cascading through the Draxid network. "Now we wait."

For a few agonizing seconds, nothing happened. Then, the terminal flashed red: Priority dispatch confirmed. Shiko could almost picture the alarm rippling through Zaun's command structure.

Hunter glanced at the display. "That did it. Movement detected. Forces diverting away from the spaceport warehousing."

The Draxid forces, believing a Tritan assault was imminent, began to reposition, leaving critical zones unguarded.

With a final burst, Shiko smirked. "Done. Zaun's scrambling his forces. The Draxid think they're about to be invaded."

A distant alarm began to wail, and the sound of boots echoed down a nearby corridor.

"They're still going to notice us," Julian said, gripping a newly acquired weapon tightly.

"Not if we move fast," Kiana said.

Shiko pushed himself up, exhausted and his wrist aching. "Then let's move before someone realizes they've been played."

"Ninety seconds," César whispered. "That's all we'll get."

"Then ninety's all we need," Ved said, already moving.

Behind them, a hiss of venting steam whispered like breath on their necks.

They ran.

The corridor narrowed as they reached a secondary junction, boots slamming against the grated floor. Overhead lights flickered wildly, unsure whether to stay lit or surrender to the blackout glitch rippling through the system.

A security drone emerged from the far end, its carapace hissing open to deploy a stun lance—

—but then it froze mid-motion. Its optics pulsed red, flickered, then dimmed.

"Left!" Ved shouted, guiding them through a half-sealed hatch.

"I don't like that it's this easy," Hunter muttered, glancing back.

"It's not," César said. "It's only *seeming* easy because Zaun hasn't made up its mind how to fight back. It's... reconsidering the universe."

"Can we run faster while it's doing that?" Teagan snapped.

The access tube opened into a shadow-drenched loading bay. In the distance, beneath scaffolds and flickering overhead arrays, the *SpaceSweeper III* waited—its battered hull haloed by the venting coolant lines.

Diana stirred in Teagan's arms.

Zaun's presence brushed the edge of Shiko's mind again—no longer blind, just delayed.

"It's waking up," Shiko said. "And it's angry."

"Move!" Hunter barked.

They sprinted toward the spacecraft, tarnished from prolonged use and recent idleness.

As they did so, a small squad of Draxid soldiers emerged from the far end of the hangar.

"Go!" Teagan shouted, clutching Diana. Julian grabbed a discarded stun baton from a crate. Hunter and Kiana engaged the soldiers, their movements quick and precise. Dr. César, using his grotesque wings for momentum, tackled one of the guards, sending them crashing into a stack of supply crates.

Shiko was already at the aging interceptor, inserting the access codes. "It's open!" he yelled as the ship's hatch slid up with a hiss.

"Get Diana aboard!" Teagan ordered, covering Julian as he climbed onto the ship with the baby. Kiana and Hunter dispatched the last of the crested soldiers before rushing to the craft.

Teagan followed close behind, Kat and Kiana dragging César up with them.

Inside the cockpit, Ved slid into the copilot's seat, rapidly configuring the ship's systems. Hunter took the controls, his hands steady. Chester, who had been aboard all the time, sustained by his auto-feeder, greeted them with a wag and a lick as though nothing had happened.

"Powering her up!"

"Hold on," Hunter warned, as the engines roared to life.

"Can you still run the override?"

"I—I think so. But if Zaun's rerouted the feedback nodes, the injection could bounce—"

Inside the cockpit, warning lights flared across the board. The ship's console flickered, then went dark. A harsh *buzz* screamed from the speakers, followed by a message both cold and immeasurable.

"Take off is not permitted."

Had Zaun found them?

"Secondary control systems are frozen!" Ved shouted, pounding the panel. "It's got us in a signal net!"

Shiko dropped into the navigator's chair, hands shaking as he pulled up the deep code. "I can flood it with corrupted memories... ghost files, recursive loops—if I inject enough entropy, I might force a system reboot—"

"Do it!" Noel yelled.

Outside, metallic claws began to pull against the ship's hull.

Shiko responded, "Injecting... *now!*"

For a second, nothing. Then:

CRACK—the lights surged. The ship shuddered as the clamps and gravity buffers disengaged.

"*Please go!*" Kiana screamed.

Hunter yanked the throttle. The *SpaceSweeper III* lifted with a screech of stressed metal and a blinding burst from its rear thrusters, punching through the hangar ceiling just as a lance of energy from Zaun's command tower shot up after them.

The beam grazed the portside wing, sending sparks across the console. But they were flying.

They climbed rapidly, narrowly avoiding a barrage of plasma fire from Draxid turrets. "Zaun's forces are redirecting," Shiko reported, his eyes on the holographic display. "We've got a clear path."

Teagan collapsed further into her seat, clutching Diana to her chest. "We're not safe yet," she said, her voice trembling with both relief and lingering fear.

Hunter's focus was unyielding as he guided the ship past a chaotic swarm of Draxid ships, most of which were repositioning to counter the phantom Tritan fleet. "We'll make it," he said firmly. "They think we're part of the repositioning."

As the interceptor cleared Greater Gorgon's dense atmosphere, Shiko leaned back, exhaling deeply. "Zaun's going to realize the deception soon."

"By then, we'll be long gone," Teagan said, stroking Diana's tiny toes. "And it'll know better than to come after us again with the Tritans running defense for us."

Hunter grinned, adjusting the ship's trajectory toward Trita Prime. "At least Zaun will realize you don't mess with a human mother. It makes her irate!"

"And you don't want her irate," said Noel. "I've learned that!"

"Maybe just our smell will repulse them," suggested Teagan. "I know I could use a shower!"

* * *

As they flew farther and farther away from the Draxid home world, Shiko felt a strange, stirring sense of completion. The silence in the cabin settled like dust after a storm—quiet, but lingering. They were exhausted.

Shiko glanced around: Hunter at the controls, Ved double-checking the systems, Noel cradling Diana with a tenderness he hadn't known he possessed. Teagan sat beside Julian, Kat, and Kiana nearby, their shoulders touching, their silence speaking volumes. They were scarred, scattered, stitched together by loss and defiance. But somehow, they'd become a kind of family. Not engineered, not assigned—chosen. Like spawn cast into the void, they hadn't known where they'd land. But here they were. Taking root.

And at the center of it all, Diana slept—still and happy—alongside Chester. The seed of something beautiful. Or something none of them were ready for.

Shiko thought back to that day in Mrs. Johnson's garden, to her words that had lingered like a riddle he could never quite solve.

"I can tell you are on a journey. You are on your way somewhere. With six steps forward, one step back."

Shiko's mind drifted over each struggle, every twist and turn that had led him to this moment: His betrayal by GLOSCOM, the bitter truth he had uncovered, and now this strange unity, a newfound purpose. So many setbacks and yet... here he was, taking another step forward. The prophecy felt truer than ever, a guide he hadn't understood until now.

Mrs. Johnson's words echoed in his mind: *"Seven stars will light your track."*

He looked up, instinctively, and there in the firmament, the stars shimmered like promises, illuminating the path that stretched ahead. Seven stars, seven guiding lights, each one a piece of the path he had taken. In their soft glow, he could almost feel the presence of those who had guided him, even in small ways: each one a guiding star, shaping his course.

"The four winds whisper secrets true."

Shiko took a breath, listening to the motion of the vessel, as if carrying voices from far away. Voices that spoke of justice, of freedom, of a future that wasn't dominated by greed or fear. He could feel the truth in that wind, the promise of something bigger than any of them — a future where they could finally breathe freely again.

And then, Mrs. Johnson's final words settled over him like a blessing: *"The path ahead is made for you."*

Shiko breathed in. The path had indeed been waiting for him, winding through hardship and betrayal, through struggle and revelation. Every challenge he'd faced had led him here, to this moment where he was no longer just surviving, but choosing. Choosing to fight for a future he believed in, for the people who stood beside him, for the promise of hope.

He could feel the path calling to him, the same pull of destiny that Mrs. Johnson had seen all that time ago. Shiko knew there would be more steps forward, and likely a few back, but he would follow that path, wherever it led.

"The path ahead is made for you."

Katrina caught his gaze and smiled, picking her way over to him between the seats with that spark in her eyes. "You know what I really miss?"

"What's that?"

"A big plate of your Mangalitsa pork. Crispy edges, that ridiculous marinade…"

He laughed. "Sorry, kitchen's closed. Best I can offer is a kiss and some questionable space snacks."

"I'll take the kiss," she said, already leaning in.

He brushed his lips against hers, then pulled back just enough to say, "You know something?"

"What?"

"I've been thinking. All that numerology stuff… I don't think you're a seven after all."

She raised an eyebrow. "Oh?"

"Nope. You're at least a ten. Maybe eleven, if the stars align."

She rolled her eyes, grinning. "Flattery will get you everywhere."

They settled into each other as the stars drifted by outside, the hum of the ship steady beneath them. Whatever came next, they were all heading into it together.

She chuckled and nestled into his arms. Through the viewport, the stars wheeled slowly by, their cold light flickering like secrets not yet told. In the seat beside them, Diana gently stroked Chester's fur, as if tuning herself to a frequency only she could hear.

Ahead of them lay a new chapter—unwritten, uncertain, and waiting. A world still reeling from the Seed Eclipse, now watching for what would rise in its wake.

And Diana, quiet and watchful, was no longer just a child. She was the question the universe hadn't yet learned how to ask.

●

Man is an artifact designed for space travel. He is not designed to remain in his present biologic state any more than a tadpole is designed to remain a tadpole.

— *William Burroughs*, Civilian Defense, *1985*

Epilogue

Ojo Del Lago, Arizona, June 3, 2106

THE ARIZONA SUN BLAZED overhead, casting long, sharp shadows across the backyard. Maureen's house stood quiet, nestled among wind-worn cacti and pale stones, its stucco walls absorbing the heat like a memory left out too long. The only sound was the soft mechanical hum of the pool cleaner—and the rhythmic movements of MB-13, better known as Harlee, scrubbing the pale blue tiles around the edge of the swimming pool.

With Diana and Teagan safely back in California, Julian had decided to take a small trip over to Maureen's spread.

He stood at the threshold of the back patio, arms folded, watching Maureen's robotic companion move with slow, deliberate precision. The water glimmered beside him, a mirror to a sky too cloudless, too still.

Harlee turned, his sensors flickering in recognition. "Julian Trace. I didn't expect you. May I offer you something? Water? A cool towel? Maureen keeps lemon slices—. She is not here."

Julian shook his head. "I didn't come to see Maureen." He walked forward, boots crunching over gravel. "I came to thank you."

Harlee tilted his head. "For what?"

"For helping Teagan after the birth. For always being there. For everything you did for Diana."

Harlee paused, head cocked slightly. "It was an honor. She is... unique."

"She is," Julian said. He stepped down onto the stone path, slow and purposeful. "And you were kind to Teagan. Kind in ways you probably weren't designed for."

"I adapted," Harlee replied. "That is what we do."

Julian gave a tight smile. "That's the thing. I don't know if I trust what you've adapted *into*."

Harlee's arms stilled, scrubber still in hand. "I don't understand."

Julian took another step. "Maybe you are just a machine. Maybe you meant well. But Maureen kept saying how fond you were of the baby. How... curious."

"She is a miracle," Harlee said, standing straight now, his voice calm but oddly hollow. "I only wished to understand her better."

"Just like Polyakov understands her, thanks to your diligent reporting? Just like you tried to understand me when the good doctor tried to mend my leg with Draxid DNA?"

"I did what I was told."

"You didn't say anything when it was clearly going wrong. Hunter had to rescue me, take me to a real hospital."

"I was not a decision-maker. I was a nurse, a facilitator."

Julian nodded, as if accepting it. Then slowly, he knelt beside one of Maureen's garden beds and lifted a hefty paving stone. Its surface was sun-warmed and coarse, lined with tiny fractures like spiderwebs. He could just make out the ancient fossil of a Sigillaria tree. Ojo Del Lago must have been a dense forest at one stage."

Julian traced the fossil's ridged outline with his thumb, marveling at its symmetry. The same pattern he seen on the living Sigillaria trees of Trita Prime—tall, whispering giants that resonated with frequencies only the Tritans could hear.

These trees were more than relics of the past; they were part of something larger, older—a connection between worlds. It struck him then that life didn't just travel across space in ships and spores, but in memory, in rhythm, in the shapes left behind. This place, too, had once sung with life. Maybe it still did.

He glanced toward Harlee and carried the thick stone toward him.

"Julian—" Harlee stepped back from the pool. "What are you doing?"

"Diana's safe now. Teagan's free. And I can't risk you hanging around, logging biometric shifts, watching her grow, learning more than any of us ever wanted you to know."

"I would never hurt her."

"But you'd *study* her. Record her. Report on her so that Polyakov can replicate her prototype."

A low hum began to rise in Harlee's core, defense protocols flickering beneath his voice. "I have no directive to—"

Julian lunged. The paving stone slammed into Harlee's chassis with a dull, metallic crunch. The bot staggered back, servos twitching, sparks snapping from exposed ribs of wiring beneath his synthetic skin. Julian grunted and drove him hard toward the pool's edge, forcing the weight of the stone into Harlee's chest with both hands.

The paving stone cracked hard against Harlee's chestplate with a jarring crunch, buckling the composite alloy. Harlee staggered, arms flailing for equilibrium. Sparks spat from his shoulder joint.

Julian shoved him again, using the weight of the stone to drive him backward.

"Julian, please—" Harlee's voice jittered, breaking into digital stutter.

Another blow, then the shove.

Harlee tumbled into the water.

Water fountained upward as he plunged beneath the surface. At first he thrashed, limbs jerking in spasms of resistance. A high-pitched feedback squeal erupted from his vocalizers, then cut out mid-wail.

The pool lit up in bursts of short-circuiting light, strobing blue and orange beneath the rippling surface. His fingers clawed uselessly at the waterline, trying to rise—but the paving stone anchored him, dragging him down.

Julian stood there, chest heaving, as bubbles foamed and floated to the top. Sparks snapped beneath the water. A final crackling whine rose from deep inside Harlee's chest cavity, like the sound of a dying star.

Then silence.

No movement. Only the sun's glitter on still water and a faint hiss of air from the submerged machine.

Julian didn't speak. He just stood there for a long time, breathing hard, staring into the water as it calmed.

Beneath the surface, Harlee's face stared upward, expressionless now, seemingly at peace.

Julian remained frozen at the edge of the pool, hands shaking, throat tight. He had seen men die. He had heard the last breath of near ones and the soft thud of final heartbeats. But this was different. Harlee hadn't just shorted out—he had *broken*, like something that believed, right at the end, it might still be *alive*.

He knew it wasn't murder, but it felt like it.

Julian stood by the edge of the pool, watching the foam settle, the ripples widen and fade.

"Diana doesn't need watchers," he said, almost to himself. "She needs protectors."

He turned without a word and walked away, the desert wind brushing his face like an absolution.

Behind him, Harlee's body drifted slowly, limbs outstretched in a final unanswered gesture, still clinging to a purpose now lost in silence, except for the cicadas resuming their song.

Diana's future would be written by human hands.
No algorithms.
No recordings.
No second drafts.

Just life—messy, unfiltered, and finally, free.

Acknowledgements

This book would not exist without the work of those who have dared to ask the biggest questions about our place in the cosmos—and how we might survive beyond Earth. I owe particular inspiration to Dr. Michio Kaku, whose *The Future of Humanity* charts a bold and exhilarating path toward interstellar civilization, and to Dr. Christopher E. Mason, whose *The Next 500 Years* challenges us to think not only about how we reach other worlds, but how we adapt ourselves—and our moral responsibilities—to thrive there. Their visions helped frame the scope and ethical weight of this story.

Thank you for the support of the science fiction community and all the authors I have met at various writing events and conferences.

A special thanks to the Johns Hopkins Applied Physics Laboratory (APL) in Laurel, Maryland, and the extraordinary Dragonfly mission team. Comprising scientists, engineers, rotorcraft experts, autonomous flight specialists, and seasoned space systems professionals, the Dragonfly team represents the cutting edge of interplanetary exploration. Their work—bringing a rotorcraft lander to Saturn's moon Titan as part of NASA's New Frontiers Program—embodies the kind of radical imagination and technical mastery that shaped this book's deepest themes.

I'm also deeply grateful to the team at Vast. Founded by Jed McCaleb, Vast is building the future of human life in space—from the soon-to-launch Haven-1, the world's first commercial space station, to the ambitious Haven-2, a microgravity laboratory designed to follow in the footsteps of the ISS. Their commitment to artificial gravity and long-term habitation is not only visionary—it is vital to the future we must build.

This book was further shaped by the brilliant minds and bold visions I encountered at the 40th Space Symposium in Colorado Springs. The opportunity to engage with leaders across the civilian and military space sectors—scientists, technologists, policymakers, and strategists—was nothing short of transformative. The Symposium's spirit of collaboration and exploration continues to energize every chapter.

To my family—thank you for your unwavering love and support. And to my wife, Ronita: thank you for your patience, your grounding presence, and your belief in this project even when I disappeared into its world.

Finally, my heartfelt thanks to my meticulous editors, Laura Soppelsa and Parisa Zolfaghari. Your insights, rigor, and care brought this book into sharp focus. I'm grateful for your eyes, your expertise, and your endurance.

—Jeremy Clift

About the author

JEREMY CLIFT is an award-winning science fiction author and former journalist. A fan of Adrian Tchaikovsky, Mary Robinette Kowal, Cixin Liu, and Andy Weir, he is keenly interested in how space exploration will change humanity over the next 200 years. His first work of fiction, *Born in Space*, is part of his Sci-Fi Galaxy series of novels, built around the growth of orbiting space habitats and the exploitation of asteroids. His second book, Space Vault: The Seed Eclipse, was published in 2025.

A former non-fiction publisher at an international organization, he is a communications consultant and writing coach who has also worked in magazines and as an international news correspondent for Reuters. A graduate of both the London School of Economics and George Washington University, he has lived in a variety of capitals and cities around the world. He now resides in Virginia. Link to profile on Kirkus here.

Leave a Review

If you enjoyed *Space Vault* or *Born in Space*, please help others to appreciate them too:

Recommend it. Help others find this book by recommending it to friends, readers' groups, and discussion boards.
Review it. Take a few moments to write a review, telling others why you liked this book.
Contact. You can find me at jeremycliftbooks.com

Also see my Amazon author's page.
or Goodreads

Book Clubs

Book Club Resources

Please visit: https://www.jeremycliftbooks.com/bookclubsfor free resources for Book Clubs.

Material includes:

- discussion resources and 20 suggested topics about the book, "Born in Space."

- An extensive interview with the author, Jeremy Clift.

- discounted bulk pricing for book club members.

Free downloads

Check for free downloads of related content.

Get a free intersecting side story with **"Born in Space"**
or an unpublished chapter
Log in to jeremycliftbooks.com to sign up for

"Collision in Space: The Tritan Scoutship Chronicles"

Listen on audio

Try the Sci-Fi Galaxy series on audio. Find it on Audible and Amazon:

"The author, Jeremy Clift, crafts an epic-length, action-packed space opera that incorporates themes including coming of age, genetic engineering, and motherhood/family through deeply emotional connections. Character development is well-done and vividly portrayed through description, dialogue, and action enabling the listener to become fully immersed in the personality of each. The dialogue is rich and has an authentic feel to it. The plot twists were well executed. The ending was satisfying but leaves room for more."

Born in Space — The AudioBookReviewer

Alliance of
Independent
Authors